Barney Burrell

ISBN: 978-1-7399753-0-2 (paperback)

Published by Squeeze Gut Alley Publishing

www.barneyburrell.com

Proofread by Julia Gibbs

juliaproofreader@gmail.com

British Library Cataloguing in Publication Data
A CIP catalogue record for this book is available from the British Library

For my lovely, gorgeous wife who even though she doesn't like books with violence and 'horrible stuff,' read every word I'd written after every writing session, supporting me all the way. I'm a lucky man.

Chapter 1.

Two weeks before...

Jenks was in the middle of nowhere, a few miles south of Cambridge in a windswept architectural reclamation yard looking at an antique fire surround. It would complete a room he'd been trying to decorate for the last eighteen months, but the project never really got going due to the amount of killing he'd had to do.

His phone beeped. He'd tried a few end-to-end messaging platforms, but liked Wickr's self-destruct feature for specified messages, plus breaking the level of encryption would take until any great-great-grandchildren were long dead. The message simply read *call me*. He replied, *10 mins*.

He walked across the yard passing statues, planters, piles of yellow stock bricks and an old rusty spiral staircase leading to nowhere. Locating the fire surround, he saw it was in pretty good condition. He checked the dimensions and it would fit perfectly.

Looking around, he saw an *office* sign nailed to what had been a railway goods truck many decades ago. Perhaps there was a long closed branch line nearby.

The office was barely warmer than outside, an ancient fan heater not really up to the job. A man wearing an old style flying jacket with thick sheepskin lining looked up from an old computer on a large desk overflowing with piles of paper.

Jenks got straight down to business. ‘That marble fire surround leaning against the railway sleepers – how much are you asking?’

‘Lovely one that, only came in last week...’

Jenks cut him off, smiling. ‘How much?’

‘Two grand – it’s in fabulous condition.’

Jenks knew exactly how much it was worth at a top end retail store, and what it had cost the man after hacking into his website the previous day. The man paid the paltry sum of £225 to a lady dealing with the disposal of her late mother’s house.

Jenks looked him directly in the eye, smiling but unblinking. The man felt strangely uneasy but there’d been nothing to spike the feeling.

Not breaking his stare, Jenks continued. ‘We both know two grand is way too much. Unless you’re really, *really* lucky and some unsuspecting mug walks in, it’ll still be leaning against those sleepers in two years’ time.’

Jenks pulled out a wad of £10 notes counting out £900. ‘The retail on that in a nice warm shop, cleaned up and ready to go would be twelve to thirteen hundred pounds. We’re in a draughty old shed in a muddy yard and it’s covered in moss. I’ll pay you

£900.' Jenks hadn't blinked once, psychologically reinforcing the message.

The man considered himself a good judge of people, but there was something about this customer he couldn't put his finger on. An intensity, and something else. He told himself not to be so stupid, putting the feeling down to the four cups of coffee plus a can of Red Bull.

'If you paid proper trade money for it, and you've obviously been in the game a while, you're still making a good profit. If somehow you got it *really* cheap...' Jenks let the words hang in the air. 'It's going to take thirty seconds to walk to my car and the money goes back in my pocket. No offence.'

Jenks turned his body, allowing his gaze to remain on the man's face until his head caught up with his shoulders and began to walk towards the door. Before his hand reached the handle the man blurted out, 'Yes.'

After handing over the fold of cash, Jenks told the man he didn't need a receipt, and they shook on the deal. He backed his battered Land Rover in as close as he could, and after they loaded it into the back he thanked the man again and slowly drove out, mindful of the pot holes and all the extra weight.

Stopping a few hundred yards down the road, he tapped on the Wickr app and dialled a number he knew from memory. It rang once and was answered. Jenks wasn't angry, just disappointed. 'You know I'm not available – I think it used to be called a holiday.'

The voice on the other end simply said, 'I'm really sorry old chap but we need to meet, urgently. We have a big problem. I know you said not to call until I heard from you, but this really needs your skill set. You know I wouldn't ask unless…'

Jenks cut across him, sighing, 'OK, meet me at the lock, I'm up near Cambridge at the moment. This better be good.'

They agreed a time and Jenks ended the call, pulled off the grass verge and headed towards the M11.

*

James Camburn sat on a bench at Twyford Lock, a couple of miles downstream from the market town of Bishop's Stortford in leafy Hertfordshire. He was a slender man, standing just over six foot, who conveyed a sense of authority purely from the way he carried himself.

His face bore the lines of someone who'd dealt with the type of stressful situations most people could never imagine, but he'd kept a good head of neat grey hair. As usual he was immaculately turned out in a three-piece suit, tailored shirt and silk tie. Fashions came and went but he had no interest in whether he was *in* or *out*. The cut was everything.

The air had definitely turned, with the first signs of spring blossoming along the towpath, and as far as meeting places went, he'd hung around in much less pleasant surroundings. For a few seconds he let his mind drift, as waterfowl chirped their way upstream against the flow of the slow running River Stort.

Camburn had been employed by the security services for much of his working life, cutting his teeth with five years in army intelligence. He was then head-hunted by MI5, later crossing the Thames to MI6. Technically he worked for neither now, as his department, *The Department* was so far off the grid it couldn't be seen to be connected to any agency – it didn't even have a proper name. No ties, no links, everything deniable.

Thoughts of retirement occasionally passed through his mind, but nothing could replace the buzz when a *Red BTS* file landed in his lap. He seldom questioned the intelligence in what were way beyond top secret dossiers – it was all done on trust. The trust that if the powers that be deemed the information worthy of elevation to a Red BTS file, it was to be believed without question and acted upon. Occasionally points needed to be clarified, but generally it had to work that way. He also knew it was because normal methods were not considered adequate to deal with the matter. Wheels within wheels, secrets within secrets.

Deniability was king. There would be no one to take the blame from the outer wheel if things went south. An operative had access to cover officers who possessed a range of skills, some extremely unpleasant, who could be called upon to do anything to support the operative. However, if the shit really hit the fan, you were on your own if intervention risked exposing the existence of the Department. This was precisely why the operative was paid so much, and Jenks didn't only take jobs from Camburn. He was freelance, and reserved the right to turn down a contract from any prospective employer without reason, no matter who they were.

Camburn checked his watch. It was now approaching 2.30pm, fifteen minutes until they were due to meet. He had time to smoke one of his favourite cigars – a Toscanello Rosso. Like anyone with a smattering of intelligence he knew they were bad for him, but the pleasure they gave outweighed the health concerns.

He flipped his Dunhill lighter open and rolled the cigar around the flame, savouring the moment. A large hand clamped down on his shoulder. 'Still smoking those repulsive things, I see.'

'Jesus Christ, man, you nearly gave me a heart attack.' Camburn clutched his chest and took a deep breath. 'We're not supposed to meet for another quarter of an hour, I didn't even hear you coming – you could have killed me you sneaky bastard.' 'Yes I could have,' replied Jenks. Camburn's right eye twitched slightly. 'That's not what I meant – I was talking about the shock.'

Jenks walked around to the front of the bench and sat down, relaxing Camburn with just the hint of a grin. 'That's the general idea – not to be heard or seen.'

Jenks wasn't fifteen minutes early, he'd been in the area for over an hour, secreted in the undergrowth for the last thirty minutes, perfectly still. He'd checked the area for any potential threats or watchers, happy that everything passed his internal test. He would never say safe because that assumed a situation was without risk, and when your guard came down vulnerability crept in. He'd survived this long because he went not just the extra mile, but two or three.

He leant forward and turned to face Camburn. 'You've already spoilt my day, JC, but it's good to see you – it's been a while.' Camburn smiled. 'Good to see you too, old chap.' Camburn extended his hand and the two men shook. 'You look well – been in sunnier climes?'

A deep tan on the cusp of March gave the game away somewhat, and Camburn was one of the few people Jenks could say he almost trusted completely. He also knew there was no evidence linking him to the eradication of an extremely wealthy Saudi politician, whose particular penchant was for young Egyptian girls. After the age of ten they were no longer of any interest and discarded. Or worse.

Camburn's breathing was returning to normal. 'I heard through the grapevine the Mukhabarat were extremely grateful that Saudi bastard got his comeuppance. They couldn't get near him with all his security. I don't suppose we'll ever know how he ended up at the bottom of a thirty-storey luxury apartment block looking like strawberry blancmange.' A wry smile crept up the edges of his mouth.

'No, I don't suppose we will,' replied Jenks in one slow exhale of a sentence. He knew Camburn couldn't possibly know of his involvement for certain, but guessed he'd put two and two together by keeping an eye on the international news.

*

Graham Jenkins was not a small man, but not freakishly giant enough to make him really stand out. At just over 6'3" he was obviously on the tall side, and with boots on nearer 6'5." He was naturally left-handed, but generally ambidextrous, being able to do most things from writing to shooting a gun with both hands. Like a lot of left-handers he had his anomalies. He used to bowl left-handed in cricket, but bat right-handed. He played tennis left-handed, but if he had to favour a hand to jump up to catch something, it was usually his right. This quirk proved useful during his career.

By no means classically handsome, his face was once described as *intriguing* by an old girlfriend. His short hair was an uneventful shade of brown, loosely parted at the side, but one aspect of his appearance that could never be described as boring were his eyes, which were way beyond blue – more a vivid turquoise. Whenever he was working he always wore coloured contacts, and increasingly more often when he wasn't. He didn't like being remembered.

Nobody called him Graham apart from his long dead mother. It was Jenks, just Jenks. He couldn't really remember his dad who'd been gone for long periods at a time, evidently for work, and had died when he was young. His father had a large life insurance policy which had topped up his mother's already inherited wealth, so the small family unit enjoyed a fairly comfortable lifestyle. Unfortunately his mother passed away when Jenks was in the army, having been admitted to hospital with acute stomach pains, dying within a matter of weeks.

He had fleeting memories of his father, Kenneth Jenkins – the few times he remembered him being at home seemed to be happy ones, but even when he searched the deepest corners of his mind, he couldn't really picture his face. He had no photographs of him – his late mother's house tragically caught fire between the short time she'd been admitted to hospital and when she died. The house was burnt to the ground and virtually everything lost. Unbeknown to Jenks, she purposely hadn't kept one single photograph.

The fire brigade investigation team put the likely cause down to a socket being overloaded with numerous adaptors and extension leads. Being an old house, the early occupiers had no use for multiple power points – just enough to plug in a lamp and a radio, or a television if you were particularly well-heeled. The days of numerous electronic devices were decades away, and his mother never had the house rewired. With no siblings, and his parents being only children, he was the last bearer of the Jenkins name.

His considerable strength came from not purely lifting weights, but core exercises from a variety of disciplines. Some from the Far East, which he'd studied at length, others cherry-picked from whatever form of body training developed certain muscles and suppleness.

He had virtually no body fat – his strength was the type found in professional rock climbers. He'd learnt years before it was all very well being able to lift a large hunk of iron over your head, but real core strength was the ability to hold your entire bodyweight with the fingers of one hand off a 4" ledge, twenty floors up.

Although he'd studied and relentlessly practised karate for a number of years, obtaining a black belt before his fourteenth birthday, Krav Maga was his chosen discipline. Considered the most deadly of all martial arts and practised by the legendary Israeli Special Forces, it incorporated simultaneous attack and defence. It taught the exponent extreme but controlled aggression, with the mantra that under certain circumstances you continued to hit your opponent until they were completely incapacitated.

Jenks had trained in the discipline since it was first mentioned in passing by a PE teacher at Charterhouse. One afternoon, after a rugby match had been cancelled Mr Bevan asked a few of the boys in the martial arts club if they wanted to watch a video of a display of

Krav Maga. Within a few minutes the young Graham Jenkins was fascinated. Transfixed by the discipline one second and deadly ferocity the next, he knew he wanted to explore it further.

It wasn't just the fighting style which attracted him, which at times was nothing short of brutal, but the use of the brain as well as fists, feet, knees, elbows, teeth – whatever tools the protagonist could put to best use to stop his enemy. Exponents were taught the importance of situational awareness – knowing where possible escape routes were, recognising potential threats, and mentally noting anything that could be used as a weapon.

Whilst not running around the 135 acres of school playing fields, Jenks took a keen interest in electronics and computing, learning quickly. Such was his prowess, he rewrote the software for the school's entire computing network, streamlining everything and saving the school a small fortune outsourcing their IT management. The headmaster used to joke that Jenks didn't need to leave school at all as there was a job for him starting after the final day of his last summer term.

It was at Charterhouse that he first got the tap on the shoulder whilst on a lads' weekend in Brighton. Nearing the end of his education and despite his mother assuming he would go to university, his heart was set on joining the army and doing something specialist, but he didn't quite know what. And, like the posters promised, he wanted to see the world.

He was stretching in a small park opposite a Brighton B&B on the Sunday morning of the weekend away when the approach came. All the others were too hungover to think about anything more strenuous than going down for breakfast, but Jenks wanted to run on the beach. The sun was up, the tide was out and his body was telling him to sweat out the toxins accumulated the night before.

As he leant against a tree teasing out his Achilles, he heard a voice behind him. 'I expect you'll miss Charterhouse when you leave in a couple of months.'

Jenks turned his head but kept stretching. 'Sorry, do I know you?'

'No, we've never met. Well, you've never seen *me* before. Shame you couldn't get a seat on the 4.23 on Friday afternoon – I expect that first Peroni and the sour cream and chive Pringles helped a bit though.'

Jenks straightened and faced the man. Intrigued but wary, he kept just enough space between them.

The man smiled. 'Nice reactionary gap – big enough to get a head start if you needed to run, small enough to shift position and counter any attack.'

Jenks looked directly at the man, his vivid turquoise eyes unblinking. '*Are* you going to attack me?'

'Good God no, lad, you'd probably snap me clean in half. I'm well aware you've had a black belt for years, and your mastery of other disciplines. If there were any belts darker than black, you'd undoubtedly earn those as well.'

Jenks relaxed slightly. 'What do you want and how do you know me?'

The man gestured towards a bench. 'Can we sit? I realise this must all seem rather strange, but I assure you I'm not here to make you feel uneasy. We've been watching you for quite the little while now. I have a friend on the staff at Charterhouse who mentioned about the whizz kid who revolutionised the school's computer system in his spare time. I did a little more digging and was impressed with your physical and mental capabilities. I understand you could probably be an international athlete in a few sports if you wanted to.'

'So?'

'Well…we feel someone like you could have the right attributes for a career with us.'

'And who exactly is *us*?'

'My dear chap, what I am about to say must go no further than the two of us. I'll be leaving shortly and we won't meet again unless you want to. I represent the Security Services – the Secret Service if you like, and there are opportunities for people like your good self. I'd very much like you to consider coming to London to meet a colleague of mine. No strings, just a chat.'

Jenks took a moment to digest what he'd just heard. 'Well, Mr...I'm sorry, I didn't catch your name – but then you didn't offer it.'

The man extended his hand. 'It's Camburn, James Camburn.'

Jenks continued. 'This isn't exactly what I was expecting as part of my warm up, and I suppose I can't help but be flattered, but I'm afraid I'm joining the army in September, Mr Camburn. No one knows, not even my mum – well you probably do. Thanks, but no thanks.'

Camburn sat back, slowly turning his umbrella in his hands. 'So you don't think it's worth a free trip to London?'

Jenks bent down, pulled the tongue straight in his trainers and stood. 'No, not at the moment. I've made my mind up and I'm going to follow it through. I'm joining the army and looking forward to it.'

Camburn stood. 'You're a very intriguing young man, Mr Jenkins.'

'Just Jenks, everyone calls me Jenks.'

'OK, Jenks, as I said, you have certain abilities I believe could be developed and put to great use in the service of your country. I see something very special in you, I really do, but respect your honesty and integrity. Please take my card – it says it's for a dry cleaners but it'll take you through to someone who will put you in touch with me if you change your mind – just ask the person who answers if your blazer is ready.' Jenks zipped up his hoodie. 'OK, understood.'

Jenks looked at the number on the card, then turned it over to the blank side. After a few seconds he turned it back and looked at the number again. He repeated the action six times and handed the card back.

‘No, please keep it, I do have others.’ There was a slight trace of humour in Camburn’s voice.

‘No need, I can remember it. Just a thing I can do. It’s stored away now.’ Jenks tapped the side of his head.

‘Are you sure you don’t want to know a little more about my offer?’

Jenks began to turn. ‘Nope.’ And with that he was off running towards the sand below.

Camburn shook his head as he turned to make his way back to the station. ‘Remarkable.’

*

The wind had dropped and the ducks were making better headway. Camburn turned to Jenks. ‘Everything you need is on here.’ He held up a small memory stick. ‘It’s a London job.’ Jenks inhaled but before he could say anything Camburn jumped back in. ‘I know you don’t like working in the capital what with all the cameras these days, but please, at least read the file – this one’s keeping me awake at night.’

Jenks took the stick, using it to gesticulate and make a point. ‘If I don’t like it for whatever reason, you know I’ll refuse and that’ll be the end of the matter. Non-negotiable.’

Camburn glanced at the thumb drive then at Jenks. ‘Just read it, please. The target is a very bad man.’

‘Aren’t they all?’ countered Jenks, raising his eyebrows.

‘Yes, but there’s already orphans, widows and grieving parents as a result of what he’s done so far, and he’s only just begun. It’s going to get much, much worse. The bodies will start to stack up and the chances are we’ll both know people in the pile.’

Jenks sat back against the bench, sighing slightly and pursing his lips. ‘OK, sounds serious. What’s the time frame?’

‘He arrives in two weeks, then I’m pretty sure you’ll have a three-day window in which to complete the objective.’

‘OK, you’ve spiked my interest, I’ll have a look.’

Camburn looked relieved. ‘Normal terms will of course apply – 50% if you agree to take the job and the remaining 50% upon successful completion, all to a Swiss account of your nomination.’

Jenks nodded and stood, putting the thumb drive in his trouser pocket. ‘I’ll be home in about an hour and a half – I’ve got a few things to pick up, including my dry cleaning which has been ready for three months. I’ll read and digest and call you later.’

Camburn stretched out his hand. ‘Splendid, talk later, and don’t forget to ask if your blazer is ready.’ They shook, both men grinning. Having worked with Camburn on many occasions over the years, Jenks knew if the old man was losing sleep, the problem must be serious.

*

After a decade in the army Jenks promptly resigned, having attained the rank of lieutenant colonel. His ascendency through the ranks was rapid, but the higher he climbed the further he moved away from all the reasons he joined. He already had 600 men under his command, and the next promotion would have distanced him even further, so he put his papers in.

He went travelling, getting a feel for different countries, absorbing the varied cultures, processing and storing it all away. Fluent in four languages, he could communicate well enough in a few others to get by. When his wanderlust was satiated, he dialled the number he'd committed to memory in the Brighton park years before, enquiring if his blazer was ready.

A lot had happened in the intervening years and together they'd been in more than a few scrapes, but Camburn had never let him down. There was trust between them, perhaps a little more so from Camburn, as Jenks never felt able to fully put his trust in anyone.

Camburn turned to take in the view downstream, then reached down to pick up his umbrella. 'Oh Jenks, if you…' He looked up to find he was alone.

On the drive back Jenks mused that he'd no idea how old Camburn actually was – he seemed in good enough shape, even with the cigar habit. His mind drifted back to that morning in Brighton – Camburn had seemed old all those years ago, but then everyone does when you're eighteen.

Jenks decided if he didn't pick his dry cleaning up on the way home they'd end up disposing of it, and was also out of the basics like milk and bread. A short detour wouldn't matter as he had the whole evening to examine the contents of the thumb drive and decide if he would take the job.

Ninety minutes later, after an uneventful drive back over the Dartford Bridge and along the M2, he found a space in Mortimer Street, Herne Bay – just a two-minute walk to the dry cleaners. He cut through the pay and display car park, which being out of season was empty.

Backing onto a row of semi derelict shops and a long abandoned amusement arcade, the car park was neglected, with no CCTV and more abandoned shopping trolleys than cars. No reason for anyone to be there really.

As he was halfway across, a couple of scruffy lads in their early twenties emerged from a rickety lean-to at the back of the arcade. Hoods up and jogging bottoms slung low on their arses, they shuffled towards him. The first he estimated to be about 6'4. The other was smaller, although still 5'10" or so, wearing cheap knock-off mirrored aviator style sunglasses which didn't quite sit straight. Both wore grubby baseball caps turned backwards. Jenks slipped his leather gloves on – maybe nothing, but something was spiking his sixth sense.

The men sped up, cutting diagonally across to loosely intercept him. Jenks carried on walking, expecting they were either going to ask him for a light or rob him. He stopped dead in his tracks staring straight ahead, momentarily confusing them.

The two would-be gangsters parted and slowly walked in his direction, stopping six feet in front of him. They might have wrongly assumed their next victim had stopped due to fear. *Never* assume. The taller one spoke first, and Jenks now knew he was the leader.

'Got any spare change, mate?'

Jenks confused him by looking directly at the shorter one, staying silent.

'Oi, I'm talking to you, got any spare change?'

Jenks slowly turned his head to the leader, having accomplished what he wanted. He didn't think the would-be hard men would be brave enough to work in just a pair, and his instincts were right, having seen in the reflection of the knock-off aviators two more men coming out from behind the disused toilets, creeping silently up behind him.

Jenks didn't turn. 'Hello, lads, come to join the party?' The two new guys stopped, about eight feet apart. From above, the scene resembled the number 5 on a dice, with Jenks the middle dot.

The leader couldn't work it out, and in a low voice mumbled, 'What the fuck?'

Jenks looked directly into his eyes, glad he'd left his brown contacts in. He saw pinprick pupils staring back at him. If he was on something the rest probably were as well. The threat level had just been raised.

Jenks assessed, and was happy with his reactionary gap. He had room to move and even run if he chose to and leave the young men for dust – he guessed they probably didn't undertake fifteen-mile training runs on a regular basis, but today he didn't feel like running.

The leader let his arm sway behind his baggy jogging bottoms. Right-handed, Jenks noted. Good. He knew which side the weapon was coming from.

The leader did one of those spits through his teeth which jets out in a thin line, catching the side of Jenks's trainer. 'I asked if you had any spare change and you have been extremely fucking rude and not answered my question, so I'll ask you one last time – do you?'

'Sorry, I only carry plastic.'

'That'll do, we take cards,' said the leader. The others laughed. One of the rear gunners joined in, 'Yeah, *and* PIN numbers,' which the others all thought was hilarious.

Jenks spoke to no one in particular. 'Oh come on, guys, it's not really fair odds is it – four of you and one of me.'

Aviator man spoke for the first time. 'Your bad luck, mate.'

Jenks turned towards him. 'You misunderstand – it's not good odds for you four.'

Although Jenks couldn't see his eyes, he could tell Aviator man looked to the leader to take it back up –

an almost indiscernible head movement to his right. A slight crack in the veneer.

The leader took half a step forward. 'Big talk, big man. You have no idea who we are, do you?'

Jenks slowly raised his right hand and cupped his ear. 'Did you not hear me properly? The odds are very much not in your favour. Walk away now while you still can.'

The leader hooked his right thumb inside his waistband as subtly as he could, but the movement was as obvious to Jenks as if someone had shone a spotlight on it.

'What the fuck did you say, *wanker*?' The leader accentuated the last word, stretching it out.

Jenks relaxed his body. Instinct. Muscles preparing, limbs ready to pivot in ways practised over years, hands ready to morph into house bricks. The mental rehearsal of moves leading to other moves. Infinite possibilities.

He faced the leader. 'Please don't tell me that dormant organ in your head can't muster enough power to work your ears at the same time as your potty mouth. I said, 'THE. ODDS. ARE. NOT. IN. YOUR. FAVOUR.'

Jenks could see spasms of hate and rage pulsating in the leader's temples. He watched the man's jaw tense, the muscles rippling his cheek. Aviator man started dancing from foot to foot like a boxer listening to the referee's instruction before the first bell. The two behind, probably the lowest in this particular food chain, waited for something to happen. Jenks altered his stance slightly so he could see all four in his peripheral vision by turning his head. To the uninitiated this could have been taken as a sign of weakness or fear.

Normally people just handed over cash and whatever else the gang asked for. Their victims were usually local so were often too frightened to report the robbery, wary of repercussions.

'Big mistake, big man. No one talks to me like that.' Jenks anticipated it, and sure enough the leader produced a large kitchen knife with a blade about 8" long. He'd worked himself up into such a rage, spittle and white foam formed in the corners of his mouth.

He held the knife handle up, blade down, signalling for Jenks the leading move would be a downward stab – unlike a scything diagonal swipe which Jenks would have chosen, as the odds were you would cut *something*, a downward strike limits the target area.

The leader lunged forward bringing the knife down. Jenks had anticipated – the man wasn't a trained soldier but no less a threat, armed with a deadly weapon with which he intended to inflict maximum damage. In less time than it took to blink, Jenks sidestepped, placing all his weight on his left foot whilst simultaneously shooting his right leg out. The sole of his trainer hammered into the side of the leader's knee.

The sound was sickening – like snapping a plank of wood against a wall. The leader screamed, vomiting when he saw his lower leg now pointing out at a right angle – all bones completely smashed and tendons torn apart. He would never walk again without a limp. It would remind him every day of his foolishness.

Jenks had already decided on the order of play before taking down the leader. It was obvious he would make the first move – they always did, which was how they became leader. Aviator man was No 2 in the pecking order, but was slightly further away.

Spinning around, Jenks exploded towards the rear man to his right, seeing the flash of another blade. His new assailant had as much idea about knife-craft as the last. He probably tried to impress girls down in the shelters by the King's Hall, waving it around and regaling them with stories of past imaginary battles with rival gangs.

Jenks closed the space between them as the guy raised the weapon to waist height. The knifeman presumed Jenks would keep running and dropped to what he thought was a fighting stance. Mistake.

Holding the knife up meant he couldn't strike down without turning his wrist – only a fraction of a second to complete the manoeuvre, but still too long. Jenks curled his toes under to protect them in case he got the angle slightly off, and with lightning speed kicked up at the forearm of the knifeman like a goalkeeper drop kicking a football.

It was as if he'd been hit with an iron bar – both ulna and radius bones snapped cleanly in half. The guy was in such immediate shock his eyes bulged as he dropped to the floor, but he didn't scream. Jenks saw Aviator man starting to advance and sighed – enough was enough. Pivoting round, he stamped down on the area of bone separation, then the scream came and knifeman number two passed out. In one fluid motion Jenks swept up the knife and threw it from the blade. Aviator man stopped dead in his tracks and looked down at his left leg. His fists unclenched when he saw just the hilt sticking out of his thigh, and dropped to the floor. The fourth man was disappearing into the distance.

Jenks walked slowly over. Aviator man's mouth hung open. He looked down at the knife, back at Jenks, then back at the knife. His forehead was dotted with beads of perspiration as shock coursed through his body.

'That's probably gone through your femoral artery. Now, I will explain. Imagine stabbing a car tyre. If you leave the knife in, the air escapes slowly. If you take it out, the air rushes out quickly. Your leg is nothing like a tyre by the way. That knife is the only thing saving your life as of now. If you take it out it'll be like a fire extinguisher – blood will pump out with such force you'll be dead in less than two minutes. Have I made that simple enough?'

Aviator man nodded and clenched his leg, desperately trying to keep the knife still. Jenks gently removed the man's sunglasses, ground them into the concrete and knelt down. 'I've held back with you and your big time scary gangster mates. Listen to your leader screaming. See how your other mate is unconscious. Next time I won't show restraint. Now, shall I take that knife and dispose of it for you?'

Aviator man looked down, now crying, 'Please, no.' Jenks made as if to grip the handle, and the man immediately voided his bowels, experiencing fear like never before.

Jenks withdrew his hand. 'See you around.'

The police would arrive soon due the ear-piercing screams of the leader, but Jenks guessed when they saw who the victims were, wouldn't try too hard to find their attackers. Secretly, they would in all likelihood be pleased. Jenks didn't want to be in town when the police arrived so the dry cleaning would have to wait a while longer.

Chapter 2.

For Jenks, home was a fairly large house on a desolate stretch of beach on the North Kent coast, the nearest town being Whitstable. It was plain white, with large bay windows on the ground and first floor, accessed from a private road. The windows were framed by thick white blackout curtains which automatically opened and closed in the morning and evening. The lights switched on and off with timers when he wasn't there, and everything could be remotely operated from his phone – including the tiny cameras mounted in every room and at all points of the compass outside.

Jenks owned it outright and had enough money deposited to buy his immediate neighbours out if he so chose. He didn't get to stay that much, spending a great deal of time elsewhere in the world planning, researching and executing his missions, sometimes for months at a time.

He'd inherited his mother's estate in its entirety, including the insurance payout for her house after it burnt down. Over the years his fee had gone up, and he‘d amassed enough to not have to work again.

He liked the Swiss – they loved that they had the most secretive banking system in the world, unlike the Cayman Islands or Bermuda, rarely cooperating with law enforcement, which was why he'd spread his wealth across a dozen banks.

There were a handful of people he worked with, who on occasion he allowed into his world a little. Camburn was the exception and had far greater access. He'd decided years before there was no point getting close to anyone outside his professional circle, as he'd be forced to lie to them. Logic dictated that would make the relationship false, and therefore they would not be real friends.

He could spend hours looking through his binoculars at the oystercatchers, egrets, even the odd rough-legged buzzard from his large windows facing the Swale. He could name most of the species, and enjoyed spotting the occasional visitor blown miles off course. He liked watching them resting on the mudflats before they headed off to wherever they should really be, finding it quite meditative. He was also utterly ruthless. A man who could unflinchingly dish out hurt and destruction as easily as the boy handing out leaflets for the Whitstable farmers' market.

In the immediate aftermath of a mission he'd analyse where he could improve, learn from actions which could have been executed better, filing it away in his head. But he didn't need to learn anything further about actual execution. At that, he was a master.

*

Jenks stopped at the general stores and grabbed a few essentials. Turning down towards his house, he pressed the remote clipped to the sun visor and the gates swung open.

With some difficulty he carried the heavy fire surround into the dining room, resting it carefully against the wall, planning to install it when he finally had the time. He never entertained, never threw dinner parties or intimate suppers, so the room was, for the most part, unused. For Jenks though it was an ongoing project. He enjoyed the preservation and restoration of things, stripping back the layers of the past, making good for the future.

He collected some wood from his log store and set a fire in the sitting room overlooking the beach. The seasoned logs caught quickly as he removed his trainers and peeled off his clothes. Catching sight of his reflection, he glanced at the numerous scars on his torso. He could remember what caused each one, but not the ones in his head – maybe they would never heal.

Leaving his clothes on the hearth he went upstairs to grab a shower. By the time he finished, the fire was roaring. He placed one of his trainers in the flames – not ideal for the environment, but he didn't like loose ends. The rubber sole started to melt and burn, along with the DNA of his attackers. His clothes followed, along with the other shoe and his Dents gloves. He winced slightly, but upstairs in his chest of drawers were a further twenty pairs, neatly laid side by side.

He poured himself a glass of Chenas. He'd been introduced to the delights of Beaujolais during his sabbatical and generally never drank any other wine. After arriving in France he'd purchased an old Citroen 2CV in which to explore the country from north to south, stopping frequently to observe the variety of birds also just arrived to enjoy the warm weather.

He'd parked in the town of Beaujeu and got talking to a man called Alain outside a café. Alain owned a small vineyard and produced what turned out to be exceptionally good wine, but was having serious problems with some of his equipment. Jenks offered to take a look, and with his experience in engineering was able to bring the old presses and machinery back up to scratch. Alain offered him free board and lodging in return for his services and Jenks ended up staying until the harvest, drinking more wine than he'd ever done in his life.

Whilst waiting for his encrypted laptop to go through its various checks, he scanned across the mudflats. A couple of guys he recognised as regular bait diggers were hard at work near the old wreck. The oyster beds were fully exposed, and two dog walkers were sitting on a breakwater, chatting and throwing balls from long plastic scoops. Just people doing what they do, like him.

He inserted the thumb drive and entered the password when prompted. Camburn hadn't mentioned it as it was always the same words but with a different number, 307 on from the previous one.

The screen came to life revealing a photograph of a not unpleasant looking man aged, Jenks guessed, in his late thirties. Below the photograph was a description – nothing out of the ordinary, 5’11”, chubby build, blondish wavy shoulder-length hair and a slightly angular face which usually had 3-day stubble – perhaps he trimmed it that way. He reminded Jenks of a slightly overweight surfer.

Below the description was the name Joshua Englefield III. American. Aged thirty-nine. OK, a little older than he’d guessed, but after reading further into the biography of Mr Englefield it was apparent he partied hard and enjoyed a hedonistic lifestyle. That was when he wasn’t at work at the CIA headquarters in Langley where he was employed as a senior analyst.

By the time he was halfway through his glass, Jenks’s mouth hung open. It was rapidly becoming clear why the matter had been escalated to Red BTS and passed to the Department.

*

All civilised countries have agencies who deal with the serious threats against their citizens. America has the CIA, FBI, Homeland Security, Secret Service and a host of smaller but nevertheless important groups of dedicated individuals, willing to risk their own safety for the sake of others.

Britain has MI5, MI6, GCHQ and The National Crime Agency, incorporating Special Branch. Like their overseas colleagues, they also glean intelligence from the police and armed forces. Israel has Mossad, renowned for their ruthlessness. France has the General Directorate for external security and their sister agency for internal matters – similar to MI6 and 5. It was the same all over the world. All had massive reach and capabilities, their common purpose to stop the bad men and women who would do harm to their people.

On occasions, a matter arose which couldn't be handled in the *normal* way. Constraints, exposure, legislation, accountability – incidents which would cause diplomatic relations to be ceased immediately and even start small wars, sometimes got in the way of eliminating the risk.

All recognised agencies sailed close to the wind on a daily basis, and diplomacy was tested to its very limits when things went wrong. An example, when Jenks was still a schoolboy, was Operation Flavius, which caused a top secret mission to be glaringly thrown into the international spotlight.

Now commonly known as *Death on the Rock*, Operation Flavius concerned the tracking of three IRA suspects to Gibraltar, suspected of planning to detonate a bomb at the changing of the guard outside the Governor's residence.

The suspects had been lost by the Spanish authorities who were tailing them, and not sighted again until they reappeared in Gibraltar. All three were shot dead by members of the SAS on a garage forecourt and subsequently found to be unarmed, but a viable bomb *was* found. The domino effect caused many people to lose their lives in subsequent reprisals and retaliation shootings.

The whole episode opened a can of worms, which despite the best efforts of many high up in their respective agencies, could not be closed. The powers that be ruminated on how it could have been handled differently, if only there were some other way...

In the weeks and months that followed, the *other way* was born. Coincidently, James Camburn started a new job.

The key to secrecy was keeping the secret. Obvious, but people *did* talk despite being told not to, despite being *ordered* not to and despite signing non-disclosure agreements and taking oaths. The secret might well be kept by the next person told, but as sure as eggs are eggs, the more people in on it, the chances grew it would get out, especially if there was a bad egg in the mix.

In each country operating a Department, one person was in overall command – *The Caretaker*. In the USA it was the Director of the CIA – a formidable lady called Katherine Jackson. She was technically answerable to the Director of National Intelligence, but even he was out of the loop.

Her counterpart in Great Britain was Sir John Leroux, the head of MI6 or *C*. The Prime Minister was not read in for exactly the same reasons as the American president. Even the head of MI5 was oblivious to its existence.

France, Germany, Italy, Spain, Egypt and the Israelis all had their own Department along with Canada. Certain countries would forever be excluded as even at the very top level, they just couldn't be trusted.

All Caretakers were under no illusion about the consequences of betraying the secret. They would die along with their immediate families. Brutal but effective, as in just over thirty years nothing had leaked out.

The Department mostly obtained their work through inter-agency meetings in their respective countries where only the most serious matters were discussed. There was always a chairperson to these meetings, who usually happened to be the Caretaker.

Protocol dictated that the chairperson has the opportunity to read and digest the file detailing the problem under discussion, giving ample opportunity to copy or photograph all or part of the dossier which would then become a Red BTS file, more often than not secured on a tiny memory stick.

An electronic flag was created to alert the Department of any ongoing or active operations against the target – essential to avoid compromise and the Department risking exposure by walking into a live operation, be it manned or electronic.

Each *Department* was supported by a small but utterly reliable handpicked backroom team known as *The Shop*, under the command of the *Shopkeeper*. It was to him or her the *Caretaker* would pass the Red

BTS, the *Shopkeeper* exclusively taking control from that point.

The Shop had immense reach and power, with backdoors into all intelligence databases, traffic control, CCTV and large corporations. A team could be called upon to sanitize a room or a whole building and dispose of anything. Like the Caretaker, they were fully aware of the lethal repercussions of betrayal.

It was never expected they could solve all of the world's problems – each *Department* would need thousands of staff which would drastically increase the chances of exposure, defeating the whole object. However, the small dedicated teams around the world made more than a few of the most serious ones disappear.

The British *Shop* was based in a service area within the glass city of London Docklands, a few hundred yards from Canary Wharf and No 1 Canada Square, once the tallest skyscraper in the UK. The building was in an area unused by the thousands of bankers and high earners who worked there, consisting of two units converted into one. Housed within was a main control room, separate staff areas, a room full of specialist equipment and a garage area behind a large roller shutter. It would be an understatement to describe it as secure.

*

Jenks realised he'd been holding his glass for over five minutes without taking a sip. Transfixed by what he was reading, he shook his head slightly and put his wine down. Mr Englefield was potentially the most dangerous man in the world, save for anyone about to launch a nuclear weapon, which was unlikely.

He read the file through once, leant back in his battered but comfortable recliner, closed his eyes, and thought.

When he opened them he saw the sun was sinking on the far side of the estuary, flooding the horizon with a deep orange/red hue. Jenks hadn't been asleep, he'd been busy in his head compartmentalising the facts, arranging them in an orderly fashion and forming the genesis of a plan. He then leant forward and read the whole file from start to finish again. It didn't get any better.

Chapter 3.

Jenks picked up his mobile phone, tapped on the Wickr app and dialled James Camburn. The phone rang a few times before being answered. Jenks spoke first. ‘It’s me – can you talk?’

He could hear the sound of noisy children playing in the background. It sounded like a mini riot, which wasn’t far from the truth. ‘Give me a second, I’m looking after my grandchildren for a couple of hours – my daughter’s at the gym.’

Jenks heard Camburn tell the children he had to speak to someone at the garage about booking his car in, and would be back in a minute. He heard a door open and close, and the noise disappeared.

‘OK now, have you read it?’

‘Yes, twice – I’m going over it again later but wanted to let you know it’s a go. This is potentially catastrophic. Are you sure nothing more is going to get out before he arrives?’

Camburn sounded serious. ‘As sure as I can be – this is the end game, the final move, so the payoff will be massive. London’s his last stop before disappearing, that I’m sure of.’

‘OK, I hope you’re right. Open the Shop. I’ll call you tomorrow morning with an initial list of what I need once I’ve slept on it.’

‘Righteo, splendid. The Shop is already open – I may have been a bit presumptuous but I had a feeling you’d take the job. The first fifty per cent will be in your account in ten minutes – which one do you want me to use?’

Jenks paused. ‘Put it number 7, I haven’t used it for a while.’

‘Consider it done.’ There was dead air with neither man saying anything. Camburn broke the silence. ‘It goes without saying, old chap, that this needs to be dealt with *thoroughly.’*

‘Understood, there’s absolutely no other way. Get back to the kids and let’s speak in the morning – it sounded like you’ve got your hands full.’

‘Compared to looking after them, most of this other stuff is a breeze.’

Jenks chuckled. ‘Let’s hope so. I’m going to eat then get back to it.’ He ended the call, and all records of the connection disappeared forever.

*

Jenks made himself a simple pasta meal, throwing in whatever he could find in the fridge which wasn’t showing signs of decay. He sat at his table by the window, twirling the carbonara around his fork, wondering how many people had already disappeared because of the ideals of Joshua Englefield III, and how many more would die if he failed to complete the mission.

He sat quietly, not really looking at anything, and slowly took a sip of wine. The tide was coming in and he could hear the waves washing over the shingle. The only other sound was the ticking from the old clock on the sideboard, one of the few items saved from the ashes of his late mother's house.

For a moment his mind wandered to old missions – the killing of despots, lawless tribal leaders, paedophiles, terrorists – people who needed to die so innocents could live. The men, women and children he'd saved through his actions would never know what he'd done for them, or who he was, but that didn't bother him.

This was different. If Englefield succeeded, Jenks had no doubt Camburn was right – they would both know people in the pile of bodies, had probably worked with some, maybe even owed their life to them. They might even end up on the pile themselves.

He finished his food, washed his bowl, chopping board and saucepans and put them away. Throwing another couple of logs on the fire, he sat down again to read.

This time he took notes and opened a web browser page. He pulled up maps of central London including satellite photos of the rooftops around the Soho area, and used Google Street View – a gift to the modern day spy – to take a virtual stroll around the area of the planned operation.

He looked for non-council CCTV cameras mounted on buildings adjacent to the one he was interested in, something he would have one of the Shop staff double-check to ensure no new ones had been added since Street View was filmed. He formulated approach paths, exit points and emergency escape routes should they be required. His plan was coming together as he made further entries on his shopping list.

By 10pm he was satisfied he'd done as much as he could. He tore off the piece of A4 paper and read it, turned it over to the blank side, closed his eyes for a few moments, then read it again. He completed the action six times then balled up the list and threw it in the fire. He then tore off the next four sheets and threw them into the flames. Indentation wouldn't normally go through more than two layers, and Jenks had been using a light felt tip, but better safe than sorry.

It was all committed to memory. He closed his eyes and read the list back to himself, picturing the words on the back of his eyelids. He remembered every entry, including a couple of doodles in the upper left-hand corner.

*

Joshua Englefield III wasn't coming to London as a tourist. He wasn't even coming as Joshua Englefield. He would be presenting a well-used and undetectable passport in the name of Rick Mills, acquired via the dark net. It was expensive but genuine, not a forgery, and would pass the closest of inspections from curious border staff. The package he'd paid $80,000 for came with a whole new identity and history, including a genuine social security number. The real Richard Mills would have been the exact age as Englefield, had he not died aged just three months.

The upmarket boutique hotel he'd booked for three nights in Dean Street near the junction with Old Compton Street in the heart of London's Soho district was expecting Mr Mills on Tuesday 10th March, two weeks' time, having accepted full advance payment via an American Express black card in the name of Rick Mills. He'd baulked a little at paying a further $50,000 for the card, but the benefits it offered far outweighed what were, in effect, pennies to him now. He guessed a large percentage of the fee had probably gone to a crooked Amex employee.

The best rooms in The Huntsman's Lodge Hotel were on the fourth floor, which pleased Jenks. England was still cold, with people wearing scarves, hats and thick coats, which pleased him even more.

London was mostly open farmland centuries ago, and the area called Soho a hunting ground for Deer and Boar. Named after the call shouted by the red-jacketed huntsmen at the start of the chase, and like the centre of many older cities, it was now heavily built up around a warren of alleys and thin streets.

These streets followed the lines of the original medieval byways, built to accommodate the horse and cart. Some grassy areas still survived, like St Anne's Churchyard on Wardour Street, running directly behind Old Compton Street. This was on the list.

Joshua Englefield III was visiting London to sell, although if anyone asked he was just on vacation. He considered himself a good salesman, having already amassed a not inconsiderable bank balance over the past few months, but this was the big one. This was the end of one life and the start of another.

He'd booked a procedure with one of the most renowned and discreet plastic surgeons in Geneva on the 16th March, factoring in a couple of days to appreciate the city and its fine restaurants before going under the knife, changing his appearance forever. Money would be no object, so he'd booked the Four Seasons Hotel des Bergues, reserving the *Suite Leman* overlooking the river at the cost equivalent of £3,236 per night.

He couldn't see how his sale could fail as he was dealing with a buyer he knew he could rely on, having completed nearly a dozen transactions over the past three months. Trust had been built and a good relationship cemented. He'd also ensured that any contact had stringent security measures in place.

It was most definitely a seller's market, and he was the only person in the world with a very particular stock. He'd mentioned a price to his buyer, fully expecting to have to negotiate, but it was agreed without further mention. Twenty million dollars was a lot of money anywhere, and if used wisely, would allow him to live a luxurious lifestyle for the rest of his life, after they changed the world forever.

*

Jenks was content his plan was as complete as possible at this early stage. He ran it backwards in his mind, from the end game to the planned initial contact, and then back again.

The human brain worked in mysterious ways, particularly with recall. He'd read years before about the police's use of cognitive interviewing techniques – asking the witness to free recall from the start, and then backwards from the end, then picking the recall up from a particular point.

Memories a person didn't realise were stored could be retrieved simply by getting the witness to remember in a different way – a different order. He'd found the technique helpful over the years when planning. Obstacles came to mind when reversing the plan – *what if* scenarios, and how best they could be dealt with.

He still had a lot of preparation to do, but for tonight, he would call it a day. He ruminated on what he'd read about Englefield. The research was as thorough as could be expected, with lots of detail about his lifestyle, family background, and tellingly, his work history.

The young Joshua had a fairly illustrious school career, winning prizes and accolades from kindergarten to Yale. His potential was recognised early, culminating in a full scholarship to one of the most famed and respected universities in America where he studied economics, politics and philosophy.

He came from a loving ordinary family, and had an older brother, Steven, who'd been severely injured by a roadside IED whilst on active service in Afghanistan. His brother survived, but was now living in assisted housing, due to the fact he had two prosthetic legs, a right arm that ended at the elbow and brain damage, robbing him of the power of speech. He was now only able to make sounds, like a baby having a tantrum.

Their retired parents lived in the same neighbourhood as his brother. They went to church, attended midweek prayer meetings and led a very uninteresting, unadventurous life. They visited Steven at least twice a week, always ending the trip by taking his left hand in theirs, offering up prayers that he might find peace within himself and not be in pain.

They also prayed for his attackers, that they might find clarity in their thoughts and realise what they were doing in the name of their own God was wrong. Steven often became agitated, but his parents took it all the wrong way. They thought he was trying to say amen as they asked the Lord to forgive those who trespass against us. What he was trying to say was that his parents were morons who should want the fuckers who did this to him bombed out of existence.

Fresh from graduation, Joshua applied to the CIA and was accepted as a trainee junior political analyst. He performed well and rose up the ranks, transferring to the headquarters at Langley just after his thirtieth birthday. By thirty-one he'd made senior analyst, with which came a higher security clearance.

There were a couple of notes on his file regarding minor discipline matters. These appeared to be a few choice words between Joshua and his boss, Junior Director Alicia Buckland, over his need to take the odd day off at short notice. Joshua had become *agitated and slightly aggressive in his manner* when challenged about the migraines he suffered. These only happened on a Monday.

The truth of the matter was he'd partied hard all weekend – from Friday night after work into the early hours of Monday, ingesting MDMA, lots of booze, a whole pile of grass and more than enough bumps of coke to keep him up where he wanted to be. He was mixing with an undesirable crowd, but not enough to warrant intervention. Buckland had told him if ever he needed help with anything in his life, there were support networks in place. He'd thanked her but stated he was absolutely fine. His work was so good the minor indiscretions could be overlooked. No one's perfect.

It wasn't as if he saw his party friends all the time – it was only now and again. He worked hard and didn't see why he shouldn't play hard as well – he'd earned it after all. None of the crowd knew what he really did for a living, believing he worked in insurance. He didn't see any benefit in telling them the truth as they'd think he was a spy or something. With some of the views certain individuals held, he had no doubt he'd be viewed as the antichrist, excluded from the group, and his fun would stop. They didn't even blink an eye that he was gay – he was accepted as one of the gang and not judged.

His salary had risen along with his rank, and although he earned decent money compared to his friends, he was never going to live in a mansion or drive a Porsche. It was only during the subsequent working back through his file, that the signs became apparent of something going badly wrong in Joshua Englefield's outlook on life, and his views on society.

Chapter 4.

USA, one year previously…

Around the time of Englefield's thirty-eighth birthday, Alicia Buckland had been absentmindedly looking through Facebook. She'd got home late as usual, killing time before bed randomly browsing, clicking on friends, then their friends – just being nosy and laughing at the odd photo.

Buckland was in her early forties and lived alone. Her dedication to work meant she had little time for a proper social life. She wasn't unattractive, preferring a natural look as opposed to painting her face and spending hours on her hair. She wore it in a short brown bob which complemented her elfin features and kept reasonably fit, but didn't hit the gym as often as she would've liked.

Having clicked into four degrees of separation from herself – friends of friends of friends of friends, she saw photos posted of a party in full swing. Dancing, drinking, smoking, balloons, people with their arms around each other high-kicking in unison. And right in the middle of the kickers, with what was clearly an oversized joint in his mouth and a bottle of champagne in his hand, and that stupid bead bracelet he always wore, was her employee, Joshua Englefield III.

People just having fun. Lots of fun. It was one of the other high-kickers that caught her attention. Something nudged latent memories at the back of her brain, a memory buried under layers of more important information, almost in her mind's recycling bin. She took a screenshot of the photo.

Something about the man next to Josh looked familiar, but she couldn't place him. Her job often entailed looking at thousands of photos a week, but something was niggling her about this face. She didn't know what, but knew it wasn't good.

For the next couple of days it felt like she had an itch she couldn't reach to scratch. Gasping for strong coffee after an extremely long and boring meeting, she headed to the restaurant.

Waiting to pay, she felt a tap on her shoulder. 'No muffin today?' She smiled and turned around. 'Officer Dibble, as I live and breathe – you got rid of that damn cat yet?'

Officer Dibble was her counterpart and friend Sam Dibble, Director of the Special Activities Division – the department that dealt with all clandestine investigations and missions. Well, almost all. Alicia had known Sam for years having worked together many times, Alicia's department providing analysis of intelligence which Sam's team would rely on to build a picture of their target.

They'd socialised together over the years, but nothing further ever happened. Alicia had always thought him a bit of a catch, as he looked a little like a

6'2" version of a dark-haired Brad Pitt. Sam, however, was happily married with three kids, and Alicia got on well with his wife.

In the early days of his career before promotion to management level, Sam endured daily ribbing due to having the same name as the policeman in the cartoon series *Top Cat*. People seemed to think they were the first to make the *hilarious* connection, but that all stopped as he rose up the ranks. More than a few jokers had been sent packing with their ears ringing after using a line he'd heard ten thousand times before. Alicia was just about the only person he let get away with it now.

Sam smiled and leant in to kiss her cheek. 'Hey, sweet pea, how you doing? You getting that coffee to go?

Alicia shook her head. 'After the meeting I've just had, I need a break.'

'Bad, was it?'

Alicia fake-smiled, her eyes taking on a dead look, and spoke through her teeth, her lips hardly moving. 'Human resources – how can we improve?'

Sam's mouth hung open in mock horror. 'Jeez, hun, I'm so sorry, I had no idea – you wanna sit down? Are you feeling OK? Dizzy?'

Alicia laughed. 'Yeah, I think I need to decompress for ten minutes.'

'You need a muffin, no arguments, I'm buying.'

Alicia fanned her face. 'My hero, thanks.'

Sam grabbed an extra blueberry muffin which he knew were her favourite.

'Hey, go and sit down, I'll get this. I don't want you fainting and making a mess everywhere after the hell you've been through this morning. PTSD can strike anytime, you know.'

Sam took her coffee and put it in on his tray along with the muffins and waited for the customer in front to pay.

Alicia took a seat by the big window overlooking the grassy outside seating area. It was too late for breakfast and too early for lunch so the restaurant wasn't busy. A handful of people sat around buried in laptops or looking at their phones.

Sam set the tray down. 'Here you go, that'll turn you back into a human.'

'You're a life saver.' She took a sip of coffee and leant back in her chair. 'Hey you, how's Kate and the ankle biters?'

'She's good – taken up yoga again. Now the kids are all at school she's got more free time.'

'Oh that's great, maybe I'll give her a call and tag along one of these days – my mat hasn't seen the outside of my closet for about two years. God, I used to love yoga.'

'Yeah, do that, she'd love it I'm sure. Grab lunch after as well.'

'Ah, for a normal life…those were the days.'

‘No, for real. Her friends all work so she doesn’t get to socialise much in her own time – she’d probably drag you out shopping after as well.’

Alicia slowly shook her head and pursed her lips, highlighting the stupidity of his statement. ‘A woman doesn’t need to be *dragged* shopping. We’re born with the instinct, it’s in our DNA.’

‘Yeah, my credit card would corroborate that statement.’

Alicia laughed as she tore off a piece of muffin.

Sam looked across to her. ‘And what about you? Anyone floating your boat yet?’

She laughed again. ‘Ha, I should be so lucky – I always seem to be here, and despite that, all the best ones are already taken.’

Sam mockingly wafted his face. ‘Ah shucks, you’ll make me blush. I’m sure there’s a knight in shining armour somewhere out there, you just gotta get out more.’

Alicia ruffled her eyebrows. ‘I wasn’t talking about you.’

Sam looked slightly embarrassed. ‘Oh.’

She broke into a smile, pointing her finger. ‘Ahhh, gotcha!’

‘Yeah, you got me good. Another time, another place, who knows what might’ve happened.’

They both smiled, quietly having a *what if* moment.

Alicia broke the silence. ‘Anyway if you’d dated me you’d never have met Kate – you’re a lucky man, Sam Dibble.’

'Yeah, I picked a good one there, no two ways about it and thankful every day.'

Alicia bent over and made as if looking at the floor around Sam's chair.

Sam looked down as well. 'You drop something?'

'No, just looking for the broken mould you came out of.'

Sam shook his head, smiling. They chatted about this and that, laughing together about the horror that was Human Resources. Alicia checked her watch. 'I suppose I ought to get back before this place falls apart without me.'

'Yeah, me too. No rest for the wicked, eh. Can I ask you something, Leece? If you don't mind?'

'Yeah, shoot.'

'Is everything really OK with you? We go back a long way – I might be wrong, and tell me to shut up by all means, but is there something on your mind?'

'Well.....yeah, sort of, I don't know, it's probably nothing but I just got a tingle about something.'

'And?'

She inhaled deeply, exhaling slowly. 'You know Joshua Englefield who works for me?'

'Yeah, blond-haired guy, looks a bit like a surfer who eat a few too many doughnuts and didn't do quite enough surfing.'

'That's him.'

Sam touched his finger to his lip, thinking. 'He worked on that job we had in LA last year didn't he?

The one where we took out the van on Sunset full of AK's.'

'Yep, that's him.'

Sam nodded. 'He did some good work, I recall – made the connection between one of the yacht crew and the name used to hire the van. Looks like he could do with a bit of a makeover, but got a good brain in his head. What's on your mind?'

Alicia told him about the odd Monday Josh was taking off, his occasional attitude, and killing time looking through Facebook. She rummaged in her bag for her phone. 'Give me a sec.'

She opened photos and tapped on the screen shot of the high-kickers. 'I think this was taken at his birthday recently.' She handed the phone to Sam.

'Jeez, look at the size of that doobie. Looks like a good night.'

'Take a look at the guy on his left. He's what's making me tingle. I can't place him, but something's niggling and I can't think why.'

Sam put his reading glasses on and held the handset a little closer.

His mouth was slightly open, and remained that way as he held the phone steady, moving just his eyes to look directly into Alicia's, then back at the phone.

'Have you told anyone else about this, Leece?'

'No, I wasn't sure it was anything – just a feeling in my gut.'

'We need to talk but not here. Cancel any appointments for the next hour and come to my office. We need proper privacy.'

*

Alicia brushed the crumbs off her skirt and drained the last dregs of coffee, thankful for the buzz she now felt – or was that Sam's reaction to the photo? She went directly to her department, an open plan room full of computers, whiteboards, large ultra HD screens and a separate private office at the back which was hers.

She walked past the various staff members who were at their stations. 'Hey, Eileen, how's the foot?' Eileen was her longest serving personal assistant, an African American woman with striking bleached hair cut short, who Alicia loved like a sister.

'Throbbin' like a bitch, sugar. Four hours I waited in the emergency room, four hours just to get a splinter outta my god-dammed toe, man it was a big mother though. Teach me for dancin' in bare feet.'

Alicia put her hand on Eileen's arm. 'Never stop dancing, girl – I wish I had half your moves.'

'Get outta here – I've seen you throw some shapes. Remember last year's Christmas party at the Iron Horse grill? That pole?'

Alicia laughed. 'I'll take the Fifth Amendment on that – you led an innocent country girl astray.'

'Hey, don't you go blamin' me, honey, you didn't need no leadin'.'

'Enough! Have I got anything on for the next hour that can't be changed?'

'Only that guy John Newbury from HR – he was going to talk to you about the office redesign. Seems like they found a bunch of money they gotta spend on stuff that works perfectly well anyway. Can I request a chaise longue for my corner here, maybe a hot tub as well?'

Alicia groaned, rubbing her temples. 'No more HR today, tomorrow or ever, *please*. I've been with them all morning and want to push my eyes into the back of my head. Put him off – something came up and I got to be somewhere else for a while.'

'Sure thing. When I speak to Newbury do you want me to order a dancing pole for your office so you can practise for next Christmas?'

'You're fired.'

'Yeah, yeah, yeah, who would organise your life if little old Eileen wasn't here?'

Alicia couldn't help but laugh. 'OK, final, final, final warning.'

She put her purse under her arm and walked back to the door, passing desks on her way. 'Hey, Lucy, hi, Evie, hey, Josh.'

*

Ten minutes after leaving the restaurant she knocked on Sam Dibble's door. 'Come.'

Alicia walked in to see Sam closing his laptop screen. 'That was quick – bring a chair round to my side, Leece.'

She rolled a seat up next to his. He leant forward, pressing a button on his console. 'Hi, Tiffany – no disturbances, including calls.'

'Sure thing, even the President?'

'Tiff – especially the President.'

'Haha, you got it.'

Sam turned towards Alicia. 'Let's see that photo again.'

She fished out her phone and brought up the screenshot.

Sam held out his hand. 'May I?'

He opened his laptop back up and held her phone next to the screen.

'Your gut was right – you sure you've not shared this with anyone else?'

'Oh please, Sam, I wasn't even sure I'd got anything.'

Alicia looked at the high definition photo, then back at her phone screen. 'That's him – a custody photo?'

'Yeah – arrested at a demonstration a few months ago in Washington, some sort of free speech group. He got released with a warning after threatening to punch a police horse in the face, would you believe. Take a look at his placard in this one.'

Alicia could see a homemade sign with *No more secrets* crudely painted on.

‘Who is he?’

‘Charles Black, or Chas as he likes to be called. Take a look at these as well.’

Sam swiped a series of photos, all taken at different times. Some in bars, one in what looked like a city park, and a shot taken with a long lens through a restaurant window. In many of the photos Black was with another man, slightly overweight, with his face always turned just out of shot. What could be seen though, was wavy blond shoulder length hair poking out from a knitted cap.

‘Go back to the park one.’

Sam scrolled back and Alicia confirmed what she thought she’d seen. The man in the knitted hat was gesticulating with a cigarette, and on his right wrist was a bracelet of wooden beads.

‘Jesus, is that who I think it is?’

Sam nodded. ‘You’d better believe it.’

Alicia turned to face Sam. ‘Where did you get these?’

‘From the Bureau. I’ve only just looked at them myself. As soon as you showed me the photo I was pretty sure I recognised him. Remember that seminar a few weeks ago that none of us wanted to go to?’

‘Uh-ha, all about the unseen threat in your own back yard. They were trying to remind us not to get completely hung up about ISIS, Al Qaeda and Uncle Tom Terrorist and all.’

‘That’s the one – you remember they showed us that footage and stills of peaceful demos, citizens exercising their right to protest – the land of the free and all that?'

'Sure, they wanted to remind us that an enemy could be hiding where we'd least expect to find them, i.e. right in front of us, in plain sight.'

'I just rang Chris Williams at the Bureau who presented the seminar and asked if he could send me his PowerPoint. Would you believe he was updating it when I called. Sounds like he's got himself a nice little number there, going around the country presenting it to all the field offices and staying in nice hotels on the Bureau's dime. Anyhow, he included the custody photo slide as part of his talk, as a reminder that seemingly innocent people waving quaint homemade placards might not be so nice after all.'

'So where did the other photos come from?'

'Well, Chris flagged Black up to the Bureau's Intel cell and they did a little digging. He wasn't considered high priority, but something didn't smell right so they put a loose follow on him for a few weeks. Nothing much came of it, he wasn't doing anything that raised suspicion. Just meeting his buddy and hanging out with him.'

'Englefield.'

'You got it. Anyway, Chris asked to be kept in the loop when he found out they were going to keep a long eye on him, and for a copy of the photos just in case there was anything he could use in his presentation in the future.'

'And?'

'And nothing – he didn't score many points on their risk analysis so they put it to bed.'

'So why are we sitting here huddled around your desk?'

'Because I ran his name through *our* database, the one we don't always share, and bingo.'

'So who the hell is Chas Black?'

'You remember Chelsea Manning, back when she was Bradley?'

'Of course – still sends a shiver when I hear either name.'

'Well, Black's name came up in the fallout after the big WikiLeaks data dump so he was looked at quite closely, but there was nothing solid enough to tie him to it in any meaningful way. They did shake his tree but nothing fell out. They pulled him in, turned over his apartment and examined his computer and phone but got diddly-squat. The top floor were happy – well not *happy*, but they decided to draw a line under it as they had Manning.'

'Jeez – and you said I was fast getting to your office. How did you get all this so quickly?'

'Like I said, by pure luck Chris was working on his presentation, and I literally came off the phone to the top floor just before you arrived.'

'Did you tell them about Joshua?'

'Of course, but there's more.'

Alicia made a beckoning sign with her fingers, raising her eyebrows. 'Well, go on.'

Sam nodded towards the flask on his side table 'You want coffee?'

'Er yeah. Can you talk and pour at the same time?'

'Just watch me – I can even chew gum as well and not fall over.'

'No one likes a show-off.'

Sam cracked a smile, grabbed two mugs from the table and poured what looked like two steaming quarts of strong coffee.

'Turns out our Mr Black wasn't happy with the result of Manning's handiwork.'

Almost incredulous, Alicia squealed. 'Not happy? They put 750,000 classified documents into the public domain. People disappeared as a result of it.'

'No, you misunderstand – that's exactly what I said when upstairs told me. Black boasted on various anarchy sites and bulletin boards that they'd gone about it all the wrong way. Instead of quantity he thought they should have just released the real quality ones and kept back all the rubbish. There was so much, it got diluted. Still cost a lot of lives though, but not enough for Black.'

'So why the interest in him now?'

'Black is suspected of being involved with a breakaway group from WikiLeaks. Have you heard of *Welikeleaks*?'

'Yeah, but I thought it was just another clown on the internet trying to be clever and funny.'

'Evidently not. This lot are far more dangerous. Really nasty people – mostly anarchists evidently, and they've got serious money behind them. The Agency picked up a bit of chatter, mostly on the conspiracy sites. It seems they'd love to put out personal information regarding spies, informants, handlers, even undercover sleeper officers who've been in place for months or even years.'

Alicia shook her head. 'Bastards.'

Dibble continued. 'They want addresses out there, phone numbers, even family photos. It's all at an early stage, but upstairs are starting to get concerned. You never know with these people if it's all bluster, but if they formed alliances within our industry, there's a chance it could happen.'

Alicia sat back. 'Englefield.'

'Could be.'

'What do upstairs want to do about it?'

'To see you and me.' He pulled back his cuff. 'Five minutes ago.'

Chapter 5.

UK, two weeks to mission.

Jenks put the fireguard up and took his wine glass out to the kitchen, washing and drying it and put it back in the cupboard. He set the house alarm and headed upstairs to the bathroom. Five minutes later he climbed into bed, cleared his mind and was asleep within moments.

He woke early – sunrise was just under the horizon, but the blackness of night was slowly morphing into the navy blue half-light of dawn. He felt refreshed after seven hours of deep sleep, leaving ample time for a run before his 9am call to Camburn.

The beach was deserted except for a couple of dog walkers. The lights on the Isle of Sheppey were still twinkling, and fishing boats were anchored, waiting for high water. As he set off slowly, gradually increasing his speed until he settled into a metronomic pace, his mind drifted and an image entered his head of his mother sitting under an apple tree in their large garden, crying. Jenks thought he must have been about eight. He vaguely remembered asking her what was wrong, and putting his arms around her, breathing in the familiar smell of her perfume. Long forgotten memories seemed to want to push past each other to get his attention, but it wasn't a bad feeling.

Having opened up a parental memory, he thought about his father but all he saw was a featureless figure appearing fleetingly in his very young life, then disappearing again. He tried to expand the memory, working back from the last one to the first, then back again, but nothing came. All he had was a maximum of four occasions he thought he was remembering his dad, but it was so long ago.

There were a couple of hazy recollections of a man's head appearing around his bedroom door whispering *goodnight, son*, and the last time was when his parents were arguing. All he could recall was his mother saying, 'No, Ken, I won't. This is home.'

As he ran along the beach he saw a woman bending over kissing the top of her dog's head. Jenks mind rejoined the memory of the argument and a missing part emerged – just a second or two, but it was of his father bending down to kiss the top of *his* head. 'Be a good boy for Mummy, and always remember I love you more than you will ever know.' It was in this, the *director's cut* or extended version of the memory he pictured looking up into the vivid turquoise of his father's eyes, the rest of his features lost in time.

He'd loved his mother dearly, but having left home at the age of twelve to board at Charterhouse, evidently following his father's wishes, he'd learnt quickly he didn't actually need her anymore. He had other people to patch him up when he fell over, other people to make his meals and do his washing – other people to do all the things she would have done. She'd even offered to move house so he could attend as a day pupil, but he was adamant he wanted to board – at the age of twelve he was already single-minded.

He was in Afghanistan when he received the news she was unwell. He'd graduated from Sandhurst after forty-four weeks of intensive training, where he was awarded the Queen's medal for achieving the highest scores in military, practical and academic studies. He remembered the pride on his mother's face as Prince Charles hung the medal over his head at the passing out ceremony.

His thoughts went back to a satellite telephone call with his mother on his third tour, interspersed with crackles and interference. She'd been admitted to hospital with unknown but severe stomach pains but told him not to worry, that *she* should be the one worrying, and would see him when he was next back on leave. A week later he received the news about the fire, and the likely cause. There was nothing he could do other than making sure the insurance company liaised with the hospital regarding temporary accommodation whilst the claim was processed.

A few weeks later he was dug into a rocky outcrop on the edge of the desert, watching two tents 1,200 yards away. Unwashed, surviving on field rations, shitting in a hole in the ground and with little sleep, he nevertheless remained at the ready – his only companion a fully suppressed Barratt M82 sniper rifle.

Semi-automatic, loaded with massive 50mm ordnance and fitted with the very latest optics, the weapon had an effective range of nearly 2,000 yards in the right hands.

He could have delegated the mission to one of his men, but the fact was, no one was as good as him. His vast stamina, coolness under pressure and being one of the top marksmen in the armed forces meant it was a no-brainer.

Inside one of the tents were two Taliban fighters. One making ready a digital camera, the other sharpening a long curved sword. The second tent contained two more Taliban guarding a pair of battered and bruised American airmen. The Americans had been severely mistreated – one was now blind in one eye, and both were missing most of their fingernails and a few teeth.

Shot down by a surface-to-air missile, they'd managed to parachute to safety only to be captured ten minutes later by ruthless men willing to do anything to extract information, and had subsequently been tortured. They were now minutes away from the end of their lives.

Any ground or air assault would have undoubtedly ended in their death, either at the hands of their captors or as victims of friendly fire. It was for this reason Jenks had been dropped from 10,000 feet and walked six miles through the night to where he currently lay.

He thumbed his throat mic. In a voice barely above a whisper, he transmitted. 'Control, this is Alpha One.

Subjects are exiting their tents. Confirmed four targets. Two friendlies being dragged in front of camera. This is it. Stand by for further. Do not, I repeat, do not transmit after copying this message.'

Minimum words, no need for elaboration.

He heard the acknowledgement. 'Copy that, Alpha One, radio silence will be maintained.' The truth was, no one expected the airmen to survive, but if one or two Taliban could be eliminated, at least they'd tried.

Jenks settled himself, slowing his breathing and heart rate. He'd measured wind speed, calculated the angle of drop – 1,200 yards is a very long way and bullets dipped the further they flew, even 50-calibre ones, so he made micro adjustments to the scope to compensate.

Three of the Taliban had Kalashnikovs slung casually over their shoulders – undoubtedly a gift from the Russians. They appeared relaxed, no need to be at the ready when they were in the middle of hundreds of miles of desert. The fourth was holding the sword. They would teach the great Satan a lesson when they posted footage of the infidels begging for their lives, and a close-up of their severed heads resting on the sand.

The two airmen were pulled in front of the camera and forced to kneel. He could see any fight had gone and they were resigned to their fate. He felt the slow throb of the pulse in his neck as he gently settled his finger against the trigger.

The black-robed swordsman was addressing the camera, pointing to the airmen and then the sky. Jenks exhaled slowly as the executioner stepped to the side of the first captive and spat directly at his face. The thick glob of sputum landed half in the airman's hair and half on his ear.

Three quarters of a mile away, a man the executioner didn't know existed was looking into his eyes through the cross hairs of the most advanced scope on the planet as he slowly raised the blade.

Jenks exhaled again, but didn't inhale. Between the beats of his heart he slowly squeezed the trigger. Even the slightest movement at that range would send the bullet yards from where it should be – where it deserved to be.

Before the sword began its downward trajectory, Jenks completed the last millimetre of trigger pull. Even travelling at 1,700mph, the shot would take nearly two seconds to reach its target. As the sword began its journey, so the bullet ended its own.

Jenks was already moving the barrel a fraction to the left as the swordsman's head disappeared in a puff of red mist, exploded by a piece of metal capable of passing through a railway sleeper and still killing anyone standing behind it.

Before the next man registered what had happened he was thrown back ten feet, his chest now a gaping hole where his heart and most of his lungs had been. Then, for Jenks, Lady Luck showed her pretty face. The two remaining fighters both turned simultaneously, not quite processing what had happened – one now standing in front of the other.

They hadn't heard the silenced Barrett and were too far to be able to pick out the small puff of smoke. A gift. Jenks sent the third round, keeping his eye to the sight. Just under two seconds later he saw both men drop as the bullet streaked through the first man's throat, his spine offering little resistance, and with enough velocity to remove most of the skull and brain matter of the smaller man standing behind him.

Jenks tapped his throat mic. 'Control, this is Alpha One, do you copy?'

'Alpha One, go ahead.'

'All targets down, I repeat all targets down. Full elimination of threat. Friendlies safe. Bring those boys home.'

'Roger that, Alpha One. Good job, beer is on ice.'

'Copy that, better make it a slab – I've been drinking my own piss for twenty-four hours.'

Jenks got picked up and flown back to base. The crew handed him an ice cold bottle of Bud as he strapped himself into the chopper. No beer ever tasted better.

He was walking towards the bunkhouse when his CO, Colonel Renshaw called out. 'Hey, Jenks, can you pop into my office?'

Jenks swerved right and caught up with Renshaw as they headed through the command centre and into the colonel's office.

Renshaw beckoned him to sit down. 'What you did out there couldn't be done, simple as that – I thought I'd seen everything. Those two men will be home with their families healing in a couple of days thanks to you.'

Jenks felt there was something else – Renshaw should have looked happy. He was obviously pleased about the result, but there was sadness behind his eyes.

'Thank you, sir, I had a bit of luck along the way.'

'Luck doesn't come into it, lieutenant, you make your own.'

Renshaw seemed to be trying to figure out the best way to say what he had to say next, but there was no easy way.

Jenks sensed it. 'With all due respect, sir, spit it out.'

Colonel Renshaw opened the top drawer of his desk and took out a slim file. 'Son, I'm just going to come out and say this because I know you're not big on bullshit. I'm really sorry to have to inform you that your mother passed away in hospital today.'

Jenks looked directly at Renshaw, causing him to look away from the laser-like stare of Jenks's turquoise eyes. 'Tell me everything you know.'

Renshaw looked down at the paper, thankful not to have to look at Jenks even though he knew all the details. 'She wasn't in any pain – they kept her on a very high dose of morphine and according to the doctors, hadn't really been conscious for the last week. It was pancreatic cancer. Only a matter of weeks from when she was admitted. The docs said she wouldn't have known where she was, or felt a thing.'

Jenks sat for a moment looking into space. 'What was the time of death, sir?'

Renshaw checked. 'They called it at 11.22 GMT.'

Jenks did a quick calculation in his head – England was four and a half hours behind Afghan time.

'11.22, thank you, sir.' Exactly the same time he sent his first bullet.

'You want leave, son, you got it. Take as much time as you need.'

'I'm fine thanks, sir, but appreciate the offer.' He stood up, saluted and walked across the office shutting the door behind him.

Jenks hadn't thought about that day for as long as he could remember, the whole recollection lasting a matter of seconds. As he ran on he pushed it from his mind and focused on the day ahead. He pictured again how the operation would unfold in thirteen days. Unlucky for some…

Chapter 6.

Jenks ran the last half mile along the beach, easing down before stopping at the high water mark.

He still had an hour before he was due to ring Camburn, so went to his garage. It was large enough to accommodate a workshop area, his Land Rover, a home gym and his motorcycle, a 2014 Ducati Panigale – still one of the fastest production bikes.

The difference between the quickest accelerating and thirtieth position was half a second. Jenks's machine could hit 60mph in 2.6 seconds and onwards to over 200mph. He glanced at the bike and did a quick calculation – at top speed, the distance he'd just run would have taken just over two minutes on his bike. The thought made him smile.

He spent the next thirty minutes performing a series of strenuous exercises, finishing with ten minutes of tai chi. He felt his body calming, his burning muscles cooling, and his mind clear, enabling him to focus on mission planning.

Jenks went into the kitchen, poured a pint of water and set the coffee percolator on the stove. He pulled a bag of banana slices from the freezer, defrosting a handful before adding to a large bowl of porridge and sat down to slowly eat, sip his coffee and think about the day ahead.

At 9am he dialled James Camburn. It was time to go to work.

Camburn answered on the second ring. 'Hello, old chap, I take it you're in fine fettle this morning?'

'Good morning, JC – yes, fed and watered and been out for a run. I've got a provisional list of what I need, but wanted to go over a couple of things first.'

'Of course, what's on your mind?'

Previously in the USA..

Joshua Englefield and Chas Black had started hanging out together more frequently, mostly at weekends to get wrecked, and now sometimes in the week – not just to get wasted, but to talk. Englefield liked Black, and although he hadn't spoken much at the beginning of their friendship about his thoughts on life and ideals, what Black had said resonated with him. He remembered how on his birthday they'd spent three days nonstop partying, but also had some pretty interesting deep conversations about life, the universe, and man's inhumanity to man.

Chas Black was a year older than Englefield, and the opposite in terms of looks. He wore a full beard and his brown hair, flecked with a little grey, reached the middle of his back. His face had the tell-tale signs of a heavy smoker, lined beyond his years, and unlike Englefield's chunky build, he was stick thin.

His employment history could not have been more different to Englefield's – he'd drifted from job to job, often taking a dislike to anyone in authority. He currently worked part time in a part-worn tyre depot, but was always on the lookout for something else.

Sometimes they met at each other's homes, other times hooking up with friends to debate important stuff and put the world to rights in a local bar. Occasionally they just went to the park to chat in the early evening sun, and, Englefield had noticed the posters in Black's apartment. He particularly liked one showing a protester with his clenched fist held high, his face covered by a bandana and an anarchy sign tattooed on his forearm – a red *A* within a red circle. A belief that the only real way to change things was order within anarchy.

As the months rolled by, what Black had to say made a lot of sense. Englefield thought about his brother Steven, and how he'd been reduced to mere existence due to the actions and decisions of his country.

He felt guilty about not going to see his brother more, but the truth was it upset him too much. He couldn't find anything positive in Steven's continued existence. His brother couldn't do anything for himself, having to wear a nappy and have his arse wiped by an orderly, and made noises like a baby. Joshua felt angrier each time he saw him, and the visits became less and less frequent.

He'd had arguments with his parents about it – his mother used to ring him when the gap had grown from weeks to months, and it was always the same conversation. She still clung to the belief that God would heal Steven, at least in the head.

Josh always had the same reply. 'Mum, he's a vegetable. Half his brain is in the sand in Afghanistan – Steve died the moment that bomb exploded – please don't make me feel guilty for not doing what you think I should do when I want to remember him as he was. He doesn't even know who's in the room, what's the point?'

It would always end with his mother crying, saying she would pray for him as well. Unfortunately, God never intervened.

Englefield continued to perform well at work, apart from the odd run-in with Buckland. She was always on his case when he asked for a day off. Yeah, so he wasn't actually ill, but he always took it as leave rather than a sick day. It wasn't his fault she had no life.

The more he and Black hung out, the more their bond strengthened, but Englefield was torn – he was living a double life and wanted out. He wanted to make a difference, to channel his rage into changing everything, forever. Black had great ideas but was firing a pea-shooter, not the potential cannon Englefield could supply.

And there was the big problem. Black was completely unaware Englefield worked for the CIA and would undoubtedly assume he was an agent and cut all contact with him if he found out, but he had to find out. Englefield had big ideas how to really make a difference, to change the world for the better, to end all wars – everyone on the planet equal. With Black's network and Englefield's access to data they would make the most powerful weapon – working together they could shake the world like no other. Order through anarchy. It was the only way.

*

Buckland and Dibble took the elevator to the 7th floor and into the reception area to the offices of Florence Rizzoli, director of internal security. Her PA Eleanor Trainor looked up as the doors opened. 'Hi, Sam, go right in, she's expecting you.' She smiled and nodded at Alicia as they passed her desk.

Dibble gave her a thumbs up. 'Sure thing, El – how's things with you?'

'Oh, you know, come to work, go home, eat, sleep, come back to work – repeat until fade.'

'Haha, I know the feeling – catch you later.'

They opened the internal door and walked through. 'Hi, Sam, long time no see.'

Sam smiled. 'Well that can only be a good thing – if I was seeing more of you I'd start to worry.'

'You know me better than that, and hi, you must be Alicia, nice to meet you.' Rizzoli stood up, extending her hand.

'Pleased to meet you too, ma'am.'

'Please, call me Flo. Sam and I have known each other a long time. You come highly regarded – he's mentioned you in the past.'

'Oh has he now.'

Florence smiled. 'All good, I can promise you that.'

They all laughed as she gestured towards the sofa and two armchairs by the window.

Florence Rizzoli was of Italian descent, which showed in her jet black corkscrew hair. Aged in her mid-forties, she had the look of a woman you didn't mess with. Her thick but shaped eyebrows accentuated her dark brown eyes, and like Buckland, she wore little makeup apart from mascara and subtle lipstick, when she could be bothered.

Alicia took a second to pause and look out, seeing a group of people running a trail in the distance, and felt a slight pang of envy.

Sam and Alicia took a seat next to each other on the sofa while Rizzoli sat down in one of the sumptuous armchairs.

'You've got a lovely office, Flo – great view.'

'I think it's the payoff for never letting me out of it. I'd get less time inside for murder – coffee?'

Sam spoke first. 'I'm good – Leece and I just had a bucket each downstairs.'

Alicia shook her head. 'None for me either thanks.'

Rizzoli got straight to it. 'Alicia, your instincts were spot on – you got the tingle and didn't let it drop. Those boys in training don't recognise that these days. They hammer home to the rookies to just go on the facts – what do we know and how can we find out what we don't. There's a lot to be said for listening to your gut. It may be a single fibre in a thread that can be pulled, which leads to the whole damn ball.'

‘Thank you, Flo – I did worry a little about telling Sam, but you know when you get that feeling, and it just won’t go no matter how many times you tell yourself it may be nothing?’

‘Oh I know full well, like an itch you can’t quite reach to scratch.’

‘That’s exactly how it felt, exactly.’

Rizzoli went silent, stroking the end of her nose which she always did when she was concentrating. ‘OK, here’s what I think. We’ve got a guy working for us with access to highly classified information. He’s friends with people who like to shout a lot and jump up and down because they don’t agree with the way things are.’ Sam and Alicia nodded.

‘Do you remember when you were teenagers and your parents didn’t really like some of your friends? How they thought they were a bad influence, and that somehow you’d turn out like them? But you didn’t. Maybe you liked the thrill of hanging out with people no one else liked, just because you weren’t supposed to.’

Sam raised his hand. ‘Yeeeah, but they didn’t threaten to punch police horses in the face, hang around with anarchists or potentially have been involved with the biggest data leak in American history.’

‘I get that – and don’t think I’m not taking this seriously, I am. Englefield is a concern, but I get lots of people brought to my attention with just cause to worry about. I can count on one hand the ones who follow through and actually commit crimes.'

Both Sam and Alicia looked slightly crestfallen.

'Hey, don't look at me like that – you both look like you've been sent to the naughty step. I want to follow this and see where it leads, but not like a bull in a china shop. At the moment we have you, Alicia, spotting someone in a photo that spiked something. You couldn't put your finger on it but couldn't let it go. You, Sam, recognised the person spiking Alicia, and confirmed it was someone you'd seen in a presentation by the FBI and confirmed he was a person of interest, Mr Charles Black.'

Florence started stroking her nose. 'So, Sam followed it up and found out Black was arrested at a demonstration for threatening to punch a police horse. Feelings were high, people were egging each other on, and the chances are he was on something. We also know, thanks to Sam running the name through our stand-alone system, that Black's head popped over the parapet and we were curious to find out a little more about the company he kept.'

Sam spoke. 'And it wasn't the sort of people I'd like any of my family hanging out with.'

Florence nodded. 'Quite, me neither. We now know Black was suspected of involvement in the WikiLeaks data dump back in 2010. It was thought he may have been a courier, but nothing could be proved. His home was searched, his computers seized, but he came up clean. Since then he's been off the radar until the Bureau kept a long eye on him after the horse business. And what did we glean from that? He hangs out with like-minded guys like our Joshua, and their main hobby seems to be getting off their faces. They puff out their chests and bluster about *the man* and how unfair everything is, but they're not showing any signs it goes further than that.'

Florence leant forward. 'Off the record, my predecessor was on the WikiLeaks case and had nearly two hundred people of interest, all possibly linked in some way. Black was just one of them.'

Sam looked like he was about to say something, but Alicia got in first, 'So where do we go from here – what do you want me to do?'

'Nothing, act completely normally and still bawl him out if he takes a Monday off. I'm going to get one of the covert tech guys to do a mirror copy of his hard drive tonight. What time does everyone usually leave?'

'If we haven't got an urgent job on, the office is usually clear by 7pm, 7.30 at the latest. I'm usually there until about 9, but can stay later if you need me to?'

'Thanks. Whilst it's copying I'll get him to input a key logger on Josh's system so we can go back and see exactly what he's been doing and we'll put a camera in overhead.'

Sam spoke. 'What about Black – the other half of the picture?'

‘We’ll start surveillance again, but not full technical just yet. We can always up the ante if it looks like there’s something in this. I’ve currently got forty-seven live operations targeting staff here at Langley. I guarantee virtually all of them will go nowhere. I’ve had pissed-off wives calling the anonymous tip line, reporting that their husband is passing secrets when the truth is he’s screwing some whore in the next state. I’ve even had a guy who was acting so suspiciously, his brother alerted us that something wasn’t right. When we searched his house, do you know what we found?’

‘No,’ they both said.

‘Over 600 Agency pens, dozens of staplers, and thirty bottles of photocopier toner, the large ones. The guy didn’t even own a photocopier. Turns out he got a jolt out of stealing Agency property and got addicted.’

‘Jeez, what happened to him?’

‘He got the choice of either being sacked, or transferring for a year to some shitty job basically counting paperclips in some shitty sub office, in a shitty town in the county of Shitsville.’

Alicia and Sam roared with laughter.

‘So you see, this is one of many ongoing investigations, but I’m certainly not kicking it out the park. We’ll let it run and see where it goes, and if something spikes we’ll jump on them from a great height. If I went in now and there was something at an early stage, we’re going to get almost nothing. Englefield isn’t stupid so he’ll have been careful, if indeed he is up to no good. Black will disappear as he's had his cage rattled before and won't want the attention again. Maybe they'd regroup, get others in – then we'd be completely in the dark.'

Sam and Alicia saw the situation from Rizzoli's perspective but were pleased she was taking it seriously enough to throw some resources at it.

'I think that's about it for now, folks.'

They stood and Alicia turned to Rizzoli. 'Your man tonight – what's his name? I don't want any unfortunate coincidences.'

'You're not going to believe this, it's Shaun Hacker.'

'You're putting me on right? There's no way that's his real name.'

'Believe me, it is. Hiding in plain sight I think they call it.'

Both Alicia and Sam shook their heads in disbelief and went back to work.

Chapter 7.

Kent, UK, 13 days to mission.

The phone call continued, Jenks was speaking. 'I've read the file a number of times, but what puzzles me is why we've only been given the job now? Surely there was enough for the Yanks to act beforehand – this all seems a bit last-moment even though we've got almost a fortnight to plan. There's a few ifs and buts I'm not entirely happy with.'

'Oh, in an ideal world, my boy, in an ideal world. The same thoughts occurred to me and I wasn't 100% either. I had a meeting with the Caretaker because there were a few loose ends I didn't like. The Caretaker was of the same mind.'

Camburn continued. 'I know we've always taken these things at face value and been good boys and done what we've been told. Our Caretaker was flying out for a conference last week and used it as cover to meet his counterpart in the States. I didn't want to initiate the file until I'd got an update and been briefed on the findings.'

'And?'

'The Yanks have lost Englefield.'

'What? How?'

'They had their suspicions about a year ago, but nothing concrete. It seems Englefield was keeping company with less than salubrious people. They took it seriously enough to start keeping an eye on him. They inserted a key logger into his computer at work, copied the hard drive, installed a pin hole camera and had surveillance on him and his friend as well.'

'And?'

'Well, and nothing for a good while. His work was exemplary – yes, he met with Black, but there were no useful intercepts, nothing from his computer and nothing suspicious from the camera. They also thought there was no way Black would associate with Englefield if he knew he was CIA.'

'What about Englefield's phone, home computer, laptop?'

'Well this is where it gets interesting. According to the Caretaker they only really got a break in the last few weeks, and it was working it back that they saw the whole picture. They hacked into his home Wi-Fi so if he was doing anything untoward there they'd know, but he wasn't. You would have expected him to perhaps use internet cafés but he never set foot in one. Not once.'

'So what happened to change the game?'

'Englefield put in for a month's holiday about three weeks ago and asked if he could leave at lunchtime. He told his boss he was going travelling as he hadn't done it as a student. Just a whistle-stop jaunt around the world. It was technically approved as they didn't want to do anything to spook him. He left work just after midday, and that was the last they saw of him.'

'Weren't they watching his apartment?'

'Well yes of course, but they didn't have a team on him from his place of work. They have numerous jobs running and just didn't have the manpower to cover his every move. They assumed he would go home, pack and then head off. They waited until midnight and when he didn't return they broke in and searched his apartment.'

'Did they find anything?'

'Oh yes, everything he owned, well almost everything apart from his laptop. They literally took everything apart. He was clearly a serious music nut – he had a whole wall of old records, and they took every single one out of its sleeve in case there was even a scrap of paper slipped inside one. Those guys were thorough – they took the back off an old amplifier that looked like it should have been in Dr Who's Tardis, dismantled his TV and microwave – they even defrosted all the frozen food in case he'd shoved something other than giblets up a chicken's arse.'

Camburn continued. 'All his clothes were still in the closet – no empty hangers. His passport was in a drawer, even the fridge was full. If you or I were going away on a planned trip, we'd at least chuck out the milk and butter and anything else that would go off. You wouldn't want to walk in after a month and be hit by that smell.'

They paused. Jenks spoke. ‘So he wasn’t planning on coming back then?’

‘It appears not.’

Jenks pictured the scene in his head. ‘That’s a lot to leave behind, particularly the records. Maybe he’d arranged for someone to clear it out.’ He paused for a few seconds. ‘But I’m thinking more that the payoff is going to be so big, he can spend the rest of his life rebuilding his collection from wherever he moves to.’

Camburn was quiet for a moment. ‘You don’t think he’s just doing this as part of his moral crusade then?’

‘It may well be, but he knows the consequences. All those protestors, eco warriors, hard core demonstrators, they all want a few quid in their pocket to be able to live. No, our man has thought carefully and planned this down to the last detail.’

Camburn offered some good news. ‘But they did find a thread which is why we’re talking now.’

‘Go on.’

‘He had a writing pad on his desk, but it was blank. The team leader had the presence of mind to hold it up to the light and saw faint indentation. It appears our man had thought about this and torn off the page below the one he’d written on, but had probably been using a sharp pencil. They fast-tracked it through the lab, and bingo.’

Jenks was intrigued. ‘What did they find?’

‘Well, it was a bit jumbled up as they were able to see the writing from at least two pages above. It was a cheap pad with fairly thin paper. If he’d splashed out another dollar, they wouldn't have got anything, so I'm told.'

'So what did they find?'

Camburn was obviously checking his notes. 'The name of the London hotel that's in the file, the word Eurostar ringed, and an email address – just a normal Gmail account. Oh, and the password.'

Jenks smiled. 'Nice.'

'And that's how it all came together. The Yanks had nothing, absolutely nothing until Englefield put in for leave and they turned his apartment over. It's what they found in a very short space of time that pushed it up the chain.'

'So their Caretaker wasn't even aware of Englefield at that point?'

'No, the investigation wasn't going anywhere – certainly way below the level he or she moves in. They kept him under loose surveillance for months, but he never did anything to raise the threat level – he just met his mate, had a beer and put the world to rights as far as they were aware.'

'So they fucked up then?'

'That's a bit harsh. When you consider the amount of threats they receive every day, there's only so much they can service. Had Englefield spiked a bit more they would've been all over him like a rash. Undoubtedly they would have bugged his house and car, but it's all immaterial now.'

'So they had to act quickly once they realised he'd fled the nest.'

'Precisely. For all they knew he may have actually been taking a month off and doing the things he always wished he'd done.'

Jenks wanted more information. 'So what did they find in the Gmail account?'

'Interestingly, no messages ever sent or received.'

'Hmmm, drafts?'

'Exactly.'

'How quaint.'

Camburn continued. 'The email drafts were chock-a-block – dozens of messages between Englefield and Black, but they just never got sent. It was the old trick of both having the log-in details. It's beautiful in its simplicity. Even with the most sophisticated intercepts, no one would have picked them up as they just sat on the Gmail server where they could both see them.'

'Did they sweep for any listening devices or hidden cameras in case he came back or was remote monitoring?'

'I understand so. It was clean as a whistle. Perhaps he was thinking ahead that if he was rumbled and they turned his place over but found nothing, they wouldn't have much to go on, other than the fact that his new best friend wasn't the type you'd want to bring home to meet mother.'

Jenks sighed. 'The old methods are sometimes the best – so simple.'

'Quite. But that's not all. There was another name they picked up from subsequent lab work on the pad –

Rick Mills. That name booked a first class ticket on the Eurostar from Paris to Amsterdam and from Amsterdam to London, arriving 10th March. I would hazard a guess that's the name on The Huntsman's Lodge reservation.

Jenks thought. 'Leave that with me.'

Camburn continued. 'They did quick time analysis of the draft emails and found out about the stolen data already passed on, and the big one to come.'

Jenks had another question. 'But we don't know exactly what the data was, but it's gone to someone, rather than directly out on the web like the Manning stuff?'

'Exactly. It looks like he drip fed them tasty morsels, probably for a good price, with a final large payout due before shutting up shop.'

Jenks nodded to himself. 'Makes sense, and that's why it was such a short space of time from being a nothing job right up to Red BTS.'

'Exactly. They had an urgent meeting at 8am after the lab spent all night working on the pad. Every unsent email they looked at made the whole situation go from bad to worse.'

Jenks ruminated. 'And the Caretaker was obviously at the meeting, so would have taken ownership of the whole sorry mess at that point?'

'That's my assumption. They would have let the meeting run its course, agreed with all the usual suggestions to try and trace Englefield and Black, but they were treading on very thin ice.'

'Explain.'

'They knew the big one was coming, but only in the last few days, and it was clear he was getting near fanatical. The end game is the big transfer, the real gold at the end of the rainbow. The CIA were worried, and quite rightly in my opinion, that Englefield had safeguards in place should something go wrong.'

Jenks had another question. 'So how is their Caretaker ensuring the Agency isn't pulling out all the stops to trace him themselves?'

'It was agreed that the investigation into locating Englefield was handed over to MI6 as everything pointed to the end game being in London. It was clear from the emails that he and Black would meet there, but my guess is they won't travel together. Englefield isn't stupid and knows the game too well. He'll put distance between them until the last moment.'

Jenks saw a problem. 'What if Black isn't actually going to be present – what if it's like a digital handshake?'

'Then 6 will liaise with the Agency in an effort to take Black out once Englefield is secured. Well, that's what they've been told. Langley wants to distance themselves as much as possible. If we erase the problem, nothing will come back to them. If it became known they're leaking like a sieve, well, can you imagine the fallout?'

Camburn continued. 'This is such a hot potato, it's only known to a handful of people who've been put on notice it would be considered treason if they divulged to anyone, basically anything they know about the whole affair. And, the Yanks still have the death penalty for that particular crime so as you can imagine, mouths will stay zipped.

Jenks nodded to himself. 'I see – worst case?'

'Yes, worst case scenario, the data is obviously stored digitally – I think we can safely assume that. It may be on his person or in a file already, waiting for him to push the button once he knows he's been paid. He'll have failsafes built in – maybe he has to access the file once or twice a day between certain times or it will self-disseminate to God knows who. A bit like negotiating with a gang of kidnappers and asking for proof of life before paying the ransom. If the file doesn't receive proof of life from Englefield, then out it goes, and intelligence agencies all over the world would be running around like headless chickens. Likewise if Englefield doesn't receive proof of life from Black, he'd realise he wasn't going to get the life-changing pay cheque, and with nothing to lose, put everything in the public domain anyway.'

Jenks understood the problem. 'Tricky.'

'One bit of good news is that because the messages are only held on the server, we can access the email account without leaving a digital footprint. I've got Maureen back at the Shop to monitor it, but there's been nothing of note for the last few days apart from a daily message from Black saying OK and a follow-up message from Englefield saying the same. Of course we've no way of knowing if this check-in wording will change on a pre-agreed day, so the Yanks can't even take out Black if they could find him as it would blow everything, and Black's disappeared into the ether as well.'

'I see their dilemma. The risk is way too high to apprehend Englefield or Black, if any of us could find them beforehand – it has to run to the end. Only when Englefield and I have a little chat will we know if the information's contained.'

Camburn sounded resigned. 'Unfortunately yes, our hands are well and truly tied. Now what shopping do you need in the meantime?'

'Not a huge list at the moment. I need a pre-paid credit card in the name of Hamish Wilson, preferably a Visa. I want 360-degree drone footage of the rooftops around The Huntsman's Lodge, say 200 metres in every direction. We're also going to need instant access and control of the CCTV for a square mile around the hotel, both council controlled ones and Transport for London. Send Maurs out for a walk and log any CCTV she can find in the private sector – shops, banks, cafés, anything that looks like a camera pointing towards the street.'

'Consider it done. Anything else?'

'A full leg brace. You know the sort sportsmen wear if they've had a horrendous injury. If they come left- or right-legged, I'd prefer a right but it doesn't really matter. You're also going to need to source an old oil barrel, open at one end – you know the sort pickets on strike used to light a fire in to stand around?'

'Yes, I'm old enough to remember them.'

'And put two of your best men on notice they'll be dressed as vagrants – I'll be able to give you more when I've seen the drone footage, but I want them to be really unapproachable, stinking of piss and acting drunk and aggressive.'

'No stereotyping then?'

'As if. Do you still have use of the facility in Epping Forest? I need two operatives who'll leave the hotel at the same time as me and go straight there – use your black cab for transport.'

Camburn knew where Jenks was referring to. 'The Ranger depot with the wood chipper?'

'Yes, and they'll need to pay a visit to Peppa and her friends after.'

'Understood. Anything else?

'Yes, Sildenafil. Better get two 50mg vials.'

'What the hell is that?'

'Liquid Viagra.'

Jenks could almost hear the cogs in Camburn's brain whirring round. 'Rrrright.'

'I've got a few things I can source locally. How soon can you get me the card details?'

'Hang on.' Jenks could hear Camburn call across the office. 'Maureen, I need a pre-paid Visa card, name of Hamish Wilson. How soon? Oh lovely, good.'

Camburn came back on. ‘Five mins, I’ll send you the number, valid dates and security code in a text. I’ll courier the card down with the drug.’

‘Excellent, catch up later. Oh, JC, how many people do we think have died as a result of Englefield’s disclosures?’

‘Difficult to say with any degree of certainty, my boy. The deaths have been dotted around the world. Some countries won’t reveal through fear of reprisals, even at ministerial level, but then we don’t tell the ministers why we’re asking. From speaking to the Caretaker, at least seven that we know of. They were all either undercover, Special Ops or held positions in the security service of their country. I’m aware three MI6 agents have also gone dark, so they’re probably dead as well and a US senator was found dead in his garden – he authorised a number of off-the-books operations.’

‘That’s a lot.’

‘I know – it’s the quality of the information he’s leaking. If he were releasing hundreds of thousands of names like Manning did, it would take an age to sort through them. These poor people might as well walk around with a ruddy great target painted on their chest, and we don’t know who his paymaster is, or what he’s got his hands on so far.’

Jenks was becoming more concerned. ‘This has the potential to be a real game changer.’

‘That might just be the understatement of the year, which is why we can’t let it happen, and why we need you. No shackles, no restrictions.’

‘What bothers me is how he drained this amount of information unnoticed? It seems inconceivable they don’t have more robust systems in place to detect and question chunks of top secret material and records being accessed.’

Camburn was nodding. ‘Don’t forget he works in an environment where he has access to most records and intelligence. He has a high security clearance, and as part of his everyday job would have to access at least some of the records. If he or his colleagues were pulled up every time they entered a database, they’d never get any work done. His department were not only responsible for analysis, which meant picking apart every bit of intel down to an almost sub-atomic level, but also protecting other departments ironically. The last thing anyone wants is a blue on blue situation.’

‘So he would have had access to other agencies’ systems to a certain extent, to make sure they weren’t all working on the same thing and end up tripping over each other.’

‘Up to a level, I suppose, but I just don’t know is the short answer. Perhaps there’s others involved, who knows, but he’s one of the main players. They can’t even look at it from the other way and trace it back, as they’ve no details of what files have been accessed. We can only deal with what we know.’

Jenks was slightly perplexed. ‘Wait a minute – they must’ve cross-checked the names of the people turning up dead with who’d recently accessed their files.’

‘Of course, that’s basic detective work, and they’re doing that as we speak. But, we’re talking about people who move in a very secret world here. It gets political. Various people would have cause to review a file for legitimate reasons, some up to, God knows, even vice president level. They can’t just go riding in with a posse and round everyone up. They have to tread carefully – they know they’re leaking badly, but can’t risk alerting a potential collaborator without knowing exactly who he or she is.’

Jenks nodded. ‘A real Catch-22.’

Camburn agreed. ‘Look, it’s coming from him one way or another – how he actually did it will come out in the fullness of time.’

Jenks closed the Wickr app and headed out to his car for the short drive into Whitstable, and a trawl round the charity shops.

Chapter 8.

At the same time Jenks turned the ignition key, a man sat at a table outside Le Depart Saint-Michel Café on the River Seine, overlooking Notre-Dame. He was dressed casually but warmly, with a scarf knotted around his neck. He wore a grey Magee flat cap, with his short black hair just visible. His dark beard was carefully clipped in a goatee style, but his thick-rimmed spectacles only had clear glass in them.

The cathedral was covered in scaffolding and plastic sheeting, with the sounds of men working within, carefully restoring it after the devastating fire. Paris was an hour ahead of London – it was just after 10.15 French time and chilly, so the man cupped his hands around his small café noir, and took occasional sips of his cognac. It was early, but apart from having to catch a train later, he had all the time in the world and was enjoying the jolt from the alcohol.

He'd been in Paris for three days, having travelled by train from Italy, a decision he came to regret during the journey. Had he done a little more research he would've discovered there were no direct trains. The journey took over eleven hours due to changes and a cow on the track in the middle of the French countryside.

A strikingly handsome waiter approached his table, a napkin over his arm. The man looked him up and down and liked what he saw. The waiter smiled. '*Autre chose, Monsieur*?' The man replied, '*Non, merci, l'addition s'il vous plait*,' and smiled back. The waiter disappeared and quickly returned with the bill. The man left a twenty-Euro note and strolled back to his hotel.

He walked into the lobby of the Hotel D'Aubusson and was greeted by the concierge, who never seemed to go home. '*Bonjour*, Monsieur Mills, will you be taking dinner with us tonight? I will ensure you have a good table.'

'Alas, Gaston, I'm checking out this morning, although I hope to be back.'

*

As Jenks drove towards his gates he received a text. It was the card details from Camburn. He looked at the screen, closed his eyes, then looked again. Repeating the action a further five times, the information was committed to memory. He'd use it when he got back from Whitstable.

He parked on Harbour Street and went into the Demelza shop opposite. The manager smiled as he entered, her hair an impossible shade of purple. He scanned around and couldn't find what he was looking for, but in a 50p-an-item box spotted an old-fashioned perfume atomizer and a thought came to him.

'Just that, dear?'

'Actually I was looking for a crutch, a hospital type one. My brother's really twisted his ankle and needs a bit of support.'

'Don't we all, darling,' she said, laughing far too heartily at her own joke.

'Sorry, luvvie – nothing at the moment. Have you tried the others?'

'Not yet but I'm working my way down the High Street.'

'Good idea, 50p please.'

He eventually entered the last charity shop on the High Street, pleased to see a large basket of umbrellas, walking sticks and four crutches. One was ideal, with a plastic cuff to go around the bicep, and a handle at right angles.

He took it to the counter to pay the man. 'Nothing serious, I hope?'

'No, just my idiot brother, he twisted his ankle really badly – missed the bottom rung of the ladder. He says it's not funny but I can assure you it is.'

The man laughed, 'Ooh I've done that – ouch. Call it a fiver, mate.'

'Tell you what, call it a tenner, it's for a good cause.'

'Ah cheers, mate. Hope he gets better soon.'

'So do I, I'm bloody driving him everywhere at the moment while he drives me up the wall – see you later.'

The man chuckled to himself as Jenks raised a hand to wave, closing the door behind him.

He walked back to his car and saw he still had twenty-five minutes left of his one-hour free parking. It was still only 10am and the whole day was in front of him, so he decided to do what normal people did. He went for a coffee.

Jenks walked into the delicatessen which he knew did a good brew, remembering a takeaway he'd had in the past.

One side was full of hams, cheeses and huge enticing bowls of salads which looked so good he decided to get a take-out for his lunch. The other side was a small eatery – stools against the wall so customers could sit and eat at a long counter. In the window was just one table, which was empty.

He approached the counter where a smiley lady was wiping down the coffee machine – a huge chrome unit which reminded him of cafés on the Continent.

'Morning, what can I get you?'

'Just an Americano please with a splash of milk.'

'Are you staying in or takeaway?'

'In please.'

He spotted a platter of Portuguese custard tarts. 'Those look lovely.'

'Dave made them this morning, they're my favourite, and I'm not just saying that.'

They looked too good to resist, so he ordered one. 'I'll bring it all round if you want to take a seat.'

He sipped his coffee and gazed around the interior, liking what he saw. They hadn't tried to make it look ultra-trendy or entice customers with an expensive fancy interior – it was obviously the food people came for.

Jenks took a bite from his tart, holding it out to look at – it was the best he'd ever tasted. The smiley lady came past. 'What do you think?'

'Unbelievable, I'll have another to take away please.'

'I know, I have to limit myself to one a day or I'd be the size of a house,' she said, patting her stomach.

Jenks asked her to make up a carton of mixed antipasto for him, and she busied herself around the other side. He liked the smiley lady. Very natural but attractive, and around his age, he guessed. He liked her long curly blondish hair and her smile, which made her eyes crinkle up and sparkle.

She poked her head around the door. 'Are you local?'

'Yes, quite. I had one of your coffees once before and remembered how good it was.'

'Aw thanks. I'm Alison, by the way.'

He extended his hand and they shook. 'Pleased to meet you, Alison.'

She bustled off to the kitchen and Jenks turned to gaze out at the world slowly going by. He could never have a relationship because of what he did. He would never come home to an Alison and ask her how her day had been, or tell her about his.

He was shaken out of his daydream by the sound of someone across the street shouting. 'Yoo hoo, yoo hoo.' He looked out and saw the lady with the impossibly purple hair waving at someone further down the road. And then the laugh. He closed his eyes momentarily and sighed.

Alison came out of the kitchen and guessed what he was grimacing at. 'I know, I know. You've only been here ten minutes – I get it all day.'

Jenks laughed. 'You should get danger money working here.' Alison nodded. 'You're right, I'll ask for a raise.'

He settled up and dropped a few pound coins into the tips glass. 'Cheers, really nice to meet you.'

'And you, Alison.' He picked up his food, smiling at her as he opened the door. 'I didn't catch your name.' He pretended not to hear her as he shut it, heading to his car.

Chapter 9.

USA, Three months previously..

Chas Black had called Joshua Englefield on a Sunday afternoon and asked if he fancied coming over for a beer and watching the game. Englefield had told him yes, but couldn't do a late one as he had work in the morning. Englefield was pleased, as he felt the time had come to lay his cards on the table, and the cards he'd acquired since Friday were without doubt a winning hand. His need to change things – everything, was burning more ferociously inside him with every passing day, to the extent that some mornings he woke up so angry, he felt like he couldn't start the day without smashing something.

'Yeah, man, see you about 5 – you want me to pick up pizza?'

'Cool, and get some of those chocolate cookie things in case we get the munchies later, I got some kick-ass blow you're gonna love.'

'I mean it, dude, I have to work tomorrow and keep a clear head.'

'Pussy – throw a sickie, I've still got a couple of grams of pharmaceutical grade dust that'll take the top of your head off.'

'Yeah, well I got something that'll launch you into orbit, man – it'll be like all your Christmases rolled into one, I promise you that.'

'Shit, what you got – don't keep me in suspense.'

Englefield wanted to say more, but couldn't. 'It's what I've got to show you. This'll make you higher than you've ever been before.'

'The fuck? Now you got me thinking...come on, man, give me a clue.'

'Not on the phone, this has to be face to face. You won't believe what I'm gonna tell you until you see what I gotta show you.'

Black thought his friend sounded strange. 'You're weirding me out, dude, you high?

'Straight as a die, I'll catch you about 5 – later, man.' Englefield ended the call feeling as nervous as hell.

He'd become increasingly disillusioned with his work at the Agency, convinced Chas was generally right about the way forward, but even he wasn't thinking big enough. Englefield knew the problems he was helping to solve for his country meant new and bigger ones for others – more suffering for the victims of the United States and their bully boy allies.

There was only one way that made absolute sense – order within anarchy. Anarchy per se could never work – the idea was preposterous, but anarchy with structure after all that had once been was smashed and broken would level everything, for everyone. No more bullies meant no more victims. Everything shared equally.

Englefield had thought about it a lot. The world was in such a mess. Every single leader lied to their people. By whatever title the bastards were known – presidents, chancellors, prime ministers, kings, queens, religious leaders – they never trusted the people to be able to deal with the truth. They used lies to control and manipulate everything, but never for the greater good, always just the privileged few.

He was convinced that as long as that mindset remained, there would always be injustice. Poverty would never be fully addressed – the rich would grow richer whilst the poor became poorer. Real change could never happen slowly, it had to be big, really big. Undeniable, un-spinable by the politicians and simultaneous around the world – a shockwave so big it would leave no time to engineer damage limitation lies.

His security clearance had increased over the years as he proved himself. There were very few databases he wasn't allowed to delve into. The ones beyond his grasp were open only to director level and above, and they were the ones that held the real gold. Thankfully this wasn't a problem since he had a little tinker with the workstation of Alicia Buckland, she being of sufficient height up the ladder to be able to open digital doors and peer at the bad things inside. And now, so could he.

Like all personnel working within the analysis section of the CIA, Englefield had an excellent knowledge of computing and the way information technology worked. Files within hidden files, messages masquerading as genuine enabling them to bypass security screening – back doors into forbidden areas and most importantly, electronic pathways constructed where there'd been none before, invisible to everyone but him.

He'd begun formulating his plan as the rage within him came to the boil, to the extent his mind was made up that change had to come – permanent change. He would start with little forays into databases he was barred from entering, any attempt at which would normally cause a light to come on somewhere prompting questions to be asked. He needed to test the water to see if it was safe to dive in. He just had to open the door.

The opportunity presented itself on the day of the departmental Christmas party the previous Friday. The whole floor he worked on had booked out a local bar, The Iron Horse Grill. Cocktails at 5pm followed by food, dancing, and inevitably a long night of indulgence. A chance for everyone to let their hair down and behave in a way that some would undoubtedly have to apologise for on the following Monday. Just people blowing off steam and getting into the Christmas spirit.

Normally he'd be the first to the bar and the last to leave. He'd joined in the office chat about how good last year's outing was and how this year was going to be even better, suggesting people who would undoubtedly overdo it.

He'd laid the foundations for his non-attendance on the Wednesday, coughing a little through the day and blowing his nose loudly. On Thursday he made sure it was noticed he was self-medicating, placing a bottle of Tylenol on the front of his workstation. If anyone went for a drink and asked if he wanted coffee, he declined, but twice asked for a mug of boiling water, making a play of adding powdered cold remedy to it and commenting on how disgusting it tasted.

By Friday morning his 'cold' was evident. He'd snorted three substantial lines of cocaine the night before and deliberately stayed up until the early hours, getting up after just three hours' sleep so his eyes had heavy dark bags under them. His nose was constantly running, and to anyone, it was obvious he was unwell.

Alicia Buckland had commented when he arrived for work on Friday. She actually felt sorry for him when he shuffled into the office, coughing into a tissue. 'Jeez, Josh, you look terrible – you sure you want to be here? Why don't you go home and see if you can sleep it off and join us later? It'd be a shame to miss out on tonight.'

He told her he'd be OK, it was only a cold after all, and he had stuff to clear before the weekend. He assured her if it got any worse he'd go home. She had no reason to disbelieve him – she'd seen it develop over the last couple of days. Poor man – he really didn't look good, but she had to admire him for making the effort.

By 4.30pm there was a buzz in the air – everyone began to put on their coats, and conversations were only about one subject, the night ahead. People discussed what drinks they would start with, how they would pace themselves and how so and so would undoubtedly start the dancing. There was added excitement as the bar had recently installed a mechanical bucking bronco. Alicia had stated quite categorically there was no way she was getting on it, but the general consensus was, if someone in their group tried it, they all had to.

Englefield had been rubbing his eyes a little harder than was apparent, making them very bloodshot. Everyone was ready to leave en masse as a small bus had been booked to take them all to the restaurant together. Evie came across buttoning her coat. 'Josh, you look dreadful, how are you feeling?'

At that point Alicia came out of her glass-fronted office. Joshua Englefield, the trooper who'd come in when he should have been under his duvet slowly dying, looked up, wiping his nose. 'Not that marvellous actually. I think I'll have to take a rain check tonight. I've got about another half hour to finish up, then I'm gonna go home and hibernate until Monday and mainline Tylenol.'

Alicia bent down and took a closer look at him. 'With all due respect, Josh, you look like shit. Can't the work wait until Monday?

'I promised upstairs I'd top and tail the report on that friendly fire shit last month in Afghanistan – I'm nearly done. You go have fun, I don't think I'd be much company tonight.'

Alicia patted him on the shoulder. 'Don't stay a minute longer than you have to – I hope you feel better soon.'

'I'll be in Monday. If you think I'm missing out on the debrief…'

Alicia cut him off, raising a hand. 'Hey, mister, what goes on at the Iron Horse stays at the Iron Horse. Be quick and get yourself to bed, young man.'

'Yes, Mum.' He coughed into a tissue, holding one hand to his chest.

His co-workers left as one, a gaggle of conversation filling the air like a group of schoolkids heading out on the last day of term, then silence. He waited ten minutes in case anyone came back for something they'd forgotten. The whole floor, not just his office, had departed, as most had earmarked the same day for their own celebrations.

Once he was sure he was on his own he started, having done as much preparation as he could without arousing suspicion in the week prior to party day. On Monday he'd collared Buckland as she came back from lunch, asking if she had a minute. They'd walked into her office, Englefield carrying his laptop, Alicia a coffee.

'What's up, Josh?'

‘I’m getting on pretty well with that report on the friendly fire situation. I should have it done and dusted by the end of the week but I can’t get into the database of a black op, it’s above my pay grade. It’s clear we were doing something else in that region of ’stan and my guess is it’s probably unconnected. I’m pretty sure their target was in the opposite direction, but I need to rule out any accidental engagement. I know upstairs want to bury this as soon as possible, but they can’t close the lid unless they know everything’s inside.’

‘I got you – what do you need from me?’

‘Do you mind if I take a seat and show you?’

‘Be my guest.’

Englefield wheeled a spare chair to Alicia’s side of the desk and opened his laptop, revealing a satellite photograph of sand, mountains, and more sand. The photograph had a number of red Xs. Englefield pointed to the screen.

‘This is where the depot is. This is where our boys were stationed, here and here.’ He pointed to another larger red X.

‘This is where five of our soldiers were killed by the mortar. It may have come from those hills there, in which case we’ll never know who fired it. I’ve been able to ascertain that Special Forces were likely to be here.’ He pointed to a black X.

‘They would’ve known about the two groups of friendlies here and here, but I can’t rule out anything accidental because I can’t access their report. I’m obviously not asking to see it but if you were able to, and it's clear, I can report that it didn't come from them. Upstairs are evidently chewing out the drone boys for not scanning the hills. Why they didn't even check for heat signatures when they knew our guys were vulnerable beats me. Some general dropped into the conversation during the first de-brief that it could've been blue on blue, and now they're all looking for someone to blame.'

Alicia shook her head. 'Arse covering – we're doing more and more of that.'

She continued. 'OK, I can access the team leader's report which should include a record of any ordnance used.'

Alicia Buckland had two terminals on her desk. One for general use in her day-to-day work, the other to access reports, records and files only available to those with a Top Secret clearance. At that level users had access to information for which any unauthorised disclosure would cause *grave* damage to national security. Due to her position as head of the analysis division, her clearance allowed her to view data unavailable to most other persons working within the CIA. She could request almost any type of information, and it wouldn't be questioned.

Englefield's own security clearance was at Secret level, which on first glance wasn't that different to Top Secret. It covered information that could and would cause *serious* damage to national security. The difference between *serious* and *grave* was sometimes very close, but could also be worlds apart.

Alicia moved her coffee to one side, not noticing Englefield nudging his laptop, altering the angle of the screen by just a fraction. In doing so he depressed the F12 key. Normally this would bring up a *save as* function for a document, but as he had reconfigured it, the high resolution camera was now on.

Englefield made a point of turning his chair and looking away as she logged in – her every keystroke now being recorded in absolute clarity. She typed her username on each keyboard, then her password, opening the portal to the Central Intelligence Agency's most closely guarded secrets.

Englefield couldn't see the screens but didn't need to. It was a given that unless invited to view, it would be a serious breach of protocol if he leant over to look. He would soon have the luxury of looking at anything he wanted to in the comfort of anywhere he chose to be.

Alicia remained silent as she skimmed through the CO's report. She ascertained they'd been dropped at the coordinates shown, heading north almost immediately – their target was four miles away.

She read that the hills visible on Englefield's photograph had been drone-scanned for two days solid prior to their deployment, with both high-res photography and infrared. However, once Special Ops were on the ground and moving, the drone was called away. The insurgents had, by an awful coincidence, arrived just after the eye in the sky had flown away.

'OK, I have your answer. There was a Black Op commenced just prior to our boys getting hit, but they didn't fire so much as a water pistol. Their target was in the opposite direction and they were miles away by the time our guys got hit. It's a bloody tragic set of circumstances. We can safely say the mortar didn't come from us. Those bastards moved into the hills completely undetected – they were probably hiding in a cave for God knows how long. We didn't kill our own people.'

Englefield nodded. 'Thank God for that, not that it really matters. Those poor fuckers should never have been left without drone support, it's fucking outrageous we leave them like sitting ducks all because some fucking general decides to fly his toy someplace else...'

Alicia could see Englefield was becoming agitated. 'Josh, I know this is hard for you because of your brother. With the benefit of hindsight we'd have been in and out of 'stan in a few months – not still dealing with a clusterfuck we'll never win. You're doing a great job, and never forget what you do saves boys like your brother in the future.'

'I know, I try and stay professional but every now and then it gets to me.'

'I can totally understand that. I don't know how I'd react if it were me. If you want to hand the report over to Evie or Lucy or any of the others to finish, you've got my blessing.'

‘I appreciate it, Alicia, I’m fine – rant over. I’ll get cracking and should have it ready by the end of the week.’

‘Good man.’ But Joshua Englefield was anything but.

*

He thought back to how well Monday had gone as he walked across the empty office towards the exit. There was no CCTV in the area Englefield worked in or the corridors outside. This was the CIA after all, and anyone in the building had to have come through various electronic security check points to walk around the area he worked in. His main concern was being seen by someone he wasn’t expecting.

The cleaners didn’t come until late evening, but he couldn’t assume they wouldn’t want to get their job done early, knowing everyone was out. Likewise, someone from the top floor who needed an urgent check could knock on the door unexpectedly.

He reached into his jacket pocket and took out two small industrial endoscopes. Exactly the same thing a builder uses to look into voids, rather than hacking out a piece of wall. Perfect for his requirements, they were basically high-definition cameras mounted on the end of a long piece of cable, which connected to a screen about the size of a satnav. This could be connected to another device via Bluetooth so the user could view the image on a larger screen.

Englefield left the office, instantly hit by the eerie silence, and walked a few paces down the corridor to a smoke detector. He could reach the ceiling tile on tiptoe, which he moved slightly to one side. He took out a lump of Blu-tac, sticking a piece on each tiny camera, then attached them to the smoke detector, one facing up the corridor, the other down.

He enabled the Bluetooth connection, tucking the excess wire and the screens inside the roof void and slid the tile back in place. The cameras hardly noticed, their black bodies hidden against the black case of the smoke detector. He was confident if anyone walked past they'd never spot they were on TV.

He went back into the office and sat on the nearest chair. Pairing the camera feeds to his laptop, he could see the entire corridor in both directions. If anyone approached he'd have at least thirty seconds to be back at his desk, working away like a good boy.

Englefield picked up his laptop, watching the screen the whole time. He felt a jolt of adrenaline as he pushed open the glass doors to Buckland's office, thinking about the treasures within. 'Show time,' he muttered but there was no one to hear him – just the faint whirring of computer cooling fans.

He checked his watch – 5.05pm – and set the laptop down on Buckland's desk, continually monitoring the corridor.

He hoped she hadn't changed her passwords since Monday, but thought it unlikely – that would slow things a little. Best practise was to change them regularly, but no one actually bothered.

He nudged each mouse attached to her terminals – the highly secure one to access the most secret of databases, the other for her day-to-day work in searches, emails and video calling. Both screens came to life, asking for a username and password. Carefully typing, he cleared the first obstacle. Neither screen had personal wallpaper – no pets or beach scenes or smiling couples – just a blue background. All business.

He reached into his jacket pocket, finding the tiny tear in the lining. He pushed into it, tearing a hole large enough to retrieve the memory card nestling in the hem. Inserting the card into her general use computer, he downloaded TOR deep within her system. He couldn't help smiling with the irony that the Onion Router was developed by his very own government to allow spies to exchange information without fear of exposure.

In Englefield's opinion, TOR was a thing of beauty, allowing access to the dark web but not through Google or any search engine. Like a real onion it had numerous layers, and if used correctly, was undetectable. The exchange of information continually circumnavigated the world, increasingly hiding the source with every layer added, making it impossible to find the actual location of the user.

It also wasn't known as The Dark Web for nothing. Users could access the most horrific and depraved images imaginable, order narcotics to be delivered to their door like Amazon, arrange hit men to kill their spouses – virtually anything was possible. If, for some reason, someone needed the hind legs of a dead dog, someone on TOR would facilitate.

It was the anonymity he wanted. It was impossible to accidently log in – the user had to input an exact series of letters and numbers to enter the particular area of interest to them. His own particular area of interest was data pertaining to the most secret of secrets hidden within not only the CIA database, but Homeland Security, the armed forces and the FBI.

All that information was supposed to disappear down the rabbit hole and stay there. Alicia however could see what was in the burrow, and would shortly become his very own Alice, allowing him to enter Wonderland with the push of a few buttons, whenever he wanted.

He uploaded another file. It was a highly encrypted program downloaded from TOR, which he'd tweaked slightly. He didn't trust anyone on TOR, as it wasn't beyond the realms of possibility that the writer had created a back door in order to snoop around whatever his customers chose to look at. He renamed it and buried it under multi layers of false file names. A box popped up. *Do you want to allow remote access to this computer*? He clicked yes.

Englefield withdrew the memory card and put it in an envelope which he fed into the shredder in Buckland's office. It made more noise than usual but did the job. He then shredded a handful of photocopier paper – hundreds of tiny pieces falling unseen like snow, blanketing the fragments of plastic. The cleaners would empty it later that evening.

To the side of Buckland's desk was a floor panel housing the wiring from her terminals, which fed to the servers down the corridor. He lifted his laptop down, checking the screen every few seconds for movement outside. He opened the panel and scribbled the two connection port numbers for her computers on a scrap of paper.

Every computer in every office, on every floor in every building in the CIA headquarters ,was connected to a server room which handled all the data traffic flowing in and out. The connection had to be identifiable at both ends, hence all ports, basically tiny plug sockets, were individually numbered. Replacing the panel, he headed to the server room.

The calm in the corridor hit him again. No chatter, no sounds of people going about their daily business, no anything – like being in a vacuum.

He was no stranger to the workings of the server room, having sorted out problems numerous times for his colleagues and himself. Officially if something went wrong a service request had to be generated, countersigned and sent through to IT support. In reality someone in the office usually had a go at sorting it out. Often it was as simple as isolating the server causing trouble and switching it off and on again.

After snapping on a pair of latex gloves and punching in the secret code, which everyone knew, he walked from total silence into a cacophony of cooling fans, air conditioning and the hum of electricity travelling unseen at 180,000 miles per second through hundreds of miles of wiring. He was glad of his temporary CCTV as he'd never hear footsteps above the din.

The room housed all the servers for the entire floor he worked on. Banks of cabinets bigger than a wardrobe lined each side. The heat was way above the temperature in the corridor, explaining why fire sprinklers were set into the ceiling every few feet.

Every cabinet housed eighteen drawers, with chrome handles on both sides. Each drawer could be pulled out to reveal thousands of wires, colour coded like a tiny rail system, taking their passengers – in this case packets of data – from one place to another. And like the subway, if you got the wrong train, it was likely you could get to your destination by taking a different route.

Englefield walked to the third cabinet on the left and pulled out the second from bottom drawer, laying his laptop down to monitor the corridor. Sweat beads glazed his forehead, and he could feel the uncomfortable wetness growing in size under his armpits – partly due to the heat, but mostly because he was feeling very nervous.

He pulled the drawer out until it clicked into the open position, exposing the wiring. It reminded him of tiny veins. He checked the scrap of paper, located the two port numbers relating to Alicia's terminals and gently eased the circuit board up. A row of microprocessors lined each side – the left serving her stand-alone terminal, the right her general one. At the end of each row were two empty sockets in case more capacity was needed at some future date. This was unlikely, as the system, as far as the CIA was concerned, was state of the art and futureproof.

Although the workings of a computer system are incredibly detailed and complicated, Englefield's task was relatively simple. He reached into his jacket pocket and took out a small plastic box. Carefully opening it in case he damaged the delicate terminals, he took out a processor twice the width of the ones already installed – basically an electronic bridge.

He noticed his hands were shaking, and scolded himself. Taking a deep breath, he delicately lowered his own processor over both the left and right spare port holes, carefully pushing down until he could feel everything was in the right place. With one final gentle application of pressure he felt the unit click into its new home. The bridge was built.

He then froze. Another click – one he wasn't responsible for. Without realising, he held the breath he'd just taken. Was that the sound the door made when it opened? He'd never heard it from inside the server room. He turned towards the door, knocking the laptop with his knee and spinning it ninety degrees. In a state of panic he realised he hadn't looked at the screen for about twenty seconds, and couldn't see it now. Was that enough time for someone to approach the door without him seeing?

He should've just reached out and turned the screen back. He'd read about people being so scared they were literally frozen to the spot, but never experienced the sensation until now. It was as if he'd been turned to stone.

He let out the breath, the next ones coming in short bursts – pinpricks of sweat carpeted his scalp. He knew he should move but every muscle was frozen. Another click – not so loud this time. His eyes darted around, his ears straining to locate the source above all the noise. *Shit, shit, shit.*

Diagnostics, that's what he was doing if anyone asked. But no, that would be stupid – if it was anyone other than a cleaner they would know it was bullshit. *Think, think, think.* He could hear his heart thumping in his ears like someone punching a sofa cushion to plump it up.

Click. There it was again. Perhaps it was someone entering the wrong door code and trying again. Panic was starting to overwhelm him when he caught movement in the corner of his eye. He looked diagonally up towards the door and saw the blades of a ceiling-mounted air con unit closing, then a click. The system was obviously thermostatically controlled, so when the temperature dropped the air con would shut down and the blades fold in on themselves. It made sense – no point having it on 24/7, it just activated when needed. The fact that everyone had left meant the servers were cooling, so no need for air con.

A bead of sweat began to roll down his nose, and in the tiniest fraction of a second he pictured it dropping onto the open circuits causing the whole drawer to short out, which would set his plan back catastrophically.

He slowly turned his head to one side as he felt the drip roll down, and pushing out his lower lip, blew a jet of breath upwards causing the bead to land on the floor next to the drawer. He breathed a sigh of relief. He'd now linked Alicia's two systems together – something that should never be done under any circumstances. Her terminal for general use was connected to the internet, albeit with serious security in place, but her stand-alone wasn't. But now it was, via the little bridge he'd constructed between the two systems, and one that was only open to him, if everything worked.

He pushed the drawer back into place and gathered up his laptop, checking the feed from the corridor religiously. He took a USB lead from his pocket and plugged it into the port on the back of the door keypad and connected it to his laptop. A window popped up identifying itself as the tiny program held within the lock mechanism. He clicked on settings and opened the menu, selecting *reset door code*. He clicked *yes,* entered the old door code and then a new one when prompted.

A simple Google search had revealed that if the user reset the door entry code, all previous activity would be erased, meaning no one could interrogate it to cross-reference with who was in the building at that time, should the worst happen.

He then repeated the procedure, replacing the new code with the old one, starting the time and date record all over again the next time someone opened it from outside.

He ensured he hadn't dropped or left anything, checked his laptop screen and walked out of the server room. Stopping at the smoke detector he reached up, pushing the ceiling tile aside. He could hear a pin drop in the corridor so would hear anyone coming before they saw him. He gently pulled the two cameras off, gathered up the wiring and small screens, slid the tile back into place and walked the few steps back to his office. Closing the door behind him, he leant against it and let out a sigh of relief.

Taking out the two tiny cameras, he cut the cables into tiny pieces until they looked like miniature sticks of liquorice. In the unlikely event he was stopped on the way out and searched, he was confident he'd be able to talk his way out of it. He would explain that the screens had been given to him by a friend, and he was going to ask the tech boys if they had any leads to fit.

He sat down at his workstation – the report he'd been working on was actually ready but he changed a couple of words, leaving a digital signature showing he'd last worked on it at 5.31pm. He then attached it to an email and sent it to a faceless person a few floors above. He had little doubt they'd skim-read it once then file it away forever.

Before leaving he fed the post-it note into the main office shredder, followed by a few blank sheets of paper, just to make sure. Stopping at the rest room, he pulled off a few pieces of toilet tissue, wrapped the small pieces of cable and flushed them away.

Chapter 10.

UK, 13 days to mission.

Jenks drove home, making a mental note to check his bike over and give it a run out later as it hadn't been used since before his Egypt trip. He parked next to his garage and walked straight to the kitchen and put his box of antipasto in the fridge along with the custard tart for later. He made another coffee and took the tart back out of the fridge four minutes later. They really were very good.

It was just about high tide, so he took a moment to scan the Estuary taking in the view from the Isle of Sheppey round to the old Maunsell Sea Forts machine gun platforms due north. Still standing after nearly eighty years, the rusting relics of war reminded him of the Martians in *War of the Worlds*.

The sea was relatively calm, with a few gulls bobbing around just offshore. The fishing boats had landed their catch by now so perhaps the birds had nothing really to do, other than bob around. He picked up his binoculars and focussed on the gulls, identifying three types.

He thought about missions where he'd been dug in for hours – sometimes days at a time, staying vigilant, passing the time trying to name the various species of bird in his view. Seeing the birds triggered a memory of hiding just off the shore of Lake Aguelmame Sidi Ali in Morocco a few years previously.

Jenks had been waiting two days for a meeting between the leader of a large drugs cartel and a member of the British aristocracy holding diplomatic immunity. The titled man was financing large shipments of heroin, importing them to Europe in his luxurious yacht. It was also suspected he was bringing in pounds of pure uncut heroin via the diplomatic bag. However, such were his connections, conventional methods of justice were impossible.

Whilst waiting, Jenks was transfixed by a rare visitor to the area – a bird known as Leucophaeus Atricilla, or Laughing Gull. Its unique call really did sound like someone laughing, with a distinctive *ha ha ha ha* and was quite infectious. He lay still and was able to gain its trust enough for the bird to peck a few crumbs from his outstretched hand.

Unfortunately the bird didn't want to leave the shores of the lake, or Jenks, as he saw the distant dust trails of two jeeps heading towards him from opposite directions. Its call was so distinctive, anyone would undoubtedly turn towards it. Jenks held out a few more crumbs. As the bird bent to retrieve them his arm snapped out like a striking cobra, strong fingers closing around its head. With one quick twist the neck snapped, and he threw the body into the bushes behind him.

He remembered feeling terrible about having to kill the bird, but not about shooting a member of the British aristocracy in the face and a leading drug supplier twice in the heart. Shortly after, the RSPB received a sizeable anonymous donation. Coincidently, a briefcase belonging to the titled man which had been full of large denomination notes was found empty next to his body, save for one solitary feather.

Jenks shook his head, bringing himself back to the present. He took a sip of coffee and a large bite from the tart, and opened his laptop and the website for The Huntsman's Lodge Hotel in Soho. Clicking on the photos he studied each one in detail, then opened the virtual tour video.

He ran the video six times. At the end of each one he closed his eyes, tilted his head back and thought about what he'd seen. By the end of the sixth viewing he'd committed the layout to memory, even where the light switches were.

Next, he drew himself a plan of the ground floor, marking fire, staff and public exits. He then opened Google Earth, zooming in to where the exits opened onto, noting them on his plan. He reached for his phone and rang James Camburn.

'JC, I just thought of something else. I need drone footage after it gets dark as well, say about 9pm? I'd like to see the difference at night, where the shadows cast, that sort of thing.'

'I've tasked Jo Fox to fly it this afternoon. I'll let her know to repeat the same sweep after dark.'

'OK, that's it, speak later.'

He ended the call and went back to The Huntsman's Lodge website. Ignoring all but the last page, he scrolled down and found what he was looking for. *Website designed by The Wonderful Website design team 2016.* He noted the contact details, which included their email address – *info@wonderfulwebsitedesign.co.uk*. He Googled their website and read about the company and the three main designers, Daisy Brown, Johnny Green and his brother Michael, who were also directors of the company.

Jenks then viewed the *Who's Who* section of The Huntsman's Lodge page – Rhys Evans had been general manager for just over two years. He clicked on Evans' profile and saw he was originally from Wales, and had been in the hotel trade since leaving school. Jenks looked at the photograph and saw a stocky man, clearly still fit. He went back to the profile and saw that Evans had excelled at county level rugby, but gave it up when faced with the decision to either pursue a career in the sport or continue in the hotel trade.

He opened a new search window and Googled *personalised email addresses*. One of the first ones advertised a special offer of 99p per month, down from £1.99. He clicked on the site and started to complete the application.

After he'd paid with an untraceable pre-loaded credit card, the email address *johnnygreen@wonderfulwebsitedesign.com* now existed.

Jenks pressed play on an Mpeg file on his laptop and the sounds of a busy office came through the speakers – a background hubbub of people talking in hushed tones and the sound of fingers typing on keyboards. He opened the Wickr app and dialled reservations.

'Huntsman's Lodge Hotel, Arianna speaking, how may I help you?'

Jenks detected a Latvian accent. Putting on a slightly hipster-ish voice he said, 'Oh yeah hi, Arianna, It's Johnny Green here from Wonderful Website Design – I wondered if the manager was free for a couple of minutes?'

'Mr Evans?'

'Oh, er...' Jenks held the pause for a couple of seconds. 'Erm, I'm not sure I know Mr Evans, I don't think we dealt with him last time.'

'Can I ask what it's concerning please?'

'Yah, yah, I designed your website a few years ago, but I didn't deal with Mr…'

Arianna cut in. 'Oh you must have dealt with Ray Sheehen – he moved on. Mr Evans has been the general manager here for the last two years.'

'Ah yes, that would explain it – nice guy, Ray.' Jenks was taking a bit of a chance as Ray Sheehan, for all he knew, could have been an absolute bastard to work for. If that was the case he would have to go to Plan B.

'Oh we were all sorry to see him go, he actually gave me this job.'

'That's nice. Hey, Arianna, are you from Latvia by any chance?'

'God, yes, is my accent that strong?'

'No not really, but I did a bit of work for some Latvians a few years ago and it sounded familiar.'

'Oh wow, that's so cool. Most people just think I'm Russian. You're brave though, it's not safe there really, lots of murders. That's why I came to England.'

Latvia did indeed have a huge problem with killings – Jenks had been responsible for thirty-six of them when he obliterated a house four years previously. The building was the headquarters of a notorious gang labelled the *taxi killers*. The cabs would be tailed from Riga International Airport, but only the ones picking up the first passengers off international flights – the ones travelling first or Business class – travellers with money.

They would follow the cab until the passenger got dropped off, usually at a private villa, then rob them. Their signature was that the victim always got stabbed, even if they were completely compliant, and a few had died from their injuries. It was the sort of tourist information no one really wanted.

Jenks had been hired via the dark web – he wasn't entirely sure if his employers were the government, or even the chief of police. A few minutes after the gang convened for their weekly meeting, ten large remotely fired lumps of plastic explosive completely destroyed the house, vaporising most of the inhabitants and crushing beyond recognition the few who survived the explosion.

Jenks replied, ‘I got the impression it wasn’t the friendliest of places but I was only there for a few days.’

‘Did you enjoy it?’

‘Yeah, it was a bit of a blast actually. Arianna, can I ask you, as *you* would probably know having worked there a while – have you had any problems in the last six months with the website we created for you?’

Arianna suddenly felt quite important and slightly proud that Mr Green was asking her before anyone else. Jenks heard clothing moving over leather as she sat up a little straighter in her chair. ‘No, not as far as I’m aware – oh hang on, it did crash once but I think Mr Evans sorted it out.’

‘Oh right, I did wonder if you had any problems, just the once, was it?’

‘I think so, you’d best talk to him about it, let me see if he’s free, Mr Green.’

‘Please call me Johnny, and thanks a lot, Arianna, I really appreciate it.’

Arianna liked the sound of Johnny Green’s voice. She imagined him in a pair of jeans turned up to reveal the darker outer seam, a waistcoat, thick beard and maybe a man bun – he sounded like a typical hipster, and had a lovely warm voice. The way she imagined him was ironically almost exactly how the real Johnny Green looked. 'That's no problem at all, Johnny, I'll just put you on hold for a second.'

Jenks heard the connection between them click off; Arianna's voice replaced by Heather Small from M People singing *and who do you think you are…*'

'Hello, Rhys Evans speaking.'

'Oh hi, Rhys, I appreciate you taking the time to speak to me – is it convenient at the moment?'

'Well I don't have that long, Arianna said it's something to do with our website? I have to tell you we're quite happy with it at the moment.'

'Well that's great to hear – I designed it.'

'Haha, sorry, I thought you were going to try and sell me a new one.'

'No, no, that's quite alright, we get that quite often. I know what it's like, we get bombarded every day with sales calls and emails. I'm Johnny Green from Wonderful Website Design'

'Him Johnny, yes, you and me both, how can I help you?'

'Well I was hoping to be able to help you actually. When Ray gave us the contract to…'

'Ray Sheehan? He was my predecessor, he stayed on a couple of weeks for the handover.'

'That sounds like Ray – really nice bloke.'

'Absolute diamond – he completely turned this place around.'

'And there was me thinking it was the wonderful website.'

'Well I'm sure it wasn't all just Ray!'

'Flattery will get you everywhere,' Jenks replied, laughing, pronouncing flattery as *fladdery*. 'Anyway, the reason I'm calling is about a glitch fix, if it's required.'

'A what? I'm sorry, although I run this place, between you and me I'm the least technically minded here. I can use what I need to, and thankfully it all seems to work OK. I'd have to get someone a bit more savvy than me to fix it if it all went down.'

Which was music to Jenks's ears.

'No, what I meant is, well to put it in layman's terms, even in the last four years since I made your website, programs have improved in leaps and bounds. I take it you get a lot of bookings via price comparison websites?'

'Oh God, yes.'

'Has your site ever crashed?'

Jenks knew it had because Arianna had told him a few minutes ago, but the truth was *everyone* who had a website had experienced a crash at some point.

Rhys Evans thought about it. 'Come to think, it did all go down about six months ago, literally just froze. We couldn't get into it at all and no one could make bookings. Oh God, I remember now, it was awful.'

Jenks knew the answer to his next question. 'How did you unfreeze it?'

'Well, er, I just turned the server off and on again and it seemed to sort it.'

'That's exactly what I would have done. It reboots the system and usually works. Mind you, you don't want to be having to do that too often. It does sound like you need the update.'

'Update?'

'When we built your site it was designed to deal with a lot of traffic at the same time, with extra capacity available if required. Even in the last four years the amount of comparison sites springing up linked to your system has more than doubled the inbound traffic to your server. We thought we'd futureproofed it, but occasionally demand is so high the server will say enough is enough and close itself down.'

'Ah, I see.' But Rhys Evans didn't really see, but wanted to avoid looking stupid and asking questions that a kid in junior school could probably answer. 'Go on.'

'Thankfully it's not that often it breaks, and I'm sorry you had to go through that.'

'Please don't apologise, it's just one of those things I suppose. You mentioned an update – is it expensive?'

'Oh God no, it's free. It's just an add-on to the software I installed for you. I'm basically contacting all customers with sites older than two years and giving their systems a bit more oomph.'

'Well that's what I call good customer aftercare.'

'Thanks, Rhys, from our point of view we don't want Wonderful Website Design to be thought of as anything except wonderful. A lot of our work is repeat business which means people are happy with what we do.'

'OK, it does sound like it makes sense to upgrade it, even more so if it's free – what do we have to do?'

'Well, Rhys, there's three ways we can sort it for you. None of them take very long. I can come to you, but to be honest I haven't got a window for at least a month.'

'Oh dear.'

'Or, I can send you a thumb drive with the update on it. You simply plug it in and follow the instructions on the screen. There's a few steps to follow, but anyone with a bit of computing knowledge should be able to do it.'

A thought entered Rhys Evans' head of being personally responsible for completely wrecking the entire system, costing them a fortune, and making him look an idiot in front of his entire staff. 'You mentioned three ways?'

'Yah, the other way is for me to remotely connect for a few minutes and do it for you – as if I was sitting in your seat. It doesn't affect anything else as it will just run in the background. Once it's installed, I disconnect and the job's done.'

'That sounds like the best way to me, you know what you're doing a lot more than I do.'

Jenks knew he now had Evans' complete trust. 'I'll send you over an email confirming the order and what we're going to do to sort this out. Ah, I've only got Ray's old contact details'

'Oh it's the same – *manager@huntsmanslodge.co.uk.*'

'Great, it'll take a few minutes. I'll look out for your reply then give you a call back.'

'Cool, and thanks, Johnny.'

Jenks disconnected, pressed pause on the sound file and logged into his *johnnygreen@wonderfulwebsitedesign.com* account and composed an email.

Dear Rhys,

Following our telephone conversation I'm delighted to be able to help you with the system upgrade we spoke about. As discussed, I confirm it should take no more than a few minutes, during which time you won't be able to use your terminal but all other staff will be unaffected.

I'm confident the extra capacity will be sufficient that no further updates will be required. However, if you have any further problems, please do not hesitate to contact me once we've completed the upgrade.

Once I receive your reply confirming you are happy to go ahead I will telephone you and we can go through the procedure together.

Kind regards,

Johnny Green

MD The Wonderful Website DesignTeam.

Jenks entered *manager@huntsmanslodge.co.uk* into the address field, pressed send and sat back in his chair, draining the last few drops of coffee. He fully expected Evans to reply quickly as it was clear he'd taken the bait, and they'd move to phase two.

It wasn't just stupid people who were easy to dupe. Jenks had found it easier to cause reasonably intelligent people to believe that the outright pack of lies they were being told was the truth, not doubting it for a second. He'd always been interested in the psychology of lying – the way a person will respond to someone being nice to them, or trying to help. The trick was to allay fears before they formed. If a person recognises someone's trying to help them, generally they'll try to help back, and if the victim is given a *choice* in the matter, they'll always believe they've acted freely.

Jenks remembered a surveillance job in Bristol which proved his theory. He'd been plotting the man's movements over a few days when the target turned abruptly and crossed the street towards him.

People tend to think of a foot follow as what they've seen in films and on television – someone ducking into a shop doorway or leaning casually against a wall reading a newspaper. To the professional, it couldn't be further from the truth.

Jenks always followed from the other side of the street. If someone suspects they're being tailed they generally turn around and look behind, not across the road. Another benefit was windows could be used to track the subject in their reflection – the target was unlikely to suspect anyone looking away from them, just window shopping.

On the Bristol op the target didn't actually suspect, although Jenks didn't know this at the time. The man had only been in the city for two days himself and didn't know his way around. He'd realised he was heading in the wrong direction and seeing a coffee stand, turned on his heels and headed directly towards it, and Jenks.

Seeing the man turn, Jenks walked straight up three steps and into a solicitor's practice, only needing to be out of sight for a few minutes while his target waited for his coffee.

When he walked in unsteadily, the receptionist looked like she was about to call the police to remove a drunk from the office. In an accusatory tone she called out, 'Excuse me, can I help you?'

'Oh yes, I'm so sorry, I'm a Type 1 diabetic. It's a bit embarrassing but I missed lunch and feel I'm starting to feel faint and a bit giddy. I've usually got a Mars bar on me which brings my sugar levels back up…' He braced himself against the door frame.

The receptionist jumped up, now in full help mode, feeling guilty. She took Jenks by the arm.

‘Come and sit right down – I’ve got a bar of fruit and nut in my bag, will that do?’

‘Yes,’ he said, slightly out of breath, ‘That would be great.’

The girl ran back to her desk and pushed her chair back, causing it to topple over. Turning her bag upside down, she shook the contents onto her desk. Grabbing the chocolate, she tore it open and rushed back to him.

Jenks ate four squares immediately, stealing glances out of the window.

‘Should I call an ambulance?’

‘Please no, there’s no need. I can feel it doing the trick already. Do you mind if I have a bit more?’

‘Please have it all, this must be awful for you.’

‘A couple more squares should do the trick and I’ll be out of your way.’

‘There’s no rush, stay as long as you need – do you want a cup of sweet tea? Water?’

‘No, honestly, the sugar gets into the blood pretty quickly. I’ll give it another couple of minutes.’

He glanced up and saw the vendor putting the lid on a takeaway cup and his target putting his hand inside his jacket for his wallet. Useful intelligence – the target was left-handed.

Jenks stood up, shaking his head slightly theatrically. ‘Phew, that’s better. I’ll be fine now.’

‘Are you sure? Can I call you a taxi or something?’

‘You’re so kind, but that won’t be necessary – I only live on the next street. I’m going straight home to make a sandwich.’ As he spoke he noticed his target accepting his change and start to walk off. Jenks went to hand the remaining chocolate back to the receptionist, but she held her palm up.

'Thank you for being so helpful, let me pay you for the chocolate.'

'No, don't be silly. Please keep it, I'm just glad I was able to help.'

Jenks walked towards the door, thanked the lady again, and was back on the pavement a few seconds later to pick up his follow.

A ping sounded, bringing him back from the memory, and to the new email from *manager@huntsmanslodge.co.uk*.

He moved the cursor over the new message and right-clicked, selecting *properties*. He scrolled down until he found the IP address the email had been sent from. Noting it, he dialled the direct number for the manager as shown on the reply and pressed play on his *office background sound* MP3 file.

'Rhys Evans, how can I help?'

'Hi, Rhys, it's Johnny.'

'Hi, Johnny, you've obviously seen my reply, what do I need to do?'

'Not much you'll be pleased to know.'

'Phew, OK, I'm ready.'

'Right. Press the start key in the bottom left-hand corner and go to settings, then press system. Can you see that?'

'Hang on...settings....system…OK, I'm on the system bit.'

'Excellent, now press remote desktop and turn on enable remote desktop.'

'Right, hang on…There's a box popped up saying *The identity of the remote computer cannot be verified, do you want to connect anyway*?'

'That's normal, just press yes.'

'OK, done that.'

'Great. Can you see the name of your computer anywhere?'

'Ah yes, it says Ray's Computer.'

'Good, you can change it if you want but it doesn't make any difference.'

'I'll just leave it I think. OK, what now?'

'You've just about done all you need to. I've pulled up your IP address from our records, and now you've enabled remote desktop I can do what I need to do. Once I'm done you can disable it – to be honest it's safer if it's off.'

Jenks opened the remote connection program on his laptop and inputted the information he now had.

'OK, I've finished the connection. If you look at your screen you should see your cursor move in a second.'

Jenks was now in full control of the general manager's computer which meant access to all systems within The Huntsman's Lodge, including CCTV.

Evans watched his screen, grinning like a schoolboy.

‘Wow, that’s amazing! That’s you moving the mouse!’

‘Yep, cool isn’t it.’

‘Ha, it’s like a ghost inside my computer.’

‘Right, I’m going to install the update. The screen will go blank for a short while, but I’ll stay on the phone. Yes, white coffee, no sugar please, Lizzy. Sorry, we’ve got a new machine and I haven’t had a cup yet, one of the girls is firing it up.’

Whilst they were engaging in general chit-chat, Jenks disabled the screen Rhys Evans was watching avidly, causing it to go blank. As he uploaded a Malware virus, numerous warnings popped up generated by the anti-virus protection but Jenks dismissed each one, unseen to anyone except him.

The virus deposited rogue software that would allow Jenks to remote connect unseen. Evans would disable the function once the *upgrade* was complete, but all he’d actually be doing was pushing a picture of a switch to the off position, not the real one.

There was an old saying – *I wouldn’t have believed it if I hadn’t seen it with my own eyes*, but in the digital age it meant nothing. People did still believe what they could see, and Evans would soon be looking at an outright lie, but would swear on his children’s lives it was true.

Jenks asked Evans about his previous hotel jobs as he opened the CCTV program, splitting his screen to see the individual feed from all cameras. He then started a screen recording to review all the angles later.

He then downloaded a key logger program – if other systems linked to the general manager's computer required a separate username and password, Jenks would be able to review every key pressed. He fully expected the computer would never be turned off, as someone would be sitting in the manager's chair when he was not on duty.

The two new friends chatted away as Jenks delved deeper into The Huntsman's Lodge IT system.

He was viewing the booking records, in particular a reservation for Rick Mills for three nights, commencing Tuesday 10th March 2020 – the same name as the Eurostar bookings. He opened the payment screen, noting the details of the black American Express card used. Jenks scrolled down, ticking *express checkout request*. Mr Mills now had the option of leaving the hotel without all the hassle of lining up at reception to hand over his keys. Black Amex holders don't do queues.

The official name is the Centurion card. Costing $10,000 to apply when obtained legitimately, it also carries a $5,000 annual fee. However, present one and almost anything is available to the cardholder. With no spending limit, anyone offering the metal card is immediately and inevitably treated like royalty. Another perk is the concierge service.

Recognised as one of the best in the world, the team at the end of a dedicated phone line can get the user into almost anywhere – from the best restaurants with a three-month waiting list to sold out Broadway shows. Anything is possible, even sending presents. Pick up the phone and your wish is granted.

Jenks went back to the reservations page and saw there were still rooms available on the 4th floor between 10th and 13th March.

'OK, Rhys, I'm just about done – let me know when your screen comes back on.'

'Righto, hang on, yep, back on now.'

Rhys Evans could see the cursor move then settle in the middle of the screen.

'I'm going to disconnect now so control is back to you. Are you alright disabling remote connection or do you want me to stay on the line while you do it?'

'If you don't mind. Right, erm, start, settings…' Jenks could hear the sound of the keys clicking.

'Er...system and....remote desktop. OK, do I just press disable?'

'You got it – you didn't need me at all.'

'I suppose it's just a confidence thing. I'm fine with spreadsheets and all that stuff, but I think I just panic when it comes to actually altering things the computer does.'

'You'd be surprised how many people are the same. Anyway, all done now. You might even find your system runs a little quicker as well.'

'Cool, OK let me just try something while you're on.'

Rhys Evan clicked onto and off different programs and opened a blank Word document.

‘Hey, do you know what, it does seem a bit quicker, that’s brilliant.’

There was no difference in the speed whatsoever. Nothing Jenks had done improved the performance by even a split second, but tell someone they might see something, and the chances are they’ll think they have.

‘Johnny, I can’t thank you enough for sorting this out. Look, the next time you’re in London look me up, dinner’s on me – be good to see you.’

‘Oh you definitely will, I promise.’

Jenks ended the call, pressed stop on the MP3 file and immediately dialled the hotel again. ‘Huntsman’s Lodge Hotel, Arianna speaking, how can I help you?’

A broad Scottish accent answered her. ‘Oh hi, I was wondering if you had availability – I’m coming down to London on the 10th and a friend recommended you to me.’

‘Of course, sir, we have different levels of room, do you know which type you’d prefer?’

‘My pal stayed on the fourth floor, he said the room was lovely and had a great view.’

‘I’ll just check for you. Is that a Scottish accent I detect?’

‘Oh aye, lassie, I’m from Aberdeen – do you know it?’

‘No I’m afraid I don’t, it’s a lovely accent though.’

‘Why thank you, it’s a long way up, right on the east coast. You’ve got a bit of an accent yourself, hen, where do you hail from?’

'Oh I'm originally from Latvia, but I've been here a while so it's slowly going. Right, the 10th, yes we have availability and I do have rooms available on the fourth floor. They're in our superior plus class – very comfortable and the rate includes a complimentary bottle of champagne.'

Arianna stated the price, which was agreed, and started the booking process.

'Can I have your name please, sir?'

'Aye, it's Hamish Wilson.'

'And the long number on your card please, Mr Wilson.'

Jenks closed his eyes, picturing the text message.

'4921 0060 1329 2519.'

Arianna asked for the expiry date and the last three numbers from the back of the card, which Jenks recited. 'Right, that's all gone through. We'll look forward to seeing you on the 10th, Mr Wilson.'

'That's grand. See you soon, hen, bye bye.'

Jenks then called Camburn.

'It's me. Just a quick one, make a note of this number – it's a Black Amex in the name of Rick Mills, no spending limit and it's the one Englefield used to pay for the room – might be useful to see where else he's used it.'

Jenks read over the card details, which Camburn noted down.

'OK, got that. How's it going your end?'

'I've got the room next to his booked and full control of the hotel's computer system.'

'Impressive, that's pretty damn quick. How did you...forget that. Good work though.'

'That's why you pay me so much. I'll call later if there's a useful update.'

'Splendid. I'll get Maureen to open the back door to Amex and see what else he's been spending money on.'

'Good. You sound like you're outside, you're not taking exercise by any chance are you?'

'Don't be so foolish – the sun's out and I thought I could do with a bit of fresh air, so I'm sitting in the park with a very nice sandwich. Mind you it should be, it cost seven bloody ninety nine.'

'You're madder than I am if you paid nearly eight quid for a sandwich.'

'Quite possibly, bye for now.' Camburn took another bite, not paying the slightest attention to the pretty girl walking her dog chatting on her phone.

*

Jenks reviewed his recording of the hotel's CCTV, noting dead areas between cameras. The bar was well covered, particularly the large copper counter which ran the entire width of the rear wall. His original plan needed to be altered, but it actually made his job a little easier.

It wasn't a big hotel by any means. He'd read that there'd been a tavern on that spot since the late 1600s. The street itself had housed many important figures over the centuries including Admiral Nelson who stayed in Dean Street the night before he set sail for the battle of Trafalgar. Dickens was a regular visitor, and Karl Marx lived on the street for a number of years. It was even rumoured that a young Mozart gave recitals at number 21. Joshua Englefield aka Rick Mills would be in illustrious historical company.

What did pleasantly surprise him was whilst the first three floors had ceiling-mounted cameras, the fourth did not. Jenks thought about this, and came to the conclusion that because the fourth floor housed the most expensive rooms, it would attract the type of well-heeled guests who perhaps wanted a little more privacy, taking into consideration the area of London they were in. Someone with a bit of forward thinking had designed the system for which rich guests and high end call girls would be eternally grateful. Good astute business sense.

He closed his laptop, having done all he could, and headed out to the garage to get started on the customisation of the crutch.

Chapter 11.

USA, 3 months previously..

Englefield was worried – he counted Black as his best friend. Josh wanted to change the world and shared Black's ideals, but the all-consuming concern was how Chas would react when Josh revealed he wasn't a manager in a car insurance claims department.

Chas really liked Josh as well. He didn't share the same sexual preferences, but that was about all they didn't have in common. They had the same tastes in music, drugs and a love of vintage hi-fi. They'd spent many evenings stoned, listening to the sort of music made when the high end analogue equipment they were using was – early Steely Dan, Pink Floyd and Led Zeppelin blasting out of speakers only just smaller than the average wardrobe.

Chas admired Josh's passion for change and his quest to fill the chasm where the have-nots were trapped. He'd wondered how far Josh would go, and if, when push came to shove, he could be relied upon to stand shoulder to shoulder with him in the fight. He was shortly to get the fright of his life, and the man he thought he knew would make him look as if he did nothing more radical than sew a few flags to wave at events no one attended.

Two days previously, the day of the Christmas party and his foray into the server room, Josh arrived home eager to see what secrets Alicia could pass to him from the rabbit hole. As much as he wanted to log straight in he reminded himself he had all weekend to explore, so grabbed a beer and made himself a club sandwich.

Englefield sat down, looked at the closed laptop and smiled. This really was the start. He finished his sandwich, setting his beer to the side. He could feel his heart pulsing in his neck, and took two deep breaths.

He pushed the power button and got out of his chair and walked over to his side cabinet, on top of which sat his vintage hi-fi. Consisting of a valve amplifier, turntable and pre-amp, the system pushed out more wattage than he'd ever dare use, all fed to an enormous pair of Tannoy Westminster speakers. He never tired of looking at it. The glass valves were not hidden inside a case, but visible – polished and full of wiring that glowed when the system was on, and looked even more beautiful with the lights out.

He placed his fingers around one of the valves in the pre-amp, carefully lifting it from its housing, revealing a USB connection on its base.

The USB plug came into use in 1994, twenty years after Englefield's amp was manufactured. The pre-amp connected to the main amp via gold-tipped connecting cables actually did nothing. It glowed like it should, but was merely a hiding place for a pay-as-you-go dongle he used to connect to the internet and look at things he wouldn't want his employers to find out about.

Dongles today were small and easily fit inside a vintage valve, manufactured decades before miniaturisation. With the knowhow Englefield had, it was comparatively easy to remove the inner workings of a valve and slot the dongle inside. He'd broken a couple trying, but on his third attempt was successful. The valve glowed like it should, hiding its secret in plain sight.

Every computer leaves a trace, somewhere. Connecting to the World Wide Web leaves a signature, but signatures can be forged, just like a hero's autograph bought off the internet. If you knew what you were doing, a few key strokes could make you untraceable.

Proxy servers, masking programs – it was all too easy to fool even the most skilled investigators. Throw TOR into the mix and you become invisible. A warren leading to another, within another and back out, until the path resembled a 1950s cartoon of atomic particles circling the nucleus. It was simply impossible to find the right path back to the user and identify them.

Englefield pushed the disguised dongle into his laptop and connected to the internet, noting the exact time, 18.37. He then connected the laptop to his own 32" monitor screen. He opened *enable remote connection* and then TOR, routing the connection through it. He inputted the name and IP address of Buckland's general use terminal when prompted – the one she used to send emails, book tickets, and more than a few Amazon orders. Everyone did it. No harm really.

A small box appeared displaying *connection successful*. He felt a jolt of adrenalin and took another deep breath. He was now looking at a very boring home screen – no photos of dogs, no vibrant green rolling hills or sandy beaches as a backdrop – just plain blue with icons arranged neatly around the edge.

He moved the cursor selecting *Devices and Drives*. The usual items were listed including her stand-alone printer and scanner, but the last one read *Dell XPS 8930* – her *other* terminal. He'd have to disguise this, as on the faint chance she did what he'd just done, she'd see something that shouldn't be there. He right-clicked, selecting *rename* and altered it to *Drive G.* With only six drives on her computer, drive G would never be called upon.

The big jump was next, the biggest he'd ever taken in his life. He took a long pull of beer and blew out a slow breath. He settled the cursor over the renamed *Drive G* and hesitated. Thoughts rushed into his mind that if he was caught, pressing the return key could determine if he would live or die. If he didn't press it he would probably be able to plea bargain that he didn't execute his full plan. Yes, he would still have committed serious offences which would result in a lengthy prison sentence, but he wouldn't be executed.

He lifted his right index finger, sat back in his chair and thought about Bradley Manning. He was sentenced to thirty-five years but ended up serving seven. He did the maths and thought about what he might be like in his mid to late forties if the same happened to him.

Englefield hadn't anticipated he'd consider abandoning his plan now that the portal was in place. He'd done the risky part – everything else would be done remotely and at a time of his choosing. He could work in the evenings once Buckland had gone home, or all weekend. He stared at the return key, likening it to the trigger of a gun.

An image entered his head of a scene from the Matrix. If he left his finger off the return key it would be the equivalent of taking the blue pill. Nothing would change. In pressing it, he'd be swallowing the red pill. Nothing would be the same and he would enter Wonderland. He looked at the screen, seeing the cursor exactly in the middle of the icon for Drive G. He picked his beer up, draining the last few drops. 'Fuck it.' He hit the return key.

*

The CIA is the lead security service in the USA, on a par with MI6, the FSB and Mossad. Other nations deployed the most advanced methods of espionage, eavesdropping, subterfuge and every dirty trick you would expect to find in a spy agency, but the CIA were at the top of the class. Other countries were still formidable with what they could intercept and infiltrate – even the Egyptian National Security

Agency were renowned for their development of gadgets and hardware for undercover operatives.

The CIA's protection against hackers and infiltrators was the envy of agencies around the world. They shared *some* of their methods and programs with their foreign brothers in arms, but as is often the case, kept the best for themselves.

Josh thought about the technicians who'd put together all the hardware back at the office – the hundreds of miles of wiring, rooms full of servers, internal security and backup power. He thought about those in command giving themselves a pat on the back over how brilliant they were in covering all the bases.

How could they not see the obvious flaw? Why didn't they house the server for the databases in a different room even, instead of not only putting the connections for two systems that should never be linked in the same drawer, but an inch apart? Stupid mistakes, just like the ones that cooked half his brother's brain on the hot Afghan sand.

Englefield stared at the page dominating his monitor – the CIA logo in vibrant blue with *Central Intelligence Agency* written in a semi-circle around the famous eagle head. Underneath the logo read *Above Top Secret database. Any access by persons not cleared to above top secret will be considered an act of treason, punishable by death.*

'Well, that's pretty clear then.'

Below the warning were two windows for username and password. Englefield looked intently to double-check he was actually seeing what he thought he was. *Above top secret.* The sly bitch. She wasn't just cleared to top secret level, but way beyond. This was incredible. He knew she'd worked on highly classified stuff – sometimes she'd put a notice on her door stating *entry is forbidden for any reason-telephone if urgent*. Buckland had been at the Agency long enough and proved her worth, so they'd obviously elevated her clearance to enable her to work on assignments only the most highly trusted were considered worthy of.

'Well I'll be dammed, you are one cool cookie,' he said to no one. 'Still a fucking bitch though.'

He typed *AliciaBucklandDDanalysis*, then moved to the password. Typing slowly to avoid any mistakes, he entered *ilikecoldplay*4488<>. With each key pressed, a star appeared in the box. Without hesitation he hit the return key with a flourish, lifting his finger off like Liberace ending a tune. Jackpot.

Englefield grabbed another beer and powered up his hi-fi. His record collection was extensive, built up over many years trawling second-hand shops, markets, record fairs and late night forays on eBay. Some were worth a few dollars, the more collectable ones many hundreds. He took a moment to peruse the shelves custom-built to house his collection, arranged in alphabetical order according to artist. Stopping at B, he withdrew *Hunky Dory*.

He kept his records in immaculate condition, each one in a plastic sleeve with some of the rarer ones still sealed and never played. He carefully laid the album on the turntable, blowing a tiny piece of dust off, and pushed back a small lever causing the diamond-tipped stylus arm to rise. He gently pushed the arm to the run on the groove of side one, pulling the small lever back to its original position. He twisted the volume to number 3 – loud enough to appreciate the exceptional tonal quality, but not so loud that it would distract him from what he was about to do.

The screen he was now transfixed by was markedly different to the one he was used to working on. He scanned it all, becoming familiar with the layout, his confidence growing as his head bobbed to the riff on 'Changes'.

He thought about the information he had to input when conducting his own research – the more you put in, the more likely the search would return the fewest hits giving better accuracy. Put in general terms and the results found would run to many pages.

The various fields were highlighted in dusty pink – name, pseudonym, nickname, address, frequents, known associates, date of birth, apparent age, ethnicity, country of origin, languages spoken, height, weight, build, eye colour, hair colour, hairstyle, facial hair, glasses, contact lenses, abnormalities, scars, piercings, tattoos, shoe size, left-/right-handed, missing body parts – all just to search for a person.

In the top right-hand corner was the username. He clicked on *Alicia Buckland* and a further window dropped down containing more options to click on, and they all looked intriguing.

The first line in the sub menu was titled *personal info*. 'Hmm, this could be interesting, let's see what they have to say about little ol' Leece.' A separate page opened which surprised him. It was a complete as is possible cache of data covering every aspect of her life. 'Jesus H,' he whispered to himself.

He reminded himself not to rush – he was the invisible man. He could go wherever he chose and no one would see him. Feeling like a child in a sweetshop with a fistful of money, he wanted so much to rush around and grab everything he could, but that's what an amateur would do. No, he was a professional.

He could scarcely believe his eyes – there was so much information about Buckland. It started with the obvious home address, date of birth, next of kin, but ran much, much deeper. As he scanned down his eyes widened. He asked himself why it would be on her file. Then it hit him – it was to protect her.

His mind jolted back to a day about eighteen months before. *Of course*, he thought to himself. It was been a pretty slack week with the whole office thinking about their summer holidays, and lunch breaks could last a couple of hours. He remembered some guy called Sam Dibble bursting into their office. Alicia was at the coffee machine chatting to Evie. Dibble came striding across the floor pointing at Buckland's office. 'Leece, we've got a hostage situation, one of ours.' He remembered they both rushed to the terminal he was now controlling.

The personal data stored was for this exact situation. It contained an encyclopaedic record of anything that might assist the CIA to help one of their own, should the worst case scenario happen. Blackmail, extortion, defection, and the worst of the worst – kidnap. It could be the difference between getting a colleague back, or not.

It was the story of a life and the lives of everyone connected to them. Englefield noted Buckland's home address, the code to her sophisticated house alarm and where she hid a spare key. A germ of an idea was forming.

He got up and carefully turned the record over, holding it like a precious archaeological find. Nodding to himself, he realised how useful all that he was seeing could be. It would alter his plans, no, not alter, improve.

Englefield sat perplexed. He'd meticulously planned the method of getting in and was confident nothing could be traced back to him, but was now facing a problem he hadn't anticipated – where to start? The net he was casting wasn't just large, it was massive. Buckland's security clearance meant she could access everything, so when she conducted a search – from a phrase to an exact description of a target, her terminal would reach into any database with even the loosest match.

In addition to searching intelligence judged above top secret, it would interrogate all the CIA databases, including top secret, secret, restricted and snippets anyone could look at. The hit rate would be potentially enormous, and it didn't stop there. Social security, immigration, medical, vehicle registration, firearm ownership, phone companies, internet service providers – even the coast guard. Englefield likened himself to a whale shark, the biggest fish in the world, gliding silently through deep waters with its massive jaws open, sucking everything in and filtering out what was of no use.

He decided to try a basic search to see how the system reacted and how fast results came in. Just a test really. He entered September 1st 2019 in the *from* section and December 1st 2019 in the *to* box. He moved to the location field but decided to leave the field blank. Moving his mouse slightly, the cursor flashed over *information*. He typed in *Black Ops* and hit the return button.

Englefield watched the little wheel spinning for a few seconds – *results found 137*. 'Jesus, that's a lot.'

A further box dropped down listing the file numbers and date. He clicked on the first, noting it was marked *Secret*. He skim-read the first few lines and realised it was going to take an age. He cut to the chase and pressed Ctrl and F. A box popped up allowing him to search for any given word or phrase. He typed *Black Ops* which took him straight to the body of the first report, highlighting where the phrase appeared.

Miquel Martinez has been sighted five times in the last two months in the area believed to house the entrance to the tunnel. Martinez has been closely supervising the build following the discovery of the previous attempt to tunnel from a hairdresser's owned by him in Nuevo Laredo. DEA are currently running a ***Black Op*** *supplying equipment from a hire all shop set up and run by DEA agents. It is anticipated.*

Englefield stopped reading. Boring – just some shit about a drug lord's new tunnel under the border. He realised his search had been too loose. Black Op covered anything clandestine, not just some Special Forces unit flying under the radar and killing people. He would have to think carefully about what to enter, otherwise he'd spend years sorting the wheat from the chaff.

He licked his finger and ran it around his plate, picking up the last few crumbs, and took another swig of beer, placing it on the edge of the table. He wiggled the fingers of both hands over the keyboard, as if daring them where to land, and began to type.

He kept the same dates but reduced the parameters of his search. In the *security level* box he typed *Above Top Secret*. He cleared the *other information* box and typed in *Black Ops/assassination/politician/VIP/head of state*. The wheel whirled for a few seconds before *Results found 3* appeared.

He started reading and time seemed to slow. He reached for his beer, unable to look away and knocked the bottle with his knuckles, causing it to fall to the floor and smash. The sound hardly registered as his eyes darted left to right, scarcely believing the words he was never meant to see. He leant back, burying his hands in his hair.

'Oh. My. Fucking. God.'

Chapter 12.

Kent, UK, 13 days to mission.

Jenks picked up his laptop and glanced out at the beach and beyond. A large bird was perched on a hazard pole at the end of a waste water outlet, and he could tell even at that distance it was a cormorant. Reaching for his binoculars, he took five minutes to gaze at it. Every so often it would stretch its wings and shake its head, then settle back to just looking around.

Further along the beach he could see a young boy walking slowly towards Whitstable with a small dog bouncing up and down as if suspended on elastic. He held the binoculars steady and could just make out the ball the lad was holding, not quite letting the dog reach it. He smiled to himself. There was hardly anyone around which was just how he liked it.

He swept back in the opposite direction. The bleak scene was almost as deserted apart from the bait diggers turning over the mud, collecting their worms. Three of them today when normally there'd be two. No cause for alarms to go off in Jenks's internal early warning system. He rested his elbows on the table to steady himself as he was at the very end of the focal range.

He lingered on the bait diggers for a moment longer, noticing one wasn't digging. What he thought had been a shovel the man was leaning on looked too thin – probably a walking stick. The man had his back to him and was wearing a long coat which reached down below his knees, and a hat with a wide brim tipped over his brow. Although the image was fuzzy, Jenks could just make out the body shape through the coat. The way the man was holding his weight with the stick suggested he was quite old – probably just out for a stroll and stopping for a few minutes to pass the time of day.

Kent, UK, 10 minutes before.

The old man walked along the beach leaving Whitstable town behind him, smiling at a young boy playing with his dog. He found it tiring plodding through the shingle, and took care placing his stick to steady himself due to the weakness in his hip. He hated getting old and physically weaker, his body now paying the price for the exploits of his younger self.

He felt happier as he crossed West Beach, the pebbles compressed by thousands of feet over the years. A row of beach huts stood against the sea wall – some modernised and swanky, others long forgotten and gradually collapsing. He could see a house in the distance, and as he got closer, a handful more, spaced apart with large gardens. Some had more land than others, but all had long gardens sloping down to the sea wall.

He kept his head low, his face obscured by his hat, his eyes hidden behind dark glasses. Whilst looking straight ahead he could set his gaze left, but anyone watching wouldn't be able to tell. He was holding his phone to his ear.

Passing the house with the most land around it, he saw an old Land Rover in front of a garage set to the side of the house. He looked left towards a large bay window on the ground floor. And there he was, unmistakeable – sitting at a table looking intently at a laptop screen and clearly talking, but the old man couldn't see signs of anyone else in the room.

The man in the house occasionally lifted his head, but didn't appear to be concentrating on the world outside his window – more the type of movement when someone is thinking and looks to the sky for inspiration. The man in the house then picked up a mobile phone and appeared to be ending a call. Still holding the phone, he punched at various buttons and put the phone to his ear. The previous call had been on loudspeaker so he could type at the same time, he guessed.

The old man didn't break his slow stride and continued talking.

'Do you have him in sight?'

A female voice replied, 'Yes, he's in the park on a bench eating a sandwich and just took a call.'

'Good. Tell me the exact moment he ends it, we'll keep this line open.'

A few minutes went by before the old man heard, 'OK, looks like he's about to finish, he's holding his sandwich up ready to take another bite.'

'Have you got cover?'

'Don't need it, I stole a dog and fit in perfectly – he's not given me a second glance. Stand by, call ended.'

The old man glanced towards the house and saw the man in the window put his mobile phone down at exactly the same moment.

'That's all for now, my dear, I won't need you again today.'

'What shall I do with the dog?'

'I don't care, let it go? Kill it? Do whatever you want.'

He disconnected and smiled to himself. 'Well, well, well. Graham Jenkins – it's been a long time.'

The old man cut diagonally across the mud towards the bait diggers. He could see them pull up a shovel full, turn it over, then reach down to pick out the worms and drop them into a bucket. He was slightly concerned about his footing – the last thing he wanted was to draw attention to himself by slipping over. Thankfully there was still a fair bit of shingle mixed with the mud making it firmer underfoot than if he'd been half an hour later, and the men had moved out to softer ground.

The diggers looked up as they noticed him approaching, one of them raising a hand to wave. The old man waved back.

'Good morning, gentlemen, and what a lovely morning it is.' The old man's voice was slightly clipped, and old school educated. Just occasionally, for those with a keen ear, the slightest hint of an accent crept in on certain words, but it *had* been many years since he'd last set foot in England.

'Morning to you – mind yourself out here, it's very slippery,' one of the men said, noticing the walking stick and smart shiny shoes.

'Oh I'm being very careful, thank you.' He glanced down at his stick. 'Bit of a dodgy hip, old chap. I'm OK as long as I don't try and turn cartwheels.'

Both men laughed.

'May I ask what type of bait you're digging for?'

'Rag and lug. We supply Syd's brother's shop with fresh bait every day, and a couple of others in Herne Bay.'

'Oh my, you must be out here in all weathers.'

'Every day guvnor, rain or shine, day or night, we're here.'

'How do you find them in the dark?

'Red light – worms can't see red, so they just sit there. It's actually easier at night as we can just pick 'em up.'

'I see – fascinating.'

The younger of the men spoke. 'You local, are you?'

'Well I am now actually. My wife and I moved down from London at the end of last week. Had enough of it up there and wanted to enjoy retirement by the sea. I think we're known as DFLs now aren't we? Down from London? Got the bungalow, and, oh now, what is it the youngsters say these days.....Oh yes, the tee-shirt as well.'

Both men burst out laughing. The older one said, 'Yep, DFLs, but at least you're staying. Whereabouts have you bought?'

The old man pointed towards the shore. 'Up behind the post office.'

The same man asked, 'Oh nice, what road?'

The old man didn't know any of the road names, and only knew the post office because he'd driven past it when acclimatising himself with the area. He pretended he hadn't heard.

'We've got a sea view and the sunsets so far have been rather good. Mind you, not as good as for those lucky blighters,' he said, nodding towards the beach houses. 'They've got to have the best view in the whole of Kent.'

Both men made a 'pfft' sound in unison. The older man spoke. 'Most of them are bloody second homes and empty most of the time.' He nodded towards the end house. 'See that creamy coloured one in the distance? That's some woman off the TV, Mary something, but I've never seen her and I'm out here every day. That one next to it – second home. The next one along belongs to some bloke who lives on his own.

Don't see him that much, keeps himself to himself but you occasionally see him outside doing stuff. I think he's got an old Landy. That house next to his – another second home.'

'A Landy? What the dickens is that?

'It's short for Land Rover.'

'Oh, I see, of course.'

The younger one added, 'Fit bugger he is – I've seen him out running, looks like an Olympic athlete he does. Bloody quick. And I've seen him do about a million press-ups in his garden when he's got back off a run. Flippin' mental if you ask me.'

'All sounds a bit unnecessary, I'll stick to walking, thank you, or rather hobbling these days. Well, look, it's been lovely talking to you, but I ought to get back to she who must be obeyed.'

'Eh?'

'The wife.'

Both men laughed again.

'Bye for now, gentlemen.'

'See ya, mate, be careful now.'

*

Jenks walked across to his garage, grabbing the crutch from the boot of his Land Rover on the way. Locking the door behind him, he walked over to his workbench, put the perfume atomizer down and examined the crutch from every angle.

His work area was well stocked with a large variety of tools and boxes and tins of odds and ends collected over the years, saved in case they came in handy one day.

He knew exactly what he wanted but couldn't remember where he'd put it. Just one of many things stored years ago, now ideal for the job in hand. He pictured it in his mind and closed his eyes, concentrating on nothing except the object. Looking up to the rafters where more boxes were stored, he settled on one in particular.

Jenks reached up, carefully sliding the box into his hands. On the lid was a photograph of a studious young boy in a lab coat hunched over a Bunsen burner holding a test tube. Emblazoned across the box was *My first chemistry set.* It was one of the few possessions to escape the fire which razed his mother's house to the ground, only surviving due to being stored in a garden shed.

He gently slid the lid off, revealing the contents, all still in immaculate condition, sitting in their original places in the plastic tray. The smell reminded him of childhood.

He removed a small test tube and cork and set it down on a rag. Picking up the atomizer, he unscrewed the lid and discarded the glass bottle. Selecting a drill bit the same size as the atomizer's pipe, he carefully drilled a hole through the cork.

He pushed the pipe through the hole, filled the test tube with water and replaced the cork. He then squeezed the bulb and the water squirted out, emptying the tube in one go. He tested it a few times, experimenting how hard to squeeze but the results were the same each time – the test tube emptied completely.

He then turned his attention to the crutch, removing the plastic grip from the handle, and carefully cutting off the end so it was now a cylinder open at both ends.

Using the same drill bit to bore a hole on the underside of the handle, he then wrapped a small piece of rag around the test tube and slid it into the handle.

The bulb protruded slightly but once the hand grip was back on, it would be undetectable. For now, he needed to leave it off until he received a delivery from James Camburn.

Normally in the weeks leading up to a mission he would never have so much spare time. There was still a lot to do, but much was reliant on updates from the Shop. He wouldn't have the drone footage until the following day, and unless something changed dramatically, he had the rare luxury of downtime.

He decided to give the Ducati a run out, and set about checking it over. Ten minutes later he put his tools neatly away, but there was one more thing he wanted to do before setting out.

He picked up the crutch and opened a large metal trunk bolted to the floor in the corner of the garage. Pulling out old blankets, newspapers and pieces of rag, he leant in and twisted a bolt in the left-hand corner furthest from him. He heard the click and the floor of the trunk popped up an inch. Hooking his fingers under the edge of the base, he lifted it up and climbed down the wooden staircase.

USA, same time, same day.

A man picked up his burner phone and punched in the international dialling code for Great Britain followed by a number. A long tone sounded and the call was answered. 'Hey, buddy, it's me.'

A cultured English voice replied, 'Good day, what have you got for me.'

'I've only been in an hour but – hey, are those seagulls I can hear? Didn't know you got them in London.'

'Yes they are, dear boy. I took a little jaunt to the coast to satisfy myself about something. I'm heading back up shortly. Anyway, what's the update?'

'OK, the emails are just saying the same thing every day. E writes OK then B puts the same. It's obviously a failsafe in case something happens to one of them, but it shows the game is live.'

'I understand. And you have no worries about the reliability of your man?'

'None whatsoever. He's been a good boy and stayed pretty straight, and he's delivered the stick and password every time as per our instructions. And of course he's richer.'

'Quite. Not enough to retire on but he's got four million reasons to follow it through to the end.'

'He's already told me what he's gonna spend some of it on, and he believes *Welikeleaks* will put everything out almost immediately – he swallowed that from you all the way. It's the when and where he's gonna get the merchandise he hasn't been told yet. He knows and we know it's a three-day period in central London, but the finer details are obviously gonna come through at the last moment.'

'Hmm, very canny. That's exactly how I'd do it if I were Mr E. He's covering himself until the very last moment. It's not ideal, but we've no other choice but to watch, wait and be ready when the time comes, although maybe we can tweak the end game ourselves a little.'

'What you got in mind?'

'Let me have a little think about it, nothing complicated, but a little twist to underline to all parties that we are in the driving seat, not them.'

'I like your style, buddy.'

'Please don't call me buddy, it's vulgar.'

'Whoa, OK.'

The Englishman changed the subject. 'Has there been any activity on other floors in your building?'

'Nope, she doesn't suspect a thing. People are running around, and it's only a matter of days before they put two and two together, then a large amount of doo-doo is gonna hit the fan. It'll buy us a few days as she won't say anything because she can't – that's the beauty of it. She knows shit, but the people here will just think she's holding out. By the time they realise she was a patsy, you'll be home and I'll be putting my arm around her telling her everything's gonna be OK, and I'll also be a rich man.'

The Englishman continued. 'When this is over you'll have serious decisions to make. You could buy an island somewhere hot, and fish all day, if that sort of thing appeals to you, or...'

'Or what?'

'If like me you enjoy being in the game, you may find it difficult to leave behind. If you stayed in place you'd be our best placed asset anywhere, and the rewards from our masters would be even higher. Maybe you could buy a string of islands.'

'I know, I've thought about the long term, but you can't spend it in, what do you guys call it...the clink.'

'That's what's so damn wonderful about this, it simply cannot come back to you. Mr E doesn't know anything about you, and there's no way he can find out now. Mr B has only spoken to you on the phone and has no idea of your real identity, *and* Mr B has never met me face to face. And of course he won't be around for much longer to tell anyone anyway – you, my dear boy, are bombproof. In a few days the world is going to be a very different place. My masters will hold not just all the cards, but every deck there is. Power like that has never been wielded in all of history. Now what's that phrase your fellow countrymen use – how cool is that?'

The American was nodding. 'Ice cold.'

The Englishman continued. 'Did B get over the water OK?'

'Yeah, no problems with the new passport, it flagged up to me when he entered the UK – he's doing the tourist thing for a few days until he gets the word. He wasn't happy losing the hair and beard though.'

'Needs must – let me know if anything, and I mean *anything* changes. I want to know if there's even a bit of gossip around the coffee machine which may be related to our business. Assemble the team in London and have them on standby from now on. We have to be ready to react to any changes. I'm going to head back to town now and find some good vodka.'

'You got it. You know, I quite like the idea of watching the new world from my office chair.'

'It'll be the best seat in the house, old boy. TTFN.'

The American screwed up his face. 'What?'

5 minutes later.

Whilst the American sat trying to work out exactly what the hell TTFN meant, the man with the cultured English accent dialled another number.

'Are you at work today?'

'No – day off, going fishing actually.'

'Nice day for it.'

'Exactly, it's pouring with rain up here. Hey, is that seagulls I can hear?

'Yes, never mind about that. I've just spoken to our American friend.'

'Oh yes, are they on top of things?'

'As much as they can be. Basically we can't act until we know exactly where, how and when the final exchange is. Mr E is very security conscious, as one would expect. We don't even know what name he's using now, but it certainly won't be his own. Our American friend was able to copy the email details they're using and the hotel name, but wasn't able to get anything else from the investigating team without looking like he was asking too many questions.'

'Still useful though. Any idea when we'll know more?'

The Englishman continued. 'He's not going to tell Mr B until, well, we just don't know. It'll be between the 10th and 12th, although my guess is it won't be the 12th as that's the day he's leaving London. He told Mr B he won't be around after then so we have to take it at face value.'

'I see, not ideal.'

The Englishman continued. 'Mr E has really thought this through. We're pretty sure we know where he'll be staying, but it's too risky to mount an intervention, and that's not to say he won't change hotel. Even if we broke his door down, he'll have security measures in place and if he thinks we're reneging on the deal, he's only got to push the wrong button, or not push a button and we'll lose the main part of the merchandise.'

'He's a sly one.'

'Isn't he just.'

‘So you’ve no choice but to let it run?’

The Englishman wasn’t concerned. ‘It is what it is and we’ll make it work. I think however with the uncertainty, we bring our plan forward – we’ll be in an unassailable position if we’ve got everything from both places. You’ve been very patient these last three years, but in a few days you’ll be home giving orders instead of taking them.’

‘I’m looking forward to it.’

The Englishman continued. ‘When is she back?’

‘Next Sunday, so I’ll secure the goods on Saturday evening.’

‘Excellent. And the key? You have checked it still works?’

The man became irritated. ‘I’m not an amateur, of course it works – she hasn’t changed the bloody locks.’

The Englishman wished he hadn’t mentioned it. ‘I’m sorry. I was just worried as it’s so old. You said there’s 150?’

‘About – maybe a few either way but I can do it in one go.’

‘Well you know what they say – the best things come in small packages. Now, security there, is there any chance they’ll search you?’

‘I’d be highly surprised if they did – I’ve built up a pattern of familiarity. They’ve always seen me with the same rucksack, and they like me. I’ve dropped down some very good bottles of scotch, so we all get on very well. You need have no fears, I'm one of the boys as far as they're concerned.'

'Excellent. I'll arrange for someone you know to collect them. Book your ticket and fly home on Sunday.'

'Understood.'

'Enjoy your fishing.'

The Englishman ended the call and dialled another number – it was answered immediately.

'You are to be in Scotland next Saturday – get a flight from City Airport as Aberdeen's not far from Balmoral. He'll hand it over on Saturday evening. You'll have to hire a car and drive back directly to me – we can't risk anything being picked up by airport security.

'I understand, goodbye, sir.'

Kent, UK, same time.

Jenks turned on the lights as he got to the bottom of the wooden staircase. The subterranean room was originally an air raid shelter built to withstand a more or less direct hit, with a ceiling of reinforced concrete at least two feet thick. Whoever built it had probably over-protected themselves, which was fine with him.

The entrance was clearly visible under a heavy iron trap door set into the garage floor when he bought the house, and made a perfect hidden room for items he couldn't afford to be discovered. The entrance, now disguised in the bottom of the trunk, was virtually undetectable.

He placed the crutch on the table, above which were rows of drawers of varying sizes. He opened each in turn, doing a quick mental inventory. He had enough ammunition to fight a war, and enough guns to equip a small army. One drawer contained his store of handguns, snugly held in custom cut foam. Jenks had favoured and stuck with the Glock 17 since leaving the army. He'd fired almost every type of weapon, but never found another as comfortable and reliable as the Glock, which was why he had a lot of them.

It held seventeen rounds and was quick to reload, but not quite as quick as drawing another fully loaded weapon, which was why he always carried two. Useful if you're hanging from a roof and need one hand to hold on.

Another drawer contained numerous boxes of ammunition. Jenks always used jacketed hollow point 9mm rounds, designed to expand and fragment when they entered the target, causing devastating damage. Other drawers contained a collection of devices, from traditional grenades to flash bangs. Along the far wall two cabinets housed an armoury of weapons designed for longer shots – sniper rifles. Jenks still favoured the Barrett, a gun he'd used successfully on many occasions. Arguably better weapons were available, but like a guitarist who favours one instrument above all others, the Barrett ticked all the boxes for him.

The converted shelter consisted of one main room, with a smaller area accessed from the rear. Jenks guessed it was probably for a toilet, should the Germans decide to bomb for longer than the occupants could hold out. This now contained his collection of odds and ends which could be used as they were, or adapted.

One cabinet housed electrical equipment, ranging from signal jammers to bug detectors, but on the floor next to it was a trunk he'd been given by his Egyptian contact. Jenks had received substantial payment, but his handler wanted to give him a selection of toys his colleagues had been working on as a little extra thank you.

He looked through, chuckling to himself at one item. He studied it in detail, wondering who on earth thought the idea up, but was impressed by the ingenuity. He couldn't foresee circumstances where it would be of use to him, but then circumstances could turn on a sixpence in his world.

Jenks made his way back up to the garage, closed the hatch and threw the bundle of blankets, newspapers and rags back into the trunk. He put his leathers on, grabbed his full face helmet and fired up the Ducati, growling like a powerful animal about to launch itself towards its prey. For the first time in months he set off on a ride just for the sheer pleasure of it.

Chapter 13.

USA, 3 months previously.

Joshua Englefield stared intently at the précis of the mission report, not quite believing it. Having just opened one of three hits returned from his search, he sat open-mouthed as he digested details of the assassination of a well-known prime minister's long-term mistress, and the DNA results proving he'd fathered her three children. The report outlined the blackmailing, resulting in the reversal of policy decisions, rewriting of trade agreements and lucrative contracts awarded to companies in the US.

He delved deeper, eager to see more. Peeling away the layers he came to a section marked *personnel.* Opening the sub folder revealed not only call signs, but the real identities of all personnel in the termination team. Not just names, but who they reported to at the CIA, and who sanctioned the mission – it even listed the senator who'd rubber-stamped the whole operation. He opened a new search and typed in one of the names, revealing a file as comprehensive as Buckland's. It was almost too much.

He copied the report to an encrypted memory stick and clicked on the second result. The report ran to many pages, titled *Persian Gulf, Operation Ulysses closing report*. He knew operation names were created at random by the system, so the name itself held no significance. It was what had happened in the Persian Gulf that intrigued him.

He skimmed through until he reached the first mention of Black Ops in the report. Scarcely able to comprehend, he saw that it detailed the shooting down of military drones, attributed to the Iranians. But it wasn't the Iranians.

It gave details of the American Special Forces unit who launched surface-to-air missiles against their own drones. The fact the drones had been stripped of everything except fuel and guidance systems had never come out. He guessed the Iranians recovered the wreckage, finding nothing but a shell.

The Iranians would have quickly realised that by keeping it a secret, but making the US aware that *they* knew what had really happened, it would open a whole new world of bargaining tools – even after publicly admitting responsibility. It was layer upon layer of subterfuge from both sides, but the truth was staring him in the face. He copied the salient parts of the report and stored it on the memory stick.

He read long into the night, finding it more addictive than any drug. Every file he opened contained details of actions taken not just by his country, but with their allies, and often with alleged enemies – alliances no one in their right mind would believe, but the truth was there. The effect on those nations if the world was made aware would be catastrophic.

His eyelids were starting to droop. It was 2.30am and he'd been sitting at his laptop for an entire working day. He closed down the remote connection, disconnected from the internet and opened an evidence eliminator program, erasing permanently all history for the last twenty-four hours. To be doubly sure he opened *settings,* selected *system restore* and typed 18.37 the previous day. The computer had effectively gone back in time, the last eight hours of activity ceasing to exist.

He straightened his back, feeling the effects in his neck from sitting hunched in the same position. His senses started to return and he became aware of a scratching sound. He turned and saw the stylus resting on the run out groove of *Hunky Dory*, Bowie having sung his last song seven hours previously.

He turned everything off and pushed the hidden dongle back into the vacant valve port and headed to bed. *Manning, eat your heart out*, he thought as he drifted off.

*

The following morning Englefield woke early. Considering his late night, he didn't feel too bad. A combination of hardly any booze let alone a joint or eight, combined with the excitement of getting back online, made him feel wide awake.

He fired up his coffee machine and took a large mug over to the table along with two doorstep-sized slices of toast. He noted the time – 09.12.

Establishing the remote connection, he logged back into Buckland's terminal. He'd decided when he first woke that he'd structure his searches even more carefully, but there was so much to see and it was overwhelmingly engrossing.

He'd had to check himself on a few occasions the previous night when he was opening door after door in the same file. He should've been making notes to come back to certain parts later, but it was like getting lost in a good book he couldn't put down. No, today he would start to fine tune, updating his memory stick with files, each one at least as incendiary as the last.

He worked well throughout Saturday, taking breaks and trying not to get carried away. The folder grew to include not just sanctioned assassinations and atrocities committed by his own country, but secret missions run by others for which America had provided assistance or intelligence. It included the unpleasant demise of a Chinese government official at the hands of three British MI6 officers, supported by CIA agents who'd made the introductions. He skimmed the next bit, noting it was something to do with mobile network contracts, concentrating on the mission report.

Identified in the report were not just the pseudonyms of the MI6 officers and their CIA support, but their real identities. No addresses for the

Brits, but he was sure an interested party would be able to find out, should they wish to.

By late afternoon he'd amassed ten subfolders. Some made him angry, others sad. Sad for the families left behind, sad for whole villages levelled in some godforsaken country in order that his fellow Americans and some dubious allies could extract the riches buried beneath their soil.

The villagers only wanted to dig a couple of feet down to grow the food they needed to survive, not hundreds of feet to mine for tiny pieces of a scarce and rare element, all to fuel the need of the throwaway generation for the latest gadget. Sadness turned to anger as he read how once the supply was exhausted, the contractors left that tiny piece of the planet upside down and toxic, moving on to the next site.

If the villagers became demonstrative or militant, they often disappeared. The report contained a list of the small group of CIA operatives who acted as *security*. It may well have just read *here is a list of men who killed the village elders*. 'You fuckers have no idea what's coming to you,' he snarled to himself.

Enough for one day, he thought. His plan would only work if he could bring Chas on board along with his *Welikeleaks* people. No point in doing all the hard work yet if he had no buyer. He'd considered putting it all out himself, but there had to be a payday. He was doing it for the cause, for the benefit of humanity, but there was no point if he couldn't watch the beauty of the new dawn. Someone would have to help guide the people, set the order within the anarchy. Yes, it would be beautiful – the whole world cleansed of everything that had caused it to become dirty, greedy and unfair.

He went through his security procedure and grabbed a cold beer. Collapsing on the couch, he kicked off his sneakers and reached into a small ornate box on the coffee table. Lighting a large joint, he inhaled deeply, sinking into the soft cushions. Closing his eyes and enjoying the hit from his first toke, he spoke softly. 'You'd be proud of me, Stevie boy, you really would.' As he exhaled a single tear rolled down his cheek. 'Fuckers,' he said a little louder. 'FUCKERS,' he shouted, barely able to contain his anger.

*

On Sunday Englefield slept late. Friday night had caught up with him, but Sunday was a day of rest, and that's exactly what he was planning to do. Maybe head downtown for a late lunch, maybe just order in and watch a movie. He was happy with what he now had up his sleeve. Not so much a smoking gun, more a fully armed nuke. Saturday had been very productive, and if the contents of the memory stick weren't enough to whet the appetite of *Welikeleaks*, nothing was.

After more coffee, a flick through the weekend edition of *USA Today* and a few chores, he wondered if he should call Chas. Why put it off when he now had the carrot tied firmly to the stick. Surely there was no way his friend wouldn't be anything but spellbound by what he had to show him. But how would he react when he learnt about Englefield's real profession? That was the big worry and the reason he put off making the call, but the decision was made for him. His cell phone rang.

He tried to sound as normal as possible, but his stomach was turning summersaults. 'Hey, Chas, what's up?

'Not a lot, what you doing?'

'Just chilling, thought I might head out and grab some food in a while.'

'You wanna come over and watch the game later? Maybe sink a few?'

Englefield told him he'd like to but couldn't stay late as he had work the following morning, but would be over about 5pm and pick up pizza on the way. Black clearly wanted to party, saying everything he could to convince Englefield to throw caution to the wind and indulge.

Englefield told Chas he had something important to show him which would blow his mind far higher than any illicit substance. Despite Black trying his best to get Englefield to divulge more, he refused, telling him it would be worth it and would see him later.

Englefield slumped back into the sofa, feeling the need to take a deep breath. His hands were shaking, and all he could think about was how to convince Chas in the shortest amount of time that it wasn't a set-up.

Then an idea came to him. He grabbed the false valve and fired up his laptop.

He opened the search page and typed Charles Chas Black* Anarchy* wikileaks*welikeleaks. He hit the return key and seconds later the screen displayed *five results.*

Intrigued to see how much interest Black had generated, he opened the first report. It detailed his arrest at a rally about a year back. There were a series of photos attached of Black looking very angry. Some showed him punching the air, others generally snarling and clearly very worked up. The last showed him being handcuffed behind his back.

Englefield read on, laughing when he saw the reason for the arrest – *threatening to punch a police horse in the mouth.* Englefield guessed his friend must have been pretty high that day. He continued through the report noting reference to another. He inputted the report number. 'Whoa. Shit.'

The file was part of the closing report into the Manning saga. It ran to many pages, so he pressed Ctrl and F and typed in *Chas Black.* 'You bad boy.' What he read was a bit of a revelation.

Chas Black was, along with many others, suspected of being involved in the mass dissemination of three quarters of a million classified reports. He'd been arrested and his apartment searched, but there wasn't enough evidence to get anywhere near putting before the DA. The Agency decided it wasn't a good use of resources chasing the also rans when they had the main man in custody.

Englefield thought back to the many conversations he'd had with Black, who despite hinting at bigger things and powerful contacts, had obviously kept information back. He was a bigger fish than Englefield had given him credit for, but clearly not the king of the pond. Englefield felt more confident that whoever Black's contacts were, they'd be very interested in seeing more after he reported back to them.

He delved deeper and sat stock still as he read a file which had been initiated by none other than Alicia Buckland herself. He shuddered when he saw his name mentioned for the first time, but a smile crept across his face as he read on. *That fucking nosy bitch*. And, his birthday of all days had started it all off.

He continued reading about what she'd told Sam Dibble, and he'd told someone else, and the Agency started looking at them. He opened the attached jpegs and saw both of them photographed in different places at various times over the last few months. He went back further to photos from the FBI, but the ones he appeared in weren't clear enough to identify him. In some he was facing away from the camera or turned away just enough that his face was hidden, which was pure luck.

There was one taken with a long lens in the park, and he remembered the afternoon they sat in the sun chewing the fat for a couple of hours. After reading all the reports, he built up a chronological picture of who'd been watching who, and when.

It seemed the FBI kept tabs on Black after the horse incident, even using a photo of him at the demo in one of their training packages. Buckland happened to see a photo posted on Facebook from his birthday celebrations, which kicked it all off. She'd noticed Black but couldn't place him, but Dibble could, and so started the attention directed at both of them.

He wasn't surprised the Agency had copied his hard drive and inserted a key logger program as well as the camera in the ceiling – that's exactly what he'd expect in the early stages of a slightly circumspect investigation. But they'd found nothing, which turned the heat down a fair bit.

The closing report detailed how, on the basis of all evidence gathered, it didn't score highly enough to warrant further resources. It concluded that Joshua Englefield kept less than ideal company with a known felon, believed to have anarchistic tendencies who might or might not have been involved with the WikiLeaks data dump. It concluded that the investigation would end unless further information came to light – it had been put it on the back burner.

Englefield thought about it and decided it was actually great news. Had an investigation started now, and he'd not been aware, there was a good chance he'd be found out. The fact they'd both been investigated and the matter put on ice meant that with new security protocols for future communication between them, they could fly under the radar. Nevertheless, he decided to build an extra layer of protection for himself.

He closed the reports and created a new blank folder. Going online, he downloaded a short cartoon clip of an old style bomb with a burning fuse. He moved this into the new folder along with a digital clock counting down from seventeen minutes to zero. He then selected a pirate flag as the icon for the new folder. The countdown clock would start as soon as he clicked on the bomb – the rest he'd have to bluff.

He completed his security measures and glanced at his watch – nearly 4.15 and approaching show time. Nervous as hell, he went to his bedroom closet, retrieving a piece of equipment from a shoebox which looked like an old style walkie-talkie. Looks can be deceptive, as the device was one of the most sophisticated bug sweepers available, which he'd borrowed from work and accidently forgotten to return.

He put the device in his shoulder bag along with his laptop, memory stick and the disguised dongle and headed out to his car. Sitting with his hands on the steering wheel, he went over how he'd reveal what he did for a job, and how he could help change the world. The first part was the most difficult of the whole plan – making good on his promises and getting the information wasn't a problem, but staying alive after 5pm might be.

Chapter 14.

Black hadn't even had a beer let alone any type of drug. He was so intrigued he wanted a clear head to fully appreciate the effects of whatever it was Josh was bringing. It was coming up to 5pm when he heard a car crunching onto the gravel drive. Through the spyhole he saw his friend getting out with two large pizza boxes under one arm, two smaller ones in his hand and his shoulder bag hung around his neck. As Englefield approached the door, Black opened it.

'Hey, dude, how's it going? Bring those babies in, I'm starving.'

The two friends fist-bumped as Englefield entered. 'Hey, bro, I got yours with everything on plus extra chilies.'

Black smiled and playfully poked Josh in the ribs. 'Cool, but I bet they ain't as hot as whatever else you got with you.'

Englefield put his finger to his lips and placed the boxes on the table between the sofa and Black's worn but comfortable recliner.

'What the hell, man? Whaddya mean, shush?'

Englefield leant in, beckoning Black even closer. Black mouthed *what* and screwed up his eyebrows, but did as asked. With his mouth almost touching Black's ear, Josh whispered, 'I gotta sweep for bugs. I know this might seem weird but I'll explain everything, give me two minutes, dude, yeah?'

Black stood back, both arms extended with his palms facing up. He looked left and right wafting both arms, the international signal for *be my guest*.

Englefield reached into his bag and took out the device. Black watched, slowly shaking his head. Englefield held up two fingers, mouthing *two minutes*. Black mouthed back *whatever*. Englefield walked around the apartment, covering every part of each room. If there was any type of electronic listening device he'd pick it up. Returning to the lounge, he found Black in his recliner finishing a second slice of pizza. Black pointed at two open bottles of Pacifico. 'Er, permission to talk, dude.'

Englefield held up his right index finger but said nothing. He pointed to Black's hi-fi, then at himself, then back at the hi-fi. The message was clear. Black raised his hand and gesticulated towards the record player. Josh saw there was still vinyl on the turntable, so set it playing, happy to hear Steely Dan.

Sitting down at the end of the sofa nearest Black, Englefield picked up a piece of pizza as if what he'd just done was a normal everyday occurrence. If he was honest, he didn't really feel like eating.

'What the fuck was all that about, man? What the hell have you taken? You're totally paranoid, dude, and what's with the 'no talking can I put music on' shit?'

'Parabolic microphones – they can pick up conversations from way down the street as clear as sitting here. The music fucks it up completely – we can talk without anyone being able pick up what we're saying now, they're just gonna hear Donald and Walter if they're out there.'

'Who the fuck *is* out there, man? What's the matter with you? Chill, drink your beer and for fuck's sake tell me about that thing you wouldn't talk about on the phone, the thing that's gonna get me higher than I've ever been before. I've stayed straight all day, man, just so I can appreciate it, you know, in pure form.'

'OK, OK.'

'Man, you're shaking, look at your hands – what is it, dude, tell me?'

'Chas...look, you're my best buddy. I got lots to tell you, things that'll make that long hair stand on end if you give me the chance. What I'm gonna say first, well, you're not gonna like, I can promise you that. Please hear me out, man, just five minutes and I guarantee it'll change your life forever. Please, please just trust me, that's all I ask.'

Black was shaking his head. 'I ain't never seen you like this, and I gotta say you're freaking me out. So what is it then? What's so important you couldn't trust your best bud enough to tell him over the phone?'

Englefield felt his mouth instantly dry like he was sucking on a ball of kitchen towel. His heart was racing as he drew a breath. 'I don't work for an insurance company, I never did – I work for the CIA.'

The speed of Black's movement stunned Englefield. In a fraction of a second he leapt out of his chair, having retrieved a semi-automatic 50-calibre Desert Eagle pistol from behind a cushion. It happened so quickly Englefield barely had time to register the click of the hammer being drawn back in one fluid movement. In what seemed like the blink of an eye, Black was next to Englefield, the barrel of the Eagle pushing into his temple.

Englefield was gasping for air. 'No, Chas, no, please. Hear me out – just give me two minutes, then if you still want to pull the trigger, I won't try and stop you.'

Black's eyes were bouncing between the window, door, and back to Englefield. He was half expecting to hear instructions shouted from a bull horn outside telling him drop the weapon, or the door would come crashing in. He leant in close to Englefield, his voice full of menace. 'You bastard. You fucking no good bastard. I thought you were one of us. You got ten seconds before I turn your skull inside out and use it as an ashtray.'

Englefield had little time in which to convince Black not to pull the trigger, blurting out as many words as he could without pausing for breath.

'Right listen don't shoot I'm an analyst at the CIA and I'm high up so I got access to the really big secret stuff you wouldn't believe that would rock the world to its core if it got out and I can show you examples I got with me but there's a program on my laptop which will instantly wipe everything because it needs a password. We can change the world with what I can get and I can show you right now.'

The gun didn't move. 'Keep talking.'

'It's a bit difficult with that half buried in my head. Look, you want to change the world, I want to change the world, and with the secrets I can show you, which are only the tip of an iceberg bigger than you could ever imagine, you'll realise like me that nothing will ever be the same again. We can totally change society and level it all up, end war and make sure the people have what they need. We can change the world, dude, if you'll just let me show you.'

Black was interested. 'If I even hear a fucking bird land on my porch, this thing is gonna punch a hole through you bigger than my fist, wherever I point it.' Black lowered the barrel to Englefield's groin, where he noticed a small wet patch on his crotch.

'You really are scared, aren't you.'

Englefield was shaking. 'I'm petrified, man, I never had a gun aimed at me in my life. Please point it away. Hold it by all means, but please don't point it at me.'

'So no SWAT team gonna burst in then? No flash bangs through the window?'

'No, man, I swear it. If I was setting you up do you really think I'd come in here, sweep for bugs, sit next to you and the first thing I say is like *hey, man, I lied to you, I'm CIA*.'

'Wouldn't be the smartest introduction to a raid.'

Englefield looked at the handgun still pointing at his genitals.

'The piece, man, please.'

Black stood up, gently easing the hammer forward.

'Looks like you got some serious explaining to do, so start from the beginning.'

Englefield gave him the history of his career in the CIA explaining what an analyst actually did, and the levels of secrecy he could peel away with the clearance he already had. He described how he'd enabled access to Buckland's computer, which was now connected to a terminal authorised to access above top secret reports and files. He ended by explaining how foolproof the plan was, if handled in the right way.

Black sat dumbstruck. 'That is nothing short of utterly fucking mind-explodingly brilliant, man. So you can sit at home, press a few keys and find out the real truth about say, the Kennedy assassination?'

'Oh yes. And it gets better than that. You wanna see some secrets? The stuff they don't even allow the President to see?'

Black looked at him, shaking his head, and made a *Duhh* sound. 'What do you think?'

'Well buckle up. You, my friend, are about to have your mind blown.'

Englefield reached inside his bag and withdrew his laptop and the valve.

Black pointed at the valve. 'Hey, that's a bit before laptop time, ain't it?'

Englefield pointed. 'Look at the connection.'

Black raised his eyebrows. 'Well I'll be dammed – that's a USB.'

'See inside? You can just make out my dongle – look between the filaments.'

'Well I'll be dammed again. That from your amp?'

'The pre-amp. It doesn't do shit actually, the main amp has a built-in pre-amp anyway, so it just sits there hiding in plain sight.'

Black grinned. 'You are one sneaky son of a bitch.'

'I'll take that as a compliment. Now there's other stuff I've gotta tell you about. If this goes where I think it could, we've got to have serious protection. For a start, we can never, and I mean *never* discuss anything related to this over the phones we got now. That means text messages, voicemail or anything. I've got an idea how we can chat without anyone finding out, but I gotta show you this first.'

Englefield turned the computer on, noting the exact time. 'Chas, you have to understand the stakes before I show you Wonderland. If I got caught, even at this stage it's treason and that means the chair. Man, I trust you with my life – you gotta know that from ten minutes ago, but who knows what could happen so we plan for the unthinkable.'

Black nodded. 'I hear you, man.'

'Watch, I'm gonna open that icon there with the skull and crossbones.'

Englefield clicked.

'Hey, man, what the fuck's that bomb?'

Englefield clicked on the bomb and showed Black the countdown clock. It was reading 16 mins 51 seconds.

'OK, I've built in a program that I basically need to talk to every so often. The countdown is random so I don't know how long I've got each time. I have to type in a password before it gets to zero or the entire contents of this little baby will be fried. Literally every single piece of data will be destroyed and irretrievable – and the link to the Agency. When I put the password in, the clock starts again. You with me?'

'Uh, yeah, I think so.'

'I have to be protected and so do you. Without this laptop there is no new order, no new world – same old shit forever.'

'What if I pulled my gun and told you I'd shoot you in the heart unless you gave me the password?'

'I'd let you shoot me. I'm a dead man walking, man. I'd have to leave the Agency and they'd discover how it was done and find me. No question. I don't want to look over my shoulder for the rest of my life, I wanna live. I wanna see what happens when we free everyone – I've got to make enough so when I leave the good ol' US of A, I know I'm never coming back. Man, I have so many plans and I know we can do it. Let me show you some wonders.'

Englefield inserted the thumb drive which generated a password request. He turned the computer away from Black. 'You can't watch me do this, man, I gotta put another password in.'

'OK, dude, you're the boss.'

Englefield opened the drive and turned the screen to face Black.

'What you're looking at is a document I've created from my initial digging. I spent Friday night looking at stuff, but I was going about it the wrong way. There's literally so much there that I changed the way I was searching yesterday.'

'That document looks pretty lengthy – you got all this in three days?'

'Yeah, man, and I didn't even do much today, this is all just Friday night and Saturday day. Chas, this is like nothing I've seen before. My clearance is up to Secret, then you got Top Secret, which is what I thought Buckland was cleared to. Beyond that, well, when you hit Above Top Secret you're getting stuff only a handful of people have seen.'

The atmosphere in Black's lounge was electric. Neither man spoke before Black broke the silence.

'Fuck.'

Englefield pointed. 'Start from the first one. They're in no particular order, I just picked ten as examples, and there's a whole section about Buckland – literally every detail of her life, even the code for her home alarm.'

Black raised his eyebrows. 'Useful.'

'Quite.'

Black started reading, his eyes opening wider and his jaw hanging lower the more he saw. Englefield sat watching his friend shake his head in disbelief as he worked through the document.

Black turned. 'I am literally speechless, man. We actually took out a prime fucking minister's mistress? Left three children without a mother just to blackmail him into signing anything we put under his nose?'

'Yep, and we earned billions in trade out of it.'

'And Iran – that is fucking insane. We shot our own drones down so we could blame it on them. And they knew, so told us they knew, but we...wait, this is the work of madmen. And those villages – we wiped out a bunch of people just so we could sell a few cell phones?'

Englefield's smile was a mile wide. 'Can I cook, or can I cook?'

Black was in shock. 'This *will* change the world, man, I mean, change everything, everywhere. No way could anyone come back from that sort of exposure.'

'It's not just the US, dude. Those files contain every dirty deed we've done for other countries, *with* other countries, against other countries, and you know the best bit?'

'Isn't that enough, Jeez.'

Englefield made an upward motion with his hand. 'Scroll back to that first one about the mistress.'

Black rolled the document back to the top.

'OK, see where assassination is highlighted in red. Click on that.'

Black clicked. 'No way, man. You cannot be serious.'

'Never more so. That's the mission breakdown. Operatives involved, call signs, real names, home addresses, phones, alarm codes for their houses, the authorising officer and the senator who sanctioned the whole thing. Oh, and photos of her dead body.'

Englefield turned the laptop back. 'I gotta say hello to the countdown or all this will disappear.' He opened the bomb icon and pretended to reset the clock. 'OK, we're good.'

Black was totally taken in so didn't protest. He sat motionless thinking about what he'd just seen. He turned to his friend. 'This makes Manning look like an amateur.'

'That's exactly what I said to myself. Actually, dude, I was going to ask you about him. You know where I'm coming from now. You could pick up the phone, call this in and get a nice reward. I'd be taken away and get the chair – no two ways about it. So do you trust me now?

'Yeah, yeah – sorry about the piece earlier.'

'Understandable – I knew you'd be pissed, but I gotta say I didn't expect you to pull a gun. Dude, you can move pretty fast when you want to, I was impressed, even if you did make me piss my pants a little. So, Manning – were you involved?'

Black gave one nod. 'Yeah, at the start. I picked up the first batch, but it got sloppy. They fucking arrested me, man, turned this place over, broke loads of stuff, so I was burnt. They found jack shit though – I'd already dropped it all off. They had no evidence so stopped leaning on me. Made my life very difficult for a while though – every time I went out I was paranoid I was being followed.'

'You were.'

'What?'

'Well not all the time. You wanna see your file?'

'You're shitting me.'

'That's one thing I would never do. Scroll down, it's about four pages from last.'

Black scrolled down.

'Fuck, man, it mentions you here, aren't you worried?'

Englefield shook his head. 'Not now I've read the associated reports. This is exactly why it's the perfect time. You felt the heat ten years ago, and it went away. Then the horse incident, then later you came to that bitch's attention and things warmed up again, mainly, well actually entirely because of our friendship – but they got zilch. You were a tiny spike – enough to look a little deeper, but never above intelligence gathering and there was none to gather. Do you have any idea how many snippets of information flow into the Bureau, the Agency, Homeland and the Secret Service every day?'

Black shrugged his shoulders. 'Nope.'

'Neither do I, but I bet you a dime to a dollar it's hundreds, maybe thousands. They're all mostly shit, but they gotta get looked at, and that's what they did with us. Looked, found nothing, stopped looking.'

Josh prodded his own chest. 'They're probably pissed at me for hanging out with a known trouble-maker, but I'm fucking good at my job so they tolerate it. The beauty is I can see if they start anything back up again – we're hiding in plain sight. I gotta tell you I laughed my arse off when I read about that demo arrest.'

Black smiled, putting his hand to his forehead. 'Oh God, I know. I dropped some really strong acid that morning – I thought I heard the horse tell me the Beatles were shit. Man, I couldn't even remember what I was supposed to be demonstrating about.'

Englefield became serious. 'You need to keep straight if we're both gonna stay alive. No fuck-ups. You still involved with the leaking people?'

'Yeah – I only speak to one guy though, some old posh dude from England. He was way involved with the Manning stuff but wasn't happy with how it turned out – too many people involved with too many agendas. He's now with the *Welikeleaks* dudes – and he's got a heap of serious dough behind him.'

'How often do you talk?'

'Now and again. He said way back that next time it would be done properly. Funny actually, I spoke to him about a month ago and he mentioned plans were starting to come together, but he wouldn't say what for, but he might have some stuff for me to do. Look, I'll level with you, man, he's been paying me a, well I guess you'd call it a retainer since Manning. I should have said earlier. Not much, $500 a month. They learnt lessons last time and he knows I didn't say a word. From what he's said the *Welikeleaks* people are all handpicked – tried and tested and who he knows he can trust.'

'Good strategy. You need to call him – can you do that or is contact initiated by him?'

'No, I got his number, man.' Black tapped the side of his head.

'Don't give him my name, just tell him I'm highly placed in the CIA and able to access the most incendiary information he could imagine and even more that he can't. If he's interested I can get started right away.'

Black looked like the cat who'd not just got the cream, but been given the run of the entire dairy.

'Jeez, man, this is what I've been waiting for my whole life. We can make every fucking leader fall to their knees and beg. All the dirty tricks, all the cover-ups – this will level the field for humanity. We can hold them to fucking ransom and there's nothing they can do about it.'

Englefield nodded. 'A beautiful new day is on the horizon, my friend, and *we* can make it happen. The world's eyes will open to the double-crossing, triple-crossing, the secret deals with our sworn enemies, our enemies' secret deals with our allies – it'll be the dawn of a new era. No war, no more bulldozing villages that have been in the middle of a jungle for a thousand fucking years. It makes me feel physically sick the stuff done in the name of progress.'

Chas sat back, gently shaking his head. 'We've got to make it happen, man, we are the fucking future.'

'You'd better believe it. But I want to see that future as I'm sure you do. I want to look at the beauty of the new way, the new world. Everything will break down, but society, no, humanity is going to need guidance. I'm not talking about the new boss being the same as the old boss – the world will be like a group of collectives all producing things people actually need. Yeah, selling what they don't need for a fair price to others and buying the stuff they're making. It's everything – clothes, food, gas, water. No more have-nots, no more famine, no more greed.'

Black was excited. 'They're gonna need us, man, the trusted few.'

Englefield continued. 'You'll have to leave all this behind, and I mean everything. New identity, new country, but just imagine – wherever you go, it won't be a country for much longer. Borders will be history, walls and fences torn down and that's when they'll need us. To guide, to facilitate. The trusted ones who made it all possible.'

Black looked up, closing his eyes. 'It's utopia, man.'

'It will be, but it won't be cheap. Self-protection is the key and that needs serious money. Here's what I propose you put to your English gent.'

Englefield set out his plan. He told Black to describe the files, giving as much detail as he wanted, knowing *Welikeleaks* would want to corroborate at least some of the information. He was to ensure they'd grasp how much Englefield could harvest – if it was to have the desired effect it had to be big. One massive dissemination to rock the world to its core.

Englefield stated if *Welikeleaks* wanted to play, he'd give Black the memory stick and decryption password. Black could even reveal the method he was using. They had to know they'd never get more incendiary material in a thousand years. It was now or never.

Englefield named his price. 'It's a 100K for this stick. Tell them I can get into the database every evening and all weekend so the potential is massive, but we wrap it up in about twelve weeks. If it runs longer we increase the chance of something going wrong, and there's too much at stake. It takes ages to sift through everything, but I'm getting quicker all the time. I can give you a stick every week of files even better than what you've seen so far.'

Black smiled. 'How the fuck can it get better than this?'

'Wanna see?'

'You bet.'

'Right – I've got to check the timer, give me a sec.'

Englefield spun the laptop, pressed a couple of keys, and turned it back.

'Whoa, seventeen minutes now.'

'That should be ample. OK, you ready to have your mind blown?'

'Blow away my friend.'

‘OK. I’m now remote connecting. Right, look away as I’m going to put her details in. Thanks, you can look back now.’

Black sat wide-eyed. ‘Hey, look at that home screen, that’s gotta be the most boring ever.’

‘Yep, it’s all work for her. Now, see that icon there, drive G? There’s no drive G. Watch this.’

He selected drive G and another computer’s details appeared.

‘This is the portal. This is where it’s all held. They’re fucking idiots, man – it’s like hanging your front door key inside the letter box on a piece of string. OK, look away while I log in.’

Black turned for a few seconds.

‘Right, turn back. This is the stuff no one is allowed to see apart from literally a handful of people. See all this? This is where we type what we’re searching for. You put in wide parameters and you get hundreds of hits back. The trick is to be precise, then you get the gold.’

Black studied the screen. ‘So if you put in say, I dunno, John Smith, you’d get loads back.’

‘Exactly. Now if you put in, well let’s try it and see what happens. OK, John Smith. Let’s make him aged between thirty and forty. Blond hair. Let’s put Special Forces in. Right, we’ll search just between February and April last year. Now see this other information field here? Let’s put, er, something like.....*shot.* If it doesn’t bring anything back we’ll try something else, but I want you to see this in action so you can tell your friend about it.'

Englefield pressed the return key and the machine started to search.

'Ah, here we are, two results.'

The first wasn't an above top secret report, just headed *restricted.* It concerned a John Smith from Oklahoma. Mr Smith was a chancer, a charlatan. He'd come to notice for hitting on ladies of a certain age, claiming to be a Special Forces veteran, impressing them enough to lend him money. Needless to say they never saw him or the cash again once it was handed over. The search had picked him up due to an entry in the circumstances of his arrest. It explained how a *shot* of the suspect had been taken by his last victim on her iPhone. Not the most earth-shattering of secrets.

Englefield selected the second report. Black was in a trance as he read the details. It detailed how Sergeant John Smith, a Special Forces marksman, had been deployed to the top of a building 1,300 yards from a backstreet hotel in Spain. An off-the-books, clandestine meeting between diplomats from the UK, Germany and the USA with a leading figure in ISIS didn't end well, due to the terrorist's head splitting in two as he left the hotel.

Englefield tapped the screen. 'And that's with just a guess. If *Welikeleaks* have interest in a particular person or event, I can really fine-tune the results.'

Black blinked. 'This is insane. It's like having a gun to the head of every leader that matters on the planet.'

'Wanna see something else?'

'I would say surprise me, but I know you're gonna anyway.'

Englefield cleared the search fields, typing *JFK, Assassination, other shooter.*

Black looked at the screen open-mouthed then back to Englefield.

His friend nodded towards the keyboard. 'You wanna do the honours? Go on, press it.'

Black hit the return key and the little wheel whirled around. And there it was. Black devoured the report as fast as he could and threw his arms in the air.

'Those fucking conspiracy theorists were right! All the years everyone's wondered. All those shitty cheap documentaries on cable – they were fucking right!'

'The next page has got the name of the other shooter, his photograph, and the plan showing where he was deployed to.'

Englefield started moving the cursor. He clicked on the top right-hand corner and shut the page down.

'What the fuck, man! You can't leave me hanging – who was he, I gotta see? Come on, dude, turn the page.'

'Maybe next time. Look, this was to show you the quality of the merchandise. Call your contact, tell him everything we've spoken about and what you've seen. It's 100K for the first stick, and if he likes what he sees, 250K for each one thereafter. The more he sees the more he'll want, *and* it'll get progressively better. I'll save the very best stuff for last, and that'll be the same amount he's had on all the sticks plus more. The final exchange will have to be abroad, I'm thinking maybe London. If it all comes off I'll be getting a new face and going somewhere hot to watch what happens. When they need me after that, I'll be there.'

Black couldn't get JFK out of his mind. 'You promise to show me that next page, man? You gotta promise.'

'I promise.'

'This is fucking sensational, Josh, I'll call him tonight.'

Josh looked at his watch. 'Why not try him now? I gotta shut this down and run stuff so this computer was never on this afternoon.'

'OK, man, help yourself to another beer, I'll go make the call.'

*

Chas Black opened the drawer on his bedside cabinet and took out a different phone to the one he normally used. He opened WhatsApp to dial the only number he ever used on the handset and a long international ringtone sounded.

After what seemed like an inordinately long time, a sleepy sounding cultured English voice came on the line.

'Yes, hello.'

‘Hi, it’s me. Sorry did I wake you? Thought it was late evening there?’

‘I’m not in England at the moment, it’s the early hours and I was asleep.’

‘Sorry. Look, I got something you’ll want to hear about.’

‘Please continue then.’

Black described everything he’d seen and been told that evening. The Englishman listened intently, offering the occasional *Uh-huh* and *go on*.

The Englishman now sounded fully awake. ‘And you have no doubt about the accuracy of what he’s shown you so far?’

‘None whatsoever. It’s just mind-blowing. We even logged into this Buckland woman’s computer and he showed me how he’d linked it up to the really secret shit. I actually watched him call up the report about JFK. You won’t believe what really happened.’

‘Oh I think I would, young man. Some things though are best kept secret.’

‘What do you mean?’

‘Oh I’ll explain one day. Anyway, I take it he can only access the database out of office hours?’

‘That’s what he told me – evenings and weekends – basically anytime Buckland’s not sitting at her desk.’

The call lasted just over half an hour by the time Black told him all he could remember.

‘Charles, my dear chap, this could be very fortuitous. You remember I mentioned we have ideas for something?’

‘Yeah, but you never said what.’

‘No, I didn’t, but that time is rapidly approaching, and this will fit extremely well with what we’ve been planning for some time. Here is what’s going to happen. I have to call an associate in your country who you will liaise with. He is my most trusted confidant, and you will accept anything he says as if it’s come from me. He’ll arrange delivery of a new telephone tomorrow. WhatsApp is good, but we need even better encryption from now on. Are you with me so far?’

‘Yep.’

‘And you will give the deliveryman the memory stick and the password.’

‘OK.’

‘You will see an icon for encrypted communication on the front screen of the phone – only use that. His number will be pre-set as number one, mine number two. If you have cause to ring, you will hear a message telling you the call is being diverted, this is normal. You are ringing a phone in another part of the world which will redirect the encrypted call. It’s double protection for everyone concerned.’

‘OK, what shall I tell my friend?’

‘Tell him we’d very much like to work with him. I shall think about some focussed searches I’d like him to conduct.’

‘And the money?

The Englishman continued. 'Mere chicken feed, dear boy. When you're changing the world money isn't an issue. My associates have very deep pockets so it's just pennies.'

'But he wants a lot for the final handover, millions I should guess.'

'Is he still at your house?'

'Yeah, he's still here.'

'Ask him how much he wants.'

Black walked back to the lounge where Englefield was sitting eating the last piece of cold pizza. He looked up as Black stopped in the doorway.

'What did he say?'

Black held up the handset. 'He's on hold. Wants to know how much you want for the big one.'

Unblinking, Englefield calmly replied, 'Twenty million dollars.'

Black held up his index finger, moving back to the bedroom.

'He wants twenty mill for the final payoff. The first stick is 100K and 250K for each one thereafter.'

The man replied without hesitation. 'Those terms are acceptable. You'll be paid twenty per cent of whatever we pay him. You're going to be very involved from now on, my old friend.'

Black quickly did the maths. He would clear over five million dollars even at a conservative estimate.

The Englishman sounded pleased. 'Text me his account details once we've finished this call. You've done well, but I always knew you would which is why

I kept you on the books all these years. The whole Manning thing was buggered up beyond belief – this time will be different. You're going to be a hero, old chap, and a leader of men once we put the new world order in place.'

Black nodded. 'You just have to say what you need and I'll do it.'

'Thank you. One thing's for sure, you'll have to change your recreational habits somewhat. You may be called upon at any time to complete a task. I don't want you unable to comply because you're watching pink elephants dancing on the ceiling or whatever it is those substances you're fond of make you see.'

'Yeah, OK, I understand.'

'I'm not saying become a monk, but lay off the hard stuff.'

'You can count on me.'

The Englishman was almost done. 'Very well. I need to make another call. Please thank your friend and tell him I'm looking forward to working with him. I take it he doesn't want to reveal his name to me?'

'That's one of the things he said – he's just protecting himself.'

'Very wise. Make sure he leaves the memory stick with you and the password. Tell him that as a gesture of goodwill, the $100,000 will be in his account as soon as I have the details. I'll also deposit twenty in yours.'

'Jeez, thanks.'

'You'll receive a call tomorrow from my associate in your country. Please ensure you turn the phone on, and leave it on at all times, and there will be security protocol to follow.'

'Protocol?'

'When he calls you, he'll ask if you've ordered the takeaway yet. You will reply that you thought we could eat out tonight. And likewise, if you call him. Is that clear?'

'Crystal.'

'I myself will call you on the new number from tomorrow onwards and use the same protocol. You can still call me on this number, but from your new telephone. I suggest you also use it to speak to your analyst friend – the level of encryption is the highest we know of.'

'All understood.'

Black ended the call and returned to the lounge. Englefield had his jacket on and everything packed away in his bag. He raised both palms. 'Well, what did he say?'

'He's agreed to the money, no problem, and he's gonna pay me twenty per cent of whatever you get. He's asked for your account details so he can put the money in. He'll pay us straight away.'

'Wow, OK.'

'He also said I'll get another phone delivered tomorrow and I've got to give the man the stick and the password.'

Englefield gave Black a thumbs up. 'I'm cool with that.'

'Jeez, Josh, I can't believe it's happening, it's really fucking happening.'

'We've got to be ultra careful from now on, dude. No sloppiness or getting wasted until we're on the other side of all this.'

Englefield fished around in his bag and pulled out a book on VW campers, handing it to Black.

'OK, we avoid using our phones to send anything like passwords. Here's what we'll do. I've got a copy of the same book. The password for the first stick is the first three words on page 3 with no gaps, all lower case. The next one will be the first three words on page 4, again no gaps and all lower case. You with me so far?'

Black nodded.

Englefield continued. 'It'll be the same for each stick – page 5, 6 and so on and always the first three words.'

'Cool.'

'Also, tell your man not to go at it like a bull in a china shop. I know they'll want to look at some of the names, but if they expose them all on *Welikeleaks* in one go it'll arouse suspicion. Slowly, slowly is the name of the game here.'

Black agreed. 'I'll tell him.'

Englefield recited the details of his new account in Switzerland as Black composed a text to his contact. 'OK, sent.'

The two men fist-bumped.

Black smiled at his friend. 'I'll call you tomorrow. Sounds like we're gonna be busy for a few weeks.'

Englefield swept his arm around in a wide arc. 'Busy saving the *world*, dude.' The two friends embraced. Black slapped Englefield's back, 'Love you, man.' Englefield reciprocated. 'Love you too, man – catch you later.'

Englefield walked to his car, fired up by the realisation that history would show him to be a hero. Black sat back on his sofa thinking exactly the same.

*

After ending the call to Black, the Englishman immediately dialled his other associate in America. 'Good evening, are you free to speak?'

The American was slightly surprised to receive the call. 'Yep, I'm home in my den, kids are in front of the TV. What are you doing up? It must be the middle of the night there.'

'It is. I've just received a call from our sleeper in your neck of the woods.'

'Oh really, that's interesting, what did he have to say for himself?'

The Englishman recounted the entire contents of the call. There was silence on the other end of the line.

'You there, old chap?'

The American seemed to be taking a while to process what he'd just been told.

‘Yeah, yeah, I’m here. This is perfect if we can get the timing right. I mean, we’d probably have enough without this, but....shit, the way he thought to link up Buckland’s computers is nothing short of genius. I knew Englefield was good, but not *that* good.’

‘Indeed, a very useful man to have on our side until he’s not useful anymore.’

The American chuckled. ‘You’re a bastard, you know that.’

‘Oh indeed, my boy, of the highest degree. Now, down to business.’

The Englishman outlined his plan so far, setting out how he saw the next three months would progress.

‘You need to arrange delivery of one of our phones to him tomorrow morning and make sure he hands over the stick and the password. Englefield’s using a Swiss account unsurprisingly – I’ll text you the details. And don’t forget Black has no idea *we* know his friend’s identity. Englefield told him not to mention his name.’

‘Got it.’

‘We’ve been very fortuitous with the timing. You were spot on in your thinking when you reported Black to your colleagues. Brilliant, in fact. Got all that investigation and surveillance nonsense over and done with, so they think they’ve ruled him and Englefield out of any wrongdoing. Your quick thinking was the best protection the pair of them could ever wish for.’

The American was flattered. ‘Thank you. Any update from Scotland?’

‘Yes, as a matter of fact. Our man has her diary for the next three months, and it seems the planets are aligning in our favour. She’s there all over Christmas, then away, but back around the middle of March. He can’t risk taking them until we’re almost ready as she uses the vault.’

The American nodded. ‘I agree. Where’s the final handover?’

‘Looks like London. He’s a canny one, is Mr Englefield. I have to admire his thought process in all of this. He’ll keep the details of exactly where and when until the last moment, I’m sure. You’d better arrange for a new passport and identity for Mr Black. I’m about to pay Englefield, and I told Black I’d be putting twenty thousand in his account. These anarchists like a bit of cash in their pocket, truth be known.’

‘Yeah, it’s funny how they want everyone to be equal, but they want to be a bit more equal than anyone else.’

‘Isn’t it, old chap. Look, I’d better get on. Update me tomorrow, goodnight.’

Chapter 15.

The following morning Black was up early. He'd found it hard to get to sleep – not because it was the first time in years he'd gone to bed almost straight, but mainly due to what Josh had shown him. He was excited that he was an integral part of the new beginning for mankind.

At 9.30am there was a knock on his front door. Peering through the spyhole, he saw a man in UPS uniform holding an A4 envelope. He opened the door and the man greeted him with a warm smile.

'Good morning, sir, delivery for you. I understand you have a small package for me as well.'

Black looked beyond the man, scanning the street, trying not to make it look obvious.

'Please don't be nervous, sir, to anybody watching it's a normal everyday scene. You'll make it look suspicious if you carry on doing that.'

Black looked sheepish. 'Sorry. A lot's happened in the last twenty-four hours.'

The man handed the padded envelope to Black. 'The pin is 984711 – have you got that? 984711. Would you repeat it back please?'

Black did as instructed. '984711.'

The UPS man smiled. 'Good. Please activate the phone immediately and ensure it remains charged and on at all times. Now, if I can take the stick I'll be on my way.'

'Oh yes, hang on, I hid it.'

Black went into the lounge, retrieved the memory stick and handed it to the delivery driver.

'You have the password, I understand?'

'Oh God, yes.'

Black pulled a scrap of paper out of his pocket and handed it to the man.

The delivery man took a photo of the paper.

'Thank you, sir, please burn that as soon as I've left. You'll be contacted later today on your new phone – don't miss the call.'

'I won't.'

'Thank you, sir, you have a great day now.'

Chas Black did have a good day. Filled with real purpose, he spent the next few hours tidying properly for the first time in months. He vacuumed, dusted, polished and generally got the place looking better than it had ever done. He checked his bank account for about the 10th time just to see the $23,468 balance, the recent deposit of $20,180 showing as having come from the Powerball lottery. He thought it was a nice touch that *Welikeleaks* had disguised the payment so it didn't arouse suspicion.

At 4pm his new phone rang for the first time.

'Er, hello?'

An American voice spoke. 'Have you ordered the takeaway yet?'

Black thought back to what the Englishman had told him. 'Erm....I thought we could eat out tonight.'

'Good afternoon, Mr Black, I trust you've checked your account? My associate told me he'd be making your first deposit last night.'

'Oh yeah, thanks, it's all there. Nice touch with the depositor's details.'

'Yes, no questions that way. However, in future all payments will be to your new numbered Swiss account. I'll text you the details after this call. You can feel confident of complete anonymity with your new bank. Keep using your old one for day-to-day living, but do not be tempted to make any large purchases, there'll be plenty of time later to indulge yourself.'

Black really felt part of the team now. 'You do know I've been waiting all my life for this. It's going to be a beautiful world once we've put everything out.'

'I know. Just such a shame we've had to wait so long since that clown Manning. This time we won't fail.'

Black realised he hadn't caught the man's name. 'What do I call you?'

'Well I agree with your analyst friend, no names. Just use the protocol then you'll know you're safe.'

The American continued. 'I'm arranging a new identity for you which will include a passport, new name, family history, social security number and a pre-loaded Visa card. The card will be $5,000 in credit which will come off your next payment of $50,000 for the second delivery. We'll keep to the method we used today, and the same driver will pick up from you each Monday morning. You'll also need to change your appearance for the new passport. Please cut your hair short and shave off your beard. Is that all clear?

'You sure I gotta do the hair thing?'

'Let's not start questioning our methods and reasons at this early stage.'

'Sorry, man, just attached to it, that's all.'

'I understand, but needs must. My associate told me what your buddy said, and I'm in total agreement – we won't release anything until the day of reckoning. We'll cherry-pick a few names to test the quality of the intelligence, but only a few. It's too close to the end game to risk sticking our head above the parapet now.'

Black was glad the American agreed. 'I understand. That was the problem we had last time – they didn't think it through properly. Planning for every eventuality is the key.'

'Absolutely. When it all goes out to the world, everyone will see what they need to see for maximum effect. I also suggest it'll be more secure to use the phone you're on now for communication with your friend. We're confident the encryption can't be broken, so if by some million-to-one chance the spooks ever got hold of it, it's as much use as a house brick.'

'Sounds sensible, I'll speak to my friend later and run it past him.'

'Excellent. It'll take me a couple of weeks to

organise your documents. Please get your hair cut this week and hand a passport size photo to the courier next Monday. He'll deliver your new identity the following week.'

'Cool, speak to you later.'

'Sure, goodbye for now, Mr Black.'

*

Shortly after ending the call, the American's phone rang again. He recognised the Englishman's number.

'Hi. I've just spoken to Black on his new phone. I've suggested he uses it to communicate with Englefield from now on, so we'll just have to wait and see.'

'Splendid. I take it the software won't let us down?'

'No chance. We've tried and tested it for months. Anything he receives or sends, written or speech, we'll be able to retrieve.'

'That's good. I'll give him a call after this. The more he thinks he's going to save the world, the better. Instruct your courier to book a flight every Monday and bring the memory stick directly to me.'

'Good thinking, talking of which, I've given some thought as to what I'm going to do after it happens.'

'Go on.'

The American laid out what was on his mind. 'I'm thinking I'd be better placed here if it's safe. It would be very advantageous for us to know what the ex-leading superpower intends to do once stripped of its muscle – maybe for a few months while they lick their wounds and work out what to do next.'

The Englishman sounded resigned. 'There is nothing they can do, my dear chap, they and everyone else will be at our mercy.'

'Exciting times.'

'Indeed. You've done well, my friend. It's a shame we didn't have you on board last time. Anyway, TTFN.'

The American heard the call disconnect and looked at his handset. 'TTFN? What the…'

*

The man with the cultured English accent dialled Chas Black's new number.

'Hello.'

'Have you ordered the takeaway yet?'

Black replied more quickly this time. 'I thought we could eat out tonight.'

'Hello, old chap, I understand everything is in order there. I've spoken to my associate in your country and he is *very* impressed with the way you've handled things so far. I knew I was right to keep you in the fold. Everyone at *Welikeleaks* has complete faith in you.'

'You can rely on me.'

'I just wanted to touch base to say if there's anything you need you must call my friend and he'll help. He is very resourceful in ways you cannot imagine.'

'I don't doubt that, I'm just glad to be part of the team.'

‘And a very important part. I have to go now – we’ll speak soon.’

Black felt an enormous sense of self-importance. He was a major player now – no more stupid demonstrations which didn’t even make the news half the time. He was going down in history, he was sure of that.

He decided to ring Englefield and update him. It was after 5pm so he figured his friend should have finished work by now. He dialled the number from memory using the new phone.

Englefield hadn’t long got into his car and was five minutes into his journey home. He didn’t recognise the number on the screen, answering with caution. ‘Hellooo?’

‘Hey, dude, it’s me. Lots happened today, can you talk?’

‘Yeah, I’m just hitting the freeway – what’s with the new number?’

Black filled him in on the day’s activities and his conversations with his new contact and the Englishman. He told him about the new handset, the money being deposited and the arrangements for the Monday pick-up.

Englefield was happy. ‘Sounds like you’ve been busy, dude. The new cell’s a good idea and these guys know what they’re doing – they’re being ultra careful and that’s the only way. But, we mustn’t forget we gotta have our own protection – like a failsafe, just in case.’

'What you got in mind?'

'We use your new cell until near the end, then we switch.'

'To what?'

'You understand about emails, yeah? How easy they are to trace from IP addresses and that shit?'

'Duhh, yeah.'

Englefield outlined his plan. 'Well here's the thing, it's old school but it works. I'll give you the details of an email address and the password. We'll have secondary communication via email when it gets nearer the time, but we don't send any.'

Black didn't understand. 'The fuck?'

'It's beautiful, man. I type a message but don't send it, so it stays in the drafts folder – it never leaves. When you log in with the same details you can see the message and type your response, but just save it to drafts. They can't intercept it as the fucker's never going anywhere.'

'That's cool.'

'We'll have a proof-of-life check – just a word. If either of us is compromised in any way, we type the wrong response, or we just don't respond. Whoever is left will know to get the hell out. And, we'll change the words on pre-agreed days. Then nearer the time I'll send you another phone to use at the end.'

Black was impressed. 'Sounds like you thought of everything, man. You do trust them, don't you?'

'Yeah of course, 110 per cent, but these guys will be covering their backs so we should as well. This way we keep our own little bit of control just in case it goes south.'

'Good thinking, send the details over. Hey, how was it in work today? Must have felt a bit weird after the weekend you just had.'

Englefield laughed. 'It was a bit surreal, I gotta tell you. They spent most of the day talking about the party – sounds like I missed one hell of a night. And that bitch Buckland seemed really sorry for me, what with my terrible illness and all that.'

'Haha, man, you really pulled it off – you are one cool son of a bitch.'

'You know my mother?'

'Ha – later, man.'

Englefield then sent a text to Black containing the email details, password and a short message. *Memorise this and delete the text*. A reply came straight back. *Got it*.

A few seconds later an app on the American man's phone showed new activity. He opened it, digested the contents and compiled a text to the Englishman. *They're putting own backup in place, E sent B dets of new email account. Will be using drafts to communicate near to end game. We can monitor unseen. Just arse covering in my opinion. E will be sending B a new phone as well.*

The reply came back almost instantly. *Excellent, it gets better and better.*

Chapter 16.

UK, nine days to mission.

Jenks had spent the last few days going over his plan, running it forwards and backwards, looking for anything he might have missed. He would travel to London on his bike, happy it was in excellent working order after his ride the previous Saturday.

The mini road trip went further than planned, not that he really had one. The pleasure of pointing the bike in whatever direction took his fancy led him across two counties, ending up on the Brighton sea front for a coffee before heading back. Seeing the beach reminded him of the first time he'd met Camburn.

He spent little time wondering how life would've panned out if he'd accepted Camburn's offer at the time. Occasionally events from years before entered his head, like on his run a few days previously, and they'd been a little more frequent than usual. He didn't overanalyse it, something had triggered, but he'd no idea what, or why.

Animals have what is often referred to as a sixth sense – cows lie down together before it rains and stories of dogs frantically barking to be let out just before the roof collapses surface every so often. A latent sense still lingers from way back in human evolution – a warning system buried deep in our DNA, almost dispensed with, but the faintest of embers glowing, designed to alert us of impending danger.

He'd reviewed the drone footage, committing to memory the area around The Huntsman's Lodge in daylight as well as night. He'd also received Maureen's report regarding any private CCTV, content it shouldn't prove a problem – the only two shops with cameras facing the street were not on his exfill route from the mission point.

The Sildenafil drug had been couriered down and was now safe in his underground store. He'd frequently connected to the hotel's computer to check Rick Mills' booking, pleased to see no changes.

Jenks had also stepped up his training, going for daily runs and completing his gruelling set of exercises. Even in downtime he kept himself at near peak, but having the luxury of time to plan for a mission relatively close to home meant he was at a level where he couldn't go much higher in terms of physical fitness.

Same time, same day, CIA headquarters, Langley, Virginia.

Florence Rizzoli entered the analyst's office seven floors below her own with a master key card and walked quickly towards Alicia Buckland's office. Flanked by five armed agents from internal security, it was clear from the speed she covered the floor that it wasn't a social call. Alicia was at her desk concentrating hard, unaware of the catastrophic upheaval of her life just seconds away. Her staff were in total silence, like seated statues.

The glass doors swung open and the agents fanned out around her desk whilst Rizzoli positioned herself next to Alicia. Junior director Buckland was now looking up, trying to process what was happening. It was a complete surprise and utter shock to see the woman who'd previously said *call me Flo* standing over her, all business.

Rizzoli pulled out a set of handcuffs. 'Step away from your workstation. Do not attempt to touch any key or I'll use immediate restraint.'

'Er, OK. What, I mean, what the hell is this about? I haven't done anything wrong, what do you think I've done?'

'I would advise you not to say anything at this point. Alicia Buckland, I'm arresting you for conspiracy to commit treason. You will be taken from here and questioned about your involvement.'

Alicia was dumbstruck. Rizzoli cuffed her behind her back and turned her roughly around to face the door. She could feel her prisoner start to shake. Alicia turned to Rizzoli and said quietly, 'But I came to you, why are you doing this? I honestly haven't done anything wrong.'

Rizzoli leant in close, almost touching Buckland's ear. In a voice barely above a whisper she said, 'The only way you're going to save yourself from the chair is to tell us everything you know, you got that? Best advice you'll get all day.'

Buckland was terrified. Images swirled around her head she didn't want to think about. She knew exactly how people who turned against their country were treated, and started to wet herself. She also knew the answer to her next question, but still asked, 'What about my Miranda rights, aren't you supposed to give those?'

Rizzoli leant in again, her nose brushing Buckland's hair. 'Where you're going there are no rights. You will answer anything that's asked of you. If you think by remaining silent it'll help, think again sugar plum. And as for a lawyer? Well you know the answer to that.'

Junior Director Alicia Buckland was frogmarched out of her department – the office she'd devoted thousands of hours of her own time to, dedicated to the job. The only sound came from computer fans and the footsteps of the arrest team leaving. Evie covered her eyes when she noticed the wet on the back of her boss's skirt and started to cry.

Alicia didn't look up, but cast a glance to the empty workstation belonging to Joshua Englefield III. She knew where she was headed, and wasn't sure if she was ever coming back. Rizzoli turned and addressed the staff.

'Junior Director Buckland has been removed from her post, as you may have noticed. I can't tell you anything further at present, but must warn you not to speak to anyone regarding this. In the interim, this department will temporarily come under the command of the Special Activities Division. Some of you may know Sam Dibble, the director of SAD – he has vast experience and will oversee things until further notice.'

The door closed, leaving everyone stunned.

An hour later the man with the cultured English accent felt his phone vibrate in his pocket.

'Good morning.'

'Good afternoon to you, how's London?'

'Bit chilly, but not as cold as home.'

The American continued. 'I'll bet. Anyway, Buckland was arrested an hour ago and as we thought I've been placed in temporary charge of her department. Rizzoli is mad as hell thinking she and I were duped all along by her. They've sent a deep search team to her house but it'll be a while before they report back.'

'And earlier, did your man get in and out OK?'

'Went like a dream. Damn handy having the alarm code and where she hid a spare key. The first is the easiest to find, but will still be believable – it'll just look like she's been a bit careless. It's a screwed up post-it note in the bottom of the trash can under a heap of other stuff with *Huntsman's Lodge* written on it.'

'Written?'

‘Yeah, my man paid a visit to the best forger this side of Colorado – I had plenty of examples of her handwriting, so it’s spot on.’

‘Excellent, and the others?’

‘They’re hidden well but they’ll find them, those boys never let up – they’ll dismantle a whole house rather than go away empty-handed.’

‘And what are they?’

‘The names of the three MI6 agents who’ve gone missing written on a partially burned piece of paper at the bottom of the fire pit in her yard. That Delta guy who took out the prime minister’s mistress – he was found at the bottom of a ravine. Tragic jogging accident, they’re calling it. His name is barely readable, but it’s there, just about indented into the leather on her writing desk – like she wrote it on a bit of paper which she took with her.’

The Englishman was impressed. ‘Ingenious, how did your man do that?’

‘The forger wrote the name and my man laid it on the desk and traced over the letters as lightly as he could. You can hardly see it amongst the scribbles, but the team are the best – it’ll be found.’

‘That should keep them busy for a while. And the forger? All taken care of?

‘Of course, the Delta guy’s name was the last thing he ever wrote. They had to identify him from his dental records after the fire. Looks like a gas leak caused it.’

The Englishman put on a voice of mock concern. 'Oh how tragic. Never mind, onwards and upwards. Keep me posted about Buckland.'

'Will do. My guess is they'll go in hard, and I mean really hard for a good while. No sleep, no washing, no clothes and she'll be shitting in a bucket.'

'And have you thought about the server room?'

'Yeah, lots. My initial thoughts were to get in there late one night and remove Englefield's bridge, but we don't know if he plans to connect before the big day. He'll abort if he can't and we don't know what he'd do next. Leave it in, I say – when they find it after, she'll be in the clear and probably get promoted.'

'I concur. Let it run.'

30 minutes later, same day, Kent, UK.

Jenks was in his kitchen peeling potatoes and thinking about the layout of The Huntsman's Lodge, mentally walking around the hotel when his phone rang.

'Hi, James, what's up?'

'Good afternoon, dear boy. Thought I'd give you a quick tinkle as there's been a bit of an update.'

'Go on.'

'The Agency arrested one of their own – a woman called Alicia Buckland, Englefield's boss. I just had a call from the Caretaker who's just had a call from his counterpart over there. It seems they cross-matched some of the names who've either disappeared or been found dead, and this Buckland woman called up each of their files in the last three months. They checked back to see if there was any bona fide reasons why she should access them, which is why it's taken a while, due to the security level.'

Jenks pondered. 'Would she have access to that type of material?'

'Well yes. She was a flyer, destined for the top, it appears. She was cleared above top secret and the designated emergency contact in the event of an urgent live time intelligence request. And, she was on the cusp of being made up to director anyway, and that level, in her department, carries the highest of clearances.'

Jenks had a number of questions. 'Could he have used her terminal when the office was empty?'

'Potentially, but from what I gather, Buckland was first in and the last to leave.'

'Hmm, and what's she saying?'

'She's blabbering away protesting her innocence, but it's early days. It'll take a while for proper examination of her office computers and laptop.'

'Home address?'

'They've got a team there at the moment but they've only just started so it's a waiting game, but I thought you should know.'

'So she might be the real mastermind behind all this?'

Camburn was sceptical. 'I'm not sure, lad. It doesn't fit at all with what they know about her. She's been with the Agency all her working life. Utterly dedicated it seems – no real social life, puts in more hours than anyone and was just about to be promoted. She was very highly thought of.'

'They need more then.'

'I agree, but I don't think it'll affect the handover. Englefield and Black are still the final players, even if it turns out she supplied all the intelligence.'

'OK, is that it?'

Camburn continued. 'Not quite. Your discovery of the Amex card proved very useful. Maureen got in the back door and could see exactly where he's made purchases. It seems he flew out on the first available flight after he left work for his month's holiday – our Mr Englefield, or rather Mr Mills, purchased a one-way first class ticket to Italy.'

'Then what?'

'Looks like he really is enjoying a bit of a jaunt before the big payday. He stayed in one of the best hotels on the Riviera, then boarded a train to Paris. After a few days in another swanky hotel he took the Eurostar to Amsterdam, which is where we think he is now. We've got a photo of him passing through immigration in Gare Du Nord en route to Holland. He's got a reservation on Eurostar for the afternoon of the 10th, so won't arrive in London until comparatively late.'

Jenks thought. 'Which does suggest he won't be doing business on Tuesday the 10th.'

'I tend to agree. He's changed his appearance as well – I'll send you a photo over shortly.'

‘That’s all great, but it doesn’t change anything – we still can’t touch him until the last moment.’

‘I agree, and if we miss him, we’re buggered.’

‘How do you mean?’

‘He’s paid a deposit to a top plastic surgeon in Geneva, booked in on the 16th March, oh and a ticket from City Airport to fly out early on the morning of Thursday the 12th. And, he’s booked just about the most expensive hotel in Geneva – literally thousands per night.’

‘That would make my job harder if he got a new face.’

‘And pointless – it would just be revenge. If he gets that far, everything will have gone out one way or another already.’

‘I see. If he’s arriving late on the Tuesday, flying out on Thursday morning, it’s likely the handover will be Wednesday – he can have a night out in London to celebrate his new wealth before flying off to his new life.’

‘I agree.’

‘Is *that* it?’

Camburn cleared his throat. ‘Almost. Look, this may be nothing and I have no evidence to connect it to anything we’re working on at the moment, but I think it useful to keep you in the loop of anything bubbling under at the moment.’

‘Such as?’

‘GCHQ have been picking up chatter about Russia. They monitor all the bonkers conspiracy sites full of nutters as you know, and there's talk of Russia pulling out of the G20 summit. All highly unusual, but it's appeared on a few bulletin boards already. They've researched some of the lunatics who post on them, and a couple have been proved right in the past with what initially looked like wild accusations. Slightly more worrying is the fact that known Russian agents have all travelled back to the motherland in the last few days.'

'Hmm, any ideas why?'

'Who knows with them? It could just be a changing of the guard. They know full well that *we* know full well who some of their agents are. Perhaps they want fresh faces in place.'

'Well, useful to know anyway. Call me if you hear anything else.'

'Will do. Toodle pip.'

A photo message popped up on Wickr showing a very different looking Rick Mills. He was now wearing thick-rimmed spectacles, and gone were the shoulder-length surfer dude locks, replaced by short cropped dark hair and matching black goatee beard.

Jenks stared intently at the screen then shut his eyes. Repeating the exercise six times, he deleted the photo, now memorised for instant recall.

After the daily email check-in with Black, Englefield was having the time of his life accepting with relish all that Amsterdam had to offer. He spent the first part of each day taking in some culture, from the Van Gogh and Rijks museums, to queuing for a tour of Anne Frank's house.

Afternoons were when he started to unwind, getting pleasantly stoned in coffee shops followed by a handful of magic mushrooms early each evening. He justified it as a reward for reaching near exhaustion over the last two weeks – staying up late every night and all through the weekend to assemble the final explosive collection of secrets, now safely stored on his laptop in his room safe at the Krasnapolsky.

Chapter 17.

A black facility somewhere in the USA.

Alicia Buckland lost count of the days she'd been interrogated, having no idea if it was daytime or the middle of the night. After Rizzoli pulled her out of her office, she'd been taken directly to the underground car park where they pulled a hood over her head before pushing her into a blacked out SUV. She'd tried to count time in her head and estimate the speed in an attempt to gauge how far they were going, but gave up after what might have been the second hour of travelling. She'd even tried to catch the sun's rays through her hood to determine if she was going north, south, east or west, but it was useless.

Her treatment had been ruthless from the moment she arrived at the facility. Disorientation techniques were introduced immediately as she was thrown into a small room measuring 14' square. No bed, mattress, toilet and no heat, apart from the tiny amount coming from eighteen 200-watt bulbs recessed into the ceiling behind toughened glass. The room was so bright that even with her eyes tightly shut and her hands over her face, she could still see light. Anyone else entering the room wore sunglasses.

After tumbling through the door, she scanned around, taking in her surroundings whilst shielding her eyes from the glare. The room was empty apart from one wooden chair and a bucket in the corner. Conspicuous by their absence, she noticed there were no cameras. She sat down on the chair and waited.

After a few minutes she heard footsteps, and two men walked in. One was the tallest man she'd ever seen – close to 7' and almost as wide as the doorway he'd stooped down to come through. The second was noticeably shorter – probably still over 6', but dwarfed by the first man. Both wore mirrored sunglasses.

The huge man strode up to her without saying a word and swung a colossal kick at the legs of her chair. All four immediately collapsed like they were matchwood, and Alicia hit the floor hard. The giant leant down, speaking in a low rumbling voice. 'Take your clothes off.'

Alicia was terrified, imagining the worst. 'But, look, I'll answer any questions, you don't have to make me do that. Please, I beg you, ask me anything.' The giant leant down and with one huge hand grasped the lapels of Alicia's tailored jacket and slowly pulled her up. She started to straighten her legs but the momentum continued as she was lifted clean off her feet, held in mid-air.

He pulled her level with his face, just inches apart, the smell of coffee and stale cigarettes evident on his breath. With a level of volume she'd never heard from another human being, he screamed in her face. 'Take your fucking clothes off now, bitch.' He released his grip and she dropped to the floor, her ears ringing.

Alicia knew she had no option. She also knew all about the humiliation of terrorist prisoners to break them, and a whole host of other techniques and options she would undoubtedly face. Perhaps they'd ease up once she had the opportunity to tell them everything she knew. She had to cling on to something.

She stood and started to undress. She could feel herself starting to flush as she got to her underwear. The giant screamed again, 'Who the fuck said stop, bitch, take it all off.' Resigned to having no choice, she unhooked her bra and removed her knickers. She stood blinking in the glare, trying to cover herself as best she could as the giant walked slowly towards her. In a low growl even more menacing than his scream he said, 'Drop them, bitch – hands by your sides.'

Alicia complied as the man slowly circled her, ensuring she saw him looking her up and down. 'How do you feel?'

'Terrified.'

'How do you think one of our finest soldiers felt when he was knocked into that ravine, looking at a 200-foot drop onto nothing but rocks?'

'What soldier? I honestly have no idea what you're talking about.'

'Oh, have you forgotten already? Let me refresh your memory. He was the one you pulled the file on and gave to *Welikeleaks*. Remember now?'

‘I don’t know about any soldier, and I haven’t given anything to *Welikeleaks* – I’m not a traitor, that’s the truth.’

The questioning continued for a relentless seven hours without a break, during which they made her stand the whole time. The smaller man said nothing, just watching. She was shivering from the cold and fear and desperate for a drink.

With a croaking voice she said, ‘Could I please have some water, I can hardly speak I’m so dry.’

Both men immediately turned as if they’d been waiting for her to ask, and walked to the door knocking twice. It opened immediately and they left the room. Seconds later the door swung open and the smaller man strode in pulling a heavy hose. ‘Please, please, no, please, I beg you, don’t do it.’

The man smiled as he twisted the heavy brass valve. The power of the jet knocked Alicia backwards onto the floor. She instinctively cupped her private parts with one hand and her eyes with the other as he aimed the jet at her body, driving her towards the wall. She skidded across the smooth floor until she smacked against the plain concrete wall, crying out in pain. Putting her hand to her head she saw blood on her fingers.

Her instinct was to scream at the man that he was a bastard, but knew it would accomplish nothing. She’d been in highly stressful live time situations over the years, but compared to how she felt now, they were a walk in the park. All she could do and *would* do was answer everything they asked as best she could.

The man walked back to the door and passed the hose to someone unseen as they handed him a blanket.

The man spoke for the first time. His voice calm and level, almost soothing.

'I'm going now. Take this and wrap it around yourself. We'll be back in – well, maybe one minute, maybe an hour, maybe tomorrow. When we do you'll wish we were treating you like we did today. Today we've been kind. You wait and see what happens next.'

Alicia felt adrenalin coursing through her. The man's words caused her more fear than the giant had all day – the fear of the unknown. She caught the blanket, immediately feeling its coarseness and the unmistakeable stench of stale urine.

The man left his words hanging in the air as he turned and walked to the door, knocking twice.

Alicia called after him. 'Wait, please. I need to go to the bathroom, please let me use a proper one. You can put me back here as soon as I'm done. Please, have a little humanity – I've answered everything you've asked of me.'

'No you haven't, you're a fucking lying traitor bitch. I suggest when we next speak you start giving us sensible answers. Maybe even cut a deal but quit the bullshit.'

In a small voice she pleaded. 'The toilet, please.'

The man pointed at the bucket.

She gave it one more try. 'Look I'm desperate to go, you know, both ends. There's not even any toilet tissue.'

The man shook his head as he walked out. 'You got hands.'

*

By day four the junior director of CIA analysis was a broken woman. When she wasn't being interrogated she constantly heard footsteps approaching the door, the handle turning, and the footsteps recede again. Each time her body reacted, flooding itself with huge amounts of adrenalin. Every time she calmed down the footsteps came again, utterly exhausting her.

A succession of men asked her the same questions for over seventy-two hours. Time ceased to exist as did any sleep pattern. She barely had enough strength to push off the floor and lean against the wall. Most of the time she lay curled up in a ball, the blanket pulled tightly around her naked body.

Alicia was half conscious when she heard footsteps again, immediately tensing. Something was different though. This time the sound was the click-clack of someone wearing heels.

The door opened slowly and Florence Rizzoli walked in accompanied by the giant and a man she hadn't seen before. The giant was carrying four chairs. He set two against the wall and two in the middle of the room facing each other.

Rizzoli went to take her Wayfarers off, then thought better of it. She pointed to one of the chairs. 'Sit.'

Alicia complied with some difficulty, slumping down and tucking a piece of blanket between her legs. Her hair was a greasy mess and her eyes set deep with large black rings under them. She'd been fed, but only basic sustenance, so had probably lost close to ten pounds. Without looking up she mumbled something which Rizzoli couldn't hear.

'Speak up, woman, cat got your tongue?'

In barely a whisper, she spoke. 'Please, Miss Rizzoli, I got my period yesterday, please can I have something?'

Rizzoli took a deep breath and slowly blew it out. 'Oh dear. That's unpleasant for you, but you're confusing me with someone who gives a fuck.'

Alicia had nothing. No comeback, no more energy to plead and hung her head.

Rizzoli let the silence linger for close to a minute. 'We've got something new to talk about. That's good, isn't it?'

Alicia made a noise. Not a formed word, just a faint guttural sound confirming she'd heard.

Rizzoli turned and gestured at the giant. He rose from his chair and handed her three plastic sleeves.

'Now, Alicia, as you know we've had a deep search team in your house since shortly after your arrest. What I've got here will send you to the chair. You need to level with me now because this is your last hope of staying alive. I'm always open to a deal, so it's up to you. Now do you want a bottle of cold water?'

Alicia nodded slightly. In the quietest voice she said, 'Yes please.'

Rizzoli reached into her bag and handed her a freezing bottle of mineral water but had to open the cap as Alicia didn't have the strength. She greedily gulped down half the bottle and clutched it firmly to her chest.

Rizzoli held out the three plastic sleeves, each containing one piece of paper. 'These were recovered from your house. We'll go through them one by one. If you have any sense of patriotism or decency buried somewhere within you, I suggest now is the time to drag it out and be honest with me.'

Rizzoli tapped the plastic folders with her fingernail. 'These, my little murderess, tie you to killings both here and abroad. You pulled the file on each of them and lo and behold, reference to them was found in your house. You got sloppy, sugar plum – you should've checked they were completely destroyed.'

Alicia raised her head slightly, her whole body shaking like someone with Parkinson's disease. In a barely audible voice she said, 'What paper? I haven't tried to destroy any paper, I don't know…' Rizzoli cut her off. 'Shall we have a look at them together?

Rizzoli fanned out the three plastic covers on her lap and picked up the first one.

'This is a post-it note found screwed up in the bottom of your trash can outside your house ready for the next collection. Look here, see the words? In your handwriting? Oh, don't worry, we've had it analysed. It says *Huntsman's Lodge*. I understand from Director Jackson that this name is directly linked to the most serious theft of data in our history. Why did you write it down? Eh? To pass to your courier? To give to your paymasters?

Slightly louder this time, Alicia answered. 'I've never seen it before, that's the truth.'

'OK, we'll come back to that. Now, see this one? This is a list of three names, again in your own handwriting. The three men are all serving members of MI6 and have disappeared, presumed dead. They'd been working deep undercover and were completely secure, and now they've dropped off the face of the earth. And hey, guess what – you pulled the file on a joint mission between us, the UK and Canada.'

'I don't know anything about any MI6 officers, those names mean nothing to me.'

'Well how do you explain the fact that this was found at the bottom of the fire pit in your yard? You should've checked it had all gone up in smoke, because it looks like you're going the same way.'

'I didn't write that or put it there, that's the truth.'

'OK, we'll come back to that as well. Now see this? It's a high definition photograph of your desk at home. Very nice it is too, probably an antique and very valuable?'

Alicia's voice was croaky. 'It was my father's. He left it to me when he died. He knew I loved sitting at it when I was small, playing offices.'

'Oh how touching. Well I'm afraid it's in rather a different state now. The searching agents thought there may have been hidden compartments, so it's been rather...dismantled, to say the least.'

Alicia began weeping. 'It meant so much to me.'

'I've no doubt, and there's a woman with three children in Ohio missing someone rather special to her. One of our best Delta guys. He was found in two pieces having fallen into a ravine. Looks like he was hit by a car and pushed off the road. And hey, guess what?'

'I pulled his file and wrote down his name?'

'Got it in one. Look at the photo. See there in the leather on the right-hand corner of your desk? Indentation marks. Guess what's written under the scribble?'

'His name.'

'You're catching on. Now let's take it a step further, shall we? Tell me who you're working for and where the rest of the data has gone.'

Alicia felt the tiniest flicker of strength building inside. Her whole body felt toxic, but from somewhere she found reserves she never knew she had. She lifted her head and turned towards Rizzoli.

'Look, I came to *you* with the information in the first place. I recognised that other man with Josh, and after Sam put a name to him you took up the investigation yourself. Why would I do that if I was the person behind it all? It doesn't make sense.'

Rizzoli raised her voice. 'Of course it makes fucking sense. Hiding in plain sight they call it. For God's sake, that was even the title of the FBI's training package. Of course it makes sense – you bring it to us knowing it won't go anywhere and send us off chasing shadows, while you get on with the important business of stealing our most guarded secrets and passing them off.'

Alicia had a flicker of fire in her eyes. 'I might be able to assist your investigation, Miss Rizzoli.'

'That's better, now talk.'

'Do you mind if I ask a couple of questions?'

'The floor is yours, ask away.'

'The post-it note. Did you find any others of any colour in my house, garbage, car, bag, office or anywhere I'm connected to?

'No, just the one you hid in the bottom of your trash.'

'I don't use them. Not at home, work or anywhere. We're trying to be as paperless as possible at work which is why we have to use those stupid whiteboards they've put everywhere. You would think if I were trying to hide one at home you would've found the rest of the pad somewhere. I hate the damn things. Ask anyone in the office, I'm sure they'll corroborate that.'

'Is that it? Is that the best you can do?'

Alicia pointed to the partially burnt piece of paper. 'That one there – you said it was found in the bottom of my fire pit.'

'Yes, right at the bottom.'

'And you have scene photos?'

'Of course.' Rizzoli motioned to the giant, who passed over an A4 envelope.

Alicia could feel the fight returning to her heart. 'Now I haven't seen those photos, have I?'

'Well no, obviously – what's your point?'

'I bet they show a big pile of ash at the bottom of the fire pan amongst which you found the paper.' Rizzoli studied the photo, then the one underneath. Buckland continued. 'Don't you think it's a bit strange that the only thing to escape the fire just happens to be a piece of highly flammable paper, and the only bit of the paper that's not missing is the bit with the names on? I can't sit closer than four feet because it burns so hot. Can you explain how the paper survived?'

'I'm not here to answer questions, you are. We have…' But Buckland spoke over her. 'Look at the desk photo and the indentation. Very clever, but why the hell wouldn't I write the note in the middle of the desk instead of the right-hand corner? I'll tell you why, because whoever did this saw all the other indentation in the middle where I usually write. Yes, I still send good old-fashioned letters to my family. The person who did this would've been worried it might not have been found. Look at all the marks in the middle.'

'Not much of a defence, Miss Buckland.'

'Did you know I was left-handed?'

'No.'

'If I'd written this, why would I choose to write in the most awkward place for a left-hander?'

The balance in the room had shifted. Rizzoli and the two men felt it, and Buckland wasn't finished.

'I bet my fingerprints weren't on those two bits of paper.'

'No, but that doesn't prove anything.'

'I bet you found powder residue.'

'As a matter of fact we did, indicating you wore gloves.'

'OK, why the hell would I wear gloves to write a note I was going to throw in the fire? Why would I be so careless with the other so-called clues you found? Goddammit, Rizzoli, I am one of the most highly trained women in the Agency. I was about to be promoted and I know the game of subterfuge inside out, all the tricks – I'm a fucking expert. Do you *really* think I would be so sloppy, with so much at stake, i.e. my fucking life, to leave such obviously planted clues in my own house?'

'You've got a pretty sophisticated alarm system and your locks cost more than some doors, how do...'

'Jesus Christ, we both know people who could disable that alarm within ten seconds and get through my locks in twenty.' Buckland started to shake even more, but this time through a building rage. At a volume none of those present had yet heard from her, she started shouting. 'I've answered every single fucking question you and your goons have asked, including that ape. You wanted blood, you got it.' She reached down between her legs and held up her hand, red with her menstrual flow.

Rizzoli instinctively flinched backwards. For Alicia Buckland, the fire grew with every second. She spun round in her chair and got up, the blanket falling to the ground. The giant leapt out of his chair but Buckland met him halfway.

'You stripped me, humiliated me, made me shit and piss in a bucket with no toilet paper. You asked me the same things over and over and I answered everything.'

At an unbelievable volume the giant screamed at her. 'Sit the fuck back down.'

Buckland screamed back with every ounce of strength in her body. 'No, you sit down, or why don't you just snap my neck now and get it over with. You can ask me the same questions for the next year and I'll still say the same. So just fucking do it, will you. Come on, big man, you know you want to.'

The giant's cheeks pulsated as his teeth ground together.

Rizzoli stood up, walked the two steps to Alicia and put her hand on her shoulder. In the calmest, most soothing voice she could muster, she said, 'Alicia, please come and sit back down.' The director of internal security fixed the giant with a piercing stare. 'And you, mister, stand down.'

Rizzoli's words defused the standoff and everyone returned to their seats. She pointed at the giant. 'Get a table please and bring this woman's clothes back.' The giant left the room, returning a minute later with a simple plastic picnic table and placed it between Rizzoli and Buckland, throwing the clothes on the floor. Rizzoli turned to the men. 'You two, please leave us for a few minutes.'

The giant spoke up. 'Ma'am, my orders were to...'

Rizzoli fixed him with a death stare, the calmness of her voice carrying menace. 'I don't give a fuck about your orders. I outrank you many times over *and* the person who gave you your orders, so when I say leave, you leave. Clear?'

'Yes, ma'am.'

Once the two men left, Rizzoli reached into her purse and pulled out a handful of tampons and some tissues. 'This is the best I can do, clean yourself up and get dressed.' Buckland looked at her not saying a word, unsure if Rizzoli's actions were just another ploy. She'd stopped being embarrassed by her nakedness, but wanted to be warm for the first time in four days.

Buckland wet a wad of tissues and cleaned herself up as best she could, and beyond any more humiliation, inserted a tampon. She began to feel more human as she put her clothes back on. She looked at Rizzoli, still unsure about her motives but said, 'Thank you.'

Rizzoli leant over the table, closing the gap between them. 'Miss Buckland, I have never seen anyone take what you have and not deviate from your answers. Even the most devout and fanatical terrorists crack a little after a couple of days. I've heard what you said about the evidence found at your house and you make a compelling rebuttal. I want you to take a polygraph whilst under the influence of Sodium Thiopental. Will you do that willingly?'

With more than a hint of sarcasm, Alicia replied, 'Do I really have a choice?'

'I'd rather we didn't have to fight you to find a vein. I think it's in your interests.'

'Go ahead then, let's get the party started.'

Rizzoli knocked twice on the door which was opened immediately by the massive agent. 'Bring the polygraph and tell the doctor we're going to use the drug.'

He returned two minutes later with the machine, followed by the doctor carrying a physician's bag. Alicia sat staring into space whilst the doctor inserted a cannula into her arm. He produced a syringe, flicked the air out and emptied the contents into her vein. Alicia felt the effects immediately, trying to place the unpleasant taste in her mouth, made worse by the fact she hadn't brushed her teeth since before she left for work on the morning of her arrest. It tasted like rotting onions and she began to feel nauseous.

The doctor attached the electrodes and everything was ready. Rizzoli painstakingly went over everything

Alicia had been asked over the last ninety-six hours, including the evidence found in her house. Her answers remained the same. At one point the doctor topped up the dosage but nothing changed.

After three hours Rizzoli announced they were finished, instructing the doctor to remain whilst dismissing the giant. 'I've got to make a phone call. Make sure she's OK. I'll get them to bring a mattress in and you do not leave her unattended until I get back, is that clear, doc?' The doctor nodded. 'And turn those damn lights down.'

Rizzoli left the room, and a short while later a mattress arrived and the doctor settled Buckland down, covering her with a clean blanket. Rizzoli went directly to a private office and dialled the CIA headquarters in Langley. 'Good afternoon, this is Director Florence Rizzoli, can you put me through to Director Jackson's office please.'

'Hold the line please, Miss Rizzoli, putting you through now.'

A few seconds later the line clicked open. 'Director Jackson's office, how can I help?'

'Hi, it's Director Florence Rizzoli, can you put me through to the Director please.'

'She's in conference at the moment, can I take a message.'

'No thank you. Please tell her it's me, she'll take the call.'

'Miss Rizzoli, the director left strict instructions that she...'

Rizzoli sighed. 'Just do it or start clearing your desk.'

Rizzoli heard a 'Hrmph' as the line was placed on hold, and then the familiar voice of the woman in overall charge of the CIA. 'Flo, hi, give me a second.' Rizzoli heard a hand being placed over the receiver but could still make out what was being said.

'Gentlemen, I know this is bad timing, but I have to take this. Would you all mind stepping out?'

Rizzoli heard the sound of muttering and chairs being dragged backwards, guessing they were in the Director's private conference room.

'Hi, Flo, sorry about that. I've got the Bureau, Homeland and the head of the Secret Service here. Everyone's getting their pantyhose in a twist about this Russian thing. You know they've pulled out of the G20 without giving a reason, and Putin isn't taking the President's calls.'

'Would you?'

'Haha, not if I could help it. Anyway, how's it going with Buckland?'

Rizzoli recounted everything since Buckland's arrest. Director Jackson said nothing the whole time, causing Rizzoli at one point to wonder if the call had been disconnected. 'Ma'am, are you there?'

'Yes, Flo, carry on.'

The Director of internal security told the most powerful woman in America about Buckland's answers regarding the evidence found in her house, and the use of the drugs and lie detector test. She heard

Jackson exhale. ‘My God, Flo, you really put her through it.’

‘No other way with what’s at stake. I’ve never seen anyone hold out that long if they’re lying, and to be honest I don’t think she is. God knows how Englefield managed it, but I really believe it was just him. However he did it, it was brilliant and we’ll find out how, but as of now I’ve got nothing else to go on.’

‘I agree, leave it with me. Are you planning to release her?’

‘I was going to keep her for another twenty-four hours. Sodium Thiopental takes up to thirty-six hours to leave the body, but I thought with your blessing we could place her under house arrest until we find out more.’

‘I agree. Get her home tomorrow and make her comfortable until then.’

‘Yes, ma’am. I’ll let you know if anything else comes up.’

*

Rizzoli returned to the interrogation room and dismissed the doctor. Buckland was asleep on the floor, curled in a ball under the blanket with just her head visible. Rizzoli knelt down, gently shaking her shoulder.

‘Alicia, Alicia, wake up.’

Buckland woke with a start, wide-eyed and obviously terrified.

‘Shh shh, it’s OK. No more questions, I promise.’

Buckland looked up, trying to focus on Rizzoli's face but not really understanding what was going on. Rizzoli calmly explained that for what it was worth, she believed everything Buckland had said. She told her about her conversation with Director Jackson, and that it was agreed she be placed under house arrest until they worked out exactly what had happened.

'I'm going to have you moved to a more comfortable room. It's not the Ritz but it's warm with fresh bedding and a shower. I've got a go bag with me with clean clothes – we're about the same size so they should fit. You're going to feel the effects of the drug for a while yet so it's not safe to be on your own. I'll give you a lift home tomorrow. Have you taken that all in?

'Yes, thank you. Am I fired as well?'

'No, but you are suspended from duties, and we'll keep your firearm, badge and phone for now. Better than here though. Once we've got to the bottom of all this I hope you can be reinstated, if that's what you want.'

'Maybe.'

'Look, I know you'll spend the rest of your life hating me, but hopefully one day you'll realise who we thought we were dealing with, and why we had to do what we did.'

'And what was that?'

'The most dangerous traitor this country has ever encountered. Come on, I'll help you up. Let's get you in that hot shower and some decent food down you.'

*

Director Jackson popped her head out of the conference room to see the other three most powerful people in charge of defending the USA sitting in a row on a sofa, looking like a group of schoolboys waiting to see the head teacher. She held up one finger. 'Gentlemen, sorry about that, I won't keep you long but I've got one more quick call to make.' Smiling, she closed the door again.

She pulled up a secure line and dialled the twenty-four-hour contact number for Sir John Leroux, head of MI6 and her fellow Caretaker.

The call connected and she heard 'Protocol 8914 green.' Jackson replied, 'Protocol 4381 yellow.'

'Good morning, Katherine, to what do I owe the pleasure?'

'I thought you should know we've completed the interrogation of Alicia Buckland. It's my opinion and that of Florence Rizzoli that she's innocent. God knows how Englefield pulled it off, but he has.'

Jackson recounted the extensive enhanced interrogation of Buckland, down to the last detail.

'So you basically tortured her?'

'Well that's not a term we use these days, is it, Sir John.'

'No, quite, but exactly what I would have done in your shoes. So no useful leads at all?'

'Nothing, not a thing, other than someone broke into her house and planted quite compelling evidence to suggest she was behind all this, but she's one tough cookie. I don't know how she was thinking straight by the time we got to the search results, but everything she said made nonsense of the so called evidence. She's a brilliant woman, John.'

'Hmm. Perhaps we could bring her into the fold. We can always use people like that.'

'Further down the line, maybe. While I'm on, anything your end on the Russians?'

'Unfortunately not. We've tried all the back channels, but they won't talk to us either. A wall's gone up on all communication between our nations. They've now given formal notice they won't be attending G20, and half their agents are now back in Moscow.'

'I've got the heads of our agencies sitting outside my office right now. We were just discussing it. Same as you though, we're in the dark.'

'Well let me know if they come up with any bright ideas. I'll let my shop know the update on Buckland. Let's speak soon.'

'Agreed, thanks, John.'

Same day, same time, London.

James Camburn was in a meeting with all shop staff. They checked and rechecked they hadn't missed anything in the build-up to the mission. Backdoor control into Transport for London CCTV was established, as well as the Department of Transport's separate camera system.

A person living in London is captured 300 times per day on CCTV. With over 600,000 cameras in the capital alone, it was understandable Jenks preferred not to take London based jobs, but if all went to plan he wouldn't be identifiable by a single camera.

Jenks would be checking into the hotel on Tuesday 10th March to be in place by the time Englefield arrived later that evening. The Shop had the ability to view the CCTV on board Eurostar trains as they fed to a UK-based server, then surveillance operatives would follow him from St Pancras to The Huntsman's Lodge. From thereon he was Jenks's responsibility.

Camburn felt the vibration in his suit pocket. 'Hello.'

'Good day to you, James, John here. I've just heard from my counterpart over the pond. Basically they completely rinsed Buckland – they did everything to destroy her over four solid days. The upshot is, they believe she's telling the truth and had nothing to do with the haemorrhaging of the data.'

'All down to Englefield then?'

'It would appear so, but dark forces are at play. He's had serious help and backup through persons known to Black. These *Welikeleaks* people appear to be more resourceful than perhaps we originally gave them credit for. I just have a feeling we're not seeing the big picture.'

Camburn thought for a moment. 'Do we think Englefield got help from elsewhere in the Agency?'

'Not that their Caretaker can see, but who knows. He's been very clever and we mustn't underestimate him or Black.'

Camburn continued. 'I agree. Has GCHQ found anything else of interest on this Russian saga?'

'Not a sausage I'm afraid, which makes it all the more worrying. Usually there's all sorts of daft stuff flying around, but it's literally dwindled to nothing in the past couple of days. I take it you've heard they've given formal notice they won't be at the G20?'

'Yes. Do you think the Russians are manipulating the internet again?'

'More than likely, my old friend. We'll keep digging and I'll call you if I hear anything useful.'

Same time, USA.

Sam Dibble, in his capacity as acting head of analysis, received a call from Florence Rizzoli.

'Hey, Sam, Flo here.'

'Hi, Flo, what's happening with Alicia? I'm still finding it hard to believe she's involved in this whole sorry saga.'

'She isn't.'

'Pardon me?'

'She's not involved, Sam – we put her through stuff no one should ever have to face. Anyone would've broken after two days – she lasted four and still didn't crack.'

'What about the things they found in her house?'

'That's what confirmed she was telling the truth – it was planted. Most people wouldn't have been able to argue with the facts, but she did and she was right. I don't know who's behind this, Sam, but I'll find out one day, I can promise you that.'

Dibble tasted bile in his mouth but tried not to let it show in his voice, quietly swallowing hard.

'Jeez, poor Leece. Can I talk to her? Is that allowed?'

'I don't see why not, she could do with a friend now more than ever. She won't be home until tomorrow though – we gave her a lot of drugs. We're keeping her phone and she's been formally suspended and placed under house arrest so I'd try the landline when you ring.'

'Will do. What do you think will happen to her?'

'I think she'll be completely exonerated once Englefield and Black are caught. I'm not ruling out that someone else used her log-in and passed it all to Englefield, or if he did it himself. It's an absolute clusterfuck at the moment – we don't know where to start looking.'

'OK, Flo, thanks for the update.' He sat back and smiled.

USA, two minutes later.

Dibble dialled a number from memory. The familiar long international ringing tone was answered by the Englishman within a few seconds. 'News, I take it?'

'Buckland's going to be released. Basically they believe she's been set up, but she's on a tight leash until they get to the bottom of it. She'll be home tomorrow as they pumped her full of truth juice. I'll check on her once she's back but it really doesn't affect us. They are literally running around blind not knowing where to look. By Wednesday it'll all be immaterial.'

'Excellent. I should have good news from our man in Scotland later this evening. I've got someone in place to bring the envelopes down overnight so should have it all in London by tomorrow morning. It's going to take a while to scan everything and synchronise it to go out at the same time, so I'll be very busy. Did you notice the emails have changed?'

'Yeah, I saw. Englefield's saying *Donald* and Black's replying *Walter.* Shame we've no way of knowing how long they'll keep that up before changing again.'

The Englishman continued. 'It doesn't surprise me and it doesn't matter – with our little twist it's of very little consequence. While I've got you, does the name *Jenks* mean anything to you?'

'No, should it?'

'Probably not. That doesn't surprise me either – the man's like a ghost. I'm pretty sure he's working for someone I knew from way, way back who I've had tabs on recently. I know they've been in contact with each other which can only mean one thing.'

'Which is?'

'That the Brits have a sniff something's going on, and this fellow Jenks is involved trying to help them. He's a bit of an enigma – used to be in the army then disappeared off the face of the earth. Fortunately I happen to know where he lives, and he's definitely active at the moment.'

'If he's such an enigma, how come you know where he lives? Doesn't sound like much of a ghost to me.'

'Oh it's a very long story, old chap, I'll fill you in when we next meet. We should pick somewhere neutral and meet for a proper celebration.'

'Everywhere's going to be neutral in a few days.'

The Englishman laughed. 'Ha, you're spot on there, old fruit.'

Dibble had a hint of concern in his voice. 'Look, this Jenks character – is he any threat to us?'

'My boy, that is the beauty of our whole plan. He can do what he wants but we're still going to get what *we* want.'

Kent, UK, the same time.

Jenks spent most of the afternoon in his underground store. Guns were disassembled, oiled and reassembled. Other items were cleaned and batteries checked for charge. He also reviewed the staff roster for The Huntsman's Lodge and saw that Rhys Evans would be on duty.

He wasn't planning on using the Ducati until Tuesday, when he would ride it to a lock-up garage in a mews property close to Wardour Street belonging to MI6. Camburn had arranged for it to be taken off the list of safe houses in order to negate any chance of a compromise.

Whatever he was doing though, a tiny warning light was flashing deep in his subconscious. Something he'd read perhaps, something seen or possibly heard. Whatever it was, he couldn't put his finger on it so pushed it to the back of his mind. Perhaps somewhere in the hundred trillion pathways connecting each neuron, his brain would find its own way of retrieving what was troubling him.

He'd put a couple of baked potatoes in the oven to have with the steak he'd defrosted earlier. Pouring himself a glass of Côte du Brouilly, he set up his high-powered monocular scope on a tripod in his lounge bay window – a chance to do a bit of serious birdwatching.

He took a sip and settled himself, pressing his left eye against the soft rubber eyepiece. The tide was out, so conditions were perfect for birds of all types to feast on the exposed mudflats.

He spotted something dark landing on the end of one of the sea defences. Turning the scope slightly, he saw in crystal clear detail the unmistakable sight of a black guillemot. He scanned around for another but perhaps the partner was out searching for food. Although they were almost entirely black, he thought they were beautiful, with striking bright red legs and feet. The truth was, he found all birds beautiful and fascinating.

The guillemot flew off and Jenks slowly rotated the scope towards the old wreck. The magnification was so high that as he moved he flashed over something which only registered as a blur. He adjusted the scope back and saw the faces of the two bait diggers in complete clarity. They were chatting and laughing and just doing what they always did. The small warning light glowed slightly brighter.

Travelling at close to the speed of light, fragments of memories and snippets of information had travelled millions of miles around his brain and abruptly stopped. They'd found something.

He closed his eyes, picturing what he'd just seen, but after ten minutes nothing further came to mind. Then he had an idea. Reaching for his binoculars he again focussed on the bait diggers who were now at the very edge of the focal length and slightly blurred. He closed his eyes, then looked again. He repeated the action five further times and leant back in his chair. He knew there was a connection but it wouldn't come.

He leant over the desk to retrieve his glass and took a sip, moving his laptop slightly so he could put the glass down within reach. Then it came. His brain needed one more tiny fragment of recall to nudge open the door to a forgotten memory.

Jenks cast his mind back a few days. He'd been establishing remote connection to the hotel's system then rang James Camburn. He remembered the call with Rhys Evans was on speaker so he could type. Closing his eyes and clearing his mind, he entered a near meditative state.

The memory came of a third man with the bait diggers. Old. Overcoat. Hat. Stick. Realising he was never going to have a clearer picture of the man no matter how much he thought of him chatting to the diggers, he wondered which direction he'd come from. Opening his laptop screen to replicate as closely as he could the conditions from that day, he adjusted the screen to exactly the angle he preferred and placed his phone where it was when he made the call to the hotel. He ran the entire conversation with Evans in his head, projecting himself back.

They were talking about a hotel Evans had previously worked at. Perhaps it was when Evans mentioned the amazing view, he'd made an involuntary movement and looked up for a split second. *He* also had an amazing view. That was the moment.

He slowed his breathing, keeping his eyes closed, and saw what in a film would be just a handful of frames. The old man walking past his house. Just a few steps but enough to extract detail from the amount of time between blinks.

He already knew the man had been wearing a long coat, but he thought back to the two steps the man had taken before the memory ran out. The movement of the coat. It wasn't stiff, but rippled. Expensive. Perhaps cashmere or a silk and high quality wool mix?

As Jenks relaxed his breathing further he felt his pulse slow, concentrating his thoughts on the man's lower half. Pressed trousers. Smart pressed trousers. His gaze continued down and he pictured a sheen on the man's shoes, like a mirror catching the light. Probably highly polished.

He replayed the man walking past – forwards and backwards, remembering the way he carefully placed his stick. A limp perhaps, or maybe if the shoes were expensive they would have smooth leather soles – not ideal for walking on wet stones. He figured if the man was prepared to pay a lot of money for an overcoat, then he probably had for his shoes as well. Which begged the question – why would a smartly dressed man in expensive clothes trudge across dirty wet mudflats to speak to a couple of bait diggers?

Men who were usually in view of his house.

He discounted any notion that the bait men were any sort of threat. They were clearly not spies or undercover agents of any description. He'd seen them virtually every time he'd been at home since the day he moved in – just regular guys. Who better to ask about the houses on the beach than two local guys who worked that patch every day of their working lives?

Jenks was in such a deep state he jumped when his phone rang.

'It's me.'

'Hello, James, what's up?

'Quick update from the Caretaker. You remember I told you they'd arrested Englefield's boss, well she's going to be released tomorrow. She's not quite in the clear yet but they're certain she didn't have anything to do with harvesting the files. Looks like she was set up, but they're no further forward.'

'What, nothing at all?'

'Diddly squat, lad.'

Camburn recounted the details of what the Agency had put Buckland through over four days, and the evidence found in her house.

'That sounds pretty horrific, she must be made out of granite.'

'Quite agree, old son. The other thing is Englefield and Black have changed their daily check-in word.'

'I'm not surprised – pretty good failsafe.'

Camburn went quiet for a moment. 'Lad, what would you do if you were Englefield and Black?'

Jenks thought for a while. 'If I were Englefield I'd want insurance that I was going to get my money, and it must be enough to set him up for life. I would've asked for payments each time I passed information, but he still needs the big one. He's living the high life already and the surgery he's booked must be a fortune. Then he's got to buy somewhere off the radar with no paper trail back to him. You can't use a bent Amex forever.'

'So what sort of insurance policy would you build into your master plan?'

'I'd change the parameters at the very last moment – just a tweak to what everyone thinks is going to happen, that way he stays in control.'

Camburn sighed. 'I wish I'd never asked.'

'And, if I were the *Welikeleaks* people, I'd alter the terms at the last moment as well. They've been playing an expensive long game and won't entertain it failing – or maybe they'll all just play by the rules.'

'Now I know you're being silly – there are no rules in the games we play.'

There was a short silence. 'James, can you think of any reason why someone would be...actually forget that, it's not important.'

'You sure, old boy?'

'No, but I've more important things to think about, like the fact my baked spuds are ready.'

'Well then you simply must go. Speak to you later.'

Chapter 18.

Same time, same day, Balmoral, Scotland.

Dennis Best had been employed at HM Queen Elizabeth's Scottish castle for almost three years. He'd been promoted to senior footman a year previously, his personal responsibility to maintain the monarch's private quarters. He rented a small flat a couple of miles from the castle, having declined the lodgings he was entitled to, preferring to live off site.

The glowing CV he attached to his original application showed he was easily qualified, having worked all over Europe for a number of wealthy individuals. The testimonials accompanying his CV described him as the consummate professional, eminently trustworthy and trained to a standard whereby he would complement any establishment in the service industry. However, his CV was a complete fabrication.

Before being accepted to work within the royal household, any successful applicant is required to undergo strict vetting. Checks were made with previous employers, references sought, bank accounts scrutinised and credit reference agencies searched.

Vetting, however, was not infallible. Cases had surfaced over the years whereby tabloid reporters had gained positions close to the Queen, purely to photograph what she had for breakfast and present it to the nation on the front page of their Sunday issue. Heads rolled, and Whitehall was assured the system had been tightened up and loopholes closed, but that was of no consequence to Mr Best – he knew his credentials would pass the most stringent checks. His Russian masters had invested a great deal of time and money creating an alternative life for one of their most highly regarded long-term sleeper agents.

After nearly two years in post, following the untimely death of the previous senior footman in a motorcycle accident, Best was considered his natural successor. The Queen herself had even remarked to him prior to the demise of his predecessor, that she actually preferred the way he did things. She really did have a soft spot for him and enjoyed his company.

Her Majesty was due back on the estate the following day, Sunday. Although she enjoyed residing at Buckingham Palace, it was no state secret she preferred the freedom of movement Balmoral offered. Away from London she could ride her horses, drive around the estate and live more of a normal life – as normal as life could be for the world's longest reigning monarch.

It was early evening and Best had given the rest of his staff the night off. Everything had been tidied, carpets vacuumed and surfaces dusted – there was little to do apart from a few last-minute jobs which he would attend to himself, such as changing her bed and ensuring her personal drinks cabinet was fully stocked.

He attended to his duties, checking there was enough Dubonnet, gin and vermouth, straightening the bottles so the labels were facing outwards. He polished her favourite glass, made up her bed with fresh linen and placed a small wrapped chocolate on her pillow. His predecessor never left her a treat, which was one of the reasons she liked Dennis more.

Best crossed to the double doors, silently locking them. Walking into the Queen's bedroom he took an old brass key from his pocket. The walk-in vault hidden behind the ornate French rococo style full length mirror was known only to Her Majesty. It was one of the many secrets she had a duty to keep.

The vault key was with her at all times, and was one of the few items she carried in her handbag, along with a lipstick, mints and a packet of tissues. There'd once been a spare, but it had been missing for many decades. But it wasn't missing. It had been kept since the late 1940s in a safe in the Kremlin having been *accidently* lost by a man called Anthony Blunt, and it was now in Best's hand.

Blunt, unmasked later in life as one of Britain's most notorious traitors, was employed by King George VI as the keeper of the Crown's art collection. Blunt was an extremely knowledgeable art historian who advised the King on private purchases, and later the Queen. He was instrumental in persuading the monarchy to bring out more of its collection for public display – from the King's private vault.

The King had absolute faith in Blunt, and to assist him with the upkeep of priceless works of art, entrusted him with the only other key to the vault. His Majesty regarded Blunt as not only a valued confidant, but a good friend. This was why he was so forgiving when Blunt confessed he'd inadvertently dropped his keys over the side of a motor launch whilst enjoying a day's fishing on Loch Muick, part of the Balmoral estate. Divers were sent down in an attempt to retrieve them, but it was a lost cause trying to search 540 acres of water for a bunch of keys, and the matter was forgotten.

Best put on white cotton gloves and carefully swung the mirror out on its hidden hinges. Sliding the key in, he was surprised again by how smooth the mechanism was. He'd entered the room only once before – to check what he was seeking was actually there, and to count them.

He twisted the brass handle and swung the heavy door open, revealing amongst the treasures, records of secrets so incalculably incendiary in the wrong hands, that only two other people knew of their existence. One was Sir John Leroux, the other a senior civil servant in Whitehall. Or so it was believed.

Best walked slowly around the room, about the size of an average bedroom in an average house. On his previous brief visit he hadn't quite taken in what else was stored, having gone directly to the far wall, quickly counted, and left. Three sides were covered with built-in shelving arranged around a central museum style display case.

Twinkling inside the case was a collection of the most precious gems he'd ever seen, all set in exquisite jewellery, but compared to the centrepiece resting on a bed of deep blue silk, they looked like fairground prizes. He recognised it immediately – the Koh-I-Nor diamond, astonished to think that the one displayed in the jewel room at the Tower of London was a fake.

To the right were a series of thin slats housing paintings. He carefully eased one out, noticing the signature in the right-hand corner – Picasso. Holding it at arm's length he didn't recognise it as one he'd ever seen.

Conscious of time, he walked to the back wall, and the long shelf storing what he'd come for. Looking for only the second time at the long line of envelopes, he worried he'd underestimated how much space they'd take up, so quickly retrieved the Queen's duvet cover.

The envelopes appeared to be in date order. Examining the first one, he saw that the beautiful handwriting in deep indigo ink was fading, but the date was clear – June 13th 1944. Over a year before the war ended. Across the middle he could clearly pick out *1st V1 Rocket attack London. Deception and blame protocol.* He looked at the words again. Deception and blame protocol? What the hell did that mean? Did the Brits bomb their own people to blame it on the Germans?

He examined the back of the vellum envelope, running his gloved finger around the blood red disk, embossed with an image of the King. It had clearly never been reopened since the day the King's seal was pressed into the setting wax.

He picked out random envelopes. The seal changed to that of Elizabeth II in 1953, remaining unchanged to the last envelope on the right-hand side. He smiled to himself, feeling proud of his role in the imminent shifting of world order.

Best laid out the duvet cover, carefully placing envelopes onto the linen until he'd completely cleared the shelf. He folded the cover around them and bundled it up, counting 154 in total.

Carrying it back out to the Queen's bedroom, he put the cover into a wicker basket, throwing the rest of the bedding on top. He checked the vault making sure he hadn't dropped or left anything, locked the door and swung the mirror back into place, looking the same as it had for the last 100 years.

Carrying the basket, he made his way down the long corridor towards the lift, which he would take to the basement laundry room a few doors along from what could loosely be called his office.

Reaching to press the call button, he stopped dead in his tracks, his body spasming as a booming voice called out. 'Dennis Best, stop right there.' He felt a pounding in his head as instant fear took hold. He wished he had access to a firearm, but that was of course impossible.

‘Oi, Denny boy, wait up a second.’ He turned to see the huge figure of barrel-chested Constable Rory Galbraith, a veteran Royalty Protection officer ambling down the corridor towards him. PC Galbraith was seeing out the last nine months of his service in the relative calm of Balmoral. A dream posting at the end of a career, as nothing ever really happened to warrant him having to actually do anything, apart from hourly patrols in that wing of the castle.

‘Gotcha there, wee man, you didn’t half jump, ha-ha!’

Best felt his heart begin to slow. ‘I’m not surprised, you daft sod – it’s like having a fucking battleship sneaking up behind you and sounding its horn.’

‘Sorry, pal – you feeling alright? You’re sweating.’

‘Actually, not that marvellous, feels like I’m getting flu or something. I’m nearly done now – I’m going to head home and stick my feet up for the rest of the night.’

‘You going to be alright cycling? One of the lads could drop you off in the van if you like.’

‘Cheers, Rory, but the fresh air will do me good.’

‘I’ll tell you what will do you good – two fingers of single malt, a spoonful of honey, drop of boiling water and a squeeze of lemon. Always works for me, although I don’t always bother with the honey, lemon or water.’

Best laughed, more out of relief than the quality of the joke. ‘Good idea, maybe I’ll pick up a bottle on my way home.’

PC Galbraith nodded towards the Queen's chambers. 'Can't you just er, you know, borrow one?'

'She'd know. That woman remembers everything. She's sharper than people a quarter of her age – never forgets a thing.'

PC Galbraith smiled. 'Oh well, just a thought.'

Best wagged his finger. 'And you, an upstanding officer of the law, how could you even suggest stealing from our queen.'

The officer held his hands in front of his huge chest. 'Moi? I never said a thing. Oh that reminds me, the reason I scared your Sassenach arse half to death was to ask if you knew when she's back. No one tells me anything here.'

'Choppers due at 6pm tomorrow last I heard.'

PC Galbraith smiled and rubbed his hands together. 'Och, that's good news, I'm off at four.'

'God forbid they ever make you work for a living, Rory.'

'Ya cheeky young bairn, away with you.'

'See you tomorrow, big man.'

Dennis Best arrived in his basement office and pulled out the laundry, carefully unwrapping the duvet cover and packed the envelopes into his large rucksack. He took the bedding a few doors along and threw it into a large wheeled canvas bag full of items ready to be washed.

As he cycled down to the main gate with his rucksack bulging on his back, his anxiety levels rose rapidly. He was so close to completing his three-year mission – just a guard station to pass through and he would be home and dry.

'Oi, Denny, get off and milk it!'

He turned to see two officers he knew well, laughing and waving as they walked across the lawn away from the main gate, Heckler and Koch MP3 machine guns slung over their shoulders.

Best shouted back. 'Never heard that one before, Tom!'

Ringing his bell as he freewheeled towards the gate house, a smiling Sergeant Julia Tyler peered out, raised a hand to acknowledge him, and raised the barrier.

The sliding window of the checkpoint was slightly open, and as Best passed through Sergeant Tyler called out, 'See ya, Denny.'

'Night, Jules.'

*

Riding into the quiet street where he lived, Best immediately noticed a car he didn't recognise, but behind the wheel the smiling face of a man he did. Best waved, beckoning the man to follow him into his flat. Once inside the men embraced, slapping each other's backs. The man spoke first. 'Comrade, it is good to see you again. It has been over three years, yes?'

'Vasily Yahontov, my dear friend, I can't tell you how good it is to see you too. I have it all here.' He pointed down at his rucksack. 'Will you have one drink to celebrate our success? I know you have a long way to go, but it wouldn't be right not to drink a toast to the future. What do you say?'

The man smiled and nodded. 'Anatoly, dear Anatoly, how can I say no to you. Bring me a glass.'

Dennis Best now ceased to exist. Anatoly Belinsky filled two glasses with vodka and passed one to his old friend. They knocked them together, '*Za zda-ró-vye.*' Vasily raised his glass. 'And to your health as well, comrade. We will drink properly very soon when we are victorious.'

The men said their goodbyes, and Vasily Yahontov started the 400-mile drive back to London with 154 envelopes worth more than their weight in gold.

The following morning at 9.30am, immediately after sending a message to Balmoral's director of house services stating he was ill with the flu and wouldn't be in, Anatoly Belinsky passed through immigration at Aberdeen airport. The British passport he presented in the name of Martin Hurst didn't muster a second look from the bored officer.

Chapter 19.

Sunday 8th March, two days to mission start. Virginia, USA.

Florence Rizzoli looked across at Alicia as they turned into the street where Buckland lived. Hardly a word had been exchanged on the long journey back from the interrogation facility, despite Rizzoli's best efforts to try to get Alicia to engage. With just the two of them in the car, Rizzoli hoped it might make it easier to talk, but Alicia clearly didn't want to.

'Just over there please, Miss Rizzoli, the one with the smashed-in front door – you can't miss it.'

Rizzoli momentarily took one hand off the wheel and placed it on Alicia's arm. 'Please call me Flo.'

'You said that once before I seem to remember.'

'Look, Alicia. You don't have to go home right now. It's not as you left it. Why don't I drive you to a hotel and we can arrange to at least get the place cleaned up a bit. Please. You've had enough to deal with these last few days.'

Buckland turned to Rizzoli – the look was enough to make the director of internal security realise she'd just made the understatement of her career.

'Alicia, will you promise me you're going to be OK?' Alicia said nothing. Rizzoli stopped the car but kept the engine running. She rummaged around in the door pocket, pulling out an old gas receipt. 'I spoke to Sam to let him know I was dropping you back. He's really worried and said he'd drop by. I know you guys go way back, so don't push him away – you need a friend and it can't be seen to be me because I'm officially investigating you. Hopefully not for much longer though.'

Alicia gave the slightest of nods whilst Rizzoli reached for her phone and started scrolling through. She scribbled a number on the back of the receipt. 'This is Sam's cell in case you can't remember it. I'm sorry you can't have your phone back at the moment, but your landline should still be working. I don't know what else to say.'

Rizzoli was on the verge of tears. 'Alicia, I know there's nothing I can say that will make this any better at the moment, but I do want to say this. You are, without doubt, the toughest person I've ever met, man or woman. Please stay strong for just a little longer. I know you'll come out the other end of this.'

Alicia took the receipt, picked up her purse and began to get out of the car. Rizzoli leant across to see Alicia's face when she replied, but the door just closed gently and Buckland began to walk home.

Rizzoli wiped her eyes and drove slowly away. She wanted to throw her head back and sob, but held it in, feeling rather pathetic compared to the resolve of the woman she'd just dropped off.

Alicia placed her key in the lock, then realised she didn't need it. The door had been forced by the combination of a hydraulic frame splitter and battering ram and poorly repaired, swinging open with just a push.

What she encountered caused her to draw a sharp breath and freeze. The words *utter carnage* were inadequate when describing the devastation before her. She hardly recognised her own hallway. The expensive Persian carpet she'd saved for was cut into pieces and stacked in one corner. Floorboards were missing, presumably so the searching officers could push a scope around to find any secret hiding places.

She looked right and saw bare patches on the wall where paintings had previously hung. The art lay strewn around, glass smashed and frames crudely ripped from the pictures. Her hand flew to her mouth as she looked further down the hall and saw the grandmother clock passed down from her maternal grandma lying in pieces. Glass was everywhere, and they'd even ripped the face off in case there was a hiding place behind it.

Alicia Buckland did in fact have a very secret hiding place, the image of which appeared in her mind, and she really hoped they hadn't found it.

Tears started to roll down her cheeks as she turned and walked into the lounge. If she thought it couldn't get any worse, she was wrong. It looked like someone had detonated a bomb, gathered up the debris and thrown it back into the room in no particular order.

Her expensive sofa and matching armchair were barely recognisable as furniture. The upholstery had been slashed off, cushions ripped apart and the frame dismantled – that was the problem with miniaturisation.

A single memory card not much bigger than a fingernail could now store colossal amounts of information. With the advent of the one-terabyte card, it was now almost off the scale. A tiny piece of plastic could hold half a million photos, over 220 full length high definition films or one million ebooks. More than enough space for a few highly classified documents.

She gazed around, not finding one part of her life intact. Large holes had been raked out of the walls, but the most upsetting sight was her father's treasured desk, now only fit to use as kindling.

Alicia walked into what had once been her kitchen and walked straight back out. Nothing was left. All fitted units and appliances lay strewn around her garden. Looking at the digger tracks and piles of earth, it seemed the team had narrowed the parameters of the search to individual blades of grass.

Upstairs would be the same. She didn't really need to look, but reluctantly climbed the stairs anyway. Her bathroom, the one she had waited years to be able to afford, was the same story as the kitchen. The guest room was obliterated, looking like everything had been put in a huge blender and flung back out.

It was her own bedroom which upset her most. Private things had been examined and left for her to see. She imagined the men having a good laugh, holding items aloft and making crude comments.

The utter humiliation of seeing her underwear fanned out on what was once her mattress was the final straw, the gussets carefully sliced away needlessly. Anyone searching would've been able to feel anything inside, so this was gratuitous. Resting on the pair in the middle was an old vibrator she'd completely forgotten about. She and the rest of the girls at a friend's hen party years before had received one in their goody bag. She'd thrown it in the closet when she got home and hadn't seen it since, until that moment.

Back to the carnage of her lounge, she searched for something to write on, finding the partial contents of one of her desk drawers including a plain envelope and a piece of writing pad. The pad she once used to compose letters to friends and relatives.

She instinctively turned to her desk, then remembered it didn't exist anymore. Picking up a piece of plaster board, once part of the wall, she sat on the floor and placed it on her knees. Taking a pen from her jacket, she started to write.

When she finished she walked back to the front door, careful not to put her foot through the gaps between the few floorboards that remained, and hung the letter on the hook she'd put there for the holly wreath at Christmas. Gently pulling the door closed, she made her way through the house and into the garage.

Sam Dibble had been ringing the house phone repeatedly. It rang and rang his end, but unbeknown to him no sound was heard in Alicia's house. The line was fine, but the phone was in the garden in pieces. He paced around not sure what to do. Should he go straight over? Call the police? He tried to think of reasons why she'd ignore the incessant ringing. Perhaps she was making a meal – God knows she'd want something decent after the muck she'd been eating at the facility. More likely she was probably lying in the bath, mirrors all steamed up and bubbles overflowing as she soaked away the dirt and grime of the last four days. He decided he would give her time, and try again in an hour.

Alicia closed the side door to the garage and turned the key. Thankfully there hadn't been much in there to search through, and apart from her meagre collection of tools strewn over the floor, it was as she'd left it – just an old wooden garden chair and a few empty flowerpots.

She looked down at the terracotta tubs and smiled when she remembered she'd put them there at the end of autumn, planning on planting tomatoes in the spring. Searching around the floor she found a cross-head screwdriver and walked to the up and over door. Kneeling down, she began to undo the four screws securing the door bolt housing. As she turned the fourth she thought about the search team and whispered, 'You're not as good as you thought you were.'

Laying the screws down, she dug her fingernails into the thin gap and pulled. The metal plate came away easily, revealing a void in the concrete about the size of a lunchbox. Reaching inside, she retrieved a different type of box.

Now calm, serene and focussed, she carried the box over to the chair and sat down, placing it on her lap. Opening the lid, she carefully removed a burner phone she'd purchased as part of her emergency *go* box in the event she'd have to leave the house in fear of her life.

When your job was to put away bad and ruthless individuals, there was always the lingering worry at the back of every agent's mind of someone seeking revenge turning up at your front door. Thankfully it rarely occurred, but if it did, it was handy to have a backup plan.

Alicia had ensured the contents of the box were maintained, but doubted the cell phone had any juice left as she hadn't charged it for some time. She tried to switch it on but it was completely dead. Pulling out the charging lead, she plugged it into a wall socket and sat silently back down, placing her hands on her knees and waited.

After five minutes she tried again and the screen came to life. She left it to charge and went back to the box and removed $5,000 in cash, which she placed inside one of the flowerpots. She then examined the revolver, checking the action of the fully loaded chambers.

Pulling the scrap of receipt from her pocket, she went to the phone and tapped the icon for text messages. After carefully typing the recipient's number in, she composed a short message. It didn't take long. *I'm so sorry Sam, take care, Alicia X.*

Her finger hovered over the green icon for a few moments. Special times and happy memories floated in and out of her thoughts before she let out a sigh and pressed send. She turned the phone off and walked back to the chair and settled into it, making herself comfortable.

Picking up the revolver, she pulled back the hammer, placed the barrel against her left eye and pulled the trigger, blowing the back of her skull off and splattering most of her brain onto the grey concrete wall behind her.

*

Dibble was actually at work, which was unusual for a Sunday, but his wife was out most of the day taking the kids to a friend's birthday party. He'd used the time to catch up on some closing reports and was thinking about leaving. He'd made up his mind up to drop in on Alicia unannounced and check on her welfare. His phone started skittering across his desk – he'd set it to silent so he could concentrate.

He saw a text message from a number he didn't recognise. Reading it, he immediately felt every drop of blood in his body coursing into his neck. He tried ringing the number back and heard an electronic voice.

Calls to this number are not currently being connected. Grabbing his jacket he ran out of the office towards the elevators. 'No, Leece, no, please, no.'

Frantically stabbing at the button he looked at the display to see the elevator was coming up from the ground floor. Too slow. He turned and sprinted for the stairs, taking three at a time as he made his way to the basement as fast as he could. The car pool was open every day of the week, as not everyone in the CIA had weekends off.

He ran into the fleet manager's office, pulling out his credentials. The manager looked up. 'Whoa there, where's the fire?' Dibble held out his badge quickly blurting out, 'I'm Sam Dibble, director of the Special Activities Division. I need a fast car right now.' The man opened a drawer, removing a self-carbonating requisition pad. 'OK, sir, if you can just fill this out…' Sam screamed at him. 'Just give me the fucking keys to the fastest thing you've got – this is a matter of life and death.'

A minute later Dibble was accelerating out of the underground car park, magnetic blue light thrown on the roof, and high visibility red and blue strobes flashing in the front grille. He switched the siren on and fishtailed onto the road, heading for Alicia's home. He tried the number three times, but got the same message.

He knew the route including all the shortcuts, as the Dibble household was only a couple of miles from Alicia's house, but didn't need to use them as traffic was light. Hitting nearly 100mph along some of the wider roads, he completed the usual half-hour journey in eighteen minutes.

He slammed on the brakes as he approached her drive, the car slewing to the left and coming to a stop with the rear end halfway across the road. He silenced the two tones, ripped out the keys and sprinted up the garden path. Before he got halfway he saw the envelope. 'Oh God, oh God, no, please no, God.'

He pulled the letter off the hook, ripped open the envelope and began reading the neat handwriting.

Dear Sam,

You know what you're going to find inside. I'm in the garage. You'll have to go through the house and in the side door. Please be careful as they took some of the floor up and I don't want you to get hurt.

I'm so, so sorry you have to deal with this initially, but I didn't want anyone else to find me and knew you'd come.

Please tell Florence Rizzoli I don't bear her any ill will. I know she was just doing her job, and I hope she finds out who was behind all this, if there was anyone else.

As you know, the Agency was my life since graduating. I loved my job, even the shitty bits, but knew as soon as they arrested me it was over. We both know you never come out the other end of an ordeal like this clean - there'll always be whispers and suspicion, and I'd never be fully trusted again . There was me thinking I might make it to the top one day.

Sam, you'll find $5,000 in the flowerpot near me. I had an emergency go box hidden in the floor of the garage and the money was there in case I had to check out in a hurry, which I guess I now have. Please use it to get your kids something nice or put it in their college fund. Also, please tell Kate I'm sorry, and to keep up the yoga.

You were always a special friend, my dear Sam, and in another time and place, who knows what cards fate would have dealt us, but there we go.

Take care,

All my love

Alicia XXX

Dibble stood paralysed to the spot for what seemed like an age, but was no more than a few seconds. Everything morphed and shifted around him – as if he was standing in the eye of a hurricane looking out at the madness swirling around him. He felt himself sway and came to his senses.

As he put his shoulder against the front door, it offered little resistance. He knew the downstairs well enough, having visited over the years, but stepped carefully over the gaping holes as he made his way to the garden.

Having attended more searches than he would ever be able to remember, he couldn't believe the level of destruction the team had caused. It made even the worst crack house look like the presidential suite at the Fairmont in San Francisco. Every single thing in the house was broken and spoilt. The story of a life – mementos, trinkets, memories and the special things we all keep, completely annihilated.

Stepping over rubbish that had once been something important to Alicia, he approached the side door to the garage. His heart was thumping like a blacksmith striking an anvil, his breathing coming in short bursts. He tried the handle but found the door locked. He kept repeating, 'Oh God, oh God, oh God.'

Taking a step back he kicked at the door. It instantly crashed open, swinging as far back as it could on its hinges before being catapulted back closed. He took a step forward and gingerly turned the handle, as if delaying the inevitable might make the end result different.

He took one step in and saw her. Slumped back in the chair, the blood and brain matter in her hair was still shiny and only beginning to congeal. Her left eye was just a hole, and because of the angle in which she lay, he could see through the socket directly to the wall behind. The back of her skull was completely missing, along with most of her brain.

Dibble fell to his knees, his shoulders heaving. His sobbing became more pronounced with every breath before he let out the most honest, heartfelt guttural sound he'd ever made in his life. He threw his head back and screamed, '*Noooooooooo.*'

'Oh, Leece, it was never meant to end like this. Dear sweet Jesus, no, no. If only you'd hung on, honey, I would've made it alright.'

Dibble was shaken out of the moment by loud banging on the up and over door. 'Hey, everything OK in there? You in there, Alicia? It's Harry next door.'

He called back. 'No, Harry, it's not OK. There's been an accident. I'm law enforcement, please go back home, there's nothing you can do.'

'Well I don't like it, I'm calling the cops.'

'Whatever, Harry.'

Dibble hauled himself up and turned to leave. He saw the thick wad of notes in a flowerpot but shook his head and walked out to the car, tears streaming down his face. He heard the sound of sirens fast approaching and two squad cars screeched to a halt. The officers piled out guns drawn – Dibble remained in the car holding his badge out of the window.

Using correct procedure the patrolmen kept their guns up, instructing Dibble to keep his hands where they could see them and get out of the vehicle. After a minute they established he was who he said he was, and everyone relaxed. He gave them the note and told them where they would find the body of his friend and colleague.

'Boys, there's $5,000 in the garage in a tub, make sure it's all photographed and listed. I'll make a statement, but right now I'm going back to my office. If you need me I'll be at Langley.'

Dibble didn't remember driving back. He must have stopped at red lights but wouldn't be able to tell anyone which ones. He drove down the slope and swung left towards the car pool. The manager was outside with a clipboard walking around a car, studying it. He looked up and waved at Dibble as he came to a stop by the office. 'Hey, that was quick –

did you save any lives?' Dibble didn't look at the man let alone say anything as he dropped the keys in his hand and walked off.

Heading towards the elevator, he heard the sound of laughter and saw two men in white paper suits exiting. 'Hold the door please.' One of the men put his finger on the button. As he got closer the other man spoke. 'Hi, sir, it's Director Dibble isn't it?' The man held out his hand which Dibble ignored. 'Sorry, son, not sure I know you.'

The man pointed down at his protective suit. 'We're on the deep search squad. Me and Oscar here were at that bitch's house. I was the one who found the note in the fire pit. Dirty fucking traitor. We left her a little surprise upstairs, batteries and all. Nice underwear as well – just wondered if you'd heard any news?'

Dibble growled. 'You messed with her underwear?'

'Haha, yeah – left a dildo sticking out of a nice pair of lacy ones. Wish I could've seen her face when she found it.'

Without another word Dibble swung a savage right hook at the man's face, splintering his nose and sending him to the floor screaming, blood pouring through his fingers.

'Nice one, boys – she blew her brains out about an hour ago. You should have seen her face.'

Walking quickly to his office, Dibble felt his eyes start to prickle and he began welling up again. The image of Alicia in the chair with one dead eye open and the other completely missing would forever be etched in his mind. He pulled out his phone and dialled the Englishman.

'Ah, good day to you, to what do I owe the pleasure?'

Sam tried to keep his voice calm, but his nose was blocked and he couldn't disguise the fact he was upset. 'It's Alicia, she committed suicide. I just found her.'

'And?'

'And, she was my friend.'

There was a pause on the line.

'Don't you *dare* go all fucking sentimental on me. I couldn't care less if it was your wife or your mother – you knew what you signed up for all those years ago. You want out? Then just fucking walk away.'

'OK, OK, I get it, it's just…'

'It's *just* fucking *nothing*. Our plans remain unaltered. If anything it helps us – it's a nice diversion, gives them all something else to run around chasing their tails about.'

'I know. Just thought I'd better tell you.'

'Well thanks for the call, old chap. Have a nice day.'

*

Dibble immediately called Rizzoli. She started to cry when he told her what Alicia had put in the note about not blaming her. Rizzoli pulled herself together and called Director Katherine Jackson, who then called Sir

John Leroux in London. Leroux updated Camburn, who called Jenks.

Jenks was in his garden. He'd found a nice piece of driftwood which he'd fixed into the ground, and was arranging some oyster shells around it in a rockery he was creating.

'Hi, James.'

'Can you talk at the moment?'

'Yep, just out in the garden, what's up?'

'I just had a call from the Caretaker. It seems Buckland took her own life about ninety minutes ago.'

'Details?'

'That Rizzoli woman dropped her home. Evidently she tried to get her to stay in a hotel so they could at least try and clean up some of the mess. I don't think anyone realised what lay behind her front door – it would've been quicker to demolish the house and build a new one. They literally ripped it apart.'

The line was quiet for a moment before Jenks spoke. 'Note?'

'Yes. All very sad. Sam Dibble, the one she went to see Rizzoli with, found her. Evidently he'd been trying to reach her but couldn't. He was just about to drive out to her house when he got a text from her.'

'Saying?'

'Basically that she was so sorry. We'd all know what that meant if we received it under the circumstances. He got over there quick as he could but was too late. She must have sent the message seconds before blowing her brains out.'

Camburn could hear the sound of Jenks breathing, and knew there was nothing further to say. 'Thanks for letting me know.'

Chapter 20.

UK.

The day before mission commencement.

Chas Black had done the whole tourist thing around London, even taking an open-top red bus sightseeing tour. He was sitting on a bench in St James's park eating an ice cream when his phone rang. It was a withheld number, so he stayed silent. The voice on the other end said, 'Have you ordered the takeaway yet?' He replied without hesitation. 'I thought we could eat out tonight.'

The American's voice was now familiar and Black felt much more at ease speaking to him. 'Hi, how's it going over there? Everything set?'

'Hi, man, everything's cool – bit like home except they speak funny. Still can't work out which way to look crossing the road though.'

The American chuckled. 'You be careful – how's it going with Mr E? Are you speaking to him regularly? No last minute hitches?'

'No, dude, we're all good.'

'Excellent, so you've spoken to him recently?'

'We're in daily contact, everything's cool.'

'That's what I wanted to hear, buddy. We've all waited for this moment for a long time. So just to recap, he gives the product to you, you give it to us then you both get paid.'

'That's it, simple really. Then we buckle up and enjoy the ride once you guys put it out there.'

The American wanted more. 'Are you able to say exactly when the handover will be?'

'Like I said, man, I'll call you when I've got it.'

'OK, although it would be nice to know if it's going to be tomorrow or Wednesday, or even Thursday.'

Black didn't want to give anything away, but he also didn't want to start pissing off the organisation that was going to change the world, put him on a pedestal, and pay him handsomely for making it all happen. The truth was he didn't exactly know himself. Englefield had mentioned about a last-minute change of plan to protect them, but he'd no idea what the change was. He couldn't tell his contact that as it would look like Englefield didn't trust him. 'Look, all I can say is Mr E doesn't hit town until late tomorrow evening. He's been on a little holiday himself, so I doubt he's gonna start running around as soon as he gets here.'

'OK, that's helpful. We've got a lot to put in place to make sure this all runs smoothly.'

'I know, dude, I know. I'll let you know.'

Amsterdam, the same time.

Englefield woke late following a particularly heavy night. He'd fallen in with a group of Irish guys, in Amsterdam for a stag party. He'd started chatting to them in a coffee shop just off Dam Square where he showed one of the less experienced how to roll a joint. One thing led to another, and seven hours later he stumbled into bed in his superior grade room at the Krasnapolsky.

He ordered a late breakfast, pulled out his laptop and logged into the email account and typed *Jim*. By the time he'd finished eating a one-word reply appeared in the drafts folder – *Ray*.

They'd changed the daily code word yet again, as agreed the last time they sat in the same room back in the US. Englefield had run through the protocol numerous times with Black to make sure he'd got it. They'd let the same word run for a while, then change it, then change it again. No patterns or predictability, which they figured would stop anyone interfering with their grand plan.

Englefield thought the Agency would be trying to trace him by now, or maybe they weren't? He wondered if they'd even discovered the data breach – why would they? There'd been nothing on all the chat and conspiracy sites, and Black would've heard from *Welikeleaks* if there was anything in the air. Apart from everyone wondering what the damn Ruskies were up to, there was no mention of anything else bubbling under.

He thought back to how they'd covered their tracks, and whether they'd forgotten any detail which would leave a thread, but was happy they'd covered everything. No one knew he was now Rick Mills, not even Black. He'd changed his appearance, and the new passport and Amex card he'd sourced from the dark net couldn't be traced back to him.

Black had checked into a West London hotel under his new identity, Gary Taylor. The long hippie hair and straggly beard had gone – he was now clean-shaven and sported a short back and sides. He told the receptionist he was working nights and didn't want to be disturbed for any reason, and as instructed by Englefield, disabled the GPS function on the phone supplied by *Welikeleaks*. He then immediately left the hotel and booked into a shabby bed and breakfast nearby where it was cash only, registering as Don Henley.

As per their plan, Englefield waited until 1pm before drafting another message. It would be midday in London, the time he'd told Black to expect contact. He poured another coffee and browsed some news sites. They all seemed to be asking the same question – why had Russia pulled out of the forthcoming G20 summit without giving an explanation? Experts offered opinions, but none got even close to the truth.

Englefield typed the word *Hi*. Almost immediately the word *Fidelity* appeared as the next draft.

Everything was fine. The former CIA analyst typed *Are you staying in venue B*? Again, the next draft appeared seconds later. *Yes*. Englefield composed a paragraph. *A phone will be delivered tomorrow at 9am. Wait outside for the courier. Do not use it other than to turn on. I'll text you on new phone with further instructions*. Black replied. *Understood*.

Englefield lay back on his bed and smiled – the additional layers of protection were settling into place, removing them ever further from any prying eyes that might be out there.

He planned to have an easy few hours, with a spa afternoon and massage before dinner, and an earlier bedtime than the previous night. He had a few joints worth of grass to dispose of, and it would break his heart to have to flush it away, so planned to see it off on his balcony later. Tomorrow he would be fresh – ready to catch the late afternoon Eurostar to London.

Five minutes later, Dagenham, UK.

Dagenham is an area just over the Essex border on the outskirts of East London. Home to the Ford Motor Company factory, it was once full of thriving industries owing to its proximity to the Thames and Tilbury Docks. Everything had changed now, leaving the industrial units and factories decaying and empty. The money pumped into Docklands never quite reached that far up river, and the sky seemed to be permanently slate grey. Not even the sun wanted to come to Dagenham.

The old factory had been chosen due to the distance from the main A13 and its isolated position, the surrounding units long demolished. A *for sale* sign had been nailed to the entrance of the service road for the past fifteen years, so when an approach was made from a prospective buyer, the agent couldn't believe his luck.

The man told the agent he represented a foreign company, and wished to conduct ground surveys and take measurements over a few days before deciding to take the matter further. Soil samples would need to be analysed and detailed topographic plans drawn up, so they would appreciate being left to complete their work without interruption. The agent willingly handed over the keys to the gate padlock and factory doors, telling the man to drop them back at his convenience.

Outside the factory, a handful of men walked around in reflective jackets holding tripods, digging holes and taking measurements, but not actually doing anything. From a distance it appeared a hive of activity, but it was all smoke and mirrors. Inside, the Englishman was sitting at a table in an old office.

The room would have been the manager's office, and his men had cleaned it as best they could. Compared to what was once the factory floor outside, the room was pristine – every other area was covered in layers of dust. With little glass left in the windows and skylights, the outside had blown inside for years.

On the table was a laptop, scanner and two piles of envelopes. A power lead fed through a cracked pane from outside, hooked up to a generator. The large pile was the *done* ones, the smaller one *to do*. The task had taken a lot longer than the Englishman had anticipated. Each envelope had to be scanned, the scan read and its contents digested, before being placed in its own folder on the laptop which carried the recipient's details and a personalised message.

Vasily Yahontov had driven through the night with the rucksack, only stopping to refuel in order to get back to London for Sunday morning. The Englishman originally estimated they'd have everything in place by the evening, but that had proved to be way off. Due to the amount of information the envelopes contained, he'd be unlikely to have everything finished before the following day.

The Englishman was in the process of writing a précis of the information contained in one envelope dated 9th September 1976 – the recipient's folder marked *China*. On the first page was a list of the countries involved in a joint operation – Great Britain, Germany, France and the USA. He had to re-read parts of the report, as on first inspection he couldn't believe his eyes.

His attention was diverted to activity in the corner of the screen – email activity. He enlarged the window, read the mail and sat back in his chair, cursing. '*Der'mo.*' One of his assistants looked up. 'Sir?'

‘They changed the check-in word again, and now this shit.’

‘What have they done?’

The Englishman re-read the last messages. ‘Englefield’s sending Black a phone. And, Black has moved out of the hotel and disabled GPS on the phone we gave him. Cunning bastards.’

The assistant said nothing, but the Englishman now laughed.

‘They think they’re needles in a haystack. Two new numbers in a city of millions of phones. They know we’d never identify them but it doesn’t matter, they are fools. There’s nothing they can do to take control that I haven’t already thought of. Let them play with their phones and see how they like it when I ram them up their arses.’

The same time, The Shop, London.

James Camburn was in the communal seating area eating a pork pie. He looked up as Maureen called out. ‘Sir, you’d better have a look at this.’

Camburn got up, brushed the crumbs off his waistcoat and read the new email drafts over her shoulder. ‘Cunning bastards. Well, short of fishing around The Huntsman’s Lodge, I can’t see what we can do.’

Maureen gave him a look. ‘What, capture every mobile signal within a fifty-yard radius? Have you any idea how many that is? It would take weeks to research them all. Until Jenks gets him alone in his room, we're basically stuffed.'

Chapter 21.

Tuesday 10th March. Mission is live.

Jenks made a final kit check and put his brown contacts in. He broke the crutch down to its component parts and dismantled the leg brace, placing it all in his rucksack along with clothing and other specialist kit. He'd had confirmation that nothing had changed with Rick Mills' Eurostar booking, and was aware of the new phones, but there was nothing they could do at this stage.

Ideally he would've liked a recent photo of Black and the name he was using now, but had learnt over the years to focus on what he had. It wasn't ideal, but if Black got away, he got away. They all come again sooner or later. Englefield was the main target and the retrieval of the data he had with him. Anything else was a bonus.

Jenks slid his radio into the custom mesh harness, pulling it down into the small of his back. He'd set up Bluetooth connection to his throat mic and a transmit button he'd fitted to the Ducati's handlebar. A slight movement of his left thumb was all that was required to open comms to the Shop.

They kept the call signs simple – he was Alpha One, like he'd often been in his army days. Backup units were assigned their own call signs, but due to the unbreakable nature of the encryption, first or nicknames were often used.

Jenks pulled up the top of his plain black leathers and conducted a signal check. 'Control receiving Alpha One, report signals please.'

He heard Maureen in his tiny wireless earpiece. 'Alpha One, you are R5 – loud and clear.'

'Received. I'm setting off, I'll call when closer to the RVP.'

'Received, control out.'

*

Jenks liked Maureen. He'd worked with her on many jobs over the years, and always found her calm and unflappable during a live operation.

She'd been recruited to the Shop, personally selected by Camburn, who'd been on friendly terms with her at MI6 where she'd worked in target development. People back then assumed she would remain single having shown no interest in dating. She referred to herself as a plain Jane, due to the fact that she was indeed very ordinary looking, slightly plump and with hair that seemed allergic to any attempts at styling. But everything changed when she met a man purely by chance, who stopped to help when her shopping bag split.

They got talking, he asked her to go for a coffee, and before long they were an item. Everyone who knew her was delighted, and she seemed happier than she'd ever been. The courtship was comparatively brief, and within six months they were engaged. A date had been set for Sunday 10th July 2005, and a small hotel booked for the low-key reception.

Tragically everything had to be cancelled at the last moment. On the morning of Thursday 7th July 2005 her future husband was on his way to pick up the wedding rings. They'd needed minor adjustment, and he was only planning to be away from his office for an hour at the most. Hopping onto a number 30 bus in Tavistock Square, he made his way upstairs to the back. Stepping over a large rucksack, he settled himself next to a young man aged about eighteen. The man was called Hasib Hussain, and five seconds later Maureen's fiancé was vaporised by one of the 7/7 bombs.

Camburn had called in to see her at home, not only to offer his condolences, but an opportunity for payback. She resigned from MI6 the following morning and never looked back.

The Shop was manned by just a few handpicked staff. Apart from Camburn himself, Jo Fox was the veteran, having been deployed there at its inception back in 1988. Now in her early sixties, she still ran marathons, was an expert in cyber infiltration, and held a pilot's licence as well as being the resident drone expert. Whether it was a 12" hi res camera drone or an 8,000 kilo fully laden attack missile, Jo could fly it.

Two other permanent staff were undoubtedly on the autistic spectrum, which was exactly why Camburn recruited them. Miles and Jack Moore were identical twins in their mid-thirties, lived together and were ex-GCHQ. Anyone meeting them for the first time would undoubtedly describe them as slightly odd. But, the way their brains were wired meant they had a rare ability to look at a problem from different angles simultaneously, finding alternative solutions which at first glance could look completely mad.

*

Jenks started the Ducati. He was in no rush as check-in started from 3pm. Englefield wasn't due to leave Amsterdam until late afternoon so wouldn't arrive at the hotel until after 9pm.

He'd fixed a false number plate to his bike, registered to a man in the north of England with an identical model. He'd tasked Miles to check the real bike bearing that registration was taxed and insured and not reported stolen. Automatic number plate readers were becoming common, and he didn't want to inadvertently bring attention to himself by setting one off for a minor misdemeanour.

Pulling down the smoked visor on his black helmet, he set off. Keeping well within the limit, the journey was uneventful apart from an update from Maureen.

'Alpha One receiving.'

Jenks depressed the button on the underside of his handgrip. 'Go ahead.'

'Quick update, Jack's hacked into the cameras at Central Station – we should be able to put our man on the train.'

'Received, out.'

He continued through the tunnel, joining the heavy traffic on the A13 and made his way to the RVP. Passing Tower Bridge he thumbed the transmit button. 'Control from Alpha One.'

'Go ahead.'

'Maurs, are you ready with the kill switch?'

'All good to go. All cameras within one mile radius of point zero.'

Jenks exited Ludgate Hill, and as he crossed the lights into Fleet Street, transmitted. 'On my mark, three, two, one, kill.'

Careful not to get caught directly behind or in front of any buses with onboard cameras which the Shop couldn't control, Jenks twisted the throttle and sped towards Soho. The men and women controlling and viewing the capital's CCTV were frantically picking up phones, reporting blank screens. Likewise, TFL observers had lost the feed from outside every underground station between Tower Hill and Green Park, already blaming the failure on maintenance budget cuts.

Jenks snaked his way through the side streets, not drawing any attention to himself. Londoners were used to seeing despatch riders everywhere, going too fast and taking unnecessary risks, but he kept within the limit of sensible riding, barely drawing a second glance from anyone.

Entering Wardour Street, he thumbed the button. 'Control receiving Alpha One.'

'Go ahead.'

'How's the RVP looking?'

He recognised Jo Fox's voice. 'Not clear, I repeat not clear. Two females out for a smoke break. Stand by.'

Jenks pictured her sitting on a rooftop somewhere nearby. 'Received.'

Jo Fox was staring intently at the images from the drone she was flying over Chinatown in the heart of Soho. The noise level meant the faint whirring was drowned out by the cacophony of city life. And, no one generally looks up in London.

Jenks slowed and considered looping round the block when his earpiece came to life. 'Alpha One, you are green to go, I repeat green to go. Both back inside.'

Jenks continued along Wardour Street, turning into Dansey Place, a small grubby mews which smelt strongly of rotting food and cooking oil. Most of the properties backing onto it were restaurants and food shops, apart from one, which was a safe house owned and maintained by MI6. It had a small up and over garage door secured by a combination lock. Camburn had arranged through Sir John Leroux to mark the property as unavailable due to redecoration for the next week.

The Ducati purred up to the garage and Jenks leant over, rearranged the tumblers, threw the door up and drove in. Checking around, he saw the garage was set up as requested, with a small table, mirror, stool and anglepoise lamp. The only other item was a large empty Samsonite rollercase.

He pulled off his leathers, stripping down to his boxers, socks and tee-shirt. He kept his radio strapped to his back and put on a floral pattern shirt, jeans and trainers. Fixing the transmit button inside his shirt, he sat down at the table, adjusting the lamp so the beam shone on his head.

Reaching into his rucksack, he pulled out a small bag containing the high quality wig he'd selected from his collection in the underground store. He fixed it in place with strong gum, brushing it into a centre parting. The dark brown hair fell just below his shoulders, and looking at his reflection, he was reminded of a man called Neil Oliver, a Scotsman who presented wildlife and archaeological TV programmes, which he enjoyed. He topped his new hair with an orange and green beanie hat.

With transformation nearly complete, he tore open a vacuum-sealed bag and the thin orange puffer jacket expanded to near its normal size. He gave it a couple of shakes to plump the feathers and put it on.

Before putting his rucksack into the suitcase, he took out the last three items to complete his metamorphosis. He assembled the crutch and laid it to one side while he put the full leg brace together, strapping it around his right leg. It almost stopped his knee from bending, which was exactly the look he wanted. Putting on a pair of clear-lensed trendy tortoiseshell spectacles, he was ready. 'Control from Alpha One.'

'Go ahead.'

'Confirm I am green to exit.'

There was a slight pause before Jo Fox transmitted the coast was clear, and Maureen confirmed the CCTV was again off, this time within a 100-yard radius of the hotel. Opening the garage door, Hamish Wilson limped out pulling his suitcase and started the short walk to The Huntsman's Lodge.

*

Jenks hobbled through the doors of the hotel and briefly transmitted. 'Cameras on please.' As he crossed the lobby he recognised Arianna from his review of the hotel's CCTV. She looked up to see an interesting looking disabled man approaching the desk. Not classically handsome, but he had an agreeable face and lovely hair. The Latvian liked long hair on a man.

'Good afternoon, sir, welcome to The Huntsman's Lodge, how can I help?'

Jenks looked her up and down which she mistook for being checked out, and blushed slightly. He was checking, but it was for a name badge.

'Good afternoon to you, lassie, you must be Arianna.' Jenks rested the crutch against the reception desk and held out his right hand. 'Hamish Wilson, we spoke on the phone.'

Arianna felt a slight flutter that he'd remembered her name. 'Oh hi, Mr Wilson, lovely to meet you. Let's get you checked in and I'll get someone to bring your case up.'

'Och don't worry yourself, hen, I can manage it fine.'

She blushed even more, wondering if she'd inadvertently insinuated he wasn't capable of coping.

Jenks gave her his warmest smile. 'I like to do things myself, but appreciate the offer. I refuse to be a slave to this bloody thing.' As he spoke he slapped the leg support, defusing the situation.

Normally he'd do everything possible not to draw attention, preferring to be the grey man nobody noticed. For now though, he was happy for people to remember the long-haired trendy Scotsman who walked with a crutch. It was unlikely enquiries would ever be made at the hotel, but if they were, people would remember a man who didn't exist.

Having completed registration, opting for express checkout, Jenks made his way to the lift. Once in his room he took off the leg brace and paced out the dimensions. All rooms on the fourth floor were the same size and layout, but all had a different theme.

He wasn't entirely sure what statement his room was trying to make, but everything was very modern, with bold colours that almost clashed, but not quite. He knew Englefield's room next door had more of a period feel, with faux antique furniture and hunting prints on the wall in keeping with the history of the building. He checked the view, seeing the rooftops of the smaller buildings adjacent to the hotel and the green space of St Anne's churchyard beyond.

He laid his laptop and a small Tupperware box on the bed. Taking out a device no bigger than a cigarette packet, he connected it to his laptop and remote connected to the hotel's reservation section. The two other rooms on the fourth floor were shown as reserved, but the guests would never arrive. They'd been booked by Jo Fox, fully paid up for three nights. The hotel was unlikely to resell them and would put it down to some guests having more money than sense.

Jenks's ear bud crackled into life. 'Alpha One receiving.'

'Go ahead.'

'Target has boarded the train. No delays expected.'

'All received, Maurs.'

He pushed one of his two room-key cards into the device, watching the screen as The Huntsman's Lodge system recognised it as the key to room 403. He selected *delete,* wiping the card. Calling up the reservation for room 402, Jenks selected *key write.* With one further click on *confirm,* he now had a key for Englefield's room. A few seconds later he inserted the card into the lock for room 402 and saw the light go green.

Working quickly, he inserted what looked like a normal plug adaptor into the socket under the window, plugging the lamp back into it. He then dialled a number on his mobile, silently connecting to the listening device inside, linking it to his laptop.

The ceiling light was an elaborate black cartwheel design with light bulbs made to look like candles – the perfect place to hide a tiny black fisheye camera offering a 360-degree view of the room. The miniature camera had a battery life of forty-eight hours, but Jenks hoped he wouldn't need more than twenty-four. He had no coverage of the bathroom, but was content anything said or done worth knowing about would be in the main room. Englefield had no reason to suspect anyone even knew he was staying at the hotel, so antisurveillance measures were unlikely.

He slipped silently out of room 402 and back into his own. Inserting the key card back in the writer, he cancelled it and reprogrammed it for his own room. He would have liked to keep it as a backup, but when Arianna programmed Englefield's room keys, the system would show one had already been created. If his plan went smoothly, he wouldn't need it anyway.

Jenks lay on his bed propped up against the headboard. Selecting the hotels CCTV system, he rewound the recording covering the hotel entrance, noting the exact time he appeared. He saw himself approach the desk, and minutes later limping towards the lift and disappearing inside. He made a note of the exact time he'd left the gaze of the cameras, pleased there were none in the lift or on his floor. He then recorded the same scene happening four floors below at that moment, allowing an extra minute, saving it into a file on his desktop. He would record the main lobby and lift area again later when the light had changed.

*

Englefield heard the subtle change in sound as the Eurostar powered out of the Channel Tunnel, now on the last leg of its journey into London. He turned on a new unused handset under the table and typed a short text message to the new phone Black had received from him. *Meet at the London Eye 9.45pm tomorrow for key handover.*

Black was sitting at a table finishing his meal in the outside piazza of Covent Garden. It was chilly, but he was well wrapped up, and like other die-hards around him, wanted to be able to smoke. He'd been checking his new phone like a teenager since receiving it as arranged the previous day, and quickly pulled it from his pocket when he felt the vibration. He read the message and smiled. He had to admire Englefield's ingenuity and the measures to protect them both.

He typed a quick response confirming he understood, and put the phone back in his pocket. Englefield read the message just before removing the battery and snapping the SIM card. He then wrapped everything in a carrier bag along with his other rubbish and casually deposited it into the bin of his first class carriage.

*

Jenks ate the food he'd brought with him and was watching the news when he received an update that the Eurostar had arrived at St Pancras, and the surveillance team were behind Englefield's taxi bound for Soho.

He picked up his laptop and waited. Twenty minutes later a slightly overweight man with black hair and a goatee beard sauntered into reception to check in. Joshua Englefield III aka Rick Mills had arrived.

Activating the sound feed and the fish-eye camera, Jenks waited. He watched as Englefield walked to the lift, and a few minutes later heard through the wall the door to room 402 open and shut.

Englefield did what everyone does when entering a hotel room for the first time, walking around acclimatising himself, opening drawers and cupboards. He checked out the bathroom then sat on the bed and bounced a couple of times. Jenks saw him nod, presumably agreeing with himself that it was suitably comfortable. He then went to the main wardrobe which Jenks knew contained the room safe.

It was the same as the one in his room – a state-of-the-art fingerprint-secured mini vault. He watched Englefield studying the instructions, placing his left index finger on a reader next to the handle, press the store button, then repeat the process. He opened the safe door and went to fetch something from his luggage. Even though the lens distorted the picture, Jenks could see it was a memory stick.

Jenks was now presented with a new conundrum. He was almost sure the stick contained the decryption key for the final handover, but Englefield was smart. There was no way of knowing if an inbuilt wipe program would trigger if the stick wasn't dealt with in exactly the way Englefield had set up. Jenks could easily get back in the room and pick most locks, but without Englefield's fingerprint, short of blowing the door off with plastic explosive, the safe was impenetrable. Even if he confronted Englefield early, the dissemination could be triggered by Englefield not following protocol he'd pre-programmed. Too many loose ends and unknowns left no alternative but to let events unfold.

He watched as Englefield set up his laptop on the desk, plugging it into the adaptor socket transmitting every sound. He then went to the mini bar, perused its contents and took out a small bottle of champagne. Twisting the cap off, he took a swig.

Jenks saw Englefield studying the room information card, looking back and forth between the card and his screen, and was sure he was inputting the Wi-Fi code. Englefield continued typing whilst taking occasional swigs from the bottle. Jenks saw his phone flashing, showing an incoming call.

'Good evening, old chap, it's me.'

Jenks spoke quietly. 'Hi, James.'

'Another draft email exchange just happened.'

Jenks nodded. 'I'm watching him as we speak but I can't see the screen, what's it say?

He heard Camburn's chair squeak and pictured him swivelling round to get a better look at Maureen's screen.

'This is from Englefield and reads as follows.'

All in place for tomorrow. Hendrix is on, transfer at 9pm. Part two as per my text.

Camburn continued. 'And the next draft is from Black.'

All understood.

Jenks leant against the headboard, thinking. Camburn spoke first. 'Seems like the transfer is 9pm tomorrow but what do you think this Hendrix business is?'

He ran the word around his head. 'I don't know; JC. I can hear everything in the room, but there's no music on. We know they like old stuff – perhaps they're going to do the fan pilgrimage thing, like visit the flat he died in, that's in London. Is there a Hendrix tribute act on tomorrow? I honestly have no idea, but I'll think about it.'

'And the reference to the text?

Jenks paused. 'I think it's the arrangements for Englefield to hand the decryption key to Black, that's part two, however they transfer the files. With so much money at stake he'll want to see it in his account before giving them the key to Pandora's box – it would be like selling a Rolls Royce to a punter you've never met and agreeing they can drop the money in later.'

‘Makes sense.’

‘There’s one more thing, James, I saw him put a memory stick in the room safe. My betting is it’s the decryption key. I’ve thought about getting at it but it’s too risky. Now we know the time of the transfer, unless he takes it out with him before that, we just keep behind him and watch.’

Jenks heard Camburn blowing out air. ‘As much as I’d love to get my hands on it, I concur. We know he’s fastidious with his security measures so have to assume they extend to the key. If we touch it, we could be pulling the trigger.’

The call concluded and Jenks continued to watch Englefield, who was in effect sitting next to him, separated by just eight inches of brick. He saw him pick up the room phone and heard him order a lobster salad, fries and a bottle of Chablis. He then went into the bathroom and Jenks could hear water running, making it look increasingly likely that Englefield was staying in for the night.

Dagenham.
The same time.

The Englishman finished scanning every document except one, undecided whether to destroy it. He needed to go back to his hotel and grab some badly needed rest – in his mind he still felt like the young idealist he once was, but time was catching up with his body. The pain in his hip was getting worse but he wanted to avoid taking strong painkillers as they dulled his senses, and now more than ever he needed to stay sharp.

He knew who it would be as soon as his phone started ringing, answering with a hint of irritation. 'Good evening, Sam, I take it you're calling about the latest email.'

'Well, yes.'

'I see them when you do, and would of course contact you if I felt it affected our plans.'

'You're not concerned at all? They've got phones we don't know about, and the text didn't go to the phone we got Black or his own one – the trace request was left in place so I still get updates on any phone traffic, but I've had nothing.'

The Englishman let out a sigh. 'My dear boy, don't panic over trivialities. Whatever clever plan they think they've come up with will not work, I promise you that. Englefield will come to me when he realises it's the only option.'

'I'm sure you're right. Any idea what that Hendrix crap is?'

'None at all. Let them play their word games, it changes nothing. I'll call if I need you, Sam. I'm going to head off now.'

'You OK? You sound a bit…'

'I'm just tired and my bloody hip is killing me. Tomorrow's a big day so I'm going to say toodle pip and get going.'

Room 402.
The same time.

Jenks watched Englefield eat, place his tray outside the door and disappear into the bathroom leaving his phone and laptop on the desk. Jenks sensed he was watching a man who was comfortable he'd pulled together a foolproof plan, and was now going to relax before it came to fruition.

After an hour Englefield walked naked from the bathroom and stood in front of the full length mirror, completely unaware that someone was looking at him looking at himself. He glanced down at his belly, holding the dough-like flab in each hand, shaking it slightly. He then leant in close to the mirror, seeing something.

Jenks watched him tilting his head up, concerned he'd spotted the tiny camera and instinctively drew his Glock. Englefield tilted his chin up and Jenks breathed a sigh of relief as his target put his fingers to his face and squeezed a spot.

Shortly after, Englefield climbed into bed and put the light straight out. Jenks settled himself for the night, but as he'd done on countless missions, metaphorically slept with one eye open, although it was his hearing he was relying on. He put in ear buds, connected them to his laptop and turned the volume up.

He was woken by Englefield three times during the night. Once by the volume of his snoring, once when he got up to use the toilet, and once just from the clink of the glass on the nightstand when Englefield took a sip of water.

Chapter 22.

The day.

Jenks had been dressed and ready for two hours before Englefield ambled down for breakfast. He pressed the transmit button inside his shirt. 'Control from Alpha One. Target on the move, believed going for breakfast. All units stand by in case he goes walkies after.'

'Alpha One from control all received.'

He gave Englefield five minutes, watching him take a seat, then headed down.

Jenks limped into the restaurant, gave his room number quietly to the girl on the door and headed towards the tables at the back where Englefield was being served coffee. It was a high-ceilinged room with classic black and white floor tiles and large ferns placed in well-thought-out positions. A huge chandelier hung from the ceiling, and the tables were laid with thick linen and expensive silverware. When he was within ten feet of Englefield's table, Jenks felt in his pocket for his phone and depressed the on switch quickly three times. The opening notes of YMCA sounded.

Putting the phone to his ear, Jenks acted like he was trying to keep the conversation private, but loud enough that Englefield glanced his way. 'But why?

You cannae do this, I've arranged everything... Och, well just let me know as soon as ye can if you're coming. We all need space, but this is ridiculous.' He ended the call and accidently on purpose caught Englefield's gaze.

Jenks rolled his eyes and held his phone out, shaking his head. Englefield smiled as Jenks passed. 'We've all been there, dude, good luck!' Jenks continued walking. 'Cheers, pal, I'm going to need it.'

Both men ate their breakfast. Jenks didn't once look at Englefield, but saw that he himself had been observed at least three times, having caught the glances in the reflection of the large mirror next to him – precisely why he'd chosen that particular table.

Englefield signed for his breakfast and made his way out and towards the lifts. Jenks raised the menu to shield his mouth, speaking in a whisper. 'All units from Alpha One, target on the move, stand by for further.'

The outside team responded, Jenks initialled his tab and walked lamely back to his room. He noted the exact time he arrived, adding it to his record. As he watched Englefield waiting for him to give some sign of his intentions, he rewound the few minutes he'd missed of Englefield's room movements, pleased to see he hadn't retrieved the memory stick from the safe.

It was agreed Englefield would be kept under close surveillance wherever he went for the day – sometimes you just had to let a job run. There would be men and woman on the ground who were at the top of the surveillance tree, and all would be armed. Englefield had given the time of the handover but no one knew for sure if he'd change it again.

Englefield checked his wallet, put on his jacket and walked to the door, paying no attention to the safe. If he'd taken the memory stick, Jenks would have changed the plan and joined the surveillance team, but the fact he'd left it suggested the evening handover was unaltered.

'All units, target on the move, stand by for the off.' Men and women no one would suspect were surveillance operatives moved to their pre-determined positions. Couples in nearby cafés, street cleaners, window shoppers, beggars, delivery men on bicycles – even a colourful rickshaw driven by a dreadlocked armed man carrying two fully armed faux tourists eased into position two streets away.

Everyone carried alternative jackets, hats, spectacles and scarves which would change their appearance in a second if required, reducing the chances of triggering a second look of recognition from the target.

Jenks watched Englefield exiting the lift and walking towards the exit onto Dean Street. 'All units, target is leaving hotel. Fawn coloured waist-length zip-up jacket, bottle green sweatshirt, blue jeans and white Nike trainers. Shaping up for a left left left, and out of my view.'

He heard the first unit take over. 'Control from Alpha Seven, I have the eye. Target is heading north towards Old Compton Street. Now left left left into same.'

Jo Fox's voice came over the air. 'Copy that, Alpha Ten, are you in position?'

'Control from Alpha Ten, I'm outside Compton's bar.'

'Received, he's about thirty yards from you.'

'I see him, I'll take the eye.'

Joshua Englefield ambled along, looking in windows, checking out bars and restaurants and generally being a tourist. The day was his, with only one appointment later that evening. He noticed a young woman with short cropped hair standing outside a gay nightclub with some sort of tray hung around her neck. As he got closer he saw it contained rows of rainbow badges.

The girl gave him a beaming smile. 'Hi, would you like a free badge?' Englefield stopped and looked at the lapel pins. Despite being wealthy and on the verge of incredible riches, even the most affluent couldn't resist something free. He smiled back. 'They're free, are they?'

'Yep, absolutely. What we say to people is, if they want to give a couple of pounds, it all goes to a local charity offering support to LGBTQ+ people who arrive in London and need a bit of a helping hand.'

'That's really cool, well done. Yeah, I'd love one, but let me pay you.' Englefield opened his wallet and handed the girl a twenty-pound note.

‘I’m sorry but I haven’t got much change, I’ve only been out for a little while.’

Englefield shook his head. ‘No, take it – it’s for a good cause.’

The girl thanked him profusely. ‘Here, let me put it on for you, the pins are a bit tricky.’

She leant in towards him, securing the brightly coloured badge to his left breast pocket. ‘There, that looks nice. One down, 199 to go!’

They both laughed, and Englefield continued along the road, glancing down at his bright badge, feeling proud he was making a little statement all of his own. Once out of earshot the girl pushed a switch in her pocket. ‘Control from Alpha Ten, target has GPS tracker attached, still proceeding west on the south footway towards junction with Wardour Street.’

‘Alpha Ten from Alpha Two, I have the eye. Good work, Ten.’

With all the operatives on the ground, Jo Fox standing by with a drone, and their target now unknowingly carrying a GPS tracker, Englefield was well and truly under close observation. He appeared to be following no predetermined route, behaving like any other tourist on their first trip to London.

He purchased a small guide book from a newsagent and was watched turning the foldout map around, trying to work out which direction to head in. The team followed him to Carnaby Street, once the centre of Swinging London, but now all corporate and designed to look like it hadn’t been designed. He browsed a few shops, stopped for a coffee and pastry and made his way into Oxford Street.

The rest of the day was as uneventful – not once did he turn round abruptly, double back on himself or use any of the antisurveillance techniques the team would have recognised. He was a man seemingly without a care in the world, even though in a few hours his actions would change that world forever, if he was successful.

At 5.30pm Englefield returned. The surveillance team estimated they'd covered at least six miles, during which their target had done precisely nothing of interest.

Englefield peeled off his socks and disappeared into the bathroom. Shortly after Jenks heard the sound of the toilet flushing and the bath filling. After making a coffee Englefield went back into the bathroom and Jenks heard the sound of 'All Along the Watchtower' being sung badly out of tune, and the occasional splashing of water.

Jenks used the time to recheck his equipment, paying particular attention to the perfume atomiser in the crutch handle. Opening his shoulder bag, he memorised where he'd placed each item. Now all he had left to do was sit, listen, watch and wait.

Chapter 23.

End game.

Just after 6pm Chas Black was still taking in the sights. It was his first visit to the UK and with nearly four hours until his rendezvous with Englefield, he was seeing as much as he could. He checked his watch, pulled out his phone, clicked on an app and smiled.

As he was putting the handset back into his pocket the phone *Welikeleaks* had given him rang. He recognised the voice immediately. 'Have you ordered the takeaway yet?'

'I thought we could eat out tonight.'

'My dear fellow, how are you? How's London?

'Hey, man, it's really cool. Looks just like the photos – big red buses, pretty girls and warm beer.'

The Englishman wasn't paying much attention to what Black was saying, concentrating on background noise. Standing out above the traffic rumble and horns hooting was the sound of birds – lots of birds, clearly taking off in large numbers and children squealing with delight – pigeons.

'Have you seen many of the sights? Buckingham Palace? Big Ben?'

'Yeah, I saw that clock, it's awesome. I had to laugh when I saw the Houses of Parliament, I thought to myself *you guys are gonna be out of a job soon.* Man, I can't wait for it to happen.'

'Me neither, old chap, me neither. Have you been anywhere else of note?'

'Well you guys certainly know how to honour your heroes. I'm looking at some sailor dude statue on just about the biggest pole you ever saw.'

The Englishman gesticulated towards a radio handset, making it clear to one of his men to pass it quickly. 'Ah, that's…hang on one second, I've got another call coming in – hold on and I'll get rid of it.'

The Englishman muted the phone and transmitted. 'All units, he's in Trafalgar Square, I repeat, Trafalgar Square.'

His message was answered immediately. 'Sir, this is unit three, we're two minutes out, keep him talking and if possible get a better location – it'll be packed this time of the evening.'

'Quick as you can.' The Englishman returned to his call. 'Sorry about that, bloody Vodafone trying to sell me more minutes. Now, that sailor dude as you put it, is none other than our very own Lord Nelson, the finest admiral to have ever served in the British Navy. If you've seen him you must have seen those magnificent lions as well?'

Black sounded animated. 'Man, I'm leaning on one *right now* talking to you!'

'Well I never.' The Englishman muted the phone for a few seconds. 'He's leaning against one of the lions, look for someone on their phone.'

The reply came back. ‘Sir, everyone leaning on a lion will be on their phone.’

The Englishman began to lose his temper. ‘Just do your fucking job.’

Returning to the call he said, ‘Have you noticed anything unusual about them?’

‘Er no, in what way?’

‘Well not many people know this, but they’re all wrong. A lion lies down with one of his hind legs tucked under his body. The sculptor wanted symmetry, so made them with both back legs facing the same way. Lions don’t do that in the wild.’

Black looked at the hind quarters. ‘Well I’ll be damned, you’re right.’

‘Now tonight, everything set? The money’s waiting to be transferred once we’re in receipt of the merchandise. Can you give me a rough idea of timings?’

‘Everything’s cool, man, no sweat. I should have it in my hands just before 10pm.’

‘And you’ll call me as soon as you have it?’

‘Of course.’

‘Well look, I’m heading back to town shortly and will meet you personally for the handover once you’ve got it. I might even buy you a little drink.’

As Black was listening to the Englishman he failed to notice an SUV with blackened windows pull up sharply at the kerb.

‘If we can’t celebrate this, man, what can… Hey! What the fuck...’

At the same moment as the Englishman could hear the sound of electricity sizzling, Black caught a flash of blue out of the corner of his eye. It was the last thing he saw before Charles Black's world turned the same colour as his name.

Two burly men in tee-shirts grabbed him under each armpit. Dragging him towards the waiting vehicle one of them said, 'Come on, Terry, sober up, mate, the party's over, let's get you home safe and sound.'

For anyone bothering to look, it was a familiar sight of a drunk being rescued by his friends.

*

By 7pm Englefield was dressed and ready. Jenks watched his every move intently. After standing in front of the mirror, examining his beard and opening another button on his shirt, he splashed aftershave around his neck and rubbed a few drops on each wrist. Jenks looked closely and recognised the Tom Ford cologne bottle. Englefield gave a little nod to himself and picked up his key card. Jenks thumbed his mic. 'Alpha Four from Alpha One, target on the move, confirm you're in position.'

'Affirmative – if he leaves the hotel we'll see him.'

'Copy that, Alpha One out.'

Jenks watched as Englefield walked past the wardrobe and out of the door.

From his screen, he was able to see Englefield enter the lobby a few minutes later and head away from the street door. He thumbed his mic. 'Alpha Four, he's going to the bar.'

Jenks was content Englefield wasn't just going for a quick pint. He'd left his jacket in his room and was going to while away the time before the handover, happy to unwind a little as the next two steps were simple. The labour-intensive work was done and now he only had to press a button. The second part would be to hand over the decryption key in person otherwise why keep it separate, when he could just store it on his laptop. Either way, it didn't matter.

Jenks watched the bar feed on his screen and saw Englefield talking to the steward. For an American the beer names would mean nothing, so he was probably seeking advice. He set his laptop to record the reception and main lobby, slung his bag over his shoulder and picked up the crutch – it was time to go to the pub.

The hotel bar was unimaginatively called The Fox and Hounds. Along one wall were half a dozen semi-circular booths, the ancient red leather polished smooth by hundreds of thousands of backsides over decades. They were described in the hotel's history as dating back to the thirties.

The central feature was a small circular fishpond. Lit from within, the water cast dancing patterns of light on the ceiling, but dominating the room was the bar itself. One continuous piece of copper the length of the back wall, behind which numerous shelves displayed every type of drink imaginable – it was an impressive sight.

Jenks limped out of the lift and recognised Rhys Evans talking to the concierge. Evans looked up, his attention drawn to what was obviously a serious leg brace. 'Good evening, sir, are you enjoying your stay with us?'

Jenks smiled back. 'Och aye – lovely place you have here.'

'Thank you, sir. I hope you don't mind me saying, but that's a proper bit of kit you've got on there.'

Jenks looked down. 'Oh this little thing, yeah, stops ma leg from falling off, ha-ha. No, I had a farming accident a few years back, got used to it now.'

Evans pulled a pained expression. 'Had to wear one myself for six weeks – wrecked my knee playing rugby, but nothing like that.'

'Rugby! Bugger that, too violent for me.'

'And *me* as it turned out, sir. Have a lovely evening.'

'And you, pal.'

Jenks entered the bar, spotting his target in a booth on his own. Show time.

Englefield had barely dented his first pint of Foxes Brush, a new craft beer obviously chosen for the name rather than its taste – he didn't look like he was enjoying it. Jenks limped past and they exchanged nods before Englefield said, 'Did you sort out your love life?' Jenks pretended not to recognise him from breakfast before raising his left index finger and chuckling. 'Oh yeah – still ongoing, pal,' as he continued to the bar.

He ordered a non-alcoholic lager and took a seat two tables from Englefield's booth. Jenks had picked up an *Evening Standard* and was sitting quietly flicking through. Unseen, he pressed his phone's power button three times. Englefield looked up as the YMCA ringtone started.

Jenks answered, leaving gaps as if having a real conversation.

'Well....do you know what the time is? It's nearly half seven and you only think to ring now..... well it's a bit late for that isn't it, this was supposed to be a special couple of days...well that's just selfish...if you wanted to tell me at the weekend then why didn't you…so you let me come all this way knowing you wanted to split up...well fine, suit yourself, Duncan, have a nice life.' Jenks tossed the phone on the table.

Englefield was obviously witnessing a breakup call, but his ears really pricked up when he heard the man with the funny accent call his now ex, Duncan.

Jenks downed his drink in one and got up to return to the bar. Englefield turned towards him to catch his eye. 'Hey, dude, don't mean to be rude and all that, but couldn't help overhearing just then – sounds like you got your answer.'

Jenks gave a small shake of his head. 'He's a prick. I should've seen it coming, nae bother, he can fuck right off as far as I'm concerned, I'm done with him.'

‘Plenty more fish, man, you just gotta dip your worm.’

Jenks raised one eyebrow and laughed. He looked at Englefield’s beer. ‘You don’t seem to be making much headway with that, you want something decent? My treat.’

Englefield lifted his glass and peered through it. ‘Gotta say, man, tastes like piss.’

‘That’s because it’s one of them fancy beers – all fur coat and no knickers. Let me get you a decent pint.’

‘What do you suggest?’

‘Well you cannae get heavy down here so maybe…’

‘What the hell is hee-vee?’

Jenks laughed. ‘Heavy, pal, heavy as in weighs a lot. That’s what we drink back home. It’s strong real ale. You basically got a choice here of lager, which is cold and fizzy, or bitter, which is kept warmer but it’s got more flavour.’

‘I prefer cold.’

‘I’ll get ye Stella.’

‘Stella who?’

‘Stella Artois, trust me!’

Jenks carried his glass to the bar and ordered another alcohol-free beer and a pint of Stella. The bar was getting busier, but being early March the tourist season hadn’t really started. He paid the barman and passed the pint glass from his left to his right hand, holding it between thumb and index finger.

To anyone glancing over it would appear he was trying to work out how to carry two glasses whilst using the crutch. Jenks's middle finger was completely hidden from view under the handgrip. As he pressed, 50 ml of clear tasteless liquid Viagra squirted into the beer.

A middle-aged couple at the bar were trying hard to make it look like they weren't watching the spectacle of the crippled man struggling. The woman seemingly couldn't bear it any longer and got off her stool. 'Would you like a hand with those?'

Jenks gave her a warm smile. 'Cheers, hen, I don't think there'll be much left by the time I get over there. The pint's for that fella in the booth.' The movement of the woman taking the glass from him was entirely natural, perfectly concealing the moment Jenks palmed one of his room-key cards to her.

He made his way back to Englefield followed by the woman. 'Cheers, darling, thanks very much.' Jenks nodded towards the lady as she walked away. 'Good job she was there or I'd be handing you an empty glass. Enjoy your beer, pal, it'll be better than that other shite.'

Englefield reached for his new pint as Jenks turned to return to his table. 'Hey, man, why don't you join me – you're on your own and so am I, let's have a toast to your newfound freedom.'

'Aye, why not. I'll drink to that.'

Jenks went to awkwardly get in the booth from the opposite side, but Englefield immediately shuffled further in, patting the seat. 'Hey, sit here, you can stick your leg out – gotta be more comfortable.'

Jenks thanked him and slid in, manhandling his right leg out from under the table. Englefield took three hefty swigs of his beer, rolling the last one around his mouth. 'Now that's more like it. I think me and Stella are gonna get on just fine.'

Jenks offered his outstretched hand. 'Thought so. Hamish Wilson, beer advisor to the stars.'

Englefield laughed, grabbing Jenks's hand in a firm shake. 'Rick Mills, 1st grade English beer student.' Both men laughed together, the ice broken. They engaged in the usual chit-chat, talking about the English weather and other banal topics before Englefield raised the subject of the leg brace.

'So, Hamish, how did you hurt your leg? That looks pretty serious.'

'On the farm, about, ooh, must be nearly three years ago now. I'm from Aberdeen, up on the coast. My family's farmed sheep for five generations. Dad's still up and out by 5am every morning, but I had to give it up. Got myself run over by a tractor.'

'Fucking hell man, a tractor?'

'Yep, and my own stupid fault. The feed trailer had worked loose and come off. I was fixing the coupling with my back to the tractor. Had headphones in so didn't hear a thing – certainly bloody felt it though.'

'What happened?'

'I forgot to put the brake on like an idiot and didn't hear it start to roll backwards. The back wheel rolled over my hip and femur. Smashed it all to pieces. I spent three months in hospital, and cannae go through an airport now without setting off all the alarms.'

'Jesus H, that sounds horrific, dude. Could be worse though, at least it didn't run over your balls.'

Jenks threw his head back. 'Och, can you imagine. No, thankfully that's all in working order.'

Jenks sniffed. 'Hey, you wearing Tom Ford?'

Englefield offered his wrist which Jenks smelt. 'Yeah, man, it's my favourite – you use it?'

'Love it.'

Jenks noticed the bracelet. 'Nice beads by the way.'

Englefield glanced down at his wrist. 'Thanks, man, I got them years ago in Venice Beach, Jeez that was a weekend to remember – just wish I could!'

Jenks smiled. 'Sounds like you had fun.'

Englefield shrugged his shoulders. 'So I'm told.' They both laughed again.

Englefield got another round in, Jenks stating he would have alcohol-free beer due to the painkillers he took. They continued chatting, Englefield telling him he was on a break from his job in insurance and taking in the sights of Europe.

Jenks listened intently, leaning in slightly, occasionally brushing his hair off his face. Englefield liked this guy. He liked his voice, his hair, and was beginning to think that he might just fancy him a bit. He started to wonder what Hamish Wilson, the crippled ex sheep farmer, would look like naked. Would his right leg be deformed? Would there be scars? He was aware of stirrings in his groin and felt himself begin to harden.

Jenks noticed Englefield shift a little closer – time to reel him in a little more. ‘So, what you got planned for this evening - fancy grabbing dinner somewhere?’

‘Yeah, man, that would be good, but I gotta be somewhere a little later to run an errand.’

Englefield looked at his watch, leaning in a little more. ‘Look, man, I haven’t got to do what I’ve got to do for another hour or so. I got a bottle of Taittinger in my room – what say we go and share it?’

‘Tatty what?’

Englefield roared with laughter. ‘Taittinger man, real good champagne. Come on, dude, what do you say?’

Jenks looked around the room. ‘Well there’s not much action here, yeah, why not. What room you in?’

‘Fourth floor, room 402.’

‘Cool, you go on ahead and get the tatty champagne open, I’ve got to settle up here – be two minutes behind you.’

‘You promise you’re not going to stand me up, man?’

‘Hey, Rick, I’m the one who’s been stood up. Away with you now and get those glasses filled.’

Englefield extracted himself from the booth, picking up Jenks’s newspaper on the way, using it to hide the bulge in his trousers. He couldn’t believe how horny he felt.

Jenks took the empty glasses back to the bar, allowing enough time for Englefield to clear the lift. Lowering his voice, he thumbed his mic. 'All Bravo units confirm you're ready to take positions.' Releasing the button he heard each unit checking in.

Five minutes later Jenks was knocking on the door to room 402. 'Come on in, it's open, I'm in the bathroom.'

Jenks slid into the room, locking the door behind him and quickly pulled the tiny camera off the light and put it in his pocket. He called out, 'Hey, nice place.'

Englefield emerged from the bathroom wearing a long white fluffy bathrobe, the bulge obvious.

Jenks looked down. 'Well, someone's pleased to see me again.'

Englefield chuckled as he walked to the mini bar. 'Hey, man, sorry about Duncan causing you all that shit. You wanna hug first before I pour?

Englefield stood still, arms outstretched. Jenks limped over to him, stopping just out of reach. He looked Englefield in the eye and smiled. Dropping the Scottish accent he spoke. 'You know what, it's really great to meet you, Josh.'

It was as if all the air had been sucked out of the room in a split second. In that tiniest fraction of time Englefield dropped his arms, cocked his head to one side and began to speak. 'What the f—' But the third word didn't make it out.

Jenks snapped his left arm out, landing an immense hand chop to the taut side of Englefield's neck. The effect, instantaneous.

The human neck is full of veins and arteries transporting blood to and from the brain. It also houses the cervical plexus, where eight main nerves split from the spinal column at that exact point – an essential pathway for thoughts and commands between the brain and body. Striking it firmly causes instant confusion and pain unlike any other, and Jenks had hit him hard.

The brain immediately tries to make sense of what just happened but can't – all instructions are completely scrambled. Englefield felt the room warping, his vacant eyes swivelling as he bent over. Putting his hand to his neck, he started to sway. He couldn't speak or shout out, the only sound he could muster was a gentle 'Uh, uh, uhhh' as his body started to fold up.

Jenks swung a vicious uppercut, snapping his mouth shut with such force a number of teeth fractured.

Englefield began to collapse, but Jenks caught him and threw him into a chair. Quickly pulling open the Velcro straps on his leg brace, he tossed it to one side. He looked down at Englefield slumped over but conscious, blood running down his chin, staining the fluffy white robe.

Reaching into his shoulder bag he pulled out two cable ties, quickly securing Englefield's wrists to the chair arms. Grabbing him by the hair, he lifted his face up. 'You make one sound that isn't the answer I want to hear, and the pain you're feeling in your neck will be like a shaving cut. Do you understand?'

Jenks released his grip, and Englefield's head flopped back down.

'Look at me. That was a question – remember what I just said?'

Englefield slowly lifted his head. He was having difficulty speaking, his mouth starting to swell. 'I undershtand.'

Jenks walked slowly and calmly into the bathroom as Englefield tried to make sense of the fact that the crippled man he was about to sleep with was now walking unaided. Jenks returned with all the towels and spread them on the floor around and the chair. 'Why...what are the towels for?'

Jenks cast his eyes down. 'It's such a lovely carpet, shame to mess it up.'

Dagenham.
The same time.

A handcuffed Chas Black was slowly regaining consciousness in the back of the SUV. He felt burning on his neck, and as he began to open his eyes, realised he was hooded. 'I'm not gonna fight, guys, I don't know who you think I am, but you've got the wrong man. I'm on holiday, I ain't done nothing.'

A man next to him spoke. 'That is not *entirely* true, is it, Mr Charles Black. Or would you prefer I call you Gary Taylor?' Black felt every pore on his scalp open, fear coursing through his system. He began to shake. The man had a distinctive Russian accent.

Trying to think of something to say to get out of the situation, he blurted out, 'You should know, guys, I have very powerful friends. They'll be looking for me, and they don't mess around. You heard of *Welikeleaks*? Well they got serious connections…' He felt a strong hand clamp over his mouth, forcing part of the hood between his teeth.

'Mr Black, you do not have powerful friends. You have enemies more powerful than you could ever imagine, and you're with them now.'

Black began to lose control of his bladder, and thought back to the time he had his gun pressed to Josh's head. 'I'm sorry, I think I've wet myself a bit.'

The man's voice was calm. 'It is only to be expected from a man in your position. Do not concern yourself. You have far more important things to be worried about.'

Black's teeth started to chatter. 'Wh..where are you taking me, who are you, what do you want?'

'*So* many questions. We are nearly there. Sit tight and be good, man, we reveal very soon.'

Black went quiet. He felt the vehicle turn and slow, the tyres now noisy and crunching. The SUV came to a stop and he heard an electric window lowering. A man leant in. '*Privet tovarishch.*' The driver replied, 'And hello to you, comrade, I have special delivery.'

'Go right up, the door is at back of main building.'

Black felt the vehicle continue along more gravel, bouncing around as it hit potholes. The journey lasted about a minute before the vehicle came to a stop.

'You will get out now. If you try stupid things, I will break your bones, you understand?'

'Yes.' Black was helped out of the car and stood waiting for further instruction. He could hear the faint rumble of traffic in the distance, so guessed they must be well away from any main road now. It didn't make it any better. A hand looped inside his arm and the man spoke again. 'We go inside now, I guide you.'

He was taken onto the main factory floor, long since cleared of everything apart from a chair and an old sofa. 'There is chair behind you, sit.' Black did as instructed. He heard the man walk away and a door close. He tried to sit as still as he could, but the shakes still came in spasms. The sound of another door opening caused him to turn his head, despite wearing the hood.

He listened for a sound with every fibre of his body. The whirr of a motor drifted in and out of the room but other than that, silence. He suddenly felt more uneasy, like there was a presence in the room. 'Hello? Is there someone in here?'

His reply came. A voice at the other end simply said, 'Shhhhhh.' Black went rigid. Then the sound of footsteps, and something else. With every alternate click of shoes there was a tap. Black's mind was thrown back twenty years as he pictured his grandfather who always wore boots with quarter tip heels and walked with a cane. The person was using a walking stick. As the footsteps got closer, Black's heart beat faster.

A hand gripped his shoulder causing him to jump. 'Shhhhhh.' He felt the hood being slowly lifted. Although the room wasn't particularly bright, he had to blink repeatedly having been in complete darkness since his abduction. Someone slowly walked around from behind him. 'There you are, my dear chap, that's better now, isn't it.'

Black recognised the voice immediately. 'You...'

Room 402
The same time.

Englefield tried to ignore the towels, but with his neck cramping up it was more comfortable to look down. The confusion was lifting but still nothing made any real sense. Jenks walked slowly around him. 'Now, Josh, I'm going to ask you some questions, and you need to answer honestly. Bear in mind I may already know the answer, I strongly advise you not to deviate from the truth. Are you with me so far?'

The pain in Englefield's neck was excruciating and as he spoke he felt broken teeth with his tongue. 'Who are you?'

Jenks stopped in front of him, knelt down and put his hands on Englefield's knees. He leant in until his mouth was a few inches from Englefield's ear, speaking in a whisper.

'Remember when you were small and terrified of the monster under your bed – maybe you called him the bogeyman.' Jenks leant closer still, his lips brushing Englefield's ear. 'Well I'm the one he runs away from.'

Englefield felt a shudder reverberate through his body like someone just walked over his grave. 'Wh..what do you want to know?'

'Let's start with this. How are you doing the last big transfer?'

'Transfer?'

'Careful now, Josh. You get one chance, and that was it. Tell me about the transfer tonight. You know, that thing you told me you had to do later.'

'Dropbox, the file is very big.'

'Good. I presume it will be heavily encrypted?'

'Yeah, very.'

'Good so far, Joshua. Who is the final recipient, as in who's paying you?'

Englefield stayed silent for a few seconds, which were four more than the two he was allowed before answering. Jenks cupped his hand and slammed it against Englefield's ear, compressing the air within, instantly rupturing his eardrum. A towel rammed into his mouth muted the scream.

‘I gave you one chance, and you used that already. If you fail to answer me again, the next question will be left or right.’

A stunned Englefield felt like he was sitting next to a wind machine, his ear full of whooshing sounds. Jenks removed the towel, allowing him to answer.

‘Left or right? I don’t understand, and I’m having trouble hearing you.’

Jenks reached into his bag and pulled out a ceramic paring knife, moving it one way then the other whilst looking at Englefield’s groin. ‘Left ball or right. Clear now?’ Englefield tried to nod, crying out from the pain in his neck.

‘Shall we try again? Who is the final recipient, i.e. your paymasters?’

‘*Welikeleaks*. I’m getting, or was getting twenty mill for the last batch.’

Jenks whistled. ‘How much did you get each time you passed the files up to today?’

‘Man, I’m in so much pain, please don’t hit me again, I don’t want to give a wrong answer, so if I pause it’s only because I’m trying to remember.’

‘OK, now answer.’

‘The first one was 100K, that was to show what I could do, then 250K per stick. I gave them one a week for maybe ten weeks? It might have been eleven, my head’s not straight, man.’

‘So you’ve cleared over 2.5 mill so far. That’s a lot, but maybe not enough to get a new face and disappear forever, especially at the rate you’re spending it.’

Englefield felt every hope and dream evaporating, leaving him in a vacuum which was once his life. He started to try to work out if someone had ratted him out, but who? Jenks's next question brought him back to earth.

'Where's Chas Black?'

'I honestly don't know. He's in London, not far away – that's what I was doing later. I'm supposed to meet him at the London Eye at 9.45 and hand over the decryption key – the password to open the Dropbox. He's gonna contact his man beforehand to tell him we want to see the money in our accounts before they get the key, so we were switching the terms at the last moment. They need everything otherwise the plan won't work.'

'I see – tell me about the plan, Josh.'

'You remember Bradley Manning and all the shit that stirred up?'

'Yes, good people died because of him. Go on.'

'This time it was going to be different. All the stuff I got from the Agency's files was going to be of the highest quality, not 750,000 mostly full of shit. These are revelations which will set nation against nation, anarchy would break out worldwide and society collapse. It's the only way to turn this shitty world into a fairer place.'

'And why would anarchy break out, Josh?'

'Because of all the secrets. Every nation would know all the dirty tricks everyone was pulling against each other. Assassinations, secret deals, gifting nuclear secrets to people who had no right to know. I could go on.'

'Then do.'

'Do you know who really killed Kennedy? Well I do. Did you know Chairman fucking Mao didn't really die of a heart attack and what nations worked together to take him out?'

'And how would it have worked?'

'Don't you see Hamish, oh Jeez, that's not your real name is it?'

Jenks slowly shook his head.

'Don't you see that with all the secrets out everyone would be equal? No one would have the upper hand and the people would rise up and take back control. Order would be established within anarchy.'

'You're obviously committed to the cause but how does pocketing over $22,500,000 fit in with everyone being equal?'

'Someone's got to stabilize everything – individuals like me and the other *Welikeleaks* people will be needed to guide the world, set up the new order and share everything on the planet fairly.'

'And that's why you need twenty-two and a half big ones is it?

'I gotta survive, and that means disappearing while it all plays out. Those guys are brilliant, man, they've got everything figured out.'

'I see. How do you contact them?'

'I don't, and that's the truth, I swear. Chas dealt with some old English guy who put him onto an

American dude. He's the one who arranged his new passport and all the other shit. He made it all happen, you know. Some DPS guy used to pick up the stick and password from him every week. The American sorted it all out.'

'Hmm. Tell me how you avoided detection when stealing the secrets.'

Englefield explained how he'd linked up Buckland's two computers and set up remote connection via TOR. He detailed how he'd logged on for nearly three months, working well into the night and every weekend. He explained how he knew Black, and his involvement in the original WikiLeaks data dump.

'That's a lot of information, Josh, thank you – your ingenuity is nothing short of brilliant. Just a shame you had to get Miss Buckland in so much trouble.'

Englefield looked genuinely shocked. 'What do you mean, trouble?'

'Your friend's *Welikeleaks* cherry-picked a few bits of information to test the provenance. Three MI6 agents have disappeared, presumed dead. One of your fellow countrymen, a highly decorated and brave soldier, was pushed into a ravine leaving a wife and family – there's more, but you get the gist.'

'What happened with Alicia?'

'It took a while to join the dots, but they cross-referenced the names of people turning up dead, and lo and behold she'd pulled the file on each of them, or rather you had.'

‘Is she OK? What did they do to her?’

‘You know what they do to terrorists in black sites which don’t exist? Well of course you do, you’re CIA.’

‘Will she be OK? Once they know she didn’t do anything wrong?’

Jenks circled behind Englefield and leant in. ‘*Will she be OK*? She blew the contents of her skull out within thirty minutes of being released.’

Jenks felt Englefield’s body go rigid. He dropped his head as best he could and started rocking, quietly repeating, ‘Oh no, oh no.’

Dagenham.
The same time.

Chas Black looked up at the man standing before him. He’d heard the voice many times over the years and was in no doubt it was the Englishman – the man who’d kept him on a retainer and so far paid him close to $500,000 for the memory sticks. A fellow idealist.

The Englishman stopped in front of him, one hand over the other, leaning on his cane. He was immaculately turned out, and his long cashmere overcoat stopped just below his knees. From his fedora to his highly polished brogues, he oozed refinement and sophistication. ‘Yes it’s me, Charles. In the flesh. We need to have a little chit-chat about things, my boy.’

Black was trying to make sense of the last hour but failing miserably. 'What, I mean, what the fuck's going on, man? Why am I here? Is this some sort of test? You know you can rely on me, I've never let you down have I? What's with all the Ruskies?'

'You're not exactly in a position to start demanding answers, my lad. You play ball and we'll see what the future holds for you. Does that sound fair?'

'I've been tasered, kidnapped and dumped here in fucking handcuffs for Christ's sake. I think you owe me an explanation.'

The Englishman sighed, slowly picked up his cane and swung it – the carved ivory handle striking the side of Black's head with such force he flew sideways off the chair.

The Englishman leant over and bellowed in his ear. 'Get back on the bloody chair, you little shit.'

Black felt woozy, his hair wet from the blood running from his scalp. He got on all fours holding the base of the chair tightly and hauled himself up. His breathing had become rapid, and despite the chill of the old building he was sweating.

The Englishman's voice switched back to a calm soothing tone. 'Looks like you're a bit shocked, dear boy. Let's get one thing crystal clear before we go any further. I speak, you answer. Quite simple really – are you clear on that?'

Black's voice had dropped in volume. 'Yeah, but there's no need to hit me, man, we're on the same team.'

The Englishman began to chuckle, which became a laugh, and finally a guffaw until it dissolved into a coughing fit. 'Oh God, that's funny. Oh dear me.' He cleared his throat, composing himself. 'You don't even know what the teams *are*, old fruit. *Nothing* is as it seems. You've been very useful and loyal over the years, which is the only reason you're still alive.'

Black was becoming more confused. 'I *believe*, man, you know that – I've proved myself haven't I? I want to see this through just like you do and make a better world. It's all I've wanted for years. I'm part of this.'

The Englishman tapped his cane on the floor. 'Were you going to change the arrangements for payment tonight, laddie?'

'Wh..Why do you ask that?'

Giving no hint of his intentions the Englishman took a step, reversed his cane and thrust it into Black's stomach. Black doubled over making short rasping noises as he tried to reflate his lungs.

The Englishman gave him a minute before hissing, 'Sit. Up.'

Black straightened as best he could, his breathing slowly returning to normal.

'Let's try again, shall we, this is all so unnecessary if you'd only behave yourself. Now, the payment tonight.'

'Josh told me we were gonna insist on seeing the money in our accounts before we gave you the decryption key. I know you've paid every time but he said we have to put our own measures in place. Twenty million plus my four is a lot. He said you'd agree because you didn't have any option.'

'Oh did he now. How very shrewd of him. So after he gave you the files, you were going to what, ring me and *demand* the money? *You,* little insignificant wannabe saviour of the world, were going to make demands of *me*? Have I got that right?'

'You make it sound worse than it is, I was just supposed to ring you and say we needed proof the money was in. You would've got the decryption key straight away after that.'

'Hmm. Well let's see if we can salvage things a little, shall we? When and how were you due to get the key?'

'9.45 tonight. I'm meeting him at the London Eye. The plan was we would've left enough time to see the money then transfer it elsewhere.'

'Elsewhere?'

'Josh said it was more secure if we moved it to another account, you know, just to be safe.'

'You two really have thought of everything, haven't you.'

'It's just protection, man, our whole future's on the line, so it was just, I don't know, precautions.'

'Well we'll just have to send someone else to meet young Joshua, shan't we. Next question, how is he going to transfer the files to you?'

Black dropped his head and mumbled something.

'I'm sorry, you'll have to speak up. Say again.'

In the meekest of voices Black spoke. 'I've already got them.'

'I beg your pardon?'

'I've already got all the information you're paying for. The file is massive so he's put it in a Dropbox.'

The Englishman paused, working everything he knew backwards. 'What happened to the 9pm transfer time?'

'How do you know it was nine? I told you on the phone it was just before ten.'

'It doesn't matter how I know, and I would remind you what happens when you step out of line.'

'What the fuck is going on, man?'

'I'll tell you what the fuck is going on, *man*, as you so eloquently put it. I am about to gouge one of your eyes out with the end of this cane if you do not answer the next questions truthfully and without hesitation. Have you a preference?'

'For what?'

'Which eye.'

Black's bluster disappeared. 'You don't need to do that, I'll tell you what you need to know.'

'How do you access the Dropbox?'

'I've got it on my phone. Josh sent me a new one – he said it was too much of a risk to use the ones we already had. It's in my inside pocket.'

The Englishman felt inside Black's jacket and retrieved the handset. 'What's your passcode?'

'67279 – the golden age of music.'

'What?'

‘Sixty-seven to seventy-nine. It’s when all the best music was made.’

The Englishman sighed.

Black winced as he shifted position trying to get comfortable. ‘The Dropbox icon’s on the home screen, click on that, it’ll ask for username and password.’

‘Yes, I see that. What are the details?’

‘Username *utopia4meandyou@me.com*. The password is judgementday, all lower case.’

‘How quaint. Let’s see now. Yes, that works. Good lad. So now we just need the decryption key. And what other failsafes have you two dreamed up, seeing as you obviously don’t trust me?’

‘None, man, that was it. It was just the delay in giving you the key, that was all.’

‘So you’re not due to check in with each other again before 9.45pm tonight when you meet? No secret words or other nonsense?’

‘Nope, I swear, man. I haven’t even seen him since the States.’

‘OK. I believe you. Now, young Joshua, has he changed his appearance? Disguised himself?’

Black shrugged his shoulders. ‘Like I said, I haven’t seen him since back home. He mentioned something about maybe growing a beard, changing his hair, but I can’t tell you any more than that because I honestly don’t know.

‘Well that’s a little helpful.’

Black looked uncomfortable. 'Are we still going to get paid? You're still gonna get everything like we promised.'

'Have you checked your account recently? The one we set up for you?'

'No, not for a couple of days – why?'

'Well I'll save you a job. It's empty – we've taken it all back, and I understand from my American associate you've burned through almost all of your original payment.'

'What the fuck? You fucking piece of s...'

The cane caught him directly across the bridge of the nose, shattering bone and cartilage. Black let out a piercing scream and instinctively put his manacled hands to his face, howling again when he touched what was left of his nose. Blood and mucus ran down his face as his eyelids started to flutter and close.

'You mind your language and remember your place. You're only alive because you might still be useful. Speak to me like that again and I'll rip *both* your eyes out.'

Black had no doubt the Englishman would follow up on his threat and began to pass out.

The Englishman went to the door and called out. A large man appeared and followed him onto the factory floor.

'Secure him to the chair then get all the units we can spare to the London Eye. Leave me five men here. Englefield is meeting our friend at 9.45 to hand over the decryption key. Make sure your men don't stand out. It's a wide open space so you'll have plenty of time to intercept him as he approaches, but bear in mind he's changed his appearance. You have the photo, but his hair is probably short and darker now and he may have a beard. Bring it directly to me and take Englefield somewhere quiet and dispose of him. We'll deal with this clown later.'

'*Ya ponimayu.*'

Room 402.
The same time.

Jenks pulled up a chair and sat directly in front of Englefield.

'Yes, you've caused the death of yet another good person, and you weren't even worthy of cleaning her boots. I understand she dedicated her whole working life to the service of her country, and you took it away.'

Englefield's whole body was wracked with pain. He had a hammering headache, which was marginally more painful than his neck now, plus he'd spat two pieces of tooth out and his ear was leaking fluid.

'It wasn't supposed to happen like that, I know she was good…'

'Save it, Josh. I'm not interested in hearing you getting all remorseful.'

Jenks retrieved Englefield's laptop from the desk.

'CIA issue? Don't bother responding, I know it is. Obviously password protected?'

Englefield nodded.

'Well, what is it?'

'Doobiebrother, all one word and lower case.'

Jenks carefully typed the password and hit the return key.

Englefield's eyes shot wide open. 'No wait, wait, it's doobiebrothers, I forgot, there's an s on the end.'

Too late. Jenks saw the machine momentarily come to life, then start to pixilate. Random dots of colour flooded the screen and began to dissolve in front of his eyes. He quickly turned it over and dropped the battery out.

'Oh dear, Josh.'

Englefield was frantic. 'I didn't mean it, man, it wasn't on purpose, I swear. I'm not thinking straight. Oh shit, oh shit.'

'So what just happened?'

'It's a self-destruct program like evidence eliminator, you know? If the wrong password is used it fries the hard drive instantaneously. It's too late, everything's gone.'

'Can it be retrieved even partially?'

Englefield was crying. Jenks could barely hear him. 'No. It's a CIA program. They developed it in case an agent ever got kidnapped and was forced to…well it doesn't matter now. It destroys everything in seconds.'

Jenks closed the laptop and put it in his own bag. 'The memory stick in the safe, I presume that's the decryption key?'

Englefield just shrugged his shoulders.

'Do I take it from your rather rude gesture you don't want to help me anymore?'

'Whatever, I'm a dead man walking now. The Agency will know what I did so if…'

Jenks tapped Englefield's damaged ear. Even the lightest touch sent a jolt of pain through his head. 'Save it. Shut up.'

Jenks leant in and pulled the tie cord from Englefield's robe in one swift tug, then walked to the bathroom and ran a face flannel under the cold tap. Englefield's eyes followed every movement, his breathing shallow and rapid.

'Please, I'll do anything.'

Jenks balled up the flannel and thrust it into Englefield's mouth, touching exposed nerve, and wrapped the cord tightly around Englefield's mouth. As he began to thrash around his robe fell open.

Not taking his eyes from Englefield's, Jenks lifted a pair of industrial wire cutters from his bag, making sure Englefield saw him look down at his now shrivelled penis. Englefield's eyes bulged and he tried to speak, but it was impossible.

Even with the gag, the muffled sound of a primeval scream of fear escaped as Jenks lowered the cutters and nudged Englefield's manhood, now leaking what urine he had left in him. The blood vessels in his eyes started to burst as he shook his head, the pain in his neck now superseded by utter terror.

Jenks spoke. 'Alicia Buckland, that beautiful dedicated woman was held for ninety-six hours in a floodlit room, deprived of sleep and almost all food. She was stripped naked and given a piss-stained blanket as her only comfort. She was questioned nonstop, wired up to a lie detector and pumped full of drugs. She was screamed at, threatened and humiliated beyond belief. On the third day of torture she got her period. Do you know what they did? They made her wipe the blood away with her hands. Can you imagine that? I can't.'

Jenks paused. 'And while she was in custody they tore her house to pieces leaving it only fit to be demolished. Her home, her safe place she'd worked hard all her life for was no longer there. And *you*, Joshua Englefield the *turd*, caused it all.'

The words sank in as the cutters opened out.

Dagenham.
The same time.

The Englishman went into his makeshift office and carefully packed the envelopes into the rucksack that had travelled all the way from Scotland. Everything was almost in place to ensure that in a few days, for the rest of the world, nothing would be the same again.

He looked at his watch, calculating the time in Moscow. Using end-to end-encryption he dialled a number known only to a handful of people. There was a short delay before the line rang. On the fourth ring the call was picked up.

'*Da.*'

The Englishman recognised his master's voice immediately, but still had to follow security protocol to prove he wasn't under duress. He spoke in perfect Russian. *In the summers gaily singing, of the future isn't thinking*. It was the first line to a famous Russian poem.

'My friend, it is good to hear from you.'

'I'm sorry to ring you so late, sir, I hope I didn't wake you?'

'Not at all, I was just looking over some papers. What news?'

The Englishman thought how best to précis the events of the past few hours. 'We picked Black up and have him here. I considered it essential for us to succeed.'

'I have complete faith in you, if you thought it necessary, it was.'

'Thank you, comrade. They decided to change the rules at the last moment and ask to see the money in their accounts before handing over the decryption key. And they lied about the time of the exchange.'

'So we don't have it all?'

'Hear me out, comrade – Black has told me everything. I have the files in a Dropbox already – they switched the time of transfer to make their demands. We picked up Black before he made that call to us. They must have used a code word, but it is of no importance as I have the file. Black is supposed to be meeting Englefield at 9.45 to pick up the decryption key.'

'And your men will be there instead.'

'Exactly. Their pathetic attempts at manipulation have caused their downfall.'

'And the money?'

'We have taken back our money from Black, and Englefield will be interrogated for his Swiss account details before we kill him.'

'Don't spend too much time on that, my friend, it is small change. And the documents?'

'They are scanned and in my computer. I will bring you the originals when we return tomorrow. With the files from the Americans, we possess the most powerful weapon our great nation has ever created.'

'Excellent. You have done well, my old friend. Let's hope the last piece of the puzzle falls into place.'

'That's the beauty of it, Englefield has no idea we have Black, and they are not due to check in again until they meet face to face.'

'That is good. In just a few days you will come out of the shadows and take your place at my side. Call me when it is done.'

'Yes, sir, goodnight.'

The Englishman walked back out to Black who was starting to come round. 'Not much longer. You just sit tight until we get that key, there's a good fellow.'

Black partially lifted his head, slurring, 'Then what?'

‘Well you die, of course, you cretin.’

Room 402.
The same time.

Englefield scrunched his eyes tightly shut, holding his legs together as best he could and waited for the inevitable. He then felt pain like no other as Jenks snipped his left index finger off. The muffled scream was so high-pitched it sounded like a whistle.

Jenks wrapped a wad of tissues around the severed digit and took it to the wardrobe and held it against the reader. Seconds later the decryption key was in his pocket.

‘You don’t need to exist anymore now, Josh, so bye.’

Jenks stood behind him and wrapped his left arm tightly around the front of Englefield’s neck, grasping the crook of his own right elbow. Moving his right hand back, he cupped the back of Englefield’s skull. With one strong thrust he heard and felt Englefield’s spinal cord snap and his body go limp.

He thumbed his mic. ‘Room service.’

Working quickly, he turned Englefield’s right hand upwards, placing the severed finger in his palm. He retrieved the adaptor and pushed the lamp plug back into the socket then grabbed the leg brace and crutch and waited. Seconds later there was a tap on the door. Jenks opened it and the middle-aged couple from the bar walked in wheeling the large Samsonite suitcase. The woman spoke first.

'Fire door alarm is disabled and the roof hatch is unlocked. Your room's been sanitised and your rucksack is on the plastic sheet.' Jenks nodded. 'Thanks, Teresa. I've touched the arms of that chair, the cold tap on the bathroom sink, the handle of the safe, the wardrobe door handle, the lock on the room door and that plug.' Teresa pulled out a packet of alcohol-soaked wipes. 'Leave them to me.'

The man wheeled the suitcase over and cut away the plastic ties. They lowered the body, folding it into the case, and began putting the towels and anything else belonging to the late Joshua Englefield into the suitcase with him.

As Jenks was leaving he confirmed that the man had everything he needed. The man pulled a thick carrier bag from his pocket and began to unfold it. Jenks saw the Tesco logo and gave the man a *what the hell* look. 'Bag for life, Jenks, perfect size to fit it all in once they've been through the chipper – bit ironic really.' Jenks shook his head. 'You are one sick bastard, Frank.' Frank smiled. Jenks rolled his eyes and slipped out, placing *do not disturb* sign, on the door handle, of rooms 402 and 403.

Back in his own room, he stepped straight onto the plastic sheet, pulling his wig off and stripping to his underwear. He took fresh clothes from his rucksack along with new Dents gloves and got dressed – every item was black. After stopping the audio recording he secured his laptop in his shoulder bag along with Englefield's.

Wrapping the clothes he'd been wearing in the plastic sheet, he stuffed the bundle into the rucksack along with his room key and the disassembled leg brace. Teresa and Frank had already packed his toothbrush and meagre toiletries, the only thing left to do was to pull the crutch apart and secure it on the side of the rucksack.

He depressed the transmit button. 'Bravo Two, light the fire. Bravo Three stand by for pickup, Bravo Four await further instruction.' One by one the units checked in. Jenks opened his door a fraction – clear both ways. He jogged down the hallway, through the fire escape door and up the stairs.

He located the roof hatch and saw the piece of tape holding the bolt in. Swinging it open he removed the tape and jumped up to grasp the hatch frame. The rope-like muscles in his arms went taut as he easily hauled himself up. Gently lowering the hinged cover, he heard the lock click into place.

The sky above London was overcast and the sun long since set. With little light hitting the succession of rooftops in front of him, Jenks was virtually invisible. Running along the roof of the hotel he saw the end of Dean Street and the right angle onto Old Compton Street. These were old buildings with no gaps between properties – some were higher and others lower but Jenks had memorised the terrain, and knew before he got to the next building whether he had to jump down or climb up.

Getting closer to St Anne's churchyard, he caught the sound of raucous drunken singing drifting up, and smiled. Reaching the point he'd chosen, he saw the high chain link fence across the fourteen-foot gap between the fence and the roof he was now standing on. 'Control from Alpha One, kill the cameras please, 50-metre radius of the junction of Old Compton Street and Wardour Street.' Maureen replied, 'Copy that, you're good to go.'

Jenks checked the waist strap of his rucksack and pulled it tighter. He secured his shoulder bag inside the straps and stepped out his run-up from the edge of the building back to the centre. Eight paces. He added another to compensate for his longer stride when running, and turned. Taking a deep breath, he started to sprint. A long jumper would've been proud to get as close to the plasticine as Jenks did to the edge of the building. He pushed off hard and sailed over the rarely used alley nearly thirty feet below, spreading his limbs out like a tree frog.

He hit the fence hard, but his fingers thankfully went through the gaps in the links without breaking any. He was almost at the top and quickly climbed the last few feet, swung his legs over and scampered down the other side.

He could hear the singing more clearly now, which was descending into an obscenity-filled rant between two very drunken sounding men. Not the sort of people anyone would want to approach. Jenks sprinted across the grass towards the noise, which didn't abate. As he closed in on the men he saw the raging fire in the oil drum and numerous cans and bottles strewn around.

Slowing at the last moment, he pulled off the crutch components and dropped the rucksack into the fire. Pointing at the crutch he said, 'There's a perfume bottle inside the handle, burn it and wipe down the crutch please.' The men making up Bravo Two didn't bat an eyelid or miss a drunken note.

At that moment a middle-aged couple walked casually out of The Huntsman's Lodge wheeling their heavy suitcase behind them, straight into a black cab idling outside. Over his ear bud Jenks heard, 'Bravo Three, POB.'

Jenks crouched at the gates, peering though, checking the foot traffic. A group of girls passed by, giggling and saying *oh my God* every other word. Just normal people having fun on a midweek night out. Happy the coast was clear, he silently eased himself out and rejoined everyday life. Just another ordinary Joe strolling down the road.

He headed towards Dansey Place and thumbed his mic. 'Bravo Four from Alpha One, receiving.'

'Go ahead.'

'Wardour St, junction with Shaftsbury Avenue, sixty seconds. Right to right and your right rear pocket.'

'Understood, Bravo Four out.'

Jenks retrieved Englefield's laptop from his bag and the decryption key from his pocket and headed for the pedestrian crossing at Shaftsbury Avenue. As he stepped on he bumped shoulders with a man walking towards him, busy looking at his phone. Jenks momentarily turned. 'Sorry, mate.' The man didn't look up, just mumbling, 'No problem,' and continued walking.

The exchange was so quick and slick, no one could have noticed that the laptop under Jenks's right arm was now under the right arm of the phone man. As the man walked on, he casually touched his back pocket, feeling the familiar shape of a memory stick.

Jenks was about twenty seconds from Dansey Place. 'Control from Alpha One, am I clear?'

Jo Fox came on. 'Alpha One, hold back, delivery driver finishing up.'

Jenks stopped and checked his watch. Four minutes since launching himself off the roof.

'Alpha One you are green to go, I repeat, green to go.'

'Received.'

Jenks turned the corner, walking straight to the garage, and was inside within seconds.

'Control from Alpha One, please inform JC I'll call him shortly. Cameras back on until I decamp.'

'Received, control out.'

Jenks sat at the table and set his laptop up. Using a pay-as-you-go internet dongle he logged into The Huntsman's Lodge system and selected CCTV memory. He called up the notes where he'd stored various timings, and cut sections of the recordings where he appeared in the reception and lobby, pasting in recordings of the same area, taking care guests wouldn't just appear and disappear as if by magic.

Thankfully the hotel hadn't been busy, and more importantly there were no clocks visible. He managed to match almost exactly Arianna's position at the desk after he'd been and gone at check-in. Only under intense forensic scrutiny would anyone notice an almost imperceptible flick of her head at the final edit point.

The bar and dining room were more of a problem. People had come and gone making it impossible to splice in new footage, so he substituted blank screens for the duration he'd been in both rooms. If by chance someone reviewed the recordings, it would look like the cameras were malfunctioning and had temporarily gone down. To make it more believable, he selected other time frames over the previous weeks, cutting and pasting in blank recordings. The man who didn't exist had now disappeared from any retrievable footage in The Huntsman's Lodge. His last edit was to remove Teresa and Frank's presence from the hotel.

His final task was to open the remote connection program, delete the false switch Evans thought he'd turned off, then turn the real one off.

Jenks dialled Camburn and updated him on everything he'd learnt from Englefield. He told him about Englefield's plan to change the terms of their agreement at the last moment and demand proof the money was in their accounts. Camburn was delighted when Jenks told him about the eliminator program destroying the contents of the laptop before Englefield had the chance to fill the Dropbox. The retrieval of the decryption key made Camburn even happier. Neither knew they were very wrong about the Dropbox.

'My boy, that's excellent work and it's still just after nine. We've got over half an hour until Black is supposed to pick up the key. I'll get Maureen to patch into the cameras around the Eye and get the team to pick Black up when he arrives. I'll call later with an update and we'll debrief fully tomorrow.'

'Sounds like a plan. Bravo Four should have the laptop and key back to you shortly. I'm going home – speak to you later.'

'Ride safely, lad.'

Jenks pulled on his leathers and helmet, switching the radio connection to his bike. 'Control from Alpha One, kill the cameras please – half-mile radius then give me four minutes before you turn them back on.'

'Copy that, Alpha One, stand by....cameras off, alley empty, you are green to go, I repeat, green to go.'

He eased the Ducati out of the garage, stopping briefly to lock the door. The bike purred slowly into the hustle and bustle of Chinatown and within minutes he was on the Embankment and heading home.

Chapter 24.

The unforeseen.

The multi-camera feed of the area surrounding the London Eye was on the large wall display and everyone in the Shop was watching it. Camburn paced back and forth, his eyes never leaving the screen. 'He's five minutes late. Typical bloody Yank, you would think for something this important he could at least make the effort to be on time.'

The area was still fairly busy with people milling around Jubilee Gardens, drinking and having fun. Maureen cleared her throat. 'Sir, take a look at these guys.' She walked up to the screen physically touching it, pointing out seven men in different locations. 'Look, they're all on their own scanning the area.'

'Good spot, Maurs, let the team know they might not be alone.'

Jo Fox was back and had a good point. 'Perhaps they're Black's own protection detail. Just because Englefield didn't mention it, doesn't mean to say they haven't organised their own security.'

Camburn agreed. 'They're definitely there for something. Look, they're trying so hard to look normal they look abnormal. And where's our team, I can't see them anywhere?'

Maureen pointed. 'There, there, those three on the grass, there, over there, see that guy in the tree? He's one of ours.'

Camburn nodded. 'This other mob are amateurs.'

Camburn's phone rang. 'Hello.'

He recognised Sir John Leroux's voice. 'James, it's John. I'm on my way over to you, I'll be about ten minutes – something terrible has happened.'

'What is it, John, you sound awful?'

'It's too sensitive for the phone, I'll tell you when I get there. You might want to get two large glasses of Scotch ready.'

'Can't you give me some idea?'

'The most catastrophic breach of national, strike that, international security has happened. I've just been made aware.'

'But it's all in hand, John.'

'No it's not, James.'

Kent.
The same time.

Traffic was light and Jenks made good headway, arriving home just after 10pm. He put the Ducati away, hung his leathers and helmet up and realised he was feeling very hungry. After checking through the fridge, he made himself a doorstep sandwich of cheese and piccalilli and poured himself the last of the Fleurie he'd opened a couple of days ago.

He sat back in his armchair, opened his laptop and deleted the entire sound recording made in Englefield's room – no one needed to hear what happened in there. He then wiped all recordings of the hotels CCTV and deleted the red BTS file.

He wanted some fresh air so grabbed his glass and went outside to sit on the sea wall and listen to the birds settling down for the night.

He hoped the team would capture Black, knowing he would be disposed of the same way as Englefield – ground to mincemeat and fed to the pigs up in Essex. If they didn't, he'd get his comeuppance one day. He started to rewind the mission to see what he could learn to put to use in the future. The memory sticks already handed over were a problem, but they weren't his problem – he'd fulfilled his contract. They could pick the bones out at tomorrow's debrief – tonight he was going to listen to the birds then head off to bed.

Dagenham.
The same time.

The Englishman listened to the sit rep from the London Eye. 'What do you mean there's no sign of him, could you have missed him?'

'I can't see how we could have, we have eyes everywhere. We're covering every possible foot approach to the big wheel and I have a man on the

Victoria Embankment with binoculars keeping a long eye. Maybe the time they gave for the rendezvous was wrong, like a code, like they did bringing the file transfer forward three hours.'

The Englishman exhaled. 'That's actually a very good point. Perhaps it's going to be later when there's less people around. Hold your positions, I'll go talk to Black and see if he lied to me.'

The Englishman walked back onto the factory floor and over to Black, who was making loud rasping noises – his nasal passages smashed and blocked. The Englishman slapped him hard around the head. Black didn't react other than slowly opening one eye.

'Wakey wakey, old fruit. Time for another little chat.'

Black couldn't focus, his head fuzzy and muddled. 'Wh..wha?'

'What time did you say you were supposed to meet Englefield to pick up the key?'

Black tried to clear his thoughts, but with the blows to his head was having difficulty. The Englishman could barely hear him reply, 'Key?'

'The decryption key, the memory stick with the password for the Dropbox, you fool. Did you have a code word to change the time?'

Black tried to think. 'Code...we…did it at six.'

'No, not that one, the time for you to meet Joshua at the Eye.' The Englishman was beginning to wish he hadn't hit Black so hard.

'My eye?'

‘Think man, concentrate.’ The Englishman spoke slowly and precisely. ‘Did you and Joshua agree that you would say you were going to meet at 9.45 but really it was going to be later? Come on, it’s not that difficult.’

Black looked up at the Englishman, his eyes dead like a shark. He began to try to say something.

‘Come on, come on, spit it out.’

Black’s speech was becoming more slurred and laboured. ‘Zhosh. He my fwend.’

‘Oh forget it.’

The Englishman called the team leader back. ‘It’s no good, I think he’s got brain damage. I must’ve hit him harder than I thought. No matter, Englefield wants his money and may not have even left yet. We’ll give it another hour or so and if he hasn’t shown up by then, I’ll bring him to us.’

‘How on earth will you do that, sir?’

‘You leave that to me and concentrate on your own job. Call me if there’s any sign.’

The Shop.
The same time.

Camburn saw Sir John Leroux outside the door via the monitor, about to press the buzzer. He jumped up and opened it. ‘John, come in.’

Camburn had never seen his old friend looking so flustered. Leroux pointed. ‘In private, now.’

Both men swept through the Shop towards Camburn's office. Camburn stopped briefly and addressed the small team. 'You never saw him, he wasn't here.' He looked at each person in turn. 'Clear?' They all nodded.

To describe Sir John's presence in the Shop as highly irregular would be a massive understatement – it was never supposed to happen, and this was the first time he'd set foot inside the command centre of the organisation that didn't officially exist.

Camburn shut the door and handed Leroux a large Scotch. 'What the bloody hell's the matter, John? It's all in hand. We can leave it to the politicians to pass off at least some of whatever's on the memory sticks as fakery. Yes, the shit will hit the fan, but they can put out tons of disinformation and other outlandish claims to dilute it – it can be dealt with.'

Leroux shook his head. Camburn continued. 'Englefield's dead and we have the decryption key to the Dropbox. With any luck we'll be scooping Black up soon, although he's late for the handover.'

Leroux took a large gulp of his drink, set it down and leaned in. 'James, this is a conversation I never thought we'd have. I've had a telephone call…'

Five minutes later Camburn emerged from his office ashen-faced. 'Jo, get Jenks on the line now. Scratch that, I'll ring him myself – no one is to leave this room.'

Camburn went back to his office noticing Leroux had poured himself a large refill.

*

Jenks wasn't surprised when his phone buzzed – he was expecting an update from Camburn.

'Hi, James, what news from the front?'

Camburn chose his words carefully. 'Listen to me, lad, and think back over our working relationship and our friendship; have I ever let you down or caused you to distrust me in any way?'

'James, what's the matter, you sound weird.' Jenks lowered his voice to a whisper. 'If you're under duress I need to know. Where did we meet two weeks ago?'

'Twyford Lock, now please answer the question.'

'You know I trust you, probably more than anyone.'

'Well I need you to trust me like never before. This is too sensitive to even mention over the phone. I need you in the Shop as quickly as possible. Equip yourself with whatever tools you think you might need to engage the enemy.'

'What enemy?'

'Lad, I don't know.'

'James, are you OK?'

'Jenks, we are facing a grave threat. I have a feeling you'll be in the thick of it somewhere tonight, but I can't tell you where.'

'Why not?'

'Because I don't bloody know, and I don't know who with. We need you, please come now.'

Jenks didn't need to hear anything else, he knew his old friend too well. 'On my way but I'm going to need a little help – tell Maurs to access every single camera on the A299, the M2 and through to Docklands.'

'Consider it done.'

He locked the house and ran over to the garage making straight for the metal trunk – within a minute he was in his underground store. He closed his eyes, inhaled, held the breath and slowly let it out. He repeated the action and opened his eyes, ready to focus on equipping himself. The problem was he didn't know who his enemy was, the location, terrain, or how many people he might have to deal with.

He decided what to take – too much could hinder him, too little might be the last mistake he'd ever make. He struggled with a piece of kit he'd been given by a foreign contact, and after sorting it out, pulled on his all in one leathers.

He strapped on a shoulder harness which had an additional holster in the small of his back. Arming himself with his usual Glock 17 pistols, he screwed a suppressor to one, holstering it under his right arm, slotting the other into the rear pouch. Grabbing an old flak jacket he'd kept from his army days and dyed black, he began to pull out drawers and open cupboards, filling the numerous pockets with things he thought could come in useful. He packed six additional magazines which meant with one in the spout of both guns and a full clip in each, he had 138 bullets to fire. If he needed 139, he was in trouble.

Climbing the stairs back up to the garage, he took more items from a locker and pushed them into the Ducati's small storage compartment. He was set to go. 'Control from Alpha One, leaving now. I'll tell you when to kill the cameras.'

'Received Alpha One, we're standing by.'

Jenks eased out of his drive and towards the A299 along a mile or so of winding country roads. Turning a sharp right onto the on slip, he began to twist the throttle. 'Control from Alpha One, kill them.' The reply was instant. 'All off Alpha One, you are green to go.' As he rounded the corner and caught sight of the dual carriageway, he twisted the throttle all the way round.

The ferocity of the acceleration his Ducati was capable of never ceased to amaze him. It wasn't the type of bike a rider could max out anywhere other than a German autobahn. He was still in first gear as he hit 60mph in a shade over two seconds. He dropped down to second and held on tightly as he was catapulted onto the main road, the massive engine pushing never-ending power to the rear wheel.

Traffic was light – it was now late and he could see the odd tail light in the distance. He'd completed every covert motorcycling course available over the years, trained to ride at high speed and recognise potential hazards, so confidence in his ability wasn't an issue.

The common factor was forward vision. Looking beyond the vehicle in front, observing the behaviour and braking of vehicles three or four ahead would determine what the car in front would do. Seeing it early meant more reaction time.

Dressed completely in black, Jenks would be relying on his headlight to alert drivers of his approach. However, at the speed he was travelling, by the time a driver saw him flash up in the mirror, he'd be past them and disappearing into the distance – skill, concentration and a bit of luck was everything.

The distance from Jenks's house to the Shop was about sixty miles. Within fifteen minutes he'd eaten up thirty-eight miles. He passed a few cars and slow moving lorries and was making good progress. He'd have to take the fastest route which meant going through the Dartford Crossing, which was another seven miles. At his current speed it would take him just over two and a half minutes. A minute later he heard Maureen in his ear.

'Jenks, I'm monitoring the 999 system. Someone's phoned in that a black bike just passed them on the M2 doing about warp factor 9. I've got the GPS on your phone, traffic officers are setting a stinger three miles ahead of you – how fast are you going?'

Jenks glanced at the speedometer. 'Er, about a hundred and sixty seven, but it always says you're going faster than you really are, let me know if there's any updates.'

'Received, I'll…hang on, there's more. Cancel that, they're asking for a description of clothing but the caller could only say the rider was all in black.'

'Received.'

He scanned ahead but couldn't yet see any flashing blue lights. Just before the brow of the next hill he spotted an advertising hoarding set off the road behind the hard shoulder. He checked his side mirror and saw a car a mile or so back. Turning off his lights he pulled up as hard as he dared, taking most of the speed off using both brakes.

Aware that even with his lights off the brake light would still illuminate, he released the foot pedal, using just the front brake to slow the bike sufficiently and glide in behind the hoarding. The driver would have just seen a bright red light in the distance for a few seconds then disappear into thin air.

Unfastening the storage compartment, Jenks grabbed the items he'd put in there less than twenty minutes before. He quickly slipped on the reflective vest, pulled a yellow helmet cover over his own and attached an orange petrol tank cover. In seconds he pulled back onto the motorway, settling at a steady 65mph.

As he crested the hill he saw a sea of flashing blue lights and an officer behind the wing of a Range Rover poised to deploy the stinger. His colleagues stood further back, all concentrating on the hill. Jenks slowed the bike to 45mph. None of the officers even turned their heads as he rode past. They were all looking for a madman dressed completely in black, not a sensible rider in hi-vis clothing. Hiding in plain sight was often the best way.

Jenks called in that he was through the police trap, and would be at the Shop within ten minutes after passing through the toll at Dartford. Emerging on the Essex side he peeled off onto the A13, passing wasteland which had once been the site of numerous industries, now dotted with crumbling monuments to the past, but mostly one big open area waiting to be brought back to life.

Camburn looked at his watch then looked again, unsure if he'd read it wrong the first time. Whitstable to Docklands in under half an hour was insanely quick. As Jenks approached the Shop the roller shutter started to rise. Riding straight in he saw Camburn waiting for him looking like he'd aged ten years. 'This way, lad.'

Jenks raised a hand to acknowledge the staff, pulling off his helmet, and followed Camburn directly to his office. Jenks entered first and saw another man sitting nursing a glass. Camburn pulled up another chair. 'Jenks, this is Sir John Leroux, head of MI6.' Jenks extended his hand. 'I recognise you from the press.' The men shook and Leroux nodded but said nothing, leaving Camburn to continue. 'Sir John is also the Caretaker.' Jenks looked at Camburn. 'That's a bit of a breach of protocol, isn't it? This must be serious.'

'You have no idea, my boy. Protocol is out the window tonight.'

Jenks said nothing. Camburn nodded at Leroux. Leroux cleared his throat.

'What I am about to tell you is beyond sensitive, it's possibly the biggest threat we've faced since the war. I'm afraid your security clearance does not permit me to divulge every detail…'

Jenks raised his hand. 'With the greatest respect, Sir John, you can park your bullshit security clearance speech right there. A, a man who doesn't exist can't have a security clearance, and B, the department knows my terms – I do not accept a job without complete disclosure of everything pertaining to the mission.' Leroux's face was turning a darker shade of crimson by the second.

'I've fulfilled my contract, so if you'll excuse me I'll be getting along.' Jenks began to stand as Leroux erupted with fury, shouting directly into Jenks's stone face. 'Just who the bloody hell do you think you're talking to, do you have...' Camburn exploded out of his chair pulling Leroux around by the shoulder to face him. Jenks had never seen his old friend so angry or threatening, or move so quickly.

Camburn squared up to him, inches from Leroux's face and pointed at Jenks. 'This man has killed more people for his country than anyone I know. He's risked his life on more occasions than the combined years you and I have been alive, and that's only the ones I know about. Stop being a complete arse, John, and tell him everything or I'll tender my resignation effective from now and walk out with him.'

For a moment there was silence. Leroux sat down, running his fingers through his thick grey hair. Jenks and Camburn took their seats again. Leroux looked at Jenks. 'I'm sorry. A lot's happened in the last hour. To say there's more at stake than I or anyone in my position has ever encountered would be the understatement of the century. Can we start again?' Leroux offered his hand to Jenks, which he shook. Leroux turned to Camburn. 'Sorry, James.' Camburn smiled, 'All forgotten, John, the floor is yours.' Camburn turned to see Jenks looking wide-eyed at him, and winked.

Leroux took a deep breath and composed himself. 'I've had a telephone call from the Queen. Have you ever heard the term Sovereign Sealed?' Jenks shook his head. 'Well neither had James until half an hour ago. I don't know quite where to start, so bear with me.' Leroux cleared his throat again. 'We Brits have always had an obsession with keeping records. The more potentially damaging, the more closely guarded it is. As you're well aware, the security services have done some pretty extreme things in the past, as have our armed services. I mean, that's why the Department was set up in the first place, after the business in Gibraltar.'

He poured himself another two fingers of single malt.

'Anyway, the more secret the secret *is*, the deeper it's buried. I've got access to stuff in SIS headquarters that needs a retina scan, electronic key code and fingerprint recognition to get into it. Documents in

Thames House have at least the same measures, as does the Commissioner at Scotland Yard.'

He raised the crystal glass and took a large gulp.

'But, and this is a big but, there are some documents that detail events that are…and I can't overstress this, *so* potentially damaging in the wrong hands that they've never been opened since the day they were sealed.'

Jenks went to ask a question but Leroux raised a hand. 'Let me continue, Jenks, and I may answer any questions you have – the clock is ticking. So, Great Britain has taken part in operations, sometimes alone, sometimes with other countries over the years, which were so illegal, so far off the books that it wasn't felt safe to keep any reference to them at all. I'm talking about actions taken alongside our sworn enemies against so called allies, murders of heads of state, atrocities in the name of peace and more double- and triple-crossing than you could ever imagine.

Jenks spoke. 'Examples?'

Leroux looked even more uncomfortable. Camburn picked up on it immediately. 'Go on, John.'

Leroux continued. 'OK. Now I myself have only seen the documents I've submitted, but I have a little knowledge about the contents of a few of the others. Jesus Christ, even thinking about them sends a chill through me.' Leroux rubbed his arm as if trying to warm up.

'Take for example Chairman Mao. He died in September 1976 of a heart attack. After he died everything in China started to change and open up. Today they are one of the most important trading partners with us, the Yanks, the Germans, French – well basically everyone. Mao didn't die of a heart attack, he was poisoned. It was a joint venture between us, the Germans and the Yanks.'

The temperature in the room seemed to instantly drop a few degrees, and everyone was quiet. Leroux continued.

'Gentlemen, you will remember Kim Jong-il. Another heart attack victim? Nothing of the sort – yes, his heart stopped, but only because a long-term sleeper agent slipped massive amounts of Digoxin into his meals when he was on that bloody train of his.'

Camburn spoke. 'I heard he flew into a massive rage because the North Koreans were falling behind building a power plant which brought on a heart attack.'

'Oh it did, James, it was the waiter that offered his humble condolences that Kim's latest brainchild was not going to be finished on time. Kim didn't know at that point. With all the drugs the waiter had been slipping him throughout the week, his heart basically exploded when he got angry.'

Jenks raised a finger. 'And we had a hand in that?'

'Oh, very much so. Us, America again and a couple of other nations including South Korea – it was a long-term infiltration. It was thought that if Kim could be got rid of, the regime would at last change – maybe even reunification with the south. How wrong we all were. It's ten times worse now *and* they've gone nuclear.'

Camburn was next. 'Tell me it doesn't get any worse, John.'

'Sorry, my old friend, but it does. I only know the contents of some – there's a recent one regarding help we've given Assad...'

Jenks sat bolt upright. 'Fucking Syria? Are you serious?'

Leroux nodded. 'It was something that was supposed to work against him, but it all went pear-shaped and ended up benefiting his whole regime and strengthened his position, inadvertently.'

Camburn and Jenks remained silent.

'And don't get me started about prisoner swaps. We gave the Germans Rudolph bloody Hess back as soon as the Nuremberg trials were over. It was all make-believe – the man in Spandau was an actor. They'd pick him up in a car and deposit him there heavily made up for the odd picture that *leaked* out. That's why the photos were always from a distance. It was all part of an agreement to get the best Kraut scientists over to America.'

Jenks interjected, 'But you said a minute ago it wasn't safe to keep any records of this stuff at all?'

'Yes – the original dockets, files, minutes of meetings, agreements, plans etc were all destroyed, but it was felt a record should be kept *somewhere*. A précis if you like. This all goes way back to the war. Basically King George VI was good friends with

Stewert Menzies, then head of MI6 – utterly brilliant man. The King was a very forward thinking person too, and after dinner one evening they spoke about future generations learning from the mistakes of the past.'

Jenks commented, 'But we're still making them.'

'Not the immediate future generation, but in hundreds of years. They were both of the opinion that mankind would eventually move on from conflicts, but it would be a useful history lesson, a reminder if you like of how badly man treated man. Their vision was that people could look back and ensure none of the terrible things we did in the past were repeated.'

Jenks spoke. 'So where does the Sovereign Sealed stuff come in?'

'Before everything pertaining to whatever atrocity we'd been party to was destroyed, a detailed report was handwritten and placed in an envelope. The King closed it in the presence of the head of MI6 with sealing wax and pressed the royal seal into it. The envelope was then placed in a vault in the King's private chambers at Balmoral. No one except the King and C knew. Even records of the vault's existence were destroyed. Before the King died, he briefed Princess Elizabeth, who became the sole custodian of those records when she ascended.'

Jenks let out a whistle. 'And you've seen these?'

Leroux nodded. 'A few yes, but only the envelopes. I once sought permission for one to be opened but she refused. She's a strong woman, and no one really knows the full story of how she's served her country. Like her father, she's briefed on the contents before applying the seal. She's basically the only person alive who knows everything.'

Camburn interjected, 'John, how many of these Sovereign Sealed records are there, for God's sake?'

Leroux grimaced. '154.'

Camburn and Jenks looked stunned.

Leroux continued. 'I had a telephone call from Her Majesty a little earlier. She returned to Balmoral on Sunday evening, but as she was getting ready for bed tonight she opened the vault to place some jewellery in and discovered every single one of the envelopes was missing.'

No one said anything until Camburn asked, 'But how did they get in if no one even knew about the vault?'

'Well this is where it really gets interesting, no, that's the wrong word, this is where it gets really frightening. I asked Her Majesty if any staff had been acting strangely or out of character recently. The only thing she could think of was that her head footman, a man called Dennis Best, had called in sick with the flu, and hasn't been contactable since. She thought it unusual as Best never missed a day's work.'

Camburn raised his hand. 'Do we know any more about this chap Best?'

'We do now. I got a call from my station chief on the way over and it's not good. Her Majesty spoke very highly of Best and I think they had a really good working relationship. As soon as she told me I started to worry, so instructed the Inspector from Royalty Protection to find something of Best's to fingerprint. He lifted good dabs off a tin of coke in his office and emailed them straight through to me. I got my Chief to run them through the system.'

Jenks and Camburn both spoke. 'And?'

'We got a hit. Not only did they *not* match the set Best provided when he was accepted for the post, but they came back to a man called Anatoly Belinsky, a known KGB officer who disappeared off the face of the earth a few years ago.'

Camburn interjected, 'Latex over-prints. I've seen them.'

Leroux concurred. 'My thoughts exactly. The copper despatched to take the prints once vetting was complete would've been way down the food chain, probably a wet behind the ears probationer. Once Belinsky was inked up he'd never spot them.'

Camburn shook his head again. 'Ingenious.'

'Interpol still have an outstanding warrant for Belinsky for the murder of three German intelligence officers a few years back. And, he only got the promotion to head footman after his boss wound up dead in an accident.'

Jenks pondered his next question. 'So how the hell would Belinsky get into the vault?'

Leroux puffed out his cheeks. 'Well....the answer, I think, comes from way back in history. There is only one key. An old brass one which the Queen carries everywhere with her – it never leaves her side. But, there used to be two a very long time ago.'

Camburn and Jenks spoke in unison again. '*Used* to be two?'

'Yes, but the other was presumed lost in the late forties. You remember dear old Anthony Blunt? One of the most treacherous bastards this country ever had the misfortune to breed? For many years Blunt was the keeper of the monarch's art. He was actually an expert in his field, and advised the King and later Her Majesty on purchases, and maintained the Royal Collection. He was also a close and trusted friend of old Bertie.'

Camburn shook his head. 'I think I know what's coming.'

Leroux pursed his lips. 'The King entrusted Blunt with the other key so he could access the vault where a lot of the art was stored. Don't forget this was way before the royals were persuaded to display more of their amazing collection for the nation to see. Prior to that most of it was under lock and key.'

'Blunt's key.'

'Quite. Blunt claimed to have accidently lost it overboard when he was fishing on one of the lochs. The King wasn't that fussed and the matter was forgotten. I would imagine Blunt sent the key back to Moscow in case it could be useful in the future.'

Camburn looked at the ceiling. 'That's…Jesus, we all know the Russians are masters of the long game, but that's ridiculous.'

Leroux replied, 'That's exactly why they've been so successful in the world of espionage for decades. They keep things forever in case they can make use of them in ways not apparent at the time. They placed Belinsky at Balmoral waiting for the opportune moment to strike. He's been there nearly three years, and in that time I've personally deposited four reports for the Queen to seal.'

Camburn spoke. 'I don't wish to sound flippant, John, but anything of note?'

Leroux thought back. 'Do you remember in 2018 when Russia fired on those three Ukrainian ships?'

Camburn held his head. 'Please don't tell me we had a hand in that?'

Leroux nodded. 'Unfortunately yes, with help from others. Russia took the blame and turned the situation around, so it backfired a little. Last year – the American drones that were shot down by Iran...'

Camburn finished the sentence, 'turns out it was the Americans with help from us and other NATO allies in an attempt to find an excuse to bomb the fuck out of Iran?'

'You're not far off, James.'

Jenks spoke for the first time in a few minutes. 'And with the harvesting of the equivalent from the Americans, the timing is right. And, let's not forget Russia's pulled out of the G20 next weekend. They're rapidly heading towards the end game, gentlemen. If this gets out, every nation will be at each other's throats.'

Camburn raised his head. 'Lad, if this gets out, we're potentially looking at World War III.'

Dagenham.
The same time.

The Englishman called his assistant into the office. 'We've waited long enough, it's time to bring Englefield to us. Your men are deployed, I take it?'

'Two near the gate, three patrolling the perimeter, and you and I.'

'Good. Pass me my laptop.'

'What are you going to do, sir?'

'Quite simple, my old friend, I'm now going to become Chas Black.'

The Englishman logged into the email account and typed a message, saving it into the drafts folder.

Dude, the welikeleaks people picked me up. They know about the transfer at 6pm. I had to give them the Dropbox log-in details so they could see the files were there. I'd already told them that we wanted to see the money, but they're saying they want the key first. It's totally cool though, they've shown me the money ready to go – they even said you could press the button to deposit the dough once they've got the key.

The Englishman looked up at his assistant. 'Now we wait for Englefield to reply.'

The Shop.
The same time.

Jenks spoke. 'It's all too much of a coincidence. The Russians are involved in the CIA leak. Two major breaches like this don't happen at the same time and not be connected. They must have someone deep in the Agency.'

Camburn turned to Jenks. 'I agree, but who? It's certainly wasn't Buckland, and I'd be pretty sure it isn't their Caretaker.'

Leroux joined the conversation. 'This doesn't leave the room. Katherine Jackson, the director of the CIA, is the American Caretaker. It's not her. My own personal opinion is that it wasn't Englefield, otherwise why would he have needed Black at all?'

The door burst open and Maureen came bustling in. Camburn looked up, his temper rising. 'Maureen, it must be bloody obvious we don't want to be disturbed – and when did knocking go out of fashion?'

The trusted operative ignored him and walked up to the table. 'You need to see this right now. Black just drafted another email.'

All three jumped up and followed her to her console. 'Read that. It was saved thirty seconds ago.'

The three men read the email, but Jenks spoke first. 'It's not Black.'

Camburn still seemed a little angry. 'What do you mean it's not Black?'

Jenks explained. 'If they've got Black there's no way they'd trust him to sit at a keyboard and type an email. We've seen the security protocol they've used so far. One word, phrase or even a certain symbol would be enough to alert Englefield it was a trap. They may well have Black, but it's not him typing. Remember that we got the log-in details which the CIA found in Englefield's house? That means someone in the CIA has them as well. If it's the Russians' sleeper agent…'

Camburn completed the sentence. 'He'll have passed them to his masters, and they've got Black.'

Chapter 25.

The solution.

Camburn addressed the Shop staff. 'Ladies and gentlemen, matters have come to light of which I cannot divulge the full details, but that won't affect your actions. I *can* tell you that we believe Russia is behind the *Welikeleaks* planned dissemination of the files Englefield stole from the CIA. The Russians also have in their possession equally if not more damaging secret material stolen from us. When put with the Agency's files this presents the biggest threat to world peace in living memory. Get those brains warmed up, ladies and gentlemen, we've got some serious thinking to do.'

The twins studied the messages, talking over each other. Jack stood up. 'Hendrix was the code. It's one of his songs – if six was nine. Englefield said he'd send the files at nine but Black knew he really meant six.'

Camburn turned. 'Excellent thinking, but it doesn't help us now. We must assume from the message the Russians are in possession of the final handover of the encrypted files, and are looking at the Dropbox. They just need the key.'

Miles spoke. 'Er, maybe not, sir. It will be heavily encrypted, but if they can hack into the Pentagon…'

Jack finished the sentence for him. 'Then they might be able to break the encryption eventually. Russia has the best nerds on the planet. If it were us we'd link up hundreds, maybe thousands of computers and bombard the file with a breaker program, hitting it with millions of possibles every minute. Eventually they'll get lucky. It may take years or just a day.'

Almost everyone in the room spoke in unison. 'Shit.'

Jenks took control. 'Wait. They obviously have no idea Englefield is dead. We need to buy time so we can get to them before Englefield, so to speak. Two can play at that game. Maurs, buckle up – you are about to become Joshua Englefield.'

Maureen smiled and looked up. 'Howdy.'

Leroux looked at Jenks, incredulous. '*What*?'

'Black and Englefield are going to start talking again. Maurs, type these words.' *Shit man, I was on Westminster Bridge, when you didn't show I got spooked, where are you?*

Everyone stared at the screen in silence. A message dropped into drafts.

They've got a place in Dagenham, it's cool. Make your way over here. The tube's the quickest. Let me know when you get to Dagenham East and they'll pick you up. This pad is totally amazing man, I'm gonna buy one like this!

No one spoke, allowing Jenks time to think. 'Type this reply.'

Fuck that's a relief. I wasn't sure what to do so split. I'm over near Heathrow, I booked a ticket for tomorrow morning. Think I can afford another though lol. It's gonna take a while, I'll let you know when I get there.

The reply didn't take long to arrive.

Cool man, I'll be here. They got crate loads of champagne so don't be too long.

Everyone looked at Jenks. 'Right, we've bought ourselves an hour or so. Just the small problem of narrowing the location down from 50,000 houses to one. Everyone, think – we're missing something obvious.'

The room was silent. Jenks excused himself and went to sit alone in Camburn's office. He ran everything back in his mind – what they'd gleaned from the email exchanges and what he'd been told by Englefield. Something was tickling inside his brain but he'd no idea what. He ran it forward again from the start, stopped in the middle and reversed his thought process. Nothing, except a tingle that the answer was staring him in the face but he couldn't see it. He went back into the control room.

Camburn noticed him approaching. 'Anything?'

'Nope. All I know is there's a link out there – a connection we haven't made yet.'

The control room went quiet again. After a minute of total silence Miles broke the ice, trying to lighten the mood. 'Er, anyone fancy a game of cards?'

Jenks spun round. 'What did you just say?'

'I'm sorry, Jenks, it was inappropriate, I was just being stupid.'

'Say it again.'

'It was a stupid joke and I shouldn't have said it. I just said does anyone fancy a game of cards?'

Jenks raised his hand and Miles instinctively covered his head. Jenks grabbed his shoulder, shaking it. 'That might just be it. Maurs, you checked the expenditure on his Amex card yes? And it didn't show any phone purchases, right?'

'Correct, only the air tickets, hotel bookings and the deposit to the plastic surgeon. Oh, and the train tickets.'

Jenks started walking round in circles, tapping the side of his face. He stopped, snapping his fingers. 'Do you know if concierge services are billed to his account immediately or a month in arrears?'

'Er, no.'

'Check it.'

Maureen logged into the Amex database and called up the card details. She clicked on the history of Rick Mills concierge account and slapped the desk. 'Bingo. He ordered two smartphones. One was delivered to the Krasnapolsky Hotel in Amsterdam and the other to...looks like a guest house in Earls Court.'

Jenks put his hand on Maureen's shoulder. 'Does it show details of the phones?'

Maureen scrolled to the next page. 'Oh yes. Phone and IMEI number. We've got him.'

'We haven't got the full house yet, Maurs, is the phone switched on and is GPS enabled?'

She went into another system. 'Give me a minute.' Jenks stepped back to give her room to work, and everyone waited with bated breath.

Maureen spoke. 'I'm sorry, Jenks, I tried, I really did.'

Everyone looked deflated.

'I'm afraid I can only get you within six feet of the handset.'

Jenks spun her round and planted a kiss on her cheek. 'You little beauty.'

Maureen zoomed her map in. 'Obviously I can't guarantee Black is there, but the phone is here. It's an old factory out in Dagenham just before you get to Rainham Marshes. I think it used to manufacture car parts but looks pretty derelict now.'

Jenks studied the satellite image of the site. 'I don't believe it – I went past it half an hour ago. It's just off the A13. Can you zoom in a bit more?'

Maureen increased the image until it started to pixilate. She pointed to the main road. 'Looks like there's a long service road from the A1306 with a large hard standing area behind it, probably the staff car park – bit of undergrowth then lots of empty ground.'

Camburn leant in. ‘I can get a chopper airborne from City Airport in thirty minutes.’

Jenks shook his head. ‘Get it ready to fly by all means, but I’m not going in on it – too noisy and too slow. It’s only about eight miles – I can be there in minutes.’

Leroux spoke up. ‘Do you want to wait for backup?’

Jenks shook his head. ‘No thank you, Sir John. My job, my rules. Actually there is one thing. Our imaginary Englefield is getting the tube to Dagenham East and gave the impression he was happy to be picked up. They’ll have men at the station. I could do with them out of the picture once I go in.’

Camburn spoke. ‘You leave them to me, old son, I know a particularly unpleasant individual in Ilford we use from time to time, I’ll give him a call.’

Jenks began to zip up his leathers. ‘Joanne, can you get me heat signatures from the drone?’

Jo Fox turned her chair. ‘Yep, it’s got infrared but not from here, I’m afraid. At the absolute maximum the range is five miles, then you’ve got to have enough battery power to fly it back.’

Jenks’s mouth turned up into a grin. ‘You ever been on the back of a bike before?’

Jo smiled back. ‘Er, yes! Miles, can I borrow your lid?’

Miles Moore was also a biker, but his 50cc twist and go scooter would almost fit on the back of the Ducati. He reached under his desk and pulled out his crash helmet. 'Take my jacket as well, it's a proper bike one.'

Maureen turned. 'Shame you haven't got a proper bike to go with it.'

Miles stuck two fingers up at her, smiling.

Jenks tapped Jo on the shoulder. 'Come on, girl, let's hit the road. Maurs, can you…'

'The cameras, yes I know.'

Jenks and Jo jogged out to the garage and he started the Ducati, giving it a quick rev. The ear-splitting shriek of the massive engine made her jump.

'Jesus, Jenks, let me know if you're going to do that again please.'

She stowed the drone in her backpack and Jenks turned to face her.

'We're going to be going pretty fast. Let me do the leaning, you just hold on to me, you hear? That's all you have to do. I'll drop you about two miles from the site – I don't want you closer than that.'

She nodded. Jenks climbed astride the bike and pressed the wall button to raise the roller shutter. 'You coming or not? Hop on.'

Jo climbed on, put her hands around his waist and leant into his back. It wasn't very comfortable due to all the lumps and bumps from the kit in his pockets, but she didn't care. Jenks eased out, snaking along the service roads serving the glass city – a million miles away from the drab black and white world the docks once were.

Jenks thumbed his mic. 'Control from Alpha One, can you do anything about the police?'

Camburn transmitted back. 'Maurs is on it. She's phoned in a credible bomb threat to Scotland Yard for a nightclub in Wood Green using a recognised code word. Half the Met are heading in the opposite direction from you as fast as they can.'

Jenks knew of Maureen's tragedy and grimaced. 'All received.'

Jo held on for dear life as Jenks opened the throttle. Truth be known, she was probably gripping him a little harder than she needed, but opportunities like that didn't arise every day. It had also started to rain, making the roads slippery.

With no traffic to speak of they hit over 100mph on the wider stretches, eating up the distance quicker than Jenks had estimated. He saw a sign for a lay-by up ahead and pointed at it. Jo tapped his back. They pulled up hard and Jenks lifted his visor. 'Slip through the hedge and call me as soon as the drone's up.'

She climbed off, gave Jenks a thumbs up and disappeared through a gap in the undergrowth. Within thirty seconds the quadcopter was airborne. She realised she didn't have a call sign so made one up. 'Alpha One from Pillion, she's up and inbound.'

Jenks smiled, looking up briefly, but the tiny flying spy was virtually invisible under the night sky over Dagenham. He could hear the sound of sirens in the distance but they were getting fainter. 'Give me heat signatures as soon as you can…Pillion.'

Although slower than the Ducati the drone took a direct route, flying a straight line over fields, streams and wasteland. Within a minute it was hovering high over the factory. 'Alpha One from Pillion, I can see you in the distance, hold back, you're coming in too fast. Give me a few seconds.'

'Pillion from Alpha One, I'm pulling up, but be quick.'

Jo studied the screen intently, seeing building outlines rather than clear detail. She switched to infrared and began scanning. 'Alpha One from Pillion, you've got the entrance service road running south off the main road about 100 metres long, lots of bushes and scrub along the west side. The factory building is on the east, with a large area behind it. Beyond that is more scrub and what I would guess was the car park.'

'Good, what are you picking up on infrared?'

'I've got three spikes around the rear area, looks like a perimeter patrol. There's light leaking from the south-east corner of the main building and a small spike just outside that point.'

'Could it be a car?'

'I don't think so, too small. Possibly a generator – give me a second to sweep round again and switch cameras.'

Jenks waited, the bike burbling and ticking.

'Alpha One, looks like a car parked in the rear loading area but I'm not getting heat so it's been there a while. OK, there's windows in the roof and I've got two, no, three heat sigs in the main building. One just disappeared into another smaller room in the direction of the small heat source. I'm now heading up the service road. I've got, no wait. I can't be sure, Alpha One, I got a spike for a second but it's gone now – could be an animal but I'm not picking up anything now.'

'Roger that, I'm moving in.'

Jenks shot back onto the carriageway and accelerated towards the factory, his rear wheel spinning momentarily on the wet tarmac. He saw the entrance to the service road within a minute.

Two large galvanised water tanks sat each side of the entrance. They'd previously been in front of the gates to stop vehicles entering, but had been dragged to the side by the estate agent. Jenks had a clear run in. It was almost pitch black when he turned off his lights, but he could make out just enough of the grey gravel to keep on it.

He planned to hide the bike forty metres in and continue on foot. He'd already hit 30mph when he heard an urgent transmission from Jo – all he caught was screaming, 'Jenks – men…'

The two Russians manning the entrance had turned the water tanks on their side to make a temporary shelter from the rain. Once crouching inside, even the most sophisticated infrared camera couldn't penetrate galvanised steel. Jenks saw it too late. Hearing the sound of the bike accelerating towards them, both men jumped out and grabbed the ends of a large chain lying across the road and pulled it tight. Jenks leapt off the bike as the front of the Ducati hurtled into it. Now riderless, the bike started to slew and catapulted end over end, sending up a shower of sparks as it skidded to a halt.

Jenks instinctively put himself into a tumble but hit the ground hard, his shoulder striking the ground first. With no time to check if anything was broken he dove for the cover of the bushes, drawing his silenced Glock.

The entrance was well away from any streetlights, so all three men were working blind. Jenks stayed as still as a cornered mouse. He could hear the faint crunch of someone trying to walk quietly but couldn't make out a shape. He then heard someone whispering into a radio. Of the four languages he spoke fluently, Russian was thankfully one of them.

He struggled to hear exactly what was being said, but heard one man ordering another to hold position at the gate. For Jenks, that was enough. He sighted his gun into the darkness towards the sound, firing six suppressed shots in quick succession in a tight circle. He heard the thud of a body.

Jenks sprinted over to the dark shape, scanning for the other threat. His shoulder hurt like hell, but still seemed to move in the directions it was supposed to. Gripping the man's legs, he dragged him into the bushes. The man had an earpiece and a handset on his belt, which Jenks relieved him of, pushing the earpiece into his other ear.

He checked the radio. Not state of the art, which was what he'd hoped. Perfectly good, but not sophisticated enough to identity a particular user to a base station when transmitting.

He kept behind bushes, using the cover to sprint back towards the gate. Time was paramount before others came to investigate the noise. He could just about make out the shape of the other man crouched against the water tank, using it to shield most of his body.

Jenks cupped his hands around his mouth. 'Psst.' In perfect Russian, but barely above a whisper, he called out. 'Over here, he's hurt.' A figure stepped out and Jenks squeezed the trigger three times. He heard the body drop and ran over to find the man still alive but bleeding heavily. Pulling him back to the water tank, he pushed him inside.

Jenks pulled a fragmentation grenade from his flak jacket, pulling the pin with his teeth. Just before letting the tank drop the last six inches he tossed the grenade in. 'That's for the bike, comrade.' The tank absorbed most of the blast sound, but Jenks still heard the splash as the Russian's disintegrating body hit all five sides.

The borrowed earpiece crackled and Jenks heard someone asking what the hell was going on down there. He pressed the transmit button on his newly acquired radio, and putting on an extremely pained and breathless voice, answered in fluent Russian, 'It's fine but I can't walk.'

'Is that you, Marat? 'What is wrong with your voice?'

Jenks grimaced and formed his mouth into the shape it would be if he was in intense pain, and panted. 'I turned the water tank over to shelter from the rain. I dropped it on my ankle, I think it's broken.'

'You fool, you're supposed to be patrolling. Where's Leonid? I can't raise him on the radio.'

'He went to scare some kids off who tried to get in on a motorbike. Arghh... Sorry. He was complaining his battery was loose earlier, perhaps it fell out. I can see him though and call to him.'

'Well just stay on post and tell Leonid to keep within earshot of you. We will sort your leg out later.'

'Understood.'

Jenks kept low and ran back up the other side of the bushes, heading towards the factory. 'Pillion, sit rep please.'

'Still got three signatures round the back. I just saw a fourth but he's gone back inside. One sig still static in the middle of the factory floor. You have men at your eight, eleven and two o'clock.'

'Received.'

Jenks slowed, moving through the undergrowth making less noise than a grass snake. Peering through the bushes he could see a little more thanks to the light seeping out from the factory. It wasn't bright, and he could hear the sound of a generator on the other side of the building, but it was better than nothing.

He heard a transmission. 'Base from Taras, I have to pee. One minute.'

He heard the reply. 'Be quick.'

Jenks had no idea which of the three men he couldn't see was Taras, but hoped it was the one closest to him. He reached inside his jacket and pulled on a full face balaclava and waited. He heard footsteps, and the outline of a man began to emerge. The man walked up to the bushes and settled himself in front of the prone Jenks, as the sound of a zipper being pulled down filled the air. The man waited for his flow to start, leaning forwards slightly. Jenks raised the barrel of his Glock and sent a silent round directly into the man's groin.

The man instantly straightened, throwing his head back, drawing a breath to scream. Jenks despatched him with a second shot into the roof of his mouth. The only significant sound was pieces of skull landing on the concrete before the body collapsed.

Jenks inched forward and dragged the man towards him, content he was hidden well enough under the cover of darkness. He slowly retreated back into the shadows and thumbed his mic, whispering.

'Pillion, sit rep.'

'One about forty metres directly in front of you near the south-east corner, one patrolling round the front – you're blind to him for the moment.'

'Received.'

He now had a problem. Although the bushes were thick around the rear of the factory, there was a large open gap which would have been the entrance to the staff car park. Jenks could cross it at speed, but it would mean passing through the strip of light escaping through the broken windows. He wanted to avoid a gun battle with up to four other people if at all possible, preferring a silent approach. He needed to think. Dropping the partially used magazine out of the Glock, he quietly inserted a full clip.

Keeping hold of the ejected magazine he pushed three bullets out, placing them in front of him. His stolen radio came to life again.

'Taras receiving, Stepan. I thought I heard a noise, have you heard anything?'

Jenks picked up a handful of leaves, rubbing them over the radio and transmitted. '*Nyet.*'

Stepan replied, 'What's wrong with these fucking radios, they're shit.'

Jenks kept rustling. '*Da, der'mo.*'

The man turned and slowly continued his patrol. Jenks saw the flash of a match and the glow of a cigarette. Reaching into one of his breast pockets, he removed a piece of metal five inches long. He wasn't sure why he selected it from his stock of kit, but was glad he had.

He pulled out the hinged arms of the aluminium catapult and clicked them into place as quietly as he could, grimacing when the second one clicked a little louder than the first. Reaching forward, he picked up a bullet, placed it into the small leather pouch and pulled back the thick elastic. He took aim at the bushes ten metres behind the man and opened his fingers. A fraction of a second later the man turned on his heels, looking towards the noise.

Jenks lay perfectly still in the blackness, watching. The man walked over and peered into the undergrowth. Jenks loaded another bullet and aimed at an area of small trees and brambles twenty metres closer. The man straightened and looked towards where the new sound had come from. The tangle of branches were too thick for a human to move through, so he guessed it must be an animal.

Jenks unsheathed his ceramic paring knife and waited. Picking up the last bullet, he tossed it into the bushes three feet from where he was crouching. The man walked towards the source of the sound. Jenks had no idea what a fox's bark sounded like, hoping the Russian didn't either, and let out a small yelp. He heard the man speak. 'Where are you, little one, are you hurt?'

Springing up like a gymnast, Jenks plunged the knife deep into the side of the guard's neck, pulling it towards the Adam's apple, severing veins, arteries and windpipe. Silently lowering the body he whispered, 'No, you are.'

Retreating back into the darkness, he transmitted. 'Sit rep please, Pillion.'

'The signature at the front is heading towards the north-west corner. Still unsighted on you but will come into the open in about ten seconds.

'Received.'

Jenks ran to the opposite corner putting the building between them. He wanted to try to get a look inside to gauge what sort of threat was left. Jo had told him about the possible generator, which he could now clearly hear, which meant there had to be somewhere for the wire to feed into the building. Holding himself flat against the wall he withdrew a small dentist's mirror, extending it just proud of the corner, and confirmed the ground was clear.

Dropping low, he inched along the wall and saw the generator and the cable disappearing through a small window – unfortunately much smaller than him. He could just about pick out the sound of voices inside speaking Russian, but it was difficult to hear clearly over the clatter of the diesel engine.

The window was at least eight feet from the ground with an old steel frame. Jenks was glad he had gloves on, but they'd offer little protection from an unseen shard sticking up. He was sure the people talking weren't in the room, but they were close. He jumped up, grabbing hold of the frame with one hand and hung on – no point injuring both hands. Thankfully the frames were reasonably smooth, probably the result of two generations of naughty schoolboys throwing stones at every remaining piece of glass. *Good lads*, he thought.

Pulling his body up with one arm, he gingerly put his other hand onto the frame. So far, so good. He hauled himself up another few inches and was able to see into the room. It was small and empty apart from a chair, extension lead and a table. His earpiece crackled into life with a transmission from Camburn, but he wasn't exactly in a position to reply.

On the table was a laptop, document scanner and a large open rucksack. Although he could only make out the top two inches of the vellum envelopes poking out, he had no doubt what they were. He listened to the Russian voices.

'Roman, are your men at the railway station yet?'

'I have two units of four men in vehicles either side of the exit, we will not miss him.'

'Excellent. The little shit must be well on his way now.' The man switched to English. 'The glorious day is nearly upon us, my old friend.'

Jenks hung from the window perfectly still, somewhat taken aback at hearing the cut glass tones of a cultured English accent. The situation had become a whole lot stranger.

He lowered himself down and continued around the building. The patrolling guard Jo picked up was on the other side. He and Jenks were now like two moons orbiting a planet on opposite sides to each other. He thumbed his mic, speaking as quietly and quickly as he could. 'Control, I can confirm envelopes are inside. Maintain radio silence and await further. Do not approach.' The reply was a double click, confirmation of message received.

Swiftly moving to the next corner, Jenks stopped by a pile of scrap metal nestling in brambles growing up the side of the building. He used the mirror to peer round the corner and saw the back of the guard five metres ahead. Jenks looked down and found what he wanted. Thinking back to his tactic at the gate, he didn't see why it shouldn't work again. Poking his head around the corner, in little more than a hiss he called out in Russian, 'Quick, round here.'

Jenks heard the sound of the man running through the puddles and adjusted his stance, legs two feet apart. He held the four-foot-long scaffold pole like a baseball player waiting for the pitch. As the man came hurtling around the corner Jenks swung the pole with all his strength. The sound was like a watermelon smashing on the floor. The man's face completely caved in, and he was dead before he hit the concrete. Jenks jumped over the prone body and ran around the building, heading for the entrance. It was obvious he didn't need to check for a pulse.

Sneaking a quick look through the main doors, he saw a hallway, presumably the original reception area, and a set of double doors onto the main factory floor. There was dust everywhere, and tins of paint and building materials scattered around. It looked like workmen had started to make the building more presentable then given up. Jenks retreated a few metres and whispered,

'Pillion, what can you see inside the factory?'

'Still got one static heat sig in the middle of the room which hasn't moved. Another static on the right-hand side but I can't see the other one.'

Having done a complete circuit of the building, short of climbing on the roof and dropping in like Batman, there was only one way in – through the main entrance.

Moving back towards the door, he dropped into a crouch. The bottom panes of glass on one door were missing. Having not packed a can of WD40, he didn't want to risk opening the door and alerting everyone inside of his arrival with an almighty squeak.

He eased himself through the gap, careful not to touch the sides and nudge the door. It reminded him of the kids' game *Operation*. Looking ahead he saw a door which still had a fading sign, printed with the word *Caretaker*. Safely inside, he began to rise.

The Caretaker's door exploded open and a man shot out from the darkness aiming a bone-shattering kick towards Jenks's chin. With little time to react he turned his face with a millisecond to spare, but the boot still struck him a glancing blow on the side of his head. He flew backwards hitting the wall hard, tasting blood in his mouth.

The man came at him again, raising his leg to stamp at Jenks's face. Jenks swerved left and threw a kick but his aim was slightly out, only glancing the man's balls. The bottom of Jenks's boot struck the top of the man's thigh, and the kick was hard. Jenks leapt up as the man was forced to take a step back, and sized up his opponent. The man was shorter than him but nearly twice as wide, and it was all tightly packed muscle.

Jenks was extremely strong, but lean. The man could undoubtedly lift heavier weights than him, but his thick muscle mass meant he wasn't as quick. They looked at each other's holstered pistols and the same thought went through both of their minds. Jenks sprang off his back foot, feigned to move right but ducked left. The man was fractionally too slow to react as Jenks used his height advantage and delivered a vicious elbow strike to the man's nose. The crack of bone echoed in the empty hallway.

Most fighters would go down – blood poured from the wound and the nose was clearly badly broken and pushed to one side. The man shook his head once and flew at Jenks, punching him hard in the middle of his chest. The blow felt like he'd been hit with a cannonball. Jenks staggered back and the men locked eyes. Both knew they were going to settle it hand to hand.

The man raised his fists and jumped towards Jenks swinging a vicious right hook. Jenks had a five-inch height advantage, forcing the man to aim up. He whipped his head to the side, avoiding the blow and delivered a savage kick into the man's right kidney. The man grunted and stopped momentarily. That had hurt. Jenks used the lapse in concentration to land three hard jabs in quick succession on the remains of the man's nose. As he went to swing a hard right hook towards the man's jaw, his enemy let out a huge roar and ducked his head down, causing Jenks to connect with the top of his head. Jenks felt a crack and his fist opened up. The man smiled.

Jenks knew he'd broken at least one finger. He was used to blocking out pain, but broken bones can't be bent, which meant he now only had one fist. The man charged again, but Jenks's reactions were quicker and his body lighter. He side-stepped at the last moment and kicked out hard at the side of the man's knee. The man stumbled but didn't go down. He advanced again, this time slower – clearly he had difficulty putting weight on his left leg.

Jenks sprang at him again to capitalize on the injury, but his wet shoes caused him to lose his footing, giving his opponent an opportunity he might otherwise have never had. Jenks slid into the man who swung his right arm up, clamping his hand around Jenks's neck in a vice-like grip. Jenks delivered a ferocious head-butt to the man's mouth, breaking teeth. The man spat a mixture of phlegm, blood and bits of enamel directly into Jenks's eyes – everything he'd blown out was caught in the balaclava's eye holes. The man found Jenks's right hand and squeezed – it felt like he was being electrocuted as the ends of broken bones grated together.

Jenks knew the man was expecting him to fight back, but unable to see anything, he was severely hampered. Whilst being half pushed and carried towards the corner of the lobby, Jenks lifted his feet off the floor. The unexpected weight caused his opponent to loosen his grip a fraction, which was what he'd planned. Jenks hooked his leg around the man's damaged knee forcing it inwards, opening the already torn ligaments. The man let out a howl and they began to fall.

Jenks clattered into the corner scattering aerosols, tins and paint cans. There was nowhere else to retreat to as the full weight of the man landed on him, forcing every bit of air out of his body. Jenks was stunned. The man wasted no time rearing up, pinning Jenks's arms against the floor and his neck in a crushing grip. The man clearly knew what he was doing, moving his fingers to find and depress Jenks's carotid artery.

Jenks thrashed around using up valuable oxygen – he'd barely managed to inhale before the man cut off his air supply. He knew exactly what would happen next, having used the method himself over the years. In a matter of seconds he would start to pass out, and that would be it. Game over.

His vision was starting to clear, but his eyelids were beginning to feel heavy. Catching a glimpse of something out the corner of his eye he began sweeping his arm around. The man smiled. 'Going for swim?'

Jenks grabbed the plastic tube and turned the can around, grasping the top. He had moments before his strength left him, and mustering everything he had left, flexed his shoulder up no more than an inch. It was enough pressure on the man's knee to push against his injury, and Jenks felt the weight lift a fraction – sufficient to allow him to rotate his shoulder. Snapping his left arm up, Jenks thrust the plastic pipe deep into the man's mouth and depressed the top of the aerosol, sending half a can of expanding filler directly into his opponent's throat.

The viscous white foam immediately thickened and expanded by fifty times its original volume. Jenks watched the man's cheeks puff out to an unnatural size as the foam billowed out of his mouth, causing his jaw to open wider and wider. The man immediately released his grip, frantically clawing at his mouth trying to pull the highly adhesive filler out. But it was useless. The foam had filled his lungs, which were now paralysed. The man's eyes bulged, and in an instant every blood vessel burst simultaneously, the whites turning a deep red. In seconds he was dead.

Jenks rolled off taking deep breaths, feeling life coming back into his body, but he didn't have the luxury of recovery time. Ripping off his balaclava, he wiped the mess from his eyes. He checked the third finger on his right hand and saw it sticking out at a right angle. He looked around and saw the remains of a roll of duct tape and tore off a strip. Gritting his teeth, he pulled the broken digit out straight and taped it tightly against his middle finger. The pain shot a bolt of adrenalin through his body, which was the kick start it needed.

Running at the double doors to the factory floor, he kicked them open and swerved right, the gun held ramrod straight in his left hand sweeping back and forth for threats. Five metres in front of him sat Chas Black, tied to a chair with his head resting on his chest.

Reclining on a beaten up sofa against the wall, he saw an elderly man. A well-dressed elderly man. Jenks spat out his command. 'Don't move, either of you.'

Jenks couldn't make out the man's features properly due to the wide-brimmed hat pulled down over his eyes, but saw his mouth move. 'He can't and I won't.' Jenks swept the Glock between the two men, flicking his head towards the man in the chair. 'Chas Black?'

The old man nodded. 'Very astute, young man.'

Jenks momentarily kept his aim on Black and shot him in the forehead.

With the speed of a boxer's jab, he raised the gun, extinguished the overhead light illuminating his own face, and sighted the weapon back on the Englishman's centre mass, all in less than a second.

'Very impressive, old chap. Bit of a sharp shooter, aren't you.' He nodded towards Black slumped dead in the chair. 'He'd served his purpose so you've saved me a job.' The man paused. 'I thought if anyone got a sniff of this they'd send you.' The man swept his arms around. 'Welcome to my humble temporary abode.'

Jenks cocked his pistol. 'Keep your hands on your knees, old man, while you've still got a kneecap to hold.'

'Ooh, OK, you're the boss.' The Englishman did as instructed.

Jenks really wanted to kill him at that moment, but needed to know more. He knew the man had already collected the memory sticks, bar the last big handover, and the Department had no way of knowing if the information they contained had already been stored or sent elsewhere. If the man turned up dead, Jenks was under no illusion that whoever he was working for would put it all out in the open regardless. You don't sit on a weapon that powerful and not use it.

He glanced around the dusty floor and back at the man, now lit by just the small trickle of light escaping from the office doorway. 'Where's your walking stick?'

The man lifted his head slightly. 'Walking stick? I don't use a stick.'

'Perhaps you forgot, it's behind the sofa.'

The man didn't speak. Jenks did.

'You came to where I live and spoke to the men digging for bait.'

'I have absolutely no idea…'

'Look at the floor.'

Jenks watched the man's head moving left to right.

The man raised the fingers of one hand. 'And?'

'Look at the dust. *Step click step. Step click step.* You can see the stick marks between every pace. Look – back and forth to that room. *And* you're wearing the same overcoat. Cashmere, is it?'

The man smiled. 'Oh you're good, very good. Yes, my walking cane is tucked under the sofa here. By the way, you look like you've hurt yourself, your shoulder's bleeding.'

'Nice try.'

'No really, there's quite a lot of blood.'

Jenks flicked his eyes to his right shoulder and saw a large patch of wet crimson on his flak jacket. It was the shoulder he'd landed on when he got thrown off his bike. 'Not as injured as your men – they're all dead.' Jenks lifted the stolen radio up. 'Shall I call them?'

'No need, young man, I have no reason to doubt you, I know your abilities.'

'Do you? There's some things I'd like to know, but I don't suppose that surprises you.'

'And why should I tell you?'

'Because I'm the one holding the gun?'

'Well it's certainly an incentive, I'll grant you that, but I must tell you something.'

Jenks nodded. 'Such as?'

'You may have killed all my men here, but if I don't check in with two heavily armed units who are very nearby in the next five minutes, they will descend on this place and you'll have to fight all over again.'

'Are you referring to the two units of four men in the two silver Range Rovers waiting outside Dagenham East for Joshua Englefield?'

Jenks saw the man's mouth twitch. 'The unconscious ones? Nasty stuff that Fluothane gas, works really quickly. Shame about all eight tyres as well. So, it's just you and me.'

The man said nothing.

'Oh, Englefield got permanently delayed, by the way – I killed him earlier tonight. What was the other thing? Ah yes, I got the decryption key for the Dropbox files, it's safe with someone else now.'

Jenks desperately needed information. He knew the Sovereign Sealed envelopes were in the next room and there was a scanner on the table, which suggested they'd already been copied to the laptop. What he didn't know was if the scanned files had already been forwarded, *and*, there was still the matter of the memory sticks and files they contained. He had a feeling the old man wasn't going to tell him willingly, but had to know if the cat was already out of the bag.

The man had been silent for a while. 'What are you thinking about, Jenks?'

Jenks wasn't surprised the Englishman knew his name – if he'd managed to track him down to his home address, the man had a lot of reach. 'You mentioned you weren't surprised *they* sent me. That was what I was thinking about.'

'As soon as we saw you talking to that old relic James Camburn, I thought somehow either the Brits or the Yanks had got a little sniff that something very bad was about to happen.'

Jenks kept the gun trained on the Englishman. 'We, as in Russia? You don't sound very Russian to me.'

The man tried to hide the irritation in his voice, but his tone had changed. 'I may have been born in England, but my heart is Russian.'

'And how do you know James?'

The Englishman shook his head. 'That, young man, is a very long story, and I don't think we've got time for a history lesson.'

Jenks's brain was in overdrive. From the outside he appeared calm and relaxed, but he was working through angles, risk, velocity, strategy and alternatives. He knew for sure he was facing the biggest risk to his life he'd ever taken. 'How did you know my name?'

The Englishman looked smug. 'Because I bloody hired you, that's how.'

Jenks looked taken aback. 'What?'

'Do you remember…of course you do. You recall your contract in Morocco a few years back, sir...I can't even remember his name now – the toff supplying pharmaceutical grade heroin? An associate of mine in Russia paid him eight million dollars in advance and never received his shipment. The old bastard thought he was bombproof so basically stuck two fingers up and kept the money. I hired you through the dark web. I have to say your security protocol was second to none. You made us jump through hoops before accepting the contract.'

Jenks changed the subject. 'So why were you watching Camburn?'

The man smiled. 'We keep tabs on a lot of your security service personnel. I will confess I don't know exactly what James does now, but it's obvious he's still very much a player in this murky world we inhabit. I decided it was best to watch him a little more closely than we've done of late, what with all this coming up. We struck lucky when I saw you on the phone to him. I had someone with eyes on Camburn as he chatted to you from a park bench. What is intriguing is how you recognised me. You barely looked up during that phone call.'

'To quote a line, it's a long story, and I don't think we've got time for a history lesson.'

The Englishman's smile disappeared. Jenks kept the gun pointed at the old man and walked over to him. 'I'm going to ask for your laptop password – will you tell me?'

The Englishman shook his head. 'For want of a better phrase, fuck you, old boy.'

Jenks sprang forward, pushing the old man's head down with the palm of his disabled hand and rammed the silencer of his Glock against the top of the Englishman's hat. 'Then there's no point keeping you alive anymore.' Jenks pulled the hammer back. 'Goodbye.'

The Englishman spoke urgently. 'Listen to this first. I know you have a half-inch scar on the inside of your right ankle. You got it when you fell off your bike the first time you tried to ride without stabilisers and gashed it on the front cog – it bled heavily. You went indoors and your mother bandaged it and told you to try again the next day, but you put your blooded sock on and went back out. Even at that age you were single-minded. You pedalled away, and after a few wobbles you were off and never fell again. You put the bike down and ran into my arms shouting, I did it, I did it.'

The Englishman felt the gun start to shake in Jenks's hand. The assassin's mouth hung open. The old man raised his head and slowly took off his hat, looking directly at Jenks. Jenks looked straight through the old man's glasses into the vibrant turquoise of his eyes, and gasped.

'Dad?'

*

Jenks took a step back, the weapon still shaking. The Englishman smiled. 'Sorry it's been so long.'

Jenks remained silent, steadying his aim as best he could with his damaged hand. The Englishman shook his head.

'I wish things could have been different, but I can't change the past. Let me show you where the CIA files are stored on the laptop. I'm not a threat, son, just look at me, I'm old now.'

Jenks gestured with the barrel of the gun towards the office door.

The Englishman began to rise from the sofa. 'Do you mind if I get my cane?'

Jenks nodded.

Leaning forward, the Englishman began to reach under the sofa, at the same time slipping his right hand inside his coat. He made a play of fumbling for the stick, and finally locating it, sat up quickly. The sound of an unsuppressed round echoed around the empty building. The old man fired again, sending a second bullet into Jenks's shoulder. Jenks cried out, the impact knocking him back two paces, and the Glock out of his hand.

The Englishman rose from the sofa, his gun trained on Jenks, and moved away from the wall. Jenks grimaced and held his shoulder as his flak jacket began to turn even darker. He was starting to double over, but turned to keep facing the old man as he began to circle him, the tap of the cane echoing around the room.

The old man pointed the gun towards the office door.

'In there, now.'

Jenks backed into the small room.

'Over by the wall.'

Jenks walked backwards with difficulty towards the wall, his breathing beginning to quicken. The old man sighted the gun again and shot Jenks in the stomach. Jenks cried out. The Englishman smiled.

'Not so big and scary now are you, *fucking amateur*. I was doing this stuff before you were born. Jesus, I thought you were better than that. You dropped the ball there, old son.'

Jenks began to slide down the wall. The old man took another step forward. 'How many of my men did you kill? Six? Well this is for them.' Sweeping the gun down, the Englishman shot Jenks a further two times in his right thigh and once in the left hip. 'Hurts, doesn't it.'

Jenks screamed and dropped to the floor, his left leg folding under his body. The Englishman surveyed his handiwork. 'Hmm, by the look of that blood soaking your leathers, I would say I nicked the femoral artery. Better keep pressure on the wound, old fruit – well, all six of them.' The Englishman laughed. 'And the hip one must *really* hurt. Not much flesh there and I should know, so it's undoubtedly shattered part of your pelvis. Oh dear me.'

Jenks pushed down on his thigh, the two entry points close together, and attempted to stifle the flow from his stomach with his injured hand, with little success. The Englishman took another step forward and swung his cane, striking Jenks hard on his blooded shoulder, causing him to roar with pain.

Jenks's head began to dip as the Englishman spoke. 'It all fell into place rather well in the end. I've got the Sovereign Sealed reports, hundreds of files from the CIA, and to be honest, not having the decryption key for the Dropbox is merely an irritant. We'll get into it eventually – you have no real understanding of our abilities, just ask the American President if you don't believe me. As soon as I give our people the log-in details, it will only be a matter of time before they break the encryption. The beautiful part is, our goal can be accomplished even without it.'

Jenks coughed heavily, slowly raising his head, his mouth and chin stained red.

The Englishman looked closely. 'Oh my, looks like you're coughing up blood now, I must have ruptured an internal organ, maybe two or three. It's not looking good – I think you're bleeding out'

Jenks cleared his throat. 'Why, Dad? Why all this? Why are you taking so much pleasure in hurting me?'

The old man laughed. 'For the third time, it's a long story, and I'm not sure we've got time for a history lesson. But I'll tell you this, the timing is perfect – we are about to change the world.'

He began to get angry. 'And it's fucking overdue. Have you any idea of what I now hold on this laptop and in these envelopes?'

Jenks let out a cry, and pushed down harder on his leg, but the flow from the wounds seemed to be increasing. 'I'm not walking out of here, we both know that. What the hell is this all about, you've obviously been planning for some time.'

'Too right, my boy. I've spent *years* laying the foundations – I've even got someone in the fucking CIA. The moment is nearly upon us when Russia will be the dominant and richest nation on the planet. We are about to change the world, and there is nothing you or anyone can do about it, with or without that fucking decryption key.'

Jenks's eyes began to flutter, and he shook his head to bring his senses back. 'I was too late anyway, wasn't I. God knows what you've sent out already – I bet *Welikeleaks* or the press, or whoever is studying them right now can't believe their eyes. How can it benefit Russia if you cause a world war?'

The old man threw his head back, hysterically laughing. 'You really are behind the curve, aren't you. My God, and you're the best they've got? No wonder it's been so easy to win. You need to think outside the box, dear boy. *Nothing's* gone out, it's all in here waiting for the reaction from the G20 leaders when they receive their highly personalised emails on Saturday evening.'

He patted the laptop. 'Do you think I'm stupid? Of course I know what would happen if we simultaneously told the whole world about all the double-crossings, assassinations, illegal deals, arms shipments to enemies blah blah blah – we've got hundreds and hundreds of examples. And as for *Welikeleaks*, I am fucking *Welikeleaks*. It's only a name, there's no big teams of likeminded warriors fighting injustice, it's just a fucking name. Everyone else – those idiots Englefield and Black and all their moronic conspiracy theory friends built it up in people's minds.'

Jenks's voice was weakening. 'What's the G20 got to do with it?' As he spoke he lowered his head onto his chest and his eyes began to close. The Englishman struck him again on the shoulder.

'Don't you fucking die on me yet – I want you to take to the grave just how fucking outwitted you were. The whole point is letting world leaders know what *we* know, and showing them the proof. I've prepared all the emails to be sent simultaneously. At that point everything shifts in our favour.'

Jenks was barely audible. ‘How?’

‘Because they’ll realise they’ve no option but to agree to whatever we demand of them from that moment on. If they fail to agree, we release files pertaining to the acts and atrocities they’ve committed. Can you imagine? That nation would lose all trust and support from their allies, and retaliation from their enemies would be assured. Here’s an example. You remember Salisbury? The poisoning? We *knew* it was a joint act between America and the UK because we were there watching them! Those men from our surveillance team got sloppy, which was why their faces were all over the news. It was you and the Yanks who smeared Novichok on the door handle – all in an attempt to turn the world against us and stir up even more anti-Russian feeling.’

Jenks’s red-stained mouth hung open. His eyes were almost closed and his chest rose and fell in shallow breaths.

The old man continued.

‘When we tell your Prime Minister and the American President what we know, they will do *anything* to prevent that information getting out. That means agreeing to trade deals, money, arms – whatever we ask for. They’ll know if they don’t agree they may as well head for the bunker. And that example is but a grain of sand in the bucket of secrets we now have.’

Jenks weakly nodded.

The Englishman stood over him. 'So there we are. Your pathetic attempts to stop us were bordering on plain amateur, it now seems. And you, the great and feared Jenks, I still can't quite believe you fell for the oldest trick in the book. Haha, *can I just get my stick*? I'll tell you this – nothing fools us more than the lies we tell ourselves. And now it's time for you to die.'

Jenks mumbled something. The old man leant in, cupping his ear. 'Repeat that, I didn't quite catch it, and I don't want to miss your final pearl of wisdom.'

Jenks spoke, barely above a whisper. 'Maybe nothing fools us more than the truths we think we believe.'

The old man began to speak. 'I think you're getting delerio...'

Jenks exploded into action. Sweeping his right leg up, he landed a colossal kick directly into the old man's crippled hip. The Englishman screamed and hit the floor hard, the gun clattering away. In a blur of movement Jenks was upon him, pinning the old man down.

He sat heavily on the Englishman's chest, the old man looking up shocked, bewildered and beaten. 'What the hell *are* you?'

'Me? I'm the last person who'll have to listen to your drivel, and these are the last eyes you'll ever look into.'

'B...but I shot you. Six times. I saw you bleeding out.'

'Did you? And don't bother with all that *I am your father* shit, we're not in bloody *Star Wars*.'

The old man had terror in his eyes.

Jenks leant in closer. 'I noticed a few things about you pretty quickly. I was standing under that light before I shot it out, my face was illuminated. Look at these.' Jenks pointed to his own eyes. 'I would have thought my own father would have mentioned, even in passing, that my very distinctive eyes had completely changed colour.'

Jenks pulled off a glove, put his hand up to his left eye and removed the dark brown contact lens, one vivid turquoise eye staring back into the mirror image of the old man's eyes.

'I don't remember much about my dad, but I do remember being told I was left-handed like him. You drew your gun with your right.'

The old man stayed silent. Jenks continued.

'And do you know what else? You're the first person I've ever met who needs to wear glasses *and* contact lenses.'

Jenks slowly removed the old man's spectacles. 'Don't move now or I might hurt you.' Reaching into the old man's right eye, Jenks squeezed and removed the lens, throwing the tiny piece of turquoise plastic on the floor, revealing a dark brown iris staring back at him. The old man realised there was nothing he could say.

Jenks stood up, straddling the old man's hips. 'You said your heart will always be Russian, or something like that. Well I'm sorry but I'm going to break it.'

The old man snarled, spitting out his words. 'You could never break my heart.'

'Oh I could.'

Jenks reached behind his back and removed his backup Glock. Aiming just left centre of the man's chest, he fired six times in rapid succession. In the few seconds before the old man's brain decoded the message that his heart was no longer beating, his senses still had a moment before they shut down forever.

Jenks quickly knelt close to the man's ear. 'See.'

*

Jenks thumbed his radio. 'Control from Alpha One, receiving.'

He heard Camburn respond, and the background noise of a helicopter.

'I called, you didn't answer.'

'I've been a little busy, James. Everything is safe, the threat is neutralised.'

'Excellent work, lad. We're airborne, I'm with Sir John, we'll be with you...ETA two minutes.'

Jenks responded. 'Copy that, I need a clean-up unit here on the double, and my bike is trashed.'

'We'll get it recovered and sanitise the whole site.'

'James, I'm going to video call you on Wickr, switch to your phone.'

‘Standing by.’

Jenks pulled out his handset and dialled Camburn.

‘James, have a look at this old man. Take a screen shot and run it through every database we have access to.’ Jenks reversed the camera and held it over the Englishman’s face. Camburn responded immediately.

‘No need, I know exactly who that is. Are you sure the bastard’s dead?’

‘Yes, James, he’s dead.’

‘Well, kill him again just to make sure. We’re coming in to land now, bring it all out as soon as you can – we’ve got another leg of this journey to make.’

Chapter 26.

Everything back in place.

Jenks ran back to the factory floor and searched Black, finding one phone. Returning to the office he took what he assumed was Black's couriered phone from the old man's jacket pocket, along with the dead man's own handset. He checked the scanner had no documents under the lid, and slid the laptop into the old man's briefcase. Checking the side pocket, he saw eleven memory sticks. He zipped up the rucksack and threw it over his shoulder.

The side door opened as the chopper's skids barely touched the ground. Jenks sprinted low under the rotors and jumped in. Camburn helped haul him aboard, handed him a headset and saw Jenks properly in the light. 'Good God, man, you've been shot.'

Jenks smiled, unzipping his leathers and pointed inside. 'No, this has.'

Leroux signalled they were secure and the chopper began to ascend. As the pilot turned to acknowledge, he noticed the staining covering Jenks's leathers. 'I've got a spare flight suit in my bag back there, help yourself.'

Jenks gave him a thumbs up and once they'd levelled out, was thankful to get out of his sopping wet clothes. He handed the rucksack, phones and briefcase to Leroux. 'I don't want anything else to do with these, thanks.'

Camburn still hadn't fully closed his mouth. 'What the dickens were you wearing?'

'It was a gift from an Egyptian friend. I owe him a very, very large beer.'

'What the hell is it?'

'Well it's probably about the maddest thing they've ever dreamt up. It's made of two layers of Kevlar. A thin outer skin which slows a pistol round, and between the two layers is this gloopy red ballistic gel stuff – when exposed to air it turns runny. The inside layer is thicker and will stop the round completely. A rifle would still penetrate but not a handgun. I've got to say though, it still bloody hurts when you get shot.'

Camburn was shaking his head. 'That's utterly genius and completely insane. Just one question – what if he'd shot you in the face?'

'He wasn't going to, James. He wanted to play with me like a cat with a mouse. And there was something else – it felt like I was being paid back for something, like it was revenge.'

'You and I need to have a chat, but not now. So let me get this right – you allowed him to shoot you a number of times to make *him* talk?'

'Yep. I had to know if anything had been disseminated and there was no way he was going to tell me – he'd rather take the secret to the grave. When he thought I was dying, he couldn't wait to gloat about how stupid we were and how brilliant the Russians are. The only thing we haven't got is the log-in details for the Dropbox, but the only other people that did are dead. It'll just sit there suspended in cyberspace forever.'

Jenks pulled his headset mic a little closer. 'Where are we going?'

Leroux spoke. 'City Airport, I've got a Lear jet waiting. We have to return some stolen property.'

Jenks shrugged his shoulders.

*

The chopper flight took no more than a few minutes. Touching down on the runway, all three men briskly walked to the waiting jet and climbed aboard. The flight to Aberdeen would take just over an hour, with the last leg being a quick hop in another helicopter. Jenks settled into a seat near the back. Camburn sat across the aisle and began to speak. 'That man…'

Jenks held his hand up. 'Can we talk about it later? I've had quite a long day so I'd like to grab a bit of sleep.' Camburn looked astounded.

Jenks put earplugs in, pulled a blanket over himself and settled against the headrest. He was fast asleep within minutes.

The bump of landing woke him. He grabbed a bottle of water and followed the two older men into the waiting helicopter and they sped towards Balmoral. Within twenty minutes they touched down in the grounds of the castle and were met at the helipad by PC Rory Galbraith, who was working the night shift.

PC Galbraith drove them the short distance to one of the side entrances and key-carded them into the building. 'Follow me, gents.' The four men walked through ornate state rooms and along beautifully decorated corridors, footsteps echoing loudly in the silence before stopping at a lift. They went up two floors and fell in behind the barrel-chested veteran as they made their way to the Queen's private quarters. PC Galbraith knocked on the door which led directly into the morning room. It was 2am.

After a few moments they heard the sound of footsteps approaching. The door opened and the Queen stood on the threshold in dressing gown, nightwear and slippers. She had a large smile on her face. PC Galbraith spoke. 'Ma'am, your visitors have arrived.'

In the clear, clipped tones from another era, the Queen replied, 'Thank you, Rory, that will be all for now.'

PC Galbraith bowed and retreated.

'Sir John, James, lovely to see you again, do come in. And you must be Stuart Jenkins. Sir John has briefed me on your actions tonight.' The Queen extended her tiny hand and all three men went to shake it, Jenks last in line. He held up his bandaged fingers. 'Your Majesty, do you mind if we use the other one?'

The Queen offered her left hand. 'Do you know, of all the hundreds of thousands of hands I've shaken over the years, I think this is the first time I've…Oh wait a minute. Yes, there was a Chelsea Pensioner at my Golden Jubilee who'd lost an arm. Well, this is only the second time I've shaken with my left.'

Jenks gently took the monarch's left hand. 'Now please come in and make yourselves comfortable, you must be exhausted.'

Jenks looked at Camburn wide-eyed as if to say, *is this really happening*?

The Queen beckoned the men to follow. 'Why don't we go into the sitting room, it'll be far more comfortable.'

The three men diligently followed her through a set of double doors and into a room which the public never saw. Jenks looked around, taking in family photographs, flowers in vases and worn but obviously comfortable sofas and armchairs. In the corner sat a television, in front of which was a recliner chair with a table next to it. On the table was a newspaper open at the TV guide, with a highlighter pen next to it.

The room was beautifully decorated, which had clearly taken place about twenty years ago. It was just a comfortable, lived in room – a home.

Leroux spoke first. 'How are you, ma'am, are you well?'

'Still alive, Sir John, that's the main thing. Now will you three stop hovering and take a seat.'

All three immediately sat on one of the sofas in unison.

‘Would any of you like a drink? Tea, coffee? Gin and tonic?’ All politely declined. Leroux cleared his throat. ‘Your Majesty, the message was conveyed through the back channels to the Kremlin, and I anticipate we’ll have no problems connecting you. I think your choice of wording did the trick. I anticipate we can proceed in ten minutes or so.’

‘That’s splendid. Now, I understand you have something to return.’ Leroux passed the rucksack, and the buck over to Jenks.

‘Why don’t you bring it through, young man.’

He followed the Queen through another set of double doors, leaving the two most powerful men in the British security services on the sofa.

Jenks was now in the Queens private bed chamber. The whole evening was becoming more surreal by the minute. ‘Now let me just get the key, Mr Jenkins.’

He wasn’t sure if he should address the most powerful woman in the world in a less than formal manner, but considering he was in the Queen’s bedroom, and she was in her dressing gown, he felt protocol could possibly be relaxed.

‘Your Majesty, my friends call me Jenks, just Jenks.’

The Queen gave him a warm, genuine smile. ‘Then I should like to call you Jenks as well, if that’s alright with you?’

Jenks smiled back. ‘Of course.’

Reaching into her handbag, she removed a brass key and beckoned him to follow her to a large rococo mirror. He tried desperately not to look at the pair of them in the reflection.

The Queen chuckled. 'Look at us, what a sight – me in my nightwear with a strange man in my bedroom. What would the neighbours say.'

They both laughed. Jenks felt the ice melting, and the natural warm and human side of a woman he'd only seen on stamps and television shining through.

'Stand back a bit, Jenks.'

He watched in awe as she swung the mirror back on its hinges, revealing the vault door.

Entering, he couldn't believe what he was seeing. The Queen beckoned him to follow her to the far wall. Jenks looked down at the large display case. His eyes nearly came out on stalks when he saw the huge diamond centrepiece. 'Your Majesty, is that the...'

She cut him off. 'Yes it is, but don't tell anyone will you – it's a secret. Right, put all the envelopes on the side here, I'll sort them out tomorrow.'

Jenks unpacked the rucksack, counting the contents. '154, ma'am.'

'Jolly good, that's the lot.' She quickly flicked through them, finding the only one still sealed.

'Jenks, there's a record here pertaining to your father. I realise that must be a bit of a shock – would you like to read it?'

Jenks was staggered. 'It's OK, ma'am, leave it sealed.'

'Don't you even want to know if he's likely to be alive or dead?'

Jenks thought for a second. 'I haven't seen my dad since I was very small – I hardly remember him at all. We never had photographs in the house, so I can't even picture his face. If he's alive he's an old man now. I'm not going to be running into his arms like the last thirty years never happened.'

'That's so sad but I think I understand. You're a remarkable man and he'd be very proud of you, like I am. Now, let's go out and have a little chat, shall we?'

Jenks wasn't going to argue. He waited for the Queen to lock the vault, and started to walk towards the double doors.

'No, let's talk in here. Come and sit by the window with me.'

He followed her over to a small table which still had a tea cup and half-eaten sandwich on it. 'Excuse the mess, now make yourself comfortable. I could do with a proper drink after all that's happened. Will you join me in a G and T?'

Jenks felt he couldn't refuse. 'Do you know what, that sounds lovely.'

She went over to an antique walnut Queen Anne style cabinet, which coincidently used to belong to Queen Anne, and poured their drinks, which looked to be a lot more G than T. She dropped a couple of ice cubes in each glass and placed them on the table. Jenks took a sip.

Momentarily forgetting where he was, he coughed and blurted out, 'Christ!'

The Queen laughed. 'Oops, bit strong is it?' She took a sip of her own drink, unflinching.

They sat facing each other – the most famous person on the planet and someone who'd spent half his adult life trying not to be noticed. Jenks spoke first, nodding towards the vault.

'Ma'am, I had no idea you were so involved in, well, all this. I'm quite astonished to tell you the truth.'

She gave a little smile. 'Jenks, when I succeeded my father I made a vow to serve this country, and I hope I have. There are matters behind the scenes in which I have been involved that will never be known, and information only I am privy to. I've always enjoyed my liaison, shall we say, with my security services.'

'Ma'am, you obviously have contact with Sir John on a regular basis, but I had no idea you knew James. He's never mentioned it to me.'

'Ah, dear James. Yes, plays his cards close to his chest. I've known him for many, many years. He'd be doing Sir John's job if he hadn't been diverted to his little side project.'

Jenks had no idea if she knew about the Department or if she'd been told a little white lie about Camburn's employment for the last thirty-two years, then realised he was being naive. Of course she knew about the Department, but he wasn't going to bring it up.

'Jenks, I'm going to ask you a small favour.'

'Name it, ma'am.'

‘I want you to bring up the matter of the Sovereign Sealed documents with those two out there. I’ve done a lot of thinking since I discovered them missing.’

She took another sip of her drink and set it down, looking directly at him.

‘I come from a different era. Times were much the same as the even older days when I ascended the throne after Daddy died, but things have moved on somewhat over the last sixty-eight years. I feel as if I’m the last of a species on the verge of extinction. Does that make sense?’

Jenks thought about the numbers. Sixty-eight years.

He nodded. ‘Go on, ma’am.’

‘I’m not sure after I’ve gone they should be kept in there, or even kept at all. I love my family, but they have different values – a different outlook on life and their responsibilities. Not wishing to sound dramatic, but I’m the last of my kind and I’m ninety-four now.’

Jenks made a serious breach of protocol, but it felt like the natural thing to do. He put his hand on hers. ‘I think there’s a bit of gas left in the tank yet, ma’am.’

The Queen patted his hand. ‘I hope you’re right, but one does have to make plans.’

‘Leave it to me.’ They both reached for their drinks.

‘Jenks, Sir John appraised me of what you did tonight. If I could, I would instruct my government to request that I award you the Victoria Cross. You have shown great valour in the face of the enemy at the real risk of losing your own life. This country and the rest of the world are in your debt, but of course they can never know. I can't bestow an honour on a man who doesn't exist, but I want you to know you are more than worthy of it.'

He didn't know what to say, and blew out his cheeks. There was a tap on the door. The Queen got up and opened it and Leroux took one step in.

'Your call is waiting, Your Majesty.'

'Thank you Sir John, I'll take it in here.'

Leroux went to follow her into the bedroom, but didn't get far. The Queen flicked her fingers in the direction of the door.

'I can handle it from here, Sir John.' She turned and gave Jenks her biggest smile yet and sat back down at the table, picking up the receiver.

'Good evening, Mr Putin, are you there?'

'Good evening, Your Majesty. It is an unexpected surprise and of course a pleasure to hear from you. I have to say I am intrigued why you should want to speak at this hour.'

She cleared her throat. 'Well I shall tell you then. Please ask your advisors to leave the room and turn off whatever recording device you're using. And *please,* send your interpreter out, we both know you don't need her.'

'Of course, give me a second, Your Majesty.' She could tell he was covering the mouthpiece, but could still hear the sound of chairs being dragged back and muffled orders given. Then a click as the call became a one to one.

'It is just you and me now, ma'am.'

She could detect in his voice he wasn't looking forward to hearing what she had to say.

'Jolly good. After I've finished speaking you will be glad it was only you listening, so if there's anyone else still in the room, please ask them to leave now.'

One more chair creaked in the Kremlin, and seconds later, the sound of a door closing.

'Just really you and me now, Mr Putin?'

'You have my word, Your Majesty.'

The Queen rolled her eyes and took another sip of her gin.

'I want you to listen very carefully to what I am about to say. Please do not interrupt or insult me by any attempts at denial. I am fully aware of your involvement in events that came to a head tonight. I have all my Sovereign Sealed records back, and the information you obtained via Mr Englefield in the CIA is secure – we have also reacquired all eleven memory sticks. The head of MI6 is currently outside this room with your associate's laptop which we will attempt to examine later today.' She took another sip.

'Unless of course you decide to give me his log-in details. You should know that everyone involved in your attempt at rebalancing the world in your favour is dead. Well, apart from your long-term sleeper agent, the man I knew as Dennis Best. Do say hello from me.'

Jenks took a large gulp of his drink, utterly transfixed by the power emanating from the lady in front of him, six years from her hundredth birthday.

She continued. ‘Unless you want me to instruct my government to release details of your intentions via the diplomatic channels to all nations affected, you will do exactly as I say.’

There was a pause. Putin replied quietly. ‘Please continue, ma’am.’

‘When my security services contact your security services for assistance or information, you will give them exactly what they want. No holding back or claims that the requested information has been destroyed. I know you keep everything, just like us. If you do not, I am in a position to turn every nation on the planet against Russia. Do I make myself clear or do you want me to go over any points again?’

‘You have made your position perfectly clear, Your Majesty.’

‘I’ve been around a lot longer than you, Vladimir, and there’s information inside my head that isn’t even recorded *anywhere* now. I will give you an example. In 1967 Sir Dick White, then head of MI6 personally briefed me that GCHQ intercepted wires between your then president Mr Brezhnev, the KGB, and the man you’d inserted in NASA. The Americans don’t know this but I do. Russia was responsible for sabotaging Apollo One, causing the fire that killed those poor astronauts on the launch pad. Do you wonder what the Americans would do even all these years later if they were made aware of that information?’

For the first time in his political life Vladimir Putin was backed into a corner he couldn't escape from – the only option was surrender.

'Your Majesty, I will make the necessary arrangements for full cooperation, of that you can be assured. I will personally see to it that the log-in details you require are forwarded in the next few hours. Can I offer my apolog...'

'No you can't, Mr Putin, I'm not interested – well, it's been lovely chatting with you, please give my regards to your wife. Let's hope we can meet soon – it's been seven years now, can you believe it – seven years. Anyway, it's very late so I'll let you go. Goodbye.' And she put the phone down.

She turned to Jenks. 'You didn't hear any of that.' He made a motion of drawing a zip across his mouth. She smiled. 'Time you went home, young man.'

*

PC Galbraith met the men outside the private chambers and escorted them back to the helicopter. 'That's the most excitement we've had here for ages.'

Leroux turned to face him. 'What excitement? A helicopter didn't land, and your records will reflect that. We weren't here and you will never speak of this to anyone. Please make it clear to everyone on duty that any reference to tonight will be considered a breach of the Official Secrets Act, is that clear?'

Galbraith tapped his nose. 'Mum's the word, sir.' He then attempted his first salute since leaving

Hendon twenty-nine years earlier. Camburn spoke. 'Hmm, not bad, but you might want to tweak it a bit – you don't salute with your left hand.'

All four laughed as Camburn, Leroux and Jenks climbed aboard the chopper.

During the short journey Jenks could tell they were bursting to ask what occurred behind closed doors, but they were all wearing headsets on talk-through with the pilot.

They arrived at a deserted Aberdeen airport and were dropped next to the steps of the Lear jet. Camburn sat opposite and Leroux directly in front of Jenks. The plane took off immediately, climbing steeply before levelling off. After a few minutes the seat belt sign went off. Leroux turned around poking his head through the gap between the seats like a schoolboy on a coach trip. He and Camburn looked at each other and then back to Jenks. In unison they said, 'Well, what did she say?'

Jenks wanted to milk the moment for all it was worth – opportunities like this didn't come often. He steepled his fingers on his forehead, drawing a deep breath.

'Well, I'm afraid *neither* of you have sufficient security clearance for me to divulge anything of what I heard.'

Leroux's face momentarily flushed, then broke into a broad smile. He knelt up a little higher, extending his arm through the gap in the headrests. 'Touché, young man, touché indeed.' They shook hands and Jenks leant back in his seat.

'Before I go on, she did ask me to convey to you that she feels the time has come to find an alternative to the Sovereign Sealed records. She knows change is coming and it can't continue that way after she's gone.'

Leroux was nodding. 'It's been on my mind as well, actually. James and I will get our heads together and do some serious thinking.'

Jenks continued. 'I can tell you this though – that is one formidable lady. She can remember intelligence intercepts from over fifty years ago which could bring Russia to its knees – intelligence not in any records.'

Both men sat wide-eyed, waiting for him to continue.

'I can't tell you what she said to Putin, but as a result of the call Sir John will be receiving the log-in details for the laptop I took off the old man – that in itself will be a treasure trove. You'll also find that any diplomatic or security service requests are dealt with immediately. The flow of information and assistance will be unlike anything you've experienced before. Basically, you ask – you get.'

Camburn had been holding his breath the whole time. 'Wow.'

Leroux got up and sat next to Camburn. 'James, this presents opportunities for us like never before.'

Camburn nodded. 'For the moment yes, but after Her Majesty dies, so does our leverage. We must use it while we can.'

Jenks turned towards them. 'Once you get into the laptop and examine the files, will you share it with the Americans?'

Leroux answered, 'Good God no, man, can't see any benefit in that. We'll keep it for a rainy day.'

Jenks shook his head, smiled and closed his eyes. 'Nothing changes.'

*

An hour later they touched down at London City airport. Jenks and Camburn shook hands with Leroux, who made his way to a waiting BMW. Camburn turned to Jenks. 'Do you want me to drop you home? My car's parked here.'

'Are you sure? It's not exactly round the corner.'

'Come on, there'll be nothing on the roads, it won't take long.'

Stepping into Camburn's vintage Jag, Jenks inhaled the aroma of walnut and old leather. 'God, that takes me back – not sure where to though.'

Camburn fired up the V12 engine. 'Your father always drove Jags – wouldn't entertain any other marque, but you were too young to remember.'

Jenks gave him a glance and settled into the well-worn passenger seat, and they set off towards the Kent coast where the inky black sky was beginning to show hints of burnt orange. As they drove over the Dartford bridge Camburn turned his head.

'I think I need to fill in a few gaps for you, old chap.'

'Fill away, even older chap.'

Camburn smiled.

'The man you shot, Sebastion Paflin, was also known by the Russian name he took, Oleg Federova. Sebastion and your father were very close, joining the SIS together after university. Did you know your father went to Cambridge after leaving Charterhouse?'

'No. I don't really know anything about him.'

'Well, they were both fluent in Russian, as am I…'

Jenks interrupted. 'You're fluent in Russian? You've never mentioned that.'

'You never asked. Anyway, let me continue. What we didn't know at the time, was that Sebastion had been recruited by a man named John Cairncross…'

Jenks interrupted again. 'Not *the* John Cairncross – the so called fifth man?

'The very same, now stop interrupting. Cairncross was living in America by then but used to visit the UK, and unbeknown to us, was still active. He turned Sebastion much like Al Qaeda and ISIS do with those poor young fellows today. Sebastion and Kenneth, your father, were despatched as agents to feed back intelligence from Russia. It was a long-term deep infiltration during which Sebastion became a double agent.'

Jenks couldn't resist asking another question. 'So all this reaches back in time as far as Blunt?'

Camburn nodded. 'The Ruskies play an exceptionally long game – thank God they never took up cricket. Anyway, after a couple of years Sebastion tried to turn Ken. Your father was one of the most brilliant men I've ever met. Ken convinced Sebastion he was converted and played along for years. Seb never suspected a thing. Your father was probably the best and most valuable triple agent this country ever produced. Any questions now?'

Jenks thought for a moment. 'This Sebastion, or Oleg, knew a lot about me. He knew I had a scar on my ankle from when I fell off my bike riding without stabilisers for the first time.'

'Of course he did. Like I said, he and your father were very close. Ken was always taking photos of you – I've no doubt he would've captured that moment and probably couldn't wait to show his friend and tell him what happened.'

'OK.'

Camburn continued. 'When Ken first revealed his suspicions about Sebastion he was offered choices. He could be pulled out, and we would have understood as he had a wife and young family – you, or he could move the family abroad, i.e. closer to Russia and attempt to maintain as much contact with the two of you as possible and continue his infiltration.'

'And?'

'Ken realised if he were ever exposed, you and your mother would become instant targets. He knew he was the best opportunity we'd had for decades, maybe even ever, to feed misinformation to the Russians and quality intelligence back to us. He took a third choice and sacrificed the life he wanted for the sake of millions.'

Jenks was quiet. 'He could have made contact at some point, just to let me know he was still around.'

Camburn turned. 'Didn't you make the same sacrifice in a way? You chose to lead a distinctively different life due to decisions you made. You've both saved countless people at great cost to the life you could have had.'

Jenks thought about what he'd just heard, but couldn't think of anything else to say.

Camburn had more. 'This may come as a bit of a shock, but your father slipped back into the country on a few occasions. He attended your final awards evening at Charterhouse, and your passing out parade at Sandhurst. You wouldn't have paid him any attention though, he was a master of disguise. He even met up with Dolores one time.'

'He visited Mum?'

'Only once. It was impossible for him to make contact with you, as I'm sure you now understand.'

'James, how do you *know* all this?'

'I was his handler, lad, he fed everything back to me. I was still active in MI6 for quite some time after I'd set up the Department.'

Jenks spun around. 'What!' You've never mentioned that.'

Camburn sighed. 'It is a *secret*, old chap, and I'm pretty good at keeping them.'

Jenks sat dumbfounded. Camburn continued.

'While you were in the army, Sebastion and your father got into a bit of a standoff. I don't know how, but Seb got a sniff that Ken may have been ratting him out. He confronted him, and as Ken tried to talk his way out of it, they got into a terrible row. Seb pulled a gun, not knowing Ken was also armed, and fired but missed. Ken got off six rounds, all of them hitting Seb in his hip and upper leg – turned that side to mush. Your father got away, and that was the last report I ever had from him. Not a dicky bird from that day to this.'

'So what happened to Sebastion after my father shot him?'

'He resigned from the service with immediate effect and basically became a ghost. We put snippets of intercepts together over the years which suggested he'd become Putin's go-to man. They obviously became very close.'

'Well you certainly filled in a few gaps there, James. I just had this feeling he wanted to punish me for some reason, and not just because I was some operative sent to kill him. And this business with him pretending to be my father, I suppose he thought if push came to shove, that was just about the only thing which could make me drop my guard and give him an edge.'

Camburn nodded. 'He had a brilliant mind, so I would tend to agree. He planned everything down to the last miniscule detail, just not quite to your level though – you saw through it.'

Jenks still had an unanswered question. 'What I don't understand is how Mum got an insurance payout if my dad was still alive, at that point in time anyway.'

Camburn cast his mind back. 'Your father was independently wealthy by the time he met Dolores. He'd inherited from his father who died when he was young, and the money was put into a trust fund. When he left your mother, he also transferred a not inconsiderable sum to her. Your mother knew Ken worked for 6, but I suppose to counter any difficult questions, it was easier to explain it away as a life insurance payout. She knew he was never coming back, so that was her story.'

Jenks absorbed what he'd just heard. 'Phew. We never really spoke much about Dad – I wonder what she would've said if I'd asked her more about him?'

'She would have lied to you, to protect you, her and your father.'

Jenks nodded. 'I nearly forgot to mention, Sebastion walked past my house whilst we were planning all this. He had eyes on you as well – when you were in the park that day.'

'Hmm…doesn't surprise me. Ken knew you'd purchased a house down here after your mother died.

He would have undoubtedly mentioned it to Seb as they were, for all intents and purposes, still great friends even if your dad was selling him out at the time.'

Neither of them said anything for a few minutes before Jenks broke the silence.

'Did you know the Queen has a file with my father's name on it?'

'No, I didn't.'

'She offered to open it for me. She asked if I wanted some indication if he was alive or dead.'

Camburn smiled. 'What is she – your new BFF or something?'

Jenks laughed. 'How do you know what a BFF is?'

'My granddaughter called me it. I had to look up what it meant.'

Jenks felt the tiniest prickling in his eyes. 'That's nice.'

Camburn returned to the subject of Kenneth Jenkins' Sovereign Sealed file. 'Her Majesty obviously knows more than I. So, did you?'

'No, I told her to keep it sealed.'

Camburn indicated to pull off the main road and headed towards Jenks's drive. 'You know, lad, you're so like your father in many, many ways – in others not.'

'Thanks, I think. Do you fancy a quick one for the road? I've got a 2015 Saint-Amour that's been waiting for the right moment.'

Camburn pondered. 'Hmm, 2015, A sunny dry spring that year, then ideal conditions through to harvest with just the right amount of sun and rain. Quite a stand-out vintage. Why not.'

Jenks was surprised by his old friend yet again.

'You drink Beaujolais? You never mentioned that before.'

'You never offered me any before.'

Jenks shook his head. 'You wily old goat.'

'Less of the old, please.'

Jenks opened the gates and they drove down to the house. Dawn was rushing across the sky, filling it with deep reds and yellows, and the birds were waking up and chirping away to let everyone know they were there.

Jenks opened the bottle and carried two glasses to the bay window overlooking the estuary. Camburn was admiring the view.

'I've never been here at this time of the morning, it really is quite beautiful.'

Jenks poured the wine and took a sip. Camburn ran his around the glass and breathed in the aroma before raising it to his lips.

'Good Lord, that's exceptional. If I wasn't driving I'd sit here and finish the whole bottle with you.'

'I've got a spare room.'

'No, thank you, lad, but I'll have to get back.'

They both sat in silence, gazing out at the mudflats, now shimmering and glowing as the first of the sun's rays hit them. Two men in the distance were digging for bait.

Camburn spoke. 'Good grief, is that a redshank on the breakwater?'

Jenks was surprised yet again. 'Oh for God's sake, please don't tell me you're an ornithologist as well?'

Camburn raised his palms. 'I dabble.'

Jenks shook his head. Both men sat for a few moments, enjoying their wine and the sights and sounds of a new day unfolding.

Camburn broke the silence. 'You know what's really gnawing away at me – who Sebastian's contact was in the CIA. He or she must be high up and will soon know all connection leading back to them is now severed.'

Jenks pondered. 'Work it back like we always do. Find out exactly who had access to the information we acted on. We'd have to know about the search team, lab staff, anyone who knew anything.'

Camburn agreed. 'You're right of course. I think we can discount Katherine Jenkins. It obviously wasn't Buckland, which leaves the ones you mentioned plus Florence Rizzoli and the fellow Buckland confided in. Once we've ruled them all out, whoever's left is our man. Or woman.

The two men sat quietly again. Camburn had nearly finished his glass when Jenks turned to him.

'You know, James, I've had a chance to do a lot of thinking these past two weeks. It's been strange having all this time at home, literally on the cusp of a mission, and I've enjoyed it. I'm more than financially secure, so I've decided to delete all my contact details from the dark web and not take on any private work for the moment. Perhaps I should have done it years ago.'

'It's what you do, lad, and you're bloody good at it.'

'I know, but I want to actually get the house finished and take stock for a while. Do you know I've never spent a whole week here during a summer? I'll still take on department operations, but I'll be choosy.'

'I understand completely, there's always work there for you.'

Camburn checked his watch.

'I'd better be hitting the road.'

'Yep, I'm going to hit the sack, I might go for a run later.'

Camburn faced him. 'Are you *mad*? Put your feet up, finish that bottle tomorrow, er, today – enjoy that lovely view.'

Jenks shrugged his shoulders. 'We'll see. No rest for the wicked, eh?'

There was silence between the two men. Camburn broke it.

'For what it's worth, my old friend, I don't think you're wicked.'

Piercing turquoise eyes burned directly into Camburn's.

'What am I then, James?'

Camburn put his hand on Jenks's shoulder.

'I think....I think you're *necessary,* lad.'
Jenks smiled.
'Maybe, maybe for a while longer.'

THE END.

Epilogue.

3 months later.

Katherine Jenkins received an anonymous tip-off to check the server room controlling the computers in the analysis department. Englefield's link circuit was discovered, and Alicia Buckland was fully exonerated from any wrongdoing. She was posthumously awarded the CIA's highest award for service to her country and buried with full honours.

Sam Dibble had a major breakdown. His behaviour quickly become erratic and unstable soon after he discovered Alicia Buckland's body. He was fast-tracked for medical retirement, diagnosed with severe PTSD. He tried to convince his wife to move to the mountains but she refused, and he left, transferring the house and most of his money to her. With his injury award payment he purchased a small cabin on a remote wooded hillside 1,000 miles from his family.

Jenks's broken finger healed, and he set about doing all the jobs he hadn't previously had time for. The restoration of the Ducati would be an ongoing project, but he installed the fireplace surround and had started redecorating.

June was unseasonably hot, and taking a break from painting, he was perched on the sea wall with a mug of coffee. He'd heard reports of a red kite sighted on the Graveney Marshes, and had decided to set aside a couple of hours later that afternoon with his binoculars in case the bird decided to visit.

He was shaken out of a daydream by a voice.

'Hey, stranger, I didn't know you lived here.'

It was Alison, the smiley lady from the deli.

'Hi, Alison, yep, guilty as charged. You just out for a stroll?'

She stopped and leant against the wall. 'I don't start until two. On days like this it's lovely to walk in.'

Jenks saw her glance at his coffee.

'Fancy one? There's plenty in the pot.' He motioned to the half-full cafetière on the garden table.

She checked her watch. 'Yes, why not, that would be lovely.'

'Hop over, I'll get another mug.'

Alison realised she didn't even know his name.

'So what do I call you then, mystery man?'

He paused for a moment, wondering whether to make something up.

'Jenks.'

'Is that short for something?'

'Yeah, but generally everyone calls me Jenks.'

'Well hello, Jenks, nice to see you again.'

They were both silent for a few moments, Alison's stare unblinking. 'How the hell did I not notice your eyes before? They're amazing.'

Jenks was smiling. 'Maybe it was the light in the deli, I don't know – I've definitely not changed them since I last saw you.'

Not planning to leave the house that day, he hadn't bothered to put his brown contacts in. Alison gave her head a little shake.

They chatted away for half an hour about this and that – she was easy to talk to. Unfortunately he had to lie a couple of times which didn't sit well, but he enjoyed her company.

She checked her watch again. 'Well I better be on my way. Are you going to pop in again soon? I'm buying.'

Jenks looked at her and smiled. 'Yes, I'd like that.'

They said goodbye, and he watched as the smiley lady with the long curly hair crunched her way across the shingle.

Gathering up the mugs and coffee pot, he started to head inside. His phone vibrated in his pocket.

Opening the message, he saw three words and a jpeg attachment. It simply read, *this is him*. Jenks opened the attachment and studied it. He closed his eyes, then looked back at the photograph. He repeated the action six times, burning the image into his brain. He tapped the phone, nodded, and said quietly to himself, 'See you around.'

Perhaps by sheer coincidence, at that exact moment Sam Dibble was out in the early morning mist 5,000 miles away collecting firewood. He stopped dead in his tracks and quickly looked over his shoulder.

Feeling a shiver, as if a shadow had just passed through his body.

Thank you for reading. If you are able to leave a few words as a review on the retail site of your choice, Goodreads, BookBub or any place of your choosing that would be much appreciated.

Acknowledgements

Big thanks to my brother who pointed out some of the pitfalls of writing along the way and opened my eyes to the editing process. I've actually lost count of the drafts before Jenks became what it is now. Originally 140,000 words, at one point I really thought it was finished when I got it down to 110,000 until he pointed out I could save a further 50 words on the first page alone...oh well, start again. It was all valuable advice which will serve me well as Jenks II starts to take shape.

I'd also like to thank Julia Gibbs for her sterling work proofreading my final draft, shaving it down even more with her suggestions.

Most importantly I'd like to say a great big thank you to YOU, if you're reading this after finishing the book - it means a lot. Feel free to message me on the website barneyburrell.com and leave a comment if you fancy it.

And last but not least, France, for giving us Beaujolais.

Contact details

Website: www.barneyburrell.com
Email: barneyburrellauthor@gmail.com
Twitter @BarneyBurrell